# MURDER will TRAVEL..

# MURDER will TRAVEL

*Emily Toll*

**BERKLEY PRIME CRIME, NEW YORK**

MURDER WILL TRAVEL

A Berkley Prime Crime Book / published by arrangement with the author

All rights reserved.
Copyright © 2002 by Taffy Cannon.
Cover art by David Schweitzer.
Text design by Julie Rogers.

ISBN: 0-7394-2691-5

Berkley Prime Crime Books are published
by The Berkley Publishing Group,
a division of Penguin Putnam Inc.,
375 Hudson Street, New York, New York 10014.
The name BERKLEY PRIME CRIME and
the BERKLEY PRIME CRIME design
are trademarks belonging to Penguin Putnam Inc.

PRINTED IN THE UNITED STATES OF AMERICA

*For Ditty,*
*whose support never wavers*

# Acknowledgments

I am grateful to Brian and Sally Shore for suggesting this locale, and for hospitality showcasing the possibilities of fine wine. In Sonoma County, Don and Patricia Helfer continued that hospitality, adding invaluable information about viticulture and viniculture.

Other helpful information came from Fred Scherrer of Scherrer Winery, Winnie Kingman of the Jack London Bookstore, Reverend Jerald Stinson, Judy Greber, Leslie Scharf, Michelle Miller, Meredith Phillips, Janell Cannon, and Sue McCulloch.

Assistance on weapons and procedures was provided by Captain Dale Stockton of the Carlsbad Police Department, Lieutenant Bruce Rochester of the Sonoma County Sheriff's Department, Officer Bill Cannon of the Wheaton Police Department, and Ken Friel of North American Arms.

As always, I am indebted to Bill and Melissa Kamenjarin.

# Travelers on the Sonoma Sojourn

*Guido and Maria Ambrosino,* early seventies, retired tailor and homemaker celebrating their fiftieth anniversary, from Boston.

*Kelly Atherton,* twenty-six, a high-tech headhunter from Chicago, twin to Ryan.

*Ruth Atherton,* seventy-five, a retired teacher from Appleton, Wisconsin, grandmother of Kelly and Ryan.

*Ryan Atherton,* twenty-six, a cheese salesman from Madison, Wisconsin, twin to Kelly.

*Ginger Conner,* thirty-five, a wireless communications executive from Floritas, California, sister to Sara.

*Sara Conner,* thirty-one, a divorced paralegal from Atlanta, sister to Ginger.

*Alice and Don Harper,* midsixties, retired biotech operations manager and retired secretary from Floritas, California.

*Jessica Kincaid,* thirty, a divorced paralegal from Atlanta.

*Pat and Mark Martell,* midsixties, retired accountant and homemaker from Floritas, California.

*Haynes "Hake" Sandstrom, Esquire,* fifty-three, a Dallas attorney, and his twenty-eight-year-old trophy wife *Heidi.*

*Eleanor Whitson,* sixty-four, a widow from Pasadena, California.

# *Chapter 1*

HALF a dozen bottles of exquisite wine flowed freely, but the baby turned out to be the real icebreaker.

The infant was beautiful, even at twenty paces, peering out of her mother's arms through tiny, dark brown eyes, her dark wisps of hair covered by a lacy little cap. When mother and daughter appeared on the edge of the patio, the group gradually hushed, as more and more of them became aware of the newcomers. Silence held for a few moments, broken only by soft classical music coming from hidden speakers.

"This is my daughter, Stephanie Isabella," Angela Rutledge announced. She was their thirtyish hostess here at Villa Belladuce—slim and gracious and brimming over with nervous energy. Her own white lace trimmed a frilly, high-necked Elizabethan blouse tucked neatly into a long, royal purple skirt. Sleek black hair fell forward in graceful layers as she bent down and dropped a light kiss on her daughter's head.

A rustling breeze crossed the patio, and the moment ended. In a gentle, sybillant rush of oohs and ahs, five of the women descended on mother and child, leaving three bemused husbands to their own devices.

Lynne Montgomery was not one of those women.

Not that Lynne didn't like babies. She did indeed. She was a card-carrying, photo-toting grandmother herself and had both met and appreciated six-month-old Stephanie earlier in the day.

Right now, however, she was working. These fifteen men and women were guests on the Sonoma Sojourn Tour run by her travel agency, Booked for Travel. They had gathered here today from around the country for a weeklong visit to California's premiere wine country, and this was the first opportunity she'd had to meet them all in one place.

Lynne had been systematically chatting up her clients for hours, getting a firsthand understanding of their special needs, foibles, interests, mannerisms, and awkward prejudices. She knew how crucial it was to get a tour group to jell, and knew also that you could tell in the first hour of the first-day reception whether this was going to happen naturally. If your group flowed gently together or at least formed into a couple of comfortable subgroups, then you were more than halfway home.

If they didn't, you had a struggle ahead of you, and not a pretty one at that.

So far, this group seemed to be coalescing nicely. The Sonoma Sojourn members had spread comfortably around the stone patio, clustered in small groups around dark-green wrought-iron tables. A handsome young man tended the wine bar, and an equally attractive young woman circulated with clever canapés, many involving local cheeses. An antique wine press, artfully entwined with dried grapevines, sat in the middle of the patio, surrounded by stone planters spilling cascades of pastel annuals. More planters were scattered around the outdoor room. The sweet and spicy scent of roses wafted up from the ends of the vineyard rows below the patio.

The group would stay here at Villa Belladuce all week, making individualized daily explorations around Sonoma County: wineries, golf, cooking classes, wineries, hot-air balloon rides, wineries, historic sites, mud baths, wineries, redwood groves, shopping . . . and wineries. By night they would visit a succession of fine restaurants, beginning tonight with the legendary Marino's, just half a mile down the winding country road. And throughout it all, the Booked for Travel clients would put away enough wine to float any of the antique limos they'd be using for tomorrow's grand vineyard tour. Lynne had led this tour several times and knew that the average guest on the Sonoma Sojourn gained at least five pounds.

Villa Belladuce, their home base, was steeped in history and tradition. For over a hundred years, the venerable family-owned Sonoma Valley vineyard had survived a grapevine-destroying pest called *phylloxera,* the 1906 earthquake, Prohibition, and drought, but not the IRS. A badly timed entry into the high-end bed-and-breakfast business and a dogged tax-evasion investigation had in the end pushed the Belladuce debt over the top.

The new owners were Silicon Valley billionaires Jeff and Angela Rutledge. Angela Rutledge, now seated in a love seat, gently rocking that beautiful baby girl, loved the vineyard but had no interest in routinely hosting strangers at her home. At first, Angela had intended to cancel all bookings made prior to the property purchase. Lynne had flown north in a mild panic to argue her case, taking Angela to lunch and systematically charming the young woman—who was almost the same age as Lynne's own daughter, Jenny—into acquiescence. It was the sales job of a lifetime: part sympathetic fellow business-woman, part entertaining raconteur, part career counselor, all seasoned with a generous dose of mom. In retrospect, it was an absolutely shameless performance, and it left Lynne exhausted. But it worked.

Lynne had convinced Angela that the B and B concept might be occasional fun, and because there were half a dozen posh cottages already in place on the grounds, Angela had agreed to honor Booked for Travel's standing reservation for the first week in August.

Now Lynne returned her attention to Ruth Atherton, seventy-five, a widowed former teacher from Wisconsin, who'd been reminiscing about a trip she had taken to this same area as a young woman, half a century earlier. Ruth hadn't sampled any of the proffered wines, because alcohol interacted badly with her medications.

Ruth picked up her mineral water bottle. "Calistoga. Is that an Indian name, Lynne?"

Lynne laughed. "Not at all. There was a fellow named Sam Branner who made a fortune selling picks and shovels during the Gold Rush. Then he developed the first spa in this area in the mid–nineteenth century, using the local hot springs and patterning the place after Saratoga Springs, back in New York. The story has it that Sam was a bit of a drinker. Which is how he happened to say that his resort would be the 'Calistoga of Sarnifornia.' "

Ruth Atherton chuckled appreciatively. Though she was talking to Lynne, her eyes remained on her grown grandchildren across the patio.

"Your grandson's quite the center of attraction," Lynne noted.

Not surprising, really. This particular Sonoma Sojourn group was unusual in that so many of its members were young, in the same general age range as Lynne's own kids. The Atherton twins were only twenty-six, and the trio of young women traveling together appeared to be just a few years older. They had homed in on Ryan Atherton immediately, a logical choice, Ryan being both cute and unattached, with a wide-eyed Midwestern charm, soft brown eyes, and a shock of thick blond hair. His twin sister Kelly—who shared his wholesome good looks and had probably spent quite a few years of her life watching females goggle over Ryan—had broken away to fuss over baby Stephanie.

Ryan sat on the low stone wall that surrounded the patio, idly swirling a glass of Cabernet Franc and grinning at something one of the Atlanta paralegals had said. Sara Conner, the dark vivacious one, perched beside Ryan on the wall, both of them with their backs to the spectacular panorama behind them.

A stunning expanse of grapevines spread out behind and below the patio, trellised in graceful, undulating rows that hugged the curves of the low hills. The vines hung heavy with ripening fruit: pale golden green Chardonnay grapes, dusky red Pinot Noir, purply blue Merlot. *Véraison* had come to Sonoma quite recently, giving the thick clusters of grapes their final push toward sweet ripeness. Sweet, of course, was a relative term here; most of the wine grapes that Lynne had sampled over the years had been puckeringly tart.

Sara's sister, Ginger, a San Diego executive for a cellular phone service, sat facing the vineyard. Ginger was on her fourth glass of wine, and she hadn't taken any of the different offerings in minimal "taster" splashes, either, as had most of the others. It was a full glass each time for Ginger, who showed absolutely no effects of the alcohol.

Lynne, whose appreciation for fine wine had grown with each of the four years she'd led this tour, was keeping her own consumption to a minimum. This allowed her to maintain an informal tally of how much each of her charges had been drinking, information that would be critical once she began shepherding them around to different wineries tomorrow. Part of the appeal of this tour was that none of the guests had to do any driving, and all could therefore get quite thoroughly schnockered. Lynne needed to know who'd throw up, who would pass out, and who could put away a case without appearing more than slightly buzzed.

Hake and Heidi Sandstrom, so far making no effort whatsoever to mingle, seemed to fall into the case-capacity column. They were Texans, and Lynne knew she'd have a hard time convincing Hake to ride in the van with the masses. Hake was the kind of self-absorbed dictator who didn't let anybody tell him what to do, and his presence on this tour frankly baffled her. He was a partner at a major Dallas law firm, fifty-three, driven and intense. Heidi, his twenty-eight-year-old trophy wife, was a classic beauty and former Miss Texas runner-up. Neither seemed the type to join in group activities with strangers, and neither had objected—or really even seemed to notice—when Lynne had excused herself to move on to Ruth Atherton.

"Ryan's such a dear boy," Ruth was saying now. "I raised them, you know."

"It's the first thing Kelly told me when she called," Lynne said.

The second thing that Kelly had said was, "She's dying of cancer."

"She told me that when their parents died, they went to live with you in Appleton."

"Such a dreadful thing, that accident." Ruth Atherton shook her head. She was wearing a wig and had penciled eyebrows onto skin left translucent by her most recent round of chemotherapy. "Both of them wiped out in an instant. The twins had just turned seven, and but for the grace of God, they'd've gone, too." Her eyes took on a faraway look of pain and memory and maternal sorrow. "But I've come to realize that there's something to be said for going quickly, without warning."

Just like Monty. Lynne felt her throat close and her heart constrict as she forced down the memory of her own sudden widowhood five years ago. She willed herself to concentrate on the job at hand, breathing deeply as she watched a long-haired calico cat saunter across the patio, jump onto the stone wall, and disappear into the vineyard.

There was never an easy way to die, she believed, either for the one leaving this life or for those remaining to mourn. She had taken an instant liking to Ruth Atherton and appreciated her no-nonsense Midwestern sensibility. She knew that it would be a terrible, heart-stopping loss for Kelly and Ryan when this anchor to their childhood was gone.

"Have you decided if you'd like to join us at dinner, Ruth? I can bring you back early, if you want."

Ruth shook her head. "Actually, I was about to ask Kelly to walk me back to our cottage. These little cheese-puffy things filled me up pretty well, so I think I'll quit while I'm ahead. It's been a long day." She'd been traveling for three days, actually. Ryan had brought her from Wisconsin to Chicago, where she rested for a day and a half in Kelly's high-rise apartment before the three of them had flown into San Francisco this morning.

"Here, let me walk you over," Lynne offered. Kelly was leaning in close to Angela and her daughter, entranced. "She's enjoying the baby."

But Kelly Atherton sprang to attention when her grandmother rose to her feet, and Lynne knew she was going to insist on taking Ruth back to the cottage.

"For heaven's sake," Ruth told her fondly, "I'm going to bed, not to San Francisco. Besides, I'm enjoying talking to Lynne."

And though Kelly didn't argue, Lynne was aware of the girl watching till the two of them were out of sight, as her grandmother painstakingly and deliberately used a handsome hardwood cane to navigate the path across to Tuscany, the Atherton cottage.

⊂══✦══⊃

**WHEN** Lynne returned to the patio ten minutes later, the group had rearranged itself again. This was an excellent sign. A certain fluidity in social dynamics would enormously simplify the week to come.

Maria Ambrosino, wearing a beatific smile, now held the baby, and Angela supervised closely, with apparent approval. Maria Ambrosino was a warm, white-haired, pillowy woman, someone who would bond immediately with any baby, anywhere.

Hake and Heidi Sandstrom had not moved, and nobody had joined them. Not a problem yet, Lynne thought, though it could develop into one.

Kelly Atherton was still hovering over the baby, but Jessica Kincaid, the more quiet and reserved of the Atlanta paralegals, had rejoined Ryan Atherton and the Conner sisters at the stone wall. All but Jessica were now drinking red wine. The bartender came around at regular intervals, offering new bottles, varietals that had grown progressively more robust through the social hour.

Meanwhile, Lynne's two friends from Floritas had returned to their husbands at a large, round table near the stone wall, and Maria's husband, Guido Ambrosino, had pulled a chair over to join the foursome and Eleanor Whitson, a Pasadena widow. Alice and Don Harper were traveling with Pat and Mark Martell. The two couples were regular Booked for Travel clients and longtime friends of Lynne's. Retirees in their sixties who had reaped the benefits of some extremely well-timed genetic engineering stock options, the foursome were enjoying their retirement with a vengeance.

Lynne stopped by the wine bar for a glass of the latest offering, a five-year-old zinfandel, then pulled a chair over to their table.

"We'll have to have some kind of a party, Lynne," Pat Harper announced without preamble. "You didn't tell us the Ambrosinos are here to celebrate their fiftieth anniversary!"

Guido shifted uncomfortably in his chair. He shook his head and waved a hand dismissively in front of him. "No, no. We are just like all of you, guests on the tour." He spoke with an old-country accent and, of all the group, looked the most likely to have a vineyard as his natural habitat. In fact, if you cut out the others and got the light right, you could take a picture of him overlooking the vineyard that would make a fine cover for *Travel and Leisure.*

"Well, you're a few years ahead of us," Mark Martell told him. Mark was a pale man, neat and reserved and normally rather prim. The wine had loosened him up considerably. "Pat and I are just coming up on our fortieth." He winked at the Boston tailor. "And if these gals tell you they're going to throw you a party, you might just as well lean back and enjoy it. Because it *will* happen, I by golly guarantee it. There's nothing they like better than an excuse for a party."

As the bartender approached the table with a tray of clean glasses and a freshly opened bottle of a private reserve Merlot, Lynne heard a car engine coming up the drive fast. She had a clear view down the path to the parking area and watched in surprise as a fiery red Miata squealed to a halt, and a handsome young man jumped out, wearing black jeans and a butter-soft palomino-colored leather jacket.

Now *this* she hadn't expected. And neither, apparently, had Angela Rutledge, whose eyes opened wide and lips shrank into a tight, grim line as the man strode onto the patio, acting for all the world as if he owned the place.

"Having a party and I'm not invited?" he asked in a deep, sultry voice, flashing a sexy smile that showed dazzling white teeth.

Not altogether unreasonable, that proprietary air, since Lance Belladuce's family had owned this place for over a century. Lynne had recognized Lance immediately. He was not a man that most women would easily forget. He stood in the center of the patio now, his left hand resting on his hip, and surveyed the physical plant slowly and deliberately, looking up at the stone mansion, over toward the guest cottages, out across the rolling acres of grapevines. His thick, loosely curled, jet-black hair was cut slightly longer than the current fashion, and his skin glowed warm and golden in the setting sun. His profile would have made a dandy ancient Roman coin, and there was no doubt that he understood he was one very good-looking guy.

Lynne noticed she was holding her breath and that all conversation had stopped.

Lance Belladuce was clearly enjoying himself. He sauntered over to the wine bar, glanced at the various opened bottles, and picked one up with a delighted grin. "One of our best cabernets ever," he announced to nobody in particular as he poured himself a glass.

Angela Rutledge stood and moved slowly toward him, her eyes narrowed. She walked with a slight limp, a residual effect of an automobile accident that had nearly killed her as a teenager. "Lance, I don't think—"

He leaned down to kiss her cheek, and she recoiled, bringing the back of her hand up to touch her cheek, brushing the skin distractedly as if to banish cooties.

"Angela, you look positively delectable. Purple is definitely your color." Lance turned his attention to Maria Ambrosino, who was now holding the baby protectively. "And is this little Stephanie? Why, she's just the spitting image of you, isn't she?"

As he started toward the baby, Angela stepped into his path to block him, a mother grizzly protecting her cub. "You aren't supposed to be here," she said. "I think you'd better leave now."

He threw back his head and laughed. "I'm being evicted? That's rich now, isn't it?" He swirled the wine, held it up against the setting sun, inhaled deeply, and then sipped. When he'd finished, he offered a contented sigh. "Excellent," he pronounced.

For the first time, he seemed to notice that the party had specific members, wasn't merely an abstraction. He looked around at his fascinated audience. "Angela and I are both forgetting our manners," he apologized, charm seeping effortlessly into his tone. "I'm Lance Belladuce, and once upon a time, I used to live here. And"—his eyes halted at Lynne and flashed recognition—"you all must be the Sonoma Sojourn Tour! It's Lynne, isn't it?"

Lynne nodded and stood, extending a hand. Angela Rutledge might be unhappy, but Lynne had no quarrel with this handsome, cocky young man. "That's right. Lynne Montgomery. Nice to see you again, Lance."

He cupped his left hand over their clasped hands, his grip warm and gentle. When he bent down to kiss her cheek, Lynne offered it willingly. "Lovely as ever. Sorry I won't be doing the honors at the winery this time out, being persona non grata and all that, but I'm sure that Angela and Jeff will show you a perfectly splendid time."

Lynne could have sworn that Angela was about to start growling. And then, out of the corner of her eye, she saw someone coming down the outside staircase that led to the mansion's second floor above the garage. He was moving fast, a gaunt young man with long legs and a gangly, disjointed stride. He wore belted khakis, a white T-shirt, and wire-rimmed glasses, sported an unruly cowlick, and looked about fourteen. Lynne had seen his picture in business magazines but had always assumed that Jeff Rutledge would appear more stately and mature in person.

She'd been mistaken.

The legendarily shy billionaire electronics genius was walking so quickly he almost seemed to run. He screeched to a halt on the patio about six feet from Lance Belladuce, who'd been watching his approach with a bit of a smirk. As Rutledge glowered at him, Lance glanced at Lynne and winked.

"Jeff! Great to see you, my man!" Lance held out a hand in greeting.

"I am not your man," Jeff Rutledge replied in short, clipped syllables, ignoring the proffered handshake. "And you are not welcome here. As a matter of fact, you're trespassing. These people are guests at a private party, and you're disturbing them."

Lance clapped a hand to his chest in feigned dismay. "Disturbing your guests? Why, I wouldn't dream of it, Jeffers."

There was an element of little boys on the playground at work here, thought Lynne, of neener-neener-neener and your-mother-wears-army-boots—and it looked like somebody was about to end up with a bloody nose and a session in the principal's office.

Time to get the Booked for Travel show on the road.

Lynne backed away slowly, working at nonchalance. Whatever was happening here had nothing to do with her or her people, and the smartest thing she could do right now would be to gather the group and exit stage right, immediately. She caught the eye of the waiter. He was also their driver for the evening, so that Lynne herself could drink with her guests. He would take them down the road to Marino's for dinner at the end of this wine reception.

The reception, she realized now, was effectively over.

Lynne tilted her head and flicked her eyes toward the parking area and the van. The waiter offered a quick nod of understanding, set down his tray, and then discreetly backed off the patio and headed toward the van.

"Our dinner reservation's at seven, everyone," Lynne announced brightly, "so we'd better get going. We're eating just down the road at an utterly fabulous Italian restaurant. We'll go in two shifts in the van. Who's up first?"

Don Harper, a take-charge kind of guy, jumped right up. Don was bald and well rounded, and Lynne knew from years of socializing with the Harpers that he let very little get between him and dinner. "I'm starving," he said. "Alice, let's eat." Don read voraciously and loved Calvin Trillin, whose book title he'd just quoted. His wife, Alice, also got to her feet and was followed a moment later by Pat Martell, who murmured something about running back to the room for her purse.

Lance Belladuce, meanwhile, held up two hands placatingly and backed away from Jeff Rutledge. Rutledge seemed to take heart at his adversary's retreat, and he moved forward in a menacing fashion. He might be a geek, but he clearly understood the mechanics and occasional rewards of bullydom.

"Beat it, Belladuce," Rutledge said. His voice was deeper and stronger than his appearance suggested.

"Oh, I can tell I'm not welcome, Jeffers."

Rutledge bristled at the trivializing nickname. "Just get the hell off my property. And do it now, or I'm calling the police."

Lance offered a shiver of exaggerated fear. "Not the cops, sir, oh please, anything but that!"

The girls from Atlanta tittered, and Lance cocked his head toward the sound. Now he slowly looked around at the others on the patio, his gaze lingering on the younger women. Even under duress, Lance took the time to assess them all appreciatively. He cocked a finger at Hake Sandstrom, looking surprised, and said, "Hey, sport, fancy meeting you here!" He winked at Heidi, then turned finally to Lynne. "So sorry to interrupt your evening, Lynne, everyone. It's been a pleasure, of course."

Then, as abruptly as he'd arrived, Lance Belladuce ambled off the patio and climbed back into the Miata. The engine roared into life, and the tires spat gravel as he executed a snappy three-point turn and shot back down the driveway.

Jeff Rutledge turned and walked away, not even acknowledging his wife and daughter, leaving the patio as quickly as he'd arrived.

Angela retrieved baby Stephanie from Maria Ambrosino, and suddenly everybody was very busy. Excited voices babbled all at once, folks ran to fetch sweaters and handbags, and somebody knocked a wineglass onto the flagstone patio, where it splintered into a hundred crystal shards.

*Chapter 2*

BY the time everyone had arrived at the restaurant, Lynne was quite ready for the day to be over.

She had driven up from Floritas on Thursday in the Booked for Travel van, hightailing it up I-5 through the broiling San Joaquin Valley. Then she'd spent the next two days relaxing in San Francisco before driving up to Sonoma this morning. She loved San Francisco, and the time had been purely for herself, a sort of psychic charge-up for the week to come.

Lynne had spent the first part of the day confirming a welter of reservations for the week to come: winery tours, golf dates, restaurants, hot-air balloon rides. Some of the activities, like Wednesday's gourmet cooking class, were booked with tentative numbers, since part of the appeal of the Sonoma Sojourn was its flexibility. Guests could pick and choose among diversions up to the very moment an activity began.

The rest of the day she had devoted to welcoming her tour members and introducing them to each other, making sure everyone was comfortably settled into the well-appointed stone cottages built for the Belladuce family's bankrupting experiment in public hospitality. The cottages, named for various regions in Italy, were solidly constructed, clustered to the north of the mansion in charming drought-tolerant landscaping. Each offered a breathtaking view.

Today, the first of her Sonoma Sojourn charges had arrived in the early afternoon. The Athertons and Ambrosinos rode up from San Francisco International Airport in the same limo as Eleanor Whitson, an hour and a half before everybody else started showing up. Sara, Ginger, and Jessica had met up at Oakland International and arrived in a peppy little red rental car.

The Harpers and Martells had left Southern California at oh-dark-thirty in the Martells' SUV, which was large enough to accommodate two extensive sets of golf clubs and an impressive quantity of matched luggage. Their travel routines at this point were comfortable and well established, and Lynne was delighted to have friends on the trip.

Hake and Heidi Sandstrom had flown into Santa Rosa in their private plane and rented a Jaguar, which Hake predictably insisted on driving to dinner. Hake had made it clear from the moment he arrived that his wine expertise surpassed that of anyone else on the tour and quite possibly on the planet. He routinely visited France for the harvest, where the natives evidently fell to their knees in gratitude. No domestic wine, Hake implied—not even that deemed most exceptional, from the most exceptional wine-growing region in the nation—could ever measure up to the Real Stuff. Why he deigned to be with them at all Lynne couldn't imagine.

Dinner was California Italian, a merger of old-country flavors and ingredients with up-to-the-minute presentation and the occasional unexpected twist: shiitake mushrooms in the manicotti stuffing, razor-thin slices of sashimi layered with fresh basil and mozzarella. The Sonoma Sojourners had a back room to themselves, and they settled at two large tables.

Hake Sandstrom held court at one table with the practiced ease of one accustomed to dominating conversations wherever he turned. Seated with his wife, the Atherton twins, the

Conner sisters, and Jessica Kincaid, he seemed inspired to share his wisdom with the next generation. This included far more particulars about the contents of his wine cellar than most of his companions seemed to want to know. The young people were polite, notably the two paralegals, who undoubtedly had plenty of experience hearing out legal blowhards. Lynne had observed, however, as she waited on the Villa Belladuce patio for the van to return and whisk them off to dinner, that the four single women in the group seemed far more interested in discussing Lance Belladuce, the handsome playboy who'd disrupted the reception.

"You're probably not aware that these are the same grapes grown in Europe," Hake Sandstrom was saying now, "though often with a superior result in French vineyards. Red Burgundies are the same as Pinot Noir, red Bordeaux are Merlot or Cabernet Sauvignon, and the white wines are pretty much all Chardonnay. That includes Chablis, Macon-Villages, and Pouilly-Fuisse."

In the Marino's back room, Lynne had positioned herself to monitor conversations at both tables, from a vantage point at the second, more mature table. With this latest pontification, she decided she'd paid enough attention to Counselor Sandstrom for a while. She began to concentrate more on her own table companions and their easy camaraderie, which required almost no participation at all from her. Pat and Alice shared pictures of their grandchildren as their husbands got merrily plastered. Guido and Maria Ambrosino told everyone about the trip to Italy their kids had given them for their forty-fifth anniversary. Eleanor Whitson mentioned a recently deceased husband and an opthalmologist daughter in Seattle.

Lynne was able to pretty much stop talking altogether for a while, to relax, to discover that oyster mushrooms definitely enhanced veal saltimbocca. She now felt fairly confident that this group would work out well, and she was realizing for the first time just how tired she'd become.

The spirit of group goodwill and bonhomie lasted through cappucino (mostly decaf) and a choice of fresh apple tart or piping-hot chocolate soufflé, each topped with silky whipped cream. And then, finally, the senior Sonoma Sojourners returned to Villa Belladuce in the first van load, once again asserting the privilege of age.

By the time Lynne arrived with the second shift, the first folks had disappeared into their various cottages. Lynne watched Sara Conner, pale and glassy-eyed, clutch her sister Ginger's arm and stumble across the patio and down the path to Umbria. Ginger, who had outdrunk Sara at least two to one, was still both upright and intelligible. Only the Sandstroms, who'd announced their intention of taking a drive, hadn't yet returned. Abruzzi, their large single cottage, sat dark.

As lights went on in the various stone cottages, the colony took on the look of a small Italian hill town, romantic and charming. The only lights burning in the mansion were in the workshop over the garage, and Lynne remembered reading that Jeff Rutledge was known to work round the clock when inspired.

The evening was surprisingly chilly, and Lynne shivered as she watched everyone safely inside for the night. She then ducked into her own single room in the Campania duplex cottage she shared with Eleanor Whitson and slipped on a heavier jacket, having learned the hard way to pack for August in Sonoma as if it were December in Floritas.

Now that she could finally go to bed, she wasn't tired anymore.

She savored the crisp, clear, night air as she meandered back to the patio. The moon hung full and golden in a sky the color of ripe Merlot grapes, illuminating the gently curving rows of grapevines below. Lynne crossed to the edge of the patio where Ryan had sat with the young women earlier and admired the tranquillity of the moonlit countryside.

She could understand why Lance Belladuce, beneath his veneer of worldly indifference, had seemed to genuinely mourn the loss of the place, and why Jeff and Angela Rutledge, who could probably afford to live anywhere in the world, had chosen to put down their own roots among these ancient vines.

If there was one thing Lynne understood absolutely, it was

the urge to anchor oneself to a piece of land. As a military brat, she had spent her childhood bouncing from one base to another, getting cautiously adjusted to each location just in time to be rudely uprooted and moved somewhere else. She had yearned for the kind of hometown where folks knew each other for generations, where the sense of community arose not from the United States Navy but from a specific place, one with history and customs and mores unique unto itself.

She'd found that town when she married Monty Montgomery, a fourth-generation California surfer from the north San Diego County beach town of Floritas. What she hadn't realized then, hadn't noticed until she was up to her eyeballs in play groups and Little League and Scouts and PTA, was that the years following her father's career around the globe had fed a wanderlust that was as much a part of her as her turquoise eyes or blond hair.

Monty was never very interested in travel. Oh, he liked the out-of-doors, and they spent some wonderful family vacations camping in Yosemite and Big Sur. Monty was the dad who was always available to camp with the Boy Scouts, and when the kids were little, he often fantasized about surfing in Costa Rica and Hawaii. Later, when his business was prospering and the kids no longer living at home, he began to actually take surfin' safaris with his surf geezer buddies, some of them guys he'd grown up with long-boarding on the same beaches they now shared with Floritas High Surf PE classes.

But mostly Monty was a homebody. He considered Floritas to be God's country, and Lynne had learned to sublimate her wanderlust. This was, after all, the life she'd always claimed she wanted, and it was a mighty nice one at that.

She never stopped reading travel magazines, however. She experimented with regional and international cuisines, attended travelogues at the library, sent in *Sunset* magazine coupons for more information on offbeat cruises and remote dude ranches and obscure railroad lines. She was the mom who designed the costumes for Multicultural Day at the grade school, the Girl Scout leader who developed the troop's international themes for Thinking Day.

When the last of her kids went off to college, Lynne took a part-time job working for Maggie Chambers at Booked for Travel in downtown Floritas. Maggie had opened the agency thirty years earlier and used it to underwrite her own travel habit. Lynne started taking an occasional brief trip on her own or with a girlfriend. She visited the kids at school, went to New York and New Orleans and Savannah while Monty was surfing in Costa Rica.

She was grateful now that she had learned to travel on her own when it was an option, not a necessity. Monty's business was insurance, and after he suffered a fatal heart attack out surfing one awful January morning, it turned out that he had been one of his own best customers. Lynne was unexpectedly rich, just when Maggie wanted to free herself from the day-to-day responsibilities of Booked for Travel.

Lynne had bought the agency, and here she was.

An owl hooted somewhere off to the north, pulling her back to this starry August night in this Sonoma County vineyard. She peered in the direction of the sound, searching for the night hunter, and was rewarded a few minutes later when the dark form swooped down into the vineyard.

The quiet was broken by the roar of a Jaguar engine coming up the drive. Headlights flashed in the lot beyond the breakfast room, then abruptly cut off. Hake and Heidi Sandstrom had returned.

Lynne said good night to them, then went into her room, changed into the flannel nightgown she'd learned this country required, brushed her teeth, and collapsed into bed.

Sometime later, she was awakened by the persistent yowl of a cat. A few minutes after that, a door slammed, and the yowling ceased.

She dropped back into dreamless sleep.

❦

**LYNNE** was awake before dawn, totally alert, nerves humming, revved for the challenge of a three-vehicle, five-winery day on the summer back roads of Sonoma County. She stuck her head out long enough to determine the temperature, pulled on sweats and a jacket and her sturdy walking shoes, then slipped out into the chilly darkness for her morning walk. She moved purposefully down the paved driveway connecting mansion to highway, a driveway lined with roses rambling on wooden fences in rich and glorious bloom. She passed a spectacular single white Cherokee rosebush that seemed almost incandescent as the first purple hints of daylight began streaking in the east above the Mayacamas Mountains.

She turned right and hiked a mile or so along the deserted highway, a two-lane ribbon winding through vineyards and the occasional small orchard. Wild blackberries brambled through the roadside ditches, broken by an occasional clump of pink Naked Lady lilies. She passed the ivy-covered Marino's, where they'd eaten the night before. As she walked, she reviewed the day's itinerary for the umpteenth time, recalling Monty's aphorism that preparation was like ice in a glass of summer tea, far more obvious when there wasn't enough than when there was too much.

Today's itinerary wouldn't take them too far afield from their lodgings. They'd start out right here at Villa Belladuce with a tour of the winery, vineyard, and caves, none of which were normally open to the public. From there they'd head to Glen Ellen for the Benziger Vineyard tram tour, followed by a picnic lunch on the charming Benziger grounds. Then they'd meander back to Villa Belladuce, stopping at B. R. Cohn in Glen Ellen, and wrapping up the day with two wineries that were practically their next-door neighbors. Buena Vista was the oldest premium winery in California, and Gundlach-Bundschu—well, this was one of Lynne's personal favorites, in a class all its own.

Of course, Lynne realized, her people wouldn't get to Gundlach-Bundschu or anywhere else until she got back to Villa Belladuce and made it happen.

*Show time, Lynne.*

She crested a hill, then turned and started back. After a while, a car passed her, and she recognized the driver as Farrah, the young woman who'd been passing canapés the previous night, on her way to prepare and serve breakfast to the

Sonoma Sojourners. A bumper sticker on her car read: Sonoma Makes Fine Wines, Napa Makes Auto Parts.

The adjacent Napa Valley, on the eastern side of the Mayacamas, had long considered itself the pinnacle of California wine making. In recent years, however, Sonoma County had come into its own, and many serious oenophiles had shifted allegiance into the Sonoma-as-superior camp. Sonoma, for its part, was planting vines everywhere. Former grazing land now featured acres of vines of varying ages, apple orchards had been ripped out and replanted with grapes, and boutique wineries were tucked into every corner of the county. One of these trips, Lynne suspected, she'd find the Gravenstein Highway renamed the Pinot Noir Parkway.

She decided to return to Villa Belladuce by way of the winery, located a couple hundred yards south of the mansion and cottages. Generations ago, the women of the Belladuce family had decreed that they wanted the workplace kept separate from their home. At that point, both buildings had been relatively modest, as evidenced by the historic photos displayed in the barrel and tasting room of the winery. A grove of trees had been planted between the two buildings, with only a footpath to link them. As the winery and residence had grown over the years, so had the grove, which stood lush and virtually impenetrable today, save for the well-maintained paved pathway.

The winery had its own drive to the highway, and Lynne turned up that roadway now. She passed alongside gracefully trellised grapevines that stood eight feet tall, dripping huge clusters of photogenic fruit. She stopped for a moment to admire the dew-touched beauty of the grapes, to pick and sample one. It was, of course, quite sour. She always knew that would be the case, and yet she could never resist trying. Someday, she believed, she would sneak a wine grape and find it was as sweet and luscious as it looked.

Now she rounded the last bend in the drive and saw the low, wood-sided winery ahead of her. A scarlet Miata was parked just outside the main entrance to the building. Surely this was the car Lance Belladuce had been driving last night.

Odd. Very odd. She walked toward the car and then stopped abruptly.

Just beyond the car was Lance Belladuce himself. He lay sprawled, faceup on the gravel parking lot, one arm flung outward, the other arm draped across his chest. He was in the same clothing that he'd worn last night, but the front of that beautiful palomino leather jacket was now soaked with dark stains.

Lynne had been certified in first aid and CPR ever since her kids started kindergarten. Lance's dark eyes gazed sightlessly at the vines beyond him, and he—this man who had always been so spectacularly alive—now looked quite dead. Still, Lynne's experience with dead people was mercifully limited. What if he weren't actually dead? If he were somehow clinging to the farthest edge of life? She knew she couldn't leave him there without checking first to be sure he was beyond help.

She took a deep breath, approached tentatively, and made this a clinical exercise, the way she had when her kids had come home screaming with nasty, bloody injuries from skateboard accidents or roller skating spills. She extended her fingers cautiously and tried to find a pulse in the wrist farthest away from the rest of him, to ignore the red stains on his front and the stilled thick lashes above those lifeless eyes.

His flesh was cold and stiff, and there was no glimmer of a pulse.

She backed away slowly, then turned and sprinted toward the house, suddenly frantic to be anywhere else, to be away from him. She passed the winery building, then ran along the footpath that led through the grove to the mansion. As she emerged in the paved parking lot by the mansion, she realized that she was hopelessly winded and stopped for a moment to catch her breath. She leaned forward with her hands on her thighs, breathing deeply.

There was no need to run, she knew with absolute certainty and a wave of sudden, overwhelming sorrow.

It was way too late to help Lance Belladuce.

## Chapter 3

**DETECTIVE** Lauren Shaw was tall and broad-shouldered, a sturdy woman of around forty with restless hazel eyes and short, casually tousled brown hair. She arrived twenty-two minutes after the first sheriff's deputies answered Lynne's 911 call, taking charge with reassuring competence.

Lynne waited anxiously on the patio, positioned to quickly usher the Sonoma Sojourners into the dining room as they emerged to begin the day's itinerary. Breakfast wasn't scheduled for nearly an hour, but Lynne knew from experience that her older charges tended to rise at dawn and were often inclined to head automatically for the dining room, just in case.

Jeff and Angela Rutledge sat out on the patio, too, perched on chairs at a small table and fairly vibrating with tension. They had rushed down to the winery when Lynne first raised the alarm, even after she urged them not to go. Jeff Rutledge, she suspected, wanted to confirm that his adversary of the previous night was actually dead. Lynne had remained on the patio, reluctant to go shower lest one of her early risers decide to meander down to the winery before breakfast. She was relieved when a deputy escorted the Rutledges back to the patio with polite instructions to wait for a detective, who'd be arriving soon.

Both seemed shocked, their grim expressions locked solidly in place. A plastic two-way baby monitor lay on the table in front of Angela as she cupped her hands around a heavy mug bearing the Belladuce family crest.

Jeff had emerged fully dressed and wide awake from the mansion, wearing jeans and an old black sweatshirt faded to a dusty gray, and looking, if anything, even younger than he had the night before. Lynne had to keep reminding herself that this unprepossessing fellow had amassed at least three separate technological fortunes, that even though he kept his expression as deliberately blank as any teenage boy she'd ever known, there was a level of activity inside his brain that she could never hope to understand.

Lynne herself was fighting panic, trying to assess what the impact of this awful occurrence would be on her tour. She was not proud of this extremely selfish reaction, but business was business. At moments like this, it sometimes helped to ask herself what Monty, a world-class optimist, might have said under the circumstances. She knew immediately, could almost hear her dead husband's voice: *It'll all be downhill from here, Lynne m'love.*

Anxiety, in any case, had never much hampered Lynne's appetite. She nibbled on a flaky, custard-filled pastry and sipped a mug of fine coffee as she watched Detective Shaw walk around the corner of the mansion and approach them, all business. The detective had briefly introduced herself earlier, then headed down to the winery.

Detective Shaw smiled convivially, but only Lynne stood to greet her.

"What's going on?" Jeff Rutledge asked abruptly. "What was he doing at our winery?" The proprietary air of the question dismissed the hundred years when Lance Belladuce and his kinfolk had owned this land.

"I was hoping you might be able to tell me that, Mr. Rutledge." Detective Shaw spoke with the deference automatically accorded by law enforcement to the prominent and wealthy. Cops always said they treated everyone the same. They lied. Lynne had known this long before her son became a law enforcement officer and confirmed her lifelong suspicion.

A thin wail came from the baby monitor, and Angela straightened, instantly alert. "That's my daughter," she said. "I need to go see to her." Without waiting for a response, she picked up the monitor and headed toward the house.

With his wife gone, Jeff Rutledge looked even more like a lost and petulant adolescent. "I'm going back inside, too, officer."

Detective Shaw nodded. "In just a minute, sir, if you don't mind. I understand there was an altercation here last night."

Jeff started to glare at Lynne, the only possible source for that information, which she had in fact told the deputy earlier. Then he caught himself and offered a dismissive laugh. "Lance Belladuce made a nuisance of himself during the negotiations to buy this place. Once it was no longer necessary for us to deal with him, I told him to stay away from the premises. He showed up last night uninvited, and I asked him to leave."

He held a hand up as Detective Shaw started to speak. "I can assure you, however, that while I found him profoundly irritating, I didn't shoot him." When she gave no response, he frowned. "He *was* shot, wasn't he?"

"Why do you say that, Mr. Rutledge?" Lauren Shaw had a pleasant, neutral voice and a fine poker face.

Jeff Rutledge shrugged. "Isn't that usually how people are killed out in the country? Are you saying that he *wasn't* shot?"

Lynne recalled the profile of Jeff Rutledge published a year earlier in *GQ*. Jeff Rutledge collected guns, had a flashy personal arsenal that included everything from gargantuan handguns used in *Dirty Harry* movies to impossibly accurate sniper rifles to the Walther PPK made famous by James Bond.

"I'm saying that we'll let the coroner decide that," she answered calmly. "Now, how did Mr. Belladuce happen to show up here last night?"

"I'm sure I don't know." Jeff Rutledge turned to Lynne. "Excuse us, please." It was a dismissal so military that it carried Lynne instantly back to her childhood. Yet Jeff still hadn't made eye contact with Lynne, not even once, a characteristic he shared more with the teenage boys who'd hung out with her sons than with the officers who had terrorized her youth. An interesting hybrid.

Lynne offered an attempt at a gracious smile. "Certainly." She turned to Detective Shaw and made no effort to leave. "I have a group of fifteen people expecting to go on a back-country winery tour today. I don't think any of them even knew Lance Belladuce, so is there any reason we can't have breakfast as quickly as possible and just get out of your way then?"

The detective frowned. "The people in your group, they were here last evening when . . ." She let her voice trail off delicately.

Lynne nodded. "Except for Ruth Atherton, who wasn't feeling well and had gone to her cottage to rest. We were about to leave for dinner when Lance showed up."

"You knew Mr. Belladuce?" Detective Shaw directed the question at Lynne but then turned to Jeff Rutledge, who was beginning to sidle away. "Just a moment, please, sir," she told him crisply before returning her attention to Lynne.

"I'd met Lance on previous trips," Lynne explained. "I bring this tour to Sonoma every summer, and for the last two years, we've stayed here. We were some of the first guests when the Belladuce family opened these cottages to the public. And before that, we'd always come to the winery for a private tasting."

"Do you know if any of the people in your group knew him previously?"

Lynne shook her head. "I don't think so. After the incident out here, I'm sure anyone who actually knew him would have spoken up." She glanced apologetically at Jeff Rutledge. "The incident was discussed a bit at dinner. Anyway, I'll see that you talk to everybody before we leave, Detective."

Lynne wondered just how long this group debriefing might

take. She'd already realized there was no way to give her group their scheduled inside tour of the Villa Belladuce Winery this particular morning. *Please just step over that body there, folks, and don't mind the crime scene tape.* What she wanted to do—no, *needed* to do—was get them all away from here as quickly as possible, hoping things would be more normal when they returned in the late afternoon. At the very least, the body ought to be gone by then.

The limos were supposed to arrive at ten, and she'd already called to put them on standby. She hoped she could get the group interviewed and out of there as soon as possible.

Jeff Rutledge spoke up. "I'm not going anywhere. I live here. So why don't you talk to all these other people"—whoever the peons might be—"and then ask Rosalita, the housekeeper, to call me later." Though conspicuously lacking social skills, he seemed remarkably certain of getting his own way. Money could do that.

"Certainly, Mr. Rutledge," Detective Shaw told him with a cordial smile. "You mention a housekeeper. Who all lives in the house with you?"

He frowned. "My wife, my daughter, the housekeeper." The offhand delivery suggested that everyone had live-in help.

Detective Shaw nodded. "We'll need to speak with the housekeeper also, then, and with your wife when she has a moment. And you should be aware that several more detectives are on their way to help with this."

"I don't doubt it," he said, looking sullen. Then he loped away.

After he had gone, Detective Shaw turned her full attention to Lynne. The detective was a handsome, self-assured woman, someone, Lynne thought, it would probably be fun to meet in some other context. "You found the body, Mrs. Montgomery?"

"Yes."

"Tell me what happened."

Lynne reported briefly, then hesitated a moment. "I hope I didn't mess things up for you too badly by touching him." She shuddered. "I still can't quite believe I did. Once I saw him, I just felt like I had to check and be sure he wasn't alive, needing help. I tried to keep the Rutledges from going down there after I told them, but they insisted."

"Don't tell me what to do on my property" had been Jeff Rutledge's exact words. And so she hadn't.

"Don't worry about it, Mrs. Montgomery. I'm sure it was extremely distressing for you. You say you've known Mr. Belladuce for a number of years?"

It seemed funny to hear him called "Mister." Lance was one of those men that women instinctively call by their first names, unless they're already using terms of endearment. "Four or five, I guess. When we came here, Lance always led the tour, told the family story, brought everybody back down into the caves." Villa Belladuce, like many wineries in the area, stored much of its barreled wine in caves dug into the hillside long ago by Chinese laborers. The caves were just south of the winery.

"When was the last time you saw him? Before last night?"

"A year ago. He gave us the Villa Belladuce tour, talked about wine making, and signed a bunch of my people up for wine-of-the-month."

Lance had been *very* good at convincing her clients, particularly the women, to make significant wine purchases. He had what Lynne's mother had disapprovingly called "bedroom eyes," but none of her clients, even those her mother's age, had ever complained. And she imagined they remembered him fondly back home as they uncorked each bottle.

"Any other contact since then? Phone, E-mail, whatever?"

Lynne shook her head. "Nothing."

"What about the people in your group? Any of them been here with you before?"

"Nope."

Detective Shaw looked out into the vineyard, then turned back to Lynne and nodded toward the cottages. "You all are staying in those buildings?"

"Yes."

"And each of you has a private entrance?"

Lynne nodded. "Four of them are duplexes with interior connecting doors, and the other two are single units. I'm in a duplex with Eleanor Whitson, and our connecting door is locked, but the others are families or friends traveling together, and those are all unlocked inside."

"So someone leaving one cottage wouldn't necessarily encounter anyone else?"

"If you're suggesting that one of my tour group—"

Detective Shaw held up a hand. "I'm not suggesting anything, Mrs. Montgomery. I'm just trying to figure out who was where last night. Now. You say you went out on your own for a walk this morning?"

"Well, yes. I always take a walk first thing in the morning, and I was on my way back to shower and meet my group for breakfast. I figured I'd cut through the back way past the winery and maybe save myself a few minutes before I had to get to work."

"You thought that was a shorter route?"

"Oh, I *know* it's a shorter route. Somebody on one of my tours paced it off with a pedometer once. You learn all kinds of odd things in my job."

"And what exactly is your job?"

"Taking care of people, basically." Lynne offered a wry grin. "Would you like some coffee?"

The detective laughed. "Actually, I would, if it's not too much trouble."

"No trouble at all, Detective. There's somebody inside the dining room there whipping up a gourmet breakfast for my gang, and I know the coffee's already made, 'cause I've been drinking it. Follow me."

Lynne led her over to the dining room, where half a dozen small tables were set with white linen and fine china. Fresh roses were centered on each table in little crystal vases. A buffet at one end of the room was partly set up with fruit and assorted pastries, as well as a selection of coffees—flavored or not, decaf or high-test.

Lynne refilled her mug with hazelnut and added cream and

sweetener. She won a little bet with herself when Detective Shaw poured herself a cup of French roast, black.

Any minute now, her first folks would be stepping out to meet the day. Lynne moved to the door and peered anxiously at the patio. "I don't mean to be rude, but I really want to way-lay my people right away when they come out, so they won't wander off exploring and run into police officers or, God forbid, see that body."

"Fair enough. We'll wait on the patio. Now. You were telling me what your job is," the detective prompted, as they walked back outside.

"I own a travel agency down in Floritas, north of San Diego." Lynne took a seat facing the cottages, so nobody would appear without her seeing them first. She wanted no more surprises this morning. "My son's a cop in Floritas, if you want to check up on me. Officer David Montgomery. Anyway, I lead some special-interest tours through my agency, Booked for Travel. This is one of those tours. We'll be staying here all week, making day trips around the area."

"You take them to wine tastings? I thought most people did that on their own."

"I suppose they do," Lynne agreed. Actually, she knew perfectly well that they did. Winery tasting rooms were usually jammed with folks swirling and sniffing and sipping, especially on the weekends. "We provide transportation, so they can drink without worrying about driving. We also offer some other activities and side trips besides the wineries. It's a customized package tour, basically."

"How well do you know the people in the group?"

Lynne considered. "I've spoken with most of them on the phone when they made their travel arrangements. The Harpers and Martells I've known for years. They're regular clients, and Pat Martell and I were Girl Scout leaders together, years ago. I've known Alice Harper nearly as long as I've known Pat. Her husband Don worked with Mark Martell before they both retired. And I know Ginger Conner. Her company's one of my corporate clients, and I met her at some

Chamber of Commerce Sundowner in Floritas. The rest I met for the first time yesterday."

"And there are how many in the group?" Detective Shaw had her notebook out. Lynne got a glimpse of strong, angular handwriting, not unlike the woman herself. "Do you have some kind of roster?"

"Fifteen. There's five men and ten women."

Detective Shaw raised an eyebrow. "That kind of ratio normal?"

"Depends entirely on the tour. This one is usually mostly couples, but there are only three couples this time, the two I mentioned from Floritas and one sweet old Italian couple from Boston, the Ambrosinos. They're celebrating their fiftieth anniversary. Eleanor Whitson is a widow from Pasadena. Ruth Atherton is a terminal cancer patient from Wisconsin, here with her twin grandchildren, Kelly and Ryan. They're twenty-six. There's also three women around thirty who're traveling together: Ginger Conner, her sister, Sara, and her sister's friend, Jessica Kincaid. Sara and Jessica are paralegals in Atlanta. That's it."

Detective Shaw looked up from her notebook. "That's only thirteen."

Oh, lordie, she'd forgotten the Sandstroms. Certainly she wished she could forget the Sandstroms, or maybe just ship them back to Texas like a case of fine Cabernet Sauvignon. Except, of course, that you couldn't legally ship wine to Texas, a fact that displeased the counselor no end.

"I missed the Sandstroms, Hake and Heidi. He's a hotshot lawyer, and she's his midlife crisis wife. They're from Dallas."

"You're very thorough."

Lynne shrugged. "When people pay a lot of money for a tour, they want you to remember who they are."

The detective's smile this time was a bit warmer. "They seem to be in good hands."

Lynne rubbed her eyes. "We'll see how they feel about that when they stumble out, hungover, and have to talk to the police before breakfast." She checked her watch. "The only reason we haven't already seen some of them is that this *is* a wine country tour, and most of them were getting their money's worth last night. There was a whole lot of wine, over several hours, first here and then at dinner. First night out, not everybody knows how to pace themselves."

"So tell me about last night."

"Sure. But listen. I understand that you need to talk to my people, though I suspect what you'll get out of them about Lance's appearance last night will be like one of those psych experiments. You know, the kind where an incident's staged in front of a class and then everybody has a different perception of what happened. Like that classic movie, *Rashomon.*"

"We'll see, won't we?" Detective Shaw said easily. "And while we're waiting for the rest of your group, maybe you can start with what you saw last night."

"Sure. But when you do talk to my people, can you be, um, kind of discreet about what happened to Lance? And maybe even a little speedy? I'd like to get them out of here as quickly as I can."

Lynne was starting to get a headache. She leaned back, closed her eyes for a moment, and visualized Hake Sandstrom sniffing disdainfully at a wineglass. She snapped her eyes back open. "It's really terrible business to start off any tour with unpleasantness, much less with somebody getting killed. I need to get them away from here, and to distract them, as soon as possible. Start pouring more wine into them. Take them shopping. Make sure they're having a good time."

"Other detectives are on the way," Lauren Shaw told her. "Till they get here, that sounds doable. Actually, it sounds just fine. Now. You were saying . . ."

Detective Shaw asked another dozen questions about what Lynne had seen this morning when she first approached the winery. From there they backed up so she could give a more detailed account of the group's activities during the previous day and evening. The detective seemed particularly interested in anyone who might have taken a stroll around the grounds and gone over to look at the winery building yesterday, even though the building was normally closed on Sunday.

"Everybody was wandering around," Lynne told her, "and other than to give them general directions like 'the winery's back through the woods that way,' I didn't pay much attention. The Sandstroms didn't walk around, I don't think, because they came in later than the others and went directly to their cottage until the reception started. And Ruth Atherton was very tired when she arrived, so she went to lie down immediately. Kelly insisted that she use the wheelchair to get to her cottage, and she didn't want to, but she didn't put up much of a fuss. But if you want to know exactly where the others went, you'll have to ask them."

"Oh, I will," the detective promised, just as the Ambrosinos, their internal clocks set to eastern daylight time, emerged from the honeymoon cottage, Veneto. They spoke separately to the detective, who set herself up for the interviews on the most isolated corner of the patio. By the time Guido and Maria went in for breakfast, four more detectives had arrived, and the process moved fairly smoothly from there on out. The Harpers and Martells came out together, followed by Eleanor Whitson, who nearly fainted on learning what had happened.

Kelly Atherton showed up next and insisted on taking tea to her grandmother before she talked to anybody. Lynne, who admired the girl's devotion and spunk, helped her assemble a tray of tea, cereal, and a blueberry muffin. Lynne added a fragrant Mister Lincoln rose to the tray from an unoccupied table in the breakfast room. While she was inside, she snagged herself a chocolate croissant.

Almost as soon as Kelly left, Jessica Kincaid and Ginger Conner stumbled out into the day, reporting that Sara had decided to skip breakfast.

"Will she feel well enough to join us later?" Lynne asked diplomatically. Sara was likely to have one lollapalooza of a hangover. "Because today's the day we're going to be riding in some really cool antique limos, and that's really a lot of fun. I'll drive along separately in the van, and we'll stay in this general area all day. I could come back for Sara later if she wants. You all have the cell phones, of course, so she could call any time. Ruth Atherton is hoping to join us this afternoon, so I'll probably be coming back to pick her up, anyway."

"Oh, Sara's hungover, but she'll be fine," Ginger said offhandedly. "She should be out in a little while." Ginger herself seemed to be suffering no ill effects from the previous night's excesses.

Nor did the Sandstroms, who both seemed shocked to hear of the death but were unable to help the investigation. They picked up coffee, asked that two jalapeño omelets be sent to their cottage, and left.

Then Kelly returned, accompanied by her brother, Ryan, who looked a bit the worse for wear and announced his intention of breakfasting with his grandmother in their cottage. He waited his turn, was questioned, and took a tray back.

And to Lynne's surprise and delight, the Booked for Travel group was actually forty-five minutes ahead of schedule—the Villa Belladuce tour indefinitely postponed—when they climbed into a trio of beautifully maintained antique Cadillacs and set out for the first full day of their Sonoma Sojourn.

*Chapter 4*

"YOU can date the golden age of California wine making very precisely," Lynne Montgomery told the Booked for Travel group, "to the Paris taste-off of 1976."

Jessica Kincaid, who had been in an Atlanta preschool in 1976, glanced around and saw several heads nodding. They were waiting in Bruno's Nymph Garden at the Benziger Winery in Glen Ellen for their upcoming tram tour, and Lynne was filling the empty time with . . . well, you really couldn't call it anything else but a lecture, and Jessica was only partly paying attention. Which, she was starting to realize, was certainly her privilege. This wasn't school, after all, or work. She'd paid as much as any of these folks to be here—more, if you counted the psychic damage of the divorce that yielded the settlement she'd dipped into to pay her way—and she might just as well do whatever she felt like.

When Sara talked her into taking this trip, she'd maintained that it didn't matter whether or not Jessica knew anything about wine. Sara had been unbelievably wrong. These people were so passionate about wine that a discussion on the relative merits of zinfandel and Petite Sirah last night had seemed likely to result in fisticuffs before Lynne intervened. Jessica, whose primary distinction between wines before this trip had been red versus white, felt like a total dunce.

"Up until that point," Lynne went on now, "the French pretty much had a lock on quality wine sales, and California wines had a reputation as just barely adequate. Right up to the moment that the scores were tallied the French thought the Americans were pretty silly to even subject ourselves to such embarrassment." She grinned. "It was California Cabernet Sauvignon versus French Bordeaux red, and California Chardonnay versus French white Burgundy. And you know what happened? The top red was a Stag's Leap Cabernet, and the top white was a Chateau Montelena Chardonnay, both of them from Napa Valley, just across the Mayacamas Mountains from here. And the rest, as they say, is history. California took our wines to their turf, used their judges, and we *still* came out ahead."

"Has there been another competition?" one of the San Diego ladies asked. Jessica couldn't remember her name, but she'd noticed that the woman wasn't the least bit shy about speaking up. Since many of her questions were about things that Jessica didn't know either, this was often useful.

"Not that I'm aware of," Lynne answered. She was quite nice, Jessica thought, bright and funny and concerned that everything be just right for her group. And, unlike Jessica's mother, who knew everything and was never, ever wrong, Lynne didn't seem to mind saying when she was unsure of something.

The winery tour guide called them over and collected their tickets, Benziger wine labels featuring a tasteful russet leaf embossed on a dark marble background. Jessica was working very hard at not thinking about that handsome Lance Bella-duce being dead. She hadn't been as taken with him as Sara was last night—Sara was notoriously weak-willed where darkly handsome men were concerned—but there was no denying a certain animal magnetism. And it was truly shock-ing to think of someone who had appeared so fantastically alive being so suddenly dead. That he'd apparently been murdered was almost incomprehensible.

When they got into the tram, Jessica managed to maneuver herself in position to sit beside Ryan Atherton. Of course Sara was on his other side, Sara with her flashing dark eyes and cloud of black hair, her pert little figure and effervescent personality. Although Sara was none too peppy today, not after barfing at midnight and crawling out of bed this morning moaning how her head felt like it was being smashed between boulders. And that had been *before* she realized Lance Belladuce was dead. Jessica usually felt a bit gawky and unattractive around Sara, but last night's excesses had proven a great equalizer. Sara looked awful this morning.

The tram climbed the hillside into the vineyard, passing row after row of trellised vines. The guide stopped the tractor pulling the tram at a vista point overlooking the winery, and they all dutifully walked over to a large model of a mountain. "Sonoma Mountain was a volcano," the guide explained, "and as a result of that, it has many different soil levels." He pushed a button, and one side of the model sank to show a geological cross section.

Jessica hadn't taken any tour vacations before and hadn't been sure what to expect, but she had been to Orlando several times. This felt like a cross between a fifth-grade field trip to the science museum and the Universal Studios tour.

"These different soil levels make subtle differences in the character of the grapes we grow there," the guide went on. "This area's broken into what we call 'flavor blocks' that are farmed separately, as sort of minivineyards."

"Are you harvesting yet?" The question came from the back of the tram, from a man who wasn't with the Sonoma Sojourn tour.

The guide shook his head. "We'll start harvesting here in two or three weeks. Our Pinot and zinfandels come in the earliest. I hear that the sparkling wine harvest has already started, though. Those champagne grapes always come in first."

Everyone took the same seats on the tram when they climbed back in, after hearing rather more about geology than

Jessica really cared to know. Science had never been her strong point. At their next stop, the guide offered them the option of getting out or listening from the tram. Nobody moved, so he walked back and forth alongside the parked tram, in front of a group of exhibits.

The guide fiddled with some Venetian blinds that were rigged to explain the function of pruning to control the amount of sun reaching the grapes. Ryan leaned over and spoke quietly into her ear. "See those flavor charts?" He pointed discreetly. Each offered a continuum of flavors found within a single varietal, or type of wine.

Jessica read one of them: Fresh Green Bean—Ripe Green Olive—Blueberry—Cherry—Blackberry/Black Pepper—Generic Raisin. "Merlot looks like a salad bar," she whispered back. Ryan gave a good chuckle, and she was pleased. He had that funny Midwestern accent (though he had told her last night that her own Southern accent was the one that sounded strange) and he seemed such a cheerful, uncomplicated fellow. Which didn't mean he was, of course. Jessica had been burned by good-humored charm before.

When they reached the tasting room, she found herself standing beside him at the bar. A gracious young woman poured them each a taste of Chardonnay. Ryan swirled and sniffed and then turned to Jessica.

"An acceptable bouquet," he said softly, mimicking the twang used last night by that obnoxious Dallas lawyer. "An adequate nose." It was a pretty bad imitation, actually, but he was cute enough so it didn't matter. He took a sip, furrowed his brow, and announced, "Aged in French oak, no question about it."

Jessica giggled. "Medium toast or heavy?" Mr. Sandstrom was an overbearing gasbag, but Jessica was used to his type. Some of the lawyers in the litigation department where she and Sara worked were even worse. Last night's extensive discussion of "toasting," part of the barrel-making process, had separated the serious oenophiles from the dilettantes. Jessica had never once opened her mouth. Neither had Ryan, now that she thought about it.

"Oh medium, definitely," he responded, mock seriously. "You know, the whole time he was carrying on about that last night in the restaurant, I kept picturing, well, a *toaster.* Where barrels pop up instead of English muffins."

"And you'd need a pitchfork to get out the ones that got stuck." Jessica drained her glass, feeling suddenly giddy.

Maybe Sara had been right after all about taking this trip. Though you'd have a hard time convincing Sara of that right now. She'd skipped the tasting room altogether and gone straight for the gift shop with a couple of the older ladies. She'd said something about getting a souvenir for her son, Justin, but it was hard to imagine what a six-year-old boy would want from a winery gift shop. Jessica doubted they sold Legos or game cartridges. And a lot of the standard gift shop offerings would get a kid suspended from school in this zero-tolerance age: foil cutters, corkscrews, cheese knives.

The bartender was back. "Are you ready for another? We have a fine Merlot that was last week's Wine of the Week in the *Santa Rosa Press-Telegram.*"

"Hoo-whee!" Ryan said, thrusting his glass forward.

Jessica moved hers right beside it and for the first time noticed his watch. The background of the face showed a chunk of Swiss cheese, with little mice on the ends of the hour and minute hands. She tried to think of any guy she'd ever known who would have the nerve to wear that watch, and she came up empty. Lance Belladuce, she remembered suddenly, had worn one of those huge Rolexes that set off airport metal detectors.

Both their glasses held the prizewinning Merlot now. Emboldened, Jessica lifted her glass and turned to look Ryan in the eye. His eyes were a soft, gentle hazel, and for a moment she forgot what she was doing. Then she clinked his glass and smiled.

"Cheers!"

⊂━⧓━⊃

**HAYNES** Sandstrom, Esquire, sat in the shaded grove and surveyed his picnic lunch with considerable irritation. A couple of slivers of turkey in a French roll with way too much cheese was not Hake's idea of a sandwich, and you could just forget about that salad, a nasty little mess of sprouts and nuts and bits of oddly colored weed. Heidi nibbled her salad contentedly, but Heidi'd eat rabbit turds if you put enough hot sauce on them.

"This place is really kind of pretty, don't you think?" Heidi asked. She was always seeking assurance from him, which normally he appreciated; it pleased Hake to be considered an authority on anything you might want to know. Today, however, he found it annoying. Today, he found just about everything annoying.

"Just dandy, little darlin'," he responded shortly.

Heidi turned to him with a tiny frown on her perfect face. Seven years now since her last Miss Texas pageant, and her looks were holding splendidly. She worked out five days a week with a personal trainer in Dallas. "Do we really have to take all these tours with everybody?" she whispered.

Hake put an arm around her and offered a hearty squeeze. "Just enough to be polite," he told her, "and to take care of my business. You think you'd like fixing up a place up here?"

Her little nose wrinkled. "If it isn't too terribly old and dirty."

Hake Sandstrom, senior partner at Tammerville, Carr and Barnes, major-league rainmaker and world-class bullslinger, looked at Heidi's pouty little face and for just a moment he could hear his first wife, Susan, scornfully dismiss his *child bride*.

"Why darlin', if it's too old and dirty, we'll just rip it down and start over. Fair enough?"

Just then, a man at one of the nearby picnic tables, somebody who wasn't with their group, rose with a roar and flung a cup to the side, splashing liquid against a tree trunk. He began hollering and bellowing and cussing the kind of blue streak that you'd expect to hear in a gangster movie. Everyone looked over, startled, as the man jumped up, pawing at his mouth, dancing and stomping around like some crazed warrior from an especially belligerent jungle tribe.

When Hake finally realized what had happened—that a yellow jacket had gotten into the fellow's cup and had stung his tongue—he laughed until he choked, and Heidi had to whomp him on the back. It was the most fun he'd had since he taxied to the hanger in Santa Rosa.

Maybe today wouldn't be so terrible after all.

꘎

"... **AND** nobody ever heard from Count Harazthy again," the young man in the black apron told the group, a tinge of sadness in his voice. He stood outside the original vine-covered Buena Vista Winery building, filled with enormous old redwood barrels behind wrought-iron bars. The building was closed to the public, he'd explained, because it didn't meet earthquake safety standards. "The story, however, is that he was eaten by crocodiles down there in Nicaragua, where he was trying to set up a sugar cane plantation."

Maria Ambrosino smiled. Count Augustin Harazthy, the Hungarian who'd started the commercial wine industry in Sonoma back in the mid–nineteenth century, sounded like quite a rascal, moving restlessly from one outrageous adventure to another. Her Uncle Giancarlo, rest his soul, had been a lot like that. And Uncle Giancarlo, like the noble vagabond, had simply disappeared one day, though nobody had ever mentioned crocodiles when he vanished abruptly that long ago February. Folks had shaken their heads and muttered that they weren't really surprised, and Aunt Sophia was taken care of by other family members.

Maria stole a look at Guido, beside her. He'd picked up a handful of bark chips, stained purple with wine, and was rubbing them slowly through his fingers. She wondered if he felt as overwhelmed as she did by all of this. She supposed that Guido was probably all right. He was, after all, a gently gregarious soul who'd spent his life interacting with the public. Guido was a tailor, and a fine one at that. Even now, long after his official retirement, there were men who sought him out to cuff new trousers or let out the waistbands of old ones.

Maria, however, was most comfortable when she knew and

understood her environment. This trip was simply providing too many experiences at once for her. All these new people and strange places, and even some weird things in places where you wouldn't expect surprises. Like that sign she'd seen in the ladies' room before the tour: You Are in the Country. Occasionally the Well Water, Which Services the Rest Rooms, Has an Unusual Odor. Please Bear with Us as It Is a Natural Occurrence. Maria had lost no time getting out of *there*.

It was hard to tell if Guido was enjoying today's outing or not. Riding in the fancy old limousine was fun, of course, and the places were pretty enough, and he did appreciate the wine. She knew he would never admit feeling uncomfortable in this crowd of rich WASPs, people who under other circumstances would dismiss a retired Italian tailor without a second glance.

But Maria hadn't expected to be comfortable, and she wasn't. You couldn't tell the kids that, of course. They didn't listen. They heard what they wanted and made up the rest. When they announced they were sending her and Papa to the wine country for their anniversary, she'd known there was no way on earth that she could stop it.

"Thinking about Antonio?" she asked Guido softly now.

He nodded. Neither of them had mentioned his cousin Antonio for years, until the kids sprang the trip plans on them. Guido's cousin had moved to California half a century ago, just after Maria and Guido were married. He had begged them to go with him and his wife, Anna. The Ambrosinos remained in Boston because Maria couldn't bear to leave her mother and her sisters, and she knew that Guido had always secretly believed theirs would have been a better life if they had gone to California.

Never mind that Antonio died in Korea, and his widow stayed in California and married a Mexican. Never mind that Antonio never did, from what Maria could tell, ever do anything with wine but drink it.

It was a dream, and dreams died hard.

For herself, Maria had felt the moment they arrived at Villa Belladuce that it was a troubled place, though she would never share that feeling with Guido, who laughed at her "feelings." She had also realized as soon as she saw baby Stephanie that her own perfect vacation would be holding that dear little child on that nice old patio.

◦━◆━◦

**JEFF** Rutledge stood at his office window and looked out through the treetops toward the winery, just barely visible in the distance. The property had been overrun with cops and medical examiners and God knows who all else throughout the entire day. Lance Belladuce had been slime of the first order, and Jeff saw no reason to feign remorse at his death.

But why were they still here, those cops and technicians? Angela had been down to the winery three times, and on her last return, she'd reported that the body was finally gone. He could only hope that meant that the cops would also be gone before much longer.

But then the damned tour group would be back. He frowned. No matter what Angela said or how accustomed he was to accommodating her desires, the idea of having strangers coming and going on his property was simply unacceptable. Jeff was sorely tempted to kick them all out and tell them if they didn't like it they could talk to his attorney. But Angela was so tightly wound since those disturbing E-mails about the baby that he didn't want to say or do anything that might upset her more.

Moving here had been Angela's idea, and Jeff was sorry now to have humored her. He hadn't wanted to leave Palo Alto, hadn't been interested in owning a vineyard and winery, hadn't even, if truth be told, been all that enthusiastic about fatherhood. He'd known from the beginning that because of her accident, Angela couldn't bear children, and that had never bothered him much. They had a good thing going, just the two of them, and he had secretly feared that putting a child into their equation might render the entire relationship unstable. He had finally agreed when Angela collapsed one night in uncontrollable tears, after months of moodiness. Setting out on the road to adoption had almost totally restored her spark.

But moving to Sonoma had been a colossal mistake. In the Silicon Valley, he and Angela had been pleasantly anonymous—wealthy, of course, and then wealthier and wealthier still, but basically just another lucky geek and his wife. Part of the landscape.

Here they were objects of intense scrutiny. Different. Remarked upon no matter what they did or didn't do. The natives resented his money, lumped the Rutledges with the nouveau riche dot-commers who had swarmed north when they cashed out and found themselves floating in wealth.

Jeff had gotten over the thrill of being rich a long time ago, when he sold the first of two processes bought out by Microsoft. He and Angela had done all the obvious things then: nice cars, new houses for their parents, moving out of the cute little Eichler house in Palo Alto to a huge custom ranch house where the plumbing never did work right.

What annoyed him the most here was being tarred by the dot-com brush. The ignorant fools disparaged and dismissed him because of an association that wasn't even accurate. He'd never been personally involved with Internet technology or companies, apart from playing on-line like anybody else. But in Sonoma, all technological money was lumped together and resented. Jeff might not have been aware of any of this, actually, but Angela had social antennae that picked up everything, and she was easily hurt.

This murder would only brighten the spotlight. Damn that Lance Belladuce anyway! Alive, he had been lying scum and a colossal aggravation; dead, he was turning out to be even worse.

Jeff closed the blinds. Without thinking about what he was doing, he grabbed his keys, took the back stairs down to the garage, and roared off in his Porsche. At the end of the drive, a uniformed cop waved his arms to stop him, then jumped out of the way when it became clear that the car wasn't even going to slow down.

Jeff barely even noticed.

*Chapter 5*

**THERE** was nothing quite like drinking all day to lift the spirits of a tour group.

By the time the Sonoma Sojourn group reached Gundlach-Bundschu, the final winery of the first full day, everyone seemed to have forgotten—or at least stopped talking about—the morning's awkward beginning. Lynne regarded her group with considerable satisfaction. She'd been working triple time at creating good cheer, dredging up half-forgotten anecdotes, laughing appreciatively at Don Harper's corny jokes, sharing wine country history and gossip.

Though it was, of course, the virtually limitless wine that really turned the tide.

Now Lynne carefully surveyed the group standing around the bar in the cavelike tasting room with its stone walls and dim lighting. Some wineries worked very hard at being sophisticated, but Gundlach-Bundschu invariably aimed for funky and generally hit the mark. The list of today's wines for tasting was written casually on a chalkboard.

The operation had been owned by the same family for

nearly a century and a half, and it featured nice views, good wines, offbeat souvenirs, and one of the wittiest ad campaigns in wine history. The paneled back wall of the tasting room was hung with many of the winery's tongue-in-cheek black-and-white ads.

"Hey, Lynne," Pat Martell said, "there's the print you've got hanging in the john at the travel agency." And indeed it was, a black-and-white photograph titled "Sonoma Valley Sobriety Test #1." The picture showed a cop telling an elderly lady behind the wheel of a 1947 Kaiser: "If you can't say Gundlach-Bundschu Gewürztraminer, you shouldn't be driving!"

Lynne decided her folks were set for a while and slipped out into the warm, afternoon sunlight, past the locked entrance to the wine caves. The morning's misty haze had long since burned off, and wispy puffs of white cloud drifted lazily across a sky the soft blue of the forget-me-nots that had naturalized in Lynne's Floritas garden.

She wandered over to the edge of a patio that overlooked a small lake with a graceful fountain rising in its center. Sitting in an Adirondack chair beside a low stone wall, she punched the number of Villa Belladuce into her cell phone.

It rang. It rang and rang and rang some more. No machine picked up, no voice mail interceded. Pretty incredible, considering that the Rutledge fortune rose out of high technology. Obviously, Jeff and Angela had decided they didn't want to talk to anybody.

She let it ring ten times, then hung up and called again, prepared to give it another ten, just in case she'd called the wrong number the first time. On the seventh ring, Angela Rutledge answered, sounding slightly breathless. "Yessss?"

"It's Lynne Montgomery, Angela. How are things going back there?" That seemed sufficiently ambiguous.

Angela's response was equally oblique. "Oh. Lynne. All right, I guess."

"Are the police still there?"

Angela sighed deeply. "I'm starting to think they'll *always* be here. But most of them are gone by now. Where are you guys? When will you be back?"

"Pretty soon. We're at Gundlach-Bundschu, and that's the last stop of the day. I've been dragging things out, and I stuck in a couple unscheduled stops to slow us down a little bit more." Not to mention her impromptu talk on olive oil in the olive orchard at B. R. Cohn. First-pressing extra-virgin oils sold in winery gift shops for as much as $50 a bottle, and tiny bottles at that. These Sonoma entrepreneurs didn't miss a trick. "Our dinner reservation isn't until seven, but everybody's going to want to shower and rest up a bit first. Do you think it's all right to come back?"

"I guess," Angela answered dispiritedly.

**BUT** when the antique limos disgorged their passengers at Villa Belladuce forty minutes later, Angela was waiting for them on the patio, wearing jeans and a perky expression, hair gleaming, makeup freshly applied.

Lynne could see the edge of a thickened welt of scar tissue peeking out of Angela's cuff. Lynne had done her homework on the Rutledges before making her desperate trip north to try to save this tour. She had read about the horrific burns suffered by a teenaged Angela in a Los Angeles freeway fire after a five-car pileup. Only her face and hands had been spared, and those were the only body parts she bared, wearing high collars and long sleeves at all times, easy enough to manage in this climate.

Now Angela carried baby Stephanie in a brightly woven sling that hung across her shoulder, the kind designed by Third World mothers to carry their babies while they worked the fields.

"So, did you all have fun?" Angela asked brightly. Several bottles of wine stood with glasses on the outdoor bar, beside a platter of baked brie and crackers. "Social hour's a bit more informal tonight, but do help yourselves."

Murmurs of appreciation filled the patio, though most of the group meandered off to their cottages without stopping for refreshment. Ginger Conner and the Sandstroms sidled toward the wine bar, ready for round six, or eighty-three, or wherever they were on the day's drinking schedule. By Lynne's calculations, none of them should even be standing at this point. Hake had not only sampled many of the free offerings, he'd also ponied up for a taste of most of the premium wines available for an additional charge at many wineries.

Now Hake picked up an open bottle, curled his lip, and cocked a skeptical eyebrow at the label, then poured three glasses. Heidi's mouth tilted, slightly open, like a baby sparrow. Ginger swirled, sniffed, and slugged.

"Let's all take it easy for the next hour or so," Lynne suggested to those still loitering on the patio. "Tonight's restaurant is just down in town, so it'll only take a few minutes to get there. No need to dress up unless you really want to, but I'm sure some of us will want to freshen up a bit first."

"Me, me, me," Jessica Kincaid announced, glancing over at Ginger at the bar, then turning to Sara. The three of them were billeted together in Umbria, a two-bedroom duplex. "I call first shower."

"Do I have time for a little nap?" Alice Harper asked. She carried several bags of carefully wrapped wineglasses bearing the logos of the wineries they'd visited so far. Alice and Pat were planning a wine tasting party after they returned home, featuring some of the wines purchased on the trip. They'd decided that it would be fun to have glasses from all the wineries represented, which at the rate they were going would fill the SUV by week's end. Pat had also found a set of numbered muslin bottle covers in the Kunde gift shop, more upscale than brown paper sacks for concealing wine identities.

"Sure, go ahead," Lynne told her. "Do you need a wake-up call?"

Alice laughed. "Not as long as I have Don." She followed the others, moving languorously across to the duplex cottage she and Don shared with the Martells. Even the perpetual wine drinkers, Ginger and the Sandstroms, topped their glasses off and left. Hake was carrying one of the bottles.

Maria Ambrosino had seemed oblivious to the activity

around her, cooing at the baby from the moment she stepped onto the patio. Now Guido placed his hand lightly on his wife's shoulder, murmuring for her to come along. They walked hand in hand down the path to Veneto, the farthest cottage from the mansion. The smaller of the two single cabins was furnished as a honeymoon suite. Long rays of late-afternoon sunlight glinted off silvery hair on the two heads drawn close together.

Lynne watched the old couple with a catch in her heart and a sudden, unexpected stab of soul-searing pain. That was how she'd always pictured herself and Monty, strolling hand in hand into the sunset along some idyllic beach, Monty's surfboard lying under her umbrella by the cooler on their blanket.

Life's unfairness sometimes took her breath away.

She shook herself and turned back to Angela. They were alone now. "Have the police figured out what happened? I've been wondering all day what's going on."

Angela peered out into the vineyard. "So have I. If they've figured anything out, they sure haven't told me about it. Apparently he was shot, because they asked all kinds of questions about guns, and they were very insistent on Jeff showing them his collection, which he absolutely refused to do."

"Why?"

Angela rolled her eyes. "Because he's a staunch supporter of the Second Amendment."

The constitutional right to bear arms, as Lynne remembered, didn't involve James Bond's Walther. Better to leave this topic alone.

"They were all over the place until just a little while ago," Angela continued, "mostly over at the winery. They found a key to the winery on Lance, which he wasn't supposed to have. So even though the building was locked, I had to check to be sure everything was okay. The cops kept asking questions I couldn't answer about your people, once they realized how easy it would be for any of them to sneak out and meet Lance over there."

Lynne frowned. "But none of my people knew him." She thought suddenly of the spark of recognition in Lance's eyes when he saw Hake Sandstrom, of Lance's quick wink to Heidi. He'd even said something to Hake, like "What are *you* doing here?" She'd forgotten that and probably should tell Detective Shaw.

"I know. And the police are gone now, thank goodness," Angela said. "I'm not sure what they accomplished, if anything. I kept wishing I'd split, brought Stephanie and come along with you all, just to get away from everything."

"I'm sure it was perfectly awful," Lynne told her with absolute conviction. She remembered Angela's protestations, back when Booked for Travel was lobbying to keep these August tour reservations, that she and her husband were intensely private people. "What on earth do you suppose Lance was doing here in the middle of the night, anyway?"

Angela turned to look directly at Lynne. "I have no idea. The police seemed to think maybe he was going to sabotage something in the winery, but I can't believe that. He was always so proud of the place. Why did Lance do anything?" She frowned, seeming to register Lynne's tone of familiarity for the first time. "How well did you know him, anyway?"

"Only superficially. He wasn't involved with running the bed-and-breakfast, so we'd just see him at the winery tour and tasting when I had groups staying here. Before that, I'd see him once a year at private tastings, because of course this place was never open to the public." There was a sort of snobbery attached to wineries that remained closed to the general public, a sense of superiority to those lesser establishments that couldn't sell their wares without unseemly hustling. "Lance was always very charming, at least to me."

Angela offered a dry little chuckle. "You're female, aren't you? That's all it took for Lance. I bet he sold a lot of wine to the ladies in your groups."

"Cases," Lynne agreed cheerfully, "and they loved every minute of it." She had an image of Lance down in the caves against a backdrop of stacked oak barrels, his head thrown back in laughter at something one of her older female guests had said. Something that probably hadn't been very funny. "Hmmm. Do you suppose it was being a ladies' man that, um . . ." She couldn't figure out quite how to complete the thought. "Killed him," she finished, a moment later.

Angela didn't seem to even hear the question at first. Then she spoke softly. "It could be," she said, "but it could be all sorts of other things, too. Lance was a smooth talker and a bit of a scammer, a slippery kind of guy. He's the one we dealt with when we were trying to negotiate the deal to buy this place." She stopped and looked around for a moment. "Which maybe wasn't the best of ideas, in hindsight. But at the time . . ." Her voice trailed off.

"I get the impression that folks around Sonoma County aren't all that fond of Silicon Valley newcomers." Unabashed loathing actually seemed to be the general community reaction, but that seemed a bit harsh to mention under the circumstances.

Angela snorted. "You know, I had no idea when we came here. I figured it would be isolated and beautiful, and people would just leave us alone. Plus, of course, I was really interested in wine. I was a biochem major, and I worked for years in pharmaceutical labs, wishing I could be outside. I've taken some courses in wine making, and I really admired the work that Vincent Belladuce was doing here on the premium wines. He's a really gifted vintner. I thought the idea of raising our own grapes and making our own wine and having it be really *good* wine was incredibly cool." Her face clouded momentarily, then cleared as she pasted on her hostess smile again. "As indeed it is." She tossed her hair back, sleek as a raven's wing, and a dangling silver filigree earring danced in the golden light.

Lynne leaned in to look at Stephanie's delicate features, her wispy black hair and deep chestnut eyes. The baby was adopted, Lynne knew, and if Lynne knew it, then Lance Belladuce surely had also, being local and plugged in. That made his gratuitous comments on her resemblance to Angela all the more puzzling. Still, she could have been Angela's birth daughter, the resemblance was so strong. Her eyes were bright and alert as she followed the movements of the adults around her, and she rarely fussed. The entire time they'd been standing there talking, she hadn't let out a single unhappy peep.

"She's truly a beauty," Lynne said, offering Stephanie a finger. The baby's own tiny fingers wrapped around it like a promise.

"Yes, you are, aren't you darling?" Angela put her face close to Stephanie's and crinkled her nose. The baby's features suddenly split into a bright, toothless grin. Angela grinned back, then glanced at Lynne. "I love it when she smiles at me. It's so exciting!"

"It sure is," Lynne agreed. "When my kids first smiled at me, I used to burst into tears, I was so happy." Her own smile was rueful. "Of course, I know now that that was actually because my hormones were still out of whack, but it really was joyful." Those first smiles came not a moment too soon in the case of Jenny, who had not been an easy baby. If Jenny'd been born first, she might have been an only child.

"I should go get cleaned up myself," Lynne said. "We're going to Patina, if you'd like to join us. Bring your husband along, and Stephanie, too, if you don't have someone to leave her with."

"Oh, Rosalita lives in," Angela said offhandedly, "and that's very kind of you. I've heard Patina is really nice. But I think we want to just stay here by ourselves tonight." Her voice rang with sincerity.

"Well, if you change your mind, come on along," Lynne told her. "Patina *is* really nice. They do amazing things with crab, and I do love crab. Or if you'd like to join us tomorrow, you're more than welcome, you and Stephanie both. We're breaking up into smaller groups, and a bunch of us are going for a cooking lesson at Rosemary & Thyme in Sonoma. I've been there before, and it's a lot of fun."

Angela smiled. "I just may do that. Thanks, Lynne."

❦

**LYNNE'S** cell phone started to ring just as she stepped out of the shower. She groped for a towel and wrapped it hastily around herself as she picked up. All the Sonoma Sojourn guests had cell phones for the duration, a side deal Lynne had made with Ginger Conner, who worked for a wireless technology company. But why would any of them need her now? They'd been together all day.

Her son's voice surprised her. David ought to be at work now. He was working evenings this month, though he called it something else that she could never remember. What would have been the swing shift if police work were a factory.

"Mom, what have you gotten into up there? I had a message waiting from the Sonoma County Sheriff's Department when I got in this afternoon."

She pictured him in his crisp uniform, tall and blond like Monty, but with her eyes. "David, I'm not in any trouble."

He laughed, and it sounded enough like Monty's laugh to make her heart skip a beat. "I know. I figured I'd try you first, get your side of the story, but when you didn't answer, I started getting worried, thought maybe you were locked up or something. But Detective Shaw just assured me you're still on the loose."

"So she actually did call to check up on me, eh?" Lynne vaguely remembered mentioning David as a sort of character reference this morning on the patio. *My son, the policeman.*

"Yep. I told her we'd taken you off the Ten Most Wanted List down here and only had you coming in for the occasional random drug screen."

"You're too generous." Lynne wished for the thousandth time it were possible to hold a cell phone on her shoulder like a regular old-style corded phone, so she could stop dripping all over the carpet. She took a second towel from the stack in the closet, folded it on the upholstered armchair in her room, and sat down.

"You owe me," David said. "So what are you up to, anyway? She said you found a homicide victim this morning."

Lynne gave him the short version of the morning's experience. "It was really pretty awful," she concluded. "I don't see how you can stand it."

"Mom, I don't work homicide. I'm not a detective. Heck, we don't really even have homicides here in Floritas, other than the occasional domestic, and I've been lucky enough not to get called on one of those in a long time. But seriously, are you okay?"

Lynne thought for a moment. She had always prided herself on being scrupulously honest with her children. "Well, I wish it hadn't happened, and I wish it hadn't happened here, and I *really* wish I hadn't been the one who found that poor dead man. But yeah, I'm okay." She glanced at the clock radio beside her bed. "And if I hang up right now, I can sneak in a little nap before I have to go to dinner and be scintillating."

❦

**AFTER** dinner, when they returned to Villa Belladuce, Jessica Kincaid was surprised to find herself wide awake. After the first night's inadvertent excesses, she had deliberately paced herself today, trying only one or two wines at each of their stops and sometimes even pouring those out after tasting. At dinner she'd skipped the wine altogether, drinking iced tea and then coffee.

"I'm going to take a little walk," she told Sara. "Want to come along?" The moon hung full and ripe above the vineyard, and she felt wonderfully disconnected from the sorry realities of her life in Atlanta. She wasn't really adjusted to West Coast time, but time itself was starting to seem utterly irrelevant. She liked that.

Sara shook her head. She'd avoided tasting altogether at most wineries today, and had limited herself to one glass at dinner, but she still seemed sluggish. "I'm turning in. I need sleep." She grinned. "I also need to exercise regularly and get a better job and find a boyfriend who doesn't mind a six-year-old kid with ADHD. But for now, I'll settle for nine hours' sleep and no hangover in the morning."

As Jessica turned to leave the patio, she was suddenly aware of Ryan Atherton sitting alone at one of the far tables. His grandmother had come out to dinner tonight, the three family members sharing a quiet table in a corner of the restaurant away from the others. Kelly had picked up a rental car today, and the Athertons left before dessert and returned to Villa Belladuce early.

"Want some company?" he asked, standing up, and to Jessica it seemed the most natural thing in the world to agree.

They wandered down the long, curved drive toward the road. The guest cottages, buttoned up for the night, seeped warm light from shuttered windows. All day, Jessica realized now, everyone had made small talk without much more than an occasional bewildered allusion to the death of Lance Belladuce. Almost everybody on this tour was acting as if the whole business had been a hallucination or maybe a bad TV show. It was too big and weird a thing to have happened, Jessica thought. It simply couldn't be real. So then, just as she had all day, she forced herself to stop thinking about it. She'd gotten very good at avoidance techniques, going through her divorce.

"I think it's really sweet the way you and Kelly are so devoted to your grandmother," Jessica told Ryan as they walked along. "She seems really dear, but kind of . . . I don't know . . . feisty at the same time."

The clear night air was alive with insects chirping from rose bushes that rambled on the fences along the driveway leading from the road up to Villa Belladuce. There was an expanse of lawn here between the long driveway and the woodsy area that separated the residential part of Villa Belladuce from the winery. Across the highway were more vineyards, stretching back to the foothills of the mountains, where erosion problems on the steep hillsides made it impossible to plant vines. Since they'd arrived, she'd seen no traffic on this road other than police cars and the members of their own tour group. There was nothing in this sparsely traveled section of the valley except a few wineries and an occasional restaurant.

She shivered suddenly. They were in the middle of nowhere, and a homicidal maniac was loose. Maybe taking a walk wasn't such a hot idea after all.

But Ryan didn't seem worried. He was quiet for a moment, and the silence was a comfortable one. "Feisty. That's a good word for Gran. It's going to be really hard on Kelly when she goes."

"For you, too," she told him gently. She hoped she wasn't overstepping, but men could be so incredibly dense about these things.

"I know," he said. "But I figure it'll be hard enough when it happens, I'm not going to think about it now. Gran has all her affairs in order, and she's very matter-of-fact about everything. Of course, she's always been like that, but this is . . . oh, I don't know."

They were almost to the highway now. Despite herself, Jessica looked south to where the winery stood beyond the trees, to where that handsome, luckless man had been found dead. She heard a sudden clanging noise from that direction and then silence.

Then she heard an engine start. A dark pickup truck running without lights suddenly came out of nowhere and roared down the highway in the direction of town. Jessica felt a flash of fear and jumped back. Ryan put a protective arm around her. "Hey, take it easy."

"Sorry," she said. "Guess I'm just a little skittish."

He chuckled. "Say that again."

"Why?" She noticed that he still had his arm around her and that she liked the way it felt.

"Because I love to hear your accent."

"*My* accent? You're the one who talks funny. All clipped and flat."

"Clee-upped and flay-ut," he repeated softly. "C'mon, let's head back, Jess. Tomorrow's another busy day."

She shivered again. "A little less busy than today, I hope."

"Me, too," he agreed, and when they reached the cottage she was sharing with Sara and Ginger, he surprised her by turning and kissing her quickly on the forehead.

The forehead! Was this some Wisconsin courting ritual? The forehead indeed.

**ELEANOR** Whitson crept around the front of the Villa Belladuce mansion. She'd almost run smack into those kids, and
her nerves were shot anyway. Her goal now was simple and
desperate: sneak into her room unnoticed, tuck herself quickly
into bed, and avoid any need for explanations. Now or ever.
At first she had been just vaguely nervous, but the events of
the past half hour made it extremely important that nobody
recognize or pay any attention to her.

Usually that was easy enough to manage. Middle-aged
women, a category Eleanor realized she was definitely on the
upper end of, were pretty much invisible. They were all over
the place, of course, everywhere from Nordstrom to JCPen-
ney, from hospital volunteers to real estate salesladies. But
nobody ever really noticed them. They drove serviceable
Japanese sedans and lingered in the produce department and
waited in the lobbies of dental offices. They moved unseen
and ghostly through the world.

Eleanor herself didn't always recall middle-aged women
that she saw, and there'd been a time when she prided herself
on her powers of observation. She still did, actually, though
now she was starting to realize that being too observant could
be extremely dangerous.

Her sister-in-law, back in happier times, had once proposed
that the two of them should become international smugglers.
"We'd be perfect, Ellie," she'd argued. "Nobody notices
women our age, and when they do notice, they forget immediately. Who's ever going to suspect somebody who looks like
their mother-in-law is carrying secret codes or ancient relics?"

"Except I think that most smugglers these days are carrying
drugs," Eleanor had answered, "which I'm not about to get involved in. And anyway, I like my life the way it is. Placid and
predictable."

Those days, she realized, the placid and predictable ones,
were gone for good. She slipped into her room, ran herself a
bath, and tried to soak the events of the past thirty-six hours
out of her life.

## Chapter 6

IN the morning, before breakfast, Lynne called Detective Lauren Shaw.

"This probably doesn't mean anything," she said, "and I really hate to drag my people into anything, but when I was talking to Angela last night, I remembered something." She told the detective about Lance Belladuce's apparent recognition of Hake Sandstrom.

"Somebody else mentioned that, too," the detective replied, "and Mr. Sandstrom told us it must have been his resemblance to somebody else."

"J. R. Ewing?" Lynne asked, without thinking. Now where had *that* come from? It was years since she and Monty had watched *Dallas* on Friday nights, a bowl of buttered popcorn on the sofa between them.

Detective Shaw laughed. "Could be, I guess. Listen, I really appreciate your calling. While I have you, do you happen to remember somebody breaking a glass on the patio after Mr. Belladuce, uh, put in his appearance Sunday night?"

Lynne frowned and tried to recall. "Mostly what I remember is that I was really anxious to get everybody out of there. The glass broke at a table where a bunch of folks had been sitting. The Harpers and Martells, Eleanor Whitson, Guido Ambrosino. Me. I remember Guido started to clean it up, but I don't know if it was his glass. Why?"

"Just trying to tidy loose ends," the detective said.

"Does that mean you don't know what happened yet?"

"We're investigating a number of possibilities, Mrs. Montgomery." The words had a canned feel, suggesting the police had made no progress at all. "Have you thought of anything else that might help us?"

"Afraid not."

"Well, if you do, call me anytime. And Mrs. Montgomery?"

"Yes?"

"Your son sounded like a very nice young man."

⚬━✦━⚬

**AFTER** breakfast, Lynne wasn't particularly surprised when Angela Rutledge declined to join the group going to the cooking class in Sonoma. Lynne was pleased to see the entire Booked for Travel group animated, bustling about as folks prepared for the first individualized day's activities. From here on out, they'd be grouping and regrouping each day to pursue special personal interests, meeting up each evening for dinner together.

Now Angela retrieved Stephanie from Maria Ambrosino's arms. Mother and daughter then gaily waved off the Sonoma Sojourn groups heading out in three different directions.

Going north for the Dry Creek appellation tour were Hake and Heidi Sandstrom, Maria and Guido Ambrosino, and Ginger Conner. They climbed into a stretch limo and left first. Mark Martell and Don Harper aimed west for a day at the Bodega Harbor Golf Club, out on the rocky Pacific coast in the western part of the county. Ruth Atherton, taking a day off, retired to her cottage with a large-type book and a pot of tea.

The other seven tour members went down into town with Lynne to the large Victorian mansion that housed the Rosemary & Thyme Cooking School. Ryan Atherton was the only male in the group, but his presence was comfortable. As he got out of the van, he said, "So, I'll learn the proper way to trim the crusts off my peanut butter sandwiches?"

"If you do really well, I'll get you a set of Ginsu knives for Christmas," Kelly promised. "Then you can work your way up to . . . oh, I don't know. Grilled cheese?"

Ryan gave his twin a mock glare. "Hey, I'm a professional in the cheese industry. My grilled cheese sandwiches are masterful."

"Masterfully burned, if I remember right," Kelly shot back, playfully smacking him.

Easygoing Wendy Carr, a perky redhead in her late thirties, greeted them at the door in chef's toque and white apron, then led the Sonoma Sojourners back into her gleaming demonstration kitchen, filled with shiny copper pots and big commercial ovens and four self-contained workstations. Lilting instrumental music floated from speakers in the corners of the room, and sunlight streamed through windows overlooking a vast herb garden in the backyard.

"We're going to have fun here this morning," Wendy promised, as the group tied each other into crisply starched aprons and perched towering toques on their heads. "A lot of folks are intimidated by the idea of fancy cooking, but I got into this business because I love to cook, and I'm going to do my best to get you to share my enthusiasm. All we're doing, really, is fixing lunch. But, oh my goodness, what a lunch it will be!" She gave an orgasmic little shiver that brought chuckles, then waved a hand at an easel holding the day's menu:

*Mushroom Medley Bisque*
*Phyllo Chevre Packets*
*Herbed Shrimp Tomatoes*
*Fresh Creamed Corn*
*Chocolate Cream Puffs*

"And before we go any further," Wendy told them with a broad smile and a green-eyed wink, "you need to know that because this is an educational process, there are absolutely no calories or fat grams in any of this food."

The laughter this time came even more easily, as the group gathered around a large granite island where Wendy had placed clear glass bowls filled with prime produce: ruby red beefsteak tomatoes, shucked ears of translucent white corn, a collection of strange and vaguely ominous mushrooms. There was also a big platter of mixed red and green grapes and a smaller one of radishes and baby carrots.

"Cooking builds an appetite," Wendy told them, "and when you do this at home, some of these things *will* have a few calories. So I like to assuage my conscience by snacking on fruits and veggies while I cook. You all feel free to nibble on grapes and carrots as we go along, okay?"

Lynne had been here several times and knew that Wendy would have her people busily chopping and seeding and dicing and sautéing within ten minutes, working in subgroups on different projects, stopping at intervals to watch as she demonstrated a critical step for everyone. They'd leave with full stomachs, copies of today's recipes, and also, if history ran its usual course, with autographed copies of the handsome hardcover *Rosemary & Thyme Cookbook.*

Lynne herself planned only to eat. No cooking today, thank you very much. She was strictly a chaperon.

Lynne had pretty much given up cooking after Monty died, quickly discovering that sitting by herself at the dinner table they had shared for thirty years was simply too painful. She had also been rather surprised to realize that she actually didn't like many of the foods she'd prepared so often, meals that were her husband's favorites. Chili, for instance, was one food that Monty had adored and that she'd made by the gallon and frozen for years, even though the red-hot jalapeño-laced variety he favored gave her heartburn. Eight months after Monty's death, Lynne had taken nine carefully labeled Tupperware containers of chili out of the freezer, thawed them overnight, and put them down the disposal in the morning, sobbing as the motor roared.

After the first couple of shell-shocked weeks, when she had no idea what she had or hadn't eaten, when food appeared in her refrigerator after friends visited and stayed there till it was green and furry, she noticed that she had changed her eating habits altogether. These days, she tended to eat out or dine on Trader Joe's entrées for one while she watched the TV news. Now and then she'd have nothing for dinner but ice cream. She still *could* cook when she wanted to, was capable of producing a glorious spread for a special occasion, and she enjoyed the process. She continued to bake hundreds of cookies every Christmas, mostly to give away. But any time spent in the kitchen now, unless the grandkids were involved, was purely to indulge her own whims.

"We'll start with the end," Wendy said, "and bake our cream puff shells for dessert first, so they'll have time to cool. If you've never done this before, you might think that cream puff pastry is really tricky. Well, it's anything but. . . ."

**JEFF** Rutledge was trying to work, but having the place overrun with cops and tourists from God knows where was simply too distracting. He was having trouble with his current project anyway, and sitting around stewing about it didn't seem to be working.

So he went in search of Angela and found her feeding the baby in Stephanie's bedroom, a place that always made him feel awkward and clumsy. Mother and daughter *did* make a warm and touching picture, however. He stood in the doorway for a minute or two and just watched. Angela's head was bent low as she sang softly to Stephanie, that Disney song about a dream being a wish your heart makes. The two of them were so beautiful it took his breath away.

She felt his presence, then, and looked up, flashing a radiant smile. Angela's smile never failed to thrill him, and he blessed once again the indescribable luck that had brought her into his life.

"I'm going down to InRut," he told her. There wasn't much of a need for his presence at the Sunnyvale headquarters, but he had to get out of Villa Belladuce, and this was a destination she wouldn't question.

"When will you be back?"

He shrugged. "Tonight. Depends on how badly things are messed up down there."

She frowned. "Still having trouble?" She didn't understand, or even pretend to understand, exactly what he did, but she was unfailingly sympathetic when it didn't go well and buoyantly euphoric when it did.

"It'll be fine," he told her. "Just need to sit with Marvin and Clay for a while and hash out some stuff."

He leaned down and kissed Angela good-bye, touched Stephanie lightly on her downy and impossibly delicate little head, and split.

Sailing across the Golden Gate Bridge an hour later in his Porsche, he marveled once again at his incredible good fortune. He was, quite simply, the most successful high school dropout in America.

There might be athletes who were more famous, and there'd been robber barons and captains of industry in the past who made more money, relatively speaking. But there wasn't anybody he knew of today who had left school after tenth grade and landed on magazine covers within a decade not for being a jock or a celebrity, but for exercising intelligence and ingenuity in the course of making millions.

He considered himself an autodidact, which was technically true. The important things that he knew were almost all things he'd learned on his own, either through instinct, or through independent study, or through trial and error. His parents had insisted on leaving him in public school even though he was light-years ahead of his classmates in every field but social grace, and he had amused himself during those early adolescent years by independently studying computers and electronics and other subjects that interested him. He'd taken the GED on the sly despite his parents' disapproval, then left public high school and its bizarre social rituals for good.

He continued exploring subjects that interested him. When this required some kind of formal training, he took courses at the junior college until he turned eighteen. The idea of following a defined course of study toward a specific degree seemed utterly pointless.

By his eighteenth birthday, he'd sold several computer programs and accumulated a grubstake. He used it to move to Berkeley, where he never quite enrolled in the University of California. Maybe he couldn't have gotten in anyway, being a high school dropout and all, but it didn't really matter. He audited courses that interested him and hooked up with other computer geeks, finding a camaraderie that pleased him enormously. He was still in touch with most of those guys, though he hardly ever saw them. He'd worked for a couple of them in the early days and had employed others as time moved on. One of them was running InRut down in Sunnyvale right now.

Along the sometimes rocky road to adulthood, Jeff Rutledge had been treated badly by a number of people, often beefy athletes with girlfriends named Tiffany and IQs in the same range as their resting heartbeats. He understood perfectly the feelings of disaffected young men who shot up their high school campuses, though he had never engaged in—or even fantasized about—such activities.

He'd been a bit of a hothead when he was younger, allowing himself to be goaded into fights by Cro-Magnon morons. Twice he was suspended from high school for fighting.

Over time, he'd come to subscribe to the adage that revenge is a dish best taken cold. He never forgot a slight or an injustice done him, and he made it his business to get simply and quietly even.

A childhood spent taking things apart and putting them back together again had left him with sufficient hands-on expertise to subtly disable or destroy almost any kind of equipment. These weren't necessarily complicated measures, and he often focused on cars simply because they were conveniently located outdoors. They were also fast and easy to fiddle with. It only took seconds to squirt some epoxy into a car door lock or plop a couple of Alka-Seltzers into a car battery, giving the vehicle permanent indigestion. He discovered many amazing and creative uses for expanding resin foams besides those enumerated on the package, including his personal favorite, emptying a container into the driver's seat of a vehicle whose owner had displeased him.

He learned you could also get a lot of mileage out of scrawling graffiti slurs on rest room walls, particularly if you included phone numbers, and it was simplicity itself to carry a permanent marker. The landlord who refused to do anything about a termite-riddled apartment probably didn't like it when his own suburban home became infested with the offspring of those apartment-dwelling critters, personally delivered in the dead of night. The landlord never knew where they came from.

For Jeff, a significant part of the satisfaction of revenge was in not claiming credit. The subject might be suspicious, but he could never be certain.

When Jeff first met Angela, he was careful to keep these activities from her, certain she would disapprove. She hadn't, really, but as he became more successful and well-known, she had gently pointed out that he had far too much to lose if he were caught in a petty act of retribution. As usual, she was right. But he still sometimes acted on his instincts rather than his common sense.

What she didn't know couldn't hurt her, could it?

## Chapter 7

**LYNNE** slipped out into the herb garden behind Rosemary &
Thyme as Wendy Carr continued the group cooking lesson.

In this carefully casual place, rosemary topiaries stood scattered among clumps of cilantro and basil and oregano and
parsley. One bed held a dozen varieties of thyme, and another
offered an array of aromatic mints. Lynne moved slowly back
and forth in an old-fashioned wooden glider, watching fat
black-and-yellow bumblebees buzz among the herbs currently in bloom.

She'd been out there about fifteen minutes when Wendy
stuck her head out the door. "This a private party?"

Lynne waved at the space beside her in the glider. "Hey, it's
your garden. Have a seat."

Wendy stationed herself near the window. "Can't sit," she
said. "I need to keep an eye on how things are going. Makes
me feel more responsible, not that they're doing anything that
can get them in trouble, I don't think. But now, I absolutely
must know what's going on up at Villa Belladuce. I hear that
you were the one who found the body."

Lynne frowned. "Where'd you hear that?"

"This is a small town. People talk. So *did* you find the body?"

Lynne nodded. "Unfortunately. It was very creepy."

"I can imagine. I also hear that there was one hell of a row the night before he died, and that he punched out Jeff Rutledge."

"No physical violence. Just a lot of posturing and some yelling. Guy stuff. Lance was very cool through it all, actually. I can't imagine him punching anybody if there was a way to sweet-talk his way out of a situation instead."

"I'll give you that," Wendy agreed. "The sweet-talk part. But c'mon, tell me what happened. Don't be a tease."

"I wouldn't dream of being a tease." Lynne briefly recounted the scene on the patio. When she'd finished, she smiled at Wendy. "Your turn now. I get the impression that there are quite a few people who aren't terribly sorry Lance Belladuce is dead."

"Oh, he's a rogue, all right. Or *was,* I guess I should say. He was married twice, but Lance always had a major problem with fidelity, and I can't say that I blame his exes much for throwing him out. I went out with him myself right after I opened this place up a few years ago, and I didn't find out till after I stopped seeing him that he had two other regular girlfriends the whole time. There's a whole Sonoma sisterhood of Lance Belladuce's old girlfriends, but I don't think he left most of us very unhappy."

Wendy paused for a moment before continuing. "Although their ex-boyfriends and husbands—that's something else altogether. A lot of them were plenty angry with him."

"He was a charmer," Lynne agreed. "And a looker, too, which always seems to be a dangerous combination."

"I heard the cops were looking at unsavory business practices more than old girlfriends," Wendy said. "Lance cut a lot of corners, and plenty of people were unhappy about it."

"How so?"

"Well, part of it was just that the marketing schemes he tended to come up with were so goofy. Lance had all kinds of wild ideas and no business sense whatsoever. He was always trying to promote wine tie-ins to odd holidays, like Ground Hog's Day or Halloween. He opened some restaurants that failed, here and down in Monterey. He was a real celebrity suck-up, and he'd do special bottlings of wine named for celebrities, preferably Italian-American ones. I think his ultimate fantasies were Madonna and Robert DeNiro, not that either one was ever interested. He invested in a couple of movies and lost a bundle. Francis Coppola was like a god to him." The director had moved to the nearby Napa Valley around the time of *Godfather I* and had built a wine empire over the following decades.

"I remember Lance talking about one of his movies," Lynne said. "A few years ago, maybe the first time I brought this tour. It was about to be released, but I don't think it ever played in San Diego."

"Lance's movies, when they happened at all, tended to go straight to video," Wendy said. "But I don't think he cared all that much. It was the thrill of being a movie producer, of hanging around with movie stars on a movie set. He actually shot one of the movies at Villa Belladuce. The last one was some kind of gothic horror thing that was so bad I don't think it was even released on video."

Interesting. If Lance Belladuce was in the habit of losing big chunks of other people's money, all kinds of folks might indeed be unhappy with him. "What do you hear about the investigation, Wendy?"

"Just rumors from people who don't know any more than I do. The gossip mill is in overdrive around here, let me tell you. There were all kinds of stories floating around when Villa Belladuce was sold. Lance was handling the sale for the Belladuces, and some folks said he was taking money under the table from some of the prospective buyers."

"Why?"

"I know less than nothing about major real estate transactions, Lynne. But it would be Lance's style to be cute about it. About some part of it, anyway. I wouldn't put it past him to be playing two or three bidders against each other, getting them to sweeten the pot. And that's not even mentioning the thing Lance did that *really* upset folks in the wine business."

"Which was?" Lynne knew Wendy wanted to be begged for details, and she was more than willing to oblige. The young chef was insatiably curious and missed very little, both of which contributed to making her an excellent gossip. This morning she was in rare form.

Wendy leaned forward conspiratorially. "The story goes that on more than one occasion, Lance relabeled entire shipments of wine he was selling abroad."

Lynne frowned, confused. "Relabeled?"

Wendy nodded emphatically. "As a better blend and vintage than it actually was. That's a cardinal sin in the world of wine. It was that kind of fudging on quality that gave California wine a bad name back before the '76 Paris taste test. Now that these wines are worth serious money, everybody's extremely self-righteous about truth in labeling. I'm surprised Lance even tried to get away with it. I mean, he was reckless, but he wasn't stupid."

"Did he get caught?"

"Not by anybody official. As far as I know, his family was able to cover the whole thing up pretty well. His father was still alive then, and he managed to set things straight. Everybody liked the old man, though apparently in his youth he was a lot like Lance. But actually, it's the uncle who has the reputation for violence. Vincent."

"Vincent Belladuce? That charming old man?" Lynne could picture him clearly: a courtly gentleman, not much taller than herself, with a full head of wavy, steel-gray hair, a warm olive complexion, glittering dark eyes, and just the hint of an accent. The accent, she'd always assumed, was an affectation, since as far as she knew, the last few generations of Belladuces had been born and raised in California.

"That charming old man killed somebody in a barroom brawl in San Francisco."

"No!"

Wendy smiled. "God's truth. It was a long time ago, and I

really don't know any of the particulars. But he was convicted of manslaughter, and he spent ten years in San Quentin."

"Amazing. Still, that doesn't have anything to do with what's happening now, does it?"

"I don't know. But I wouldn't want to get Vincent mad. I think there's a reference to his past in one of the newspaper stories, if you're really interested."

On the road, particularly if she had a group with her, Lynne liked to suspend time by removing herself from the realm of current events altogether. No newspapers were delivered to Villa Belladuce, and she had deliberately avoided watching TV since her arrival, the way she always did. Of course, she hadn't previously discovered any murder victims while on tour, so this was all uncharted territory.

"I don't suppose you have any of those papers still lying around?"

"Well, of course, I do. C'mon inside and get them. I need to go in, anyway, and get everybody set up for the next steps in what they're doing."

Lynne held up a hand. "I'll pick up the papers before we leave. I'm trying to be low key about all this so nobody will get more upset than they have to. Unfortunately, we're all involved to some degree, just 'cause we were there for the ugly scene with Jeff Rutledge. Which reminds me, when Lance was talking to Angela before Jeff got there, he made some kind of reference to the baby looking just like her. But I was sure I'd heard that baby's adopted."

Wendy nodded. "She is, no question. It was a private adoption, and I heard they paid a lot of money for her, like maybe a hundred grand. White infants are hard to come by in today's adoption market. But I also remember hearing that there was something not entirely kosher about the adoption, back when it actually happened."

"Like what?"

"I don't know. Adoptions are so much more complicated than they used to be back when all the records were sealed forever. Last year, one of my friends was trying to adopt a foster child she'd been taking care of, and the birth mother changed her mind at the last minute. Just about broke my friend's heart."

"If Stephanie's was a private adoption, wouldn't the birth mother have signed off first?"

"I'd assume so, 'cause the Rutledges could certainly afford the best possible legal advice. Maybe the birth father didn't agree?"

Lynne frowned. "And they wouldn't be able to buy him off, too?"

"I don't know. And I don't see what would interest Lance about any of it. Are you sure you didn't misunderstand?"

"At the time it just felt a little off, but the more I think about it, he really did seem to be needling her. And it doesn't make any sense."

"Why should you expect it to make sense? Lance had kids of his own that he never paid much attention to. As a matter of fact, I think he may have had an illegitimate kid or two, and I know he's paid for some abortions. But that wouldn't have anything to do with what you're talking about. Unless he did know something about the adoption that the rest of us don't."

Lynne frowned. "Are you saying the Rutledges adopted a baby that Lance Belladuce fathered?"

Wendy shrugged. "Who knows? Where Lance and women are concerned, he always wrote the rules as he went along. Like I said, there could be some unhappy brothers or fathers out there. Or husbands, for that matter. Though I guess it would be a little too Hollywood for Lance to be the Rutledge baby's father, don't you think?"

"Probably," Lynne agreed.

"Of course there's also the lawsuit. The Rutledges have sued the Belladuces, you know."

No, Lynne didn't know, but the news didn't feel surprising. "About the sale of the property?"

"Sort of. There's a phylloxera problem that the Rutledges' lawyers claim wasn't revealed, and they had to rip out acres of vines to get rid of it."

"Interesting." That would explain the denuded acreage back beyond the winery, Lynne realized, newly replanted with infant vines. The baby grapevines were truly pathetic, naked stems of grafted budwood sticking out of two-foot-tall plastic collars.

Phylloxera was a nasty creature indeed, with a strong history of terrorizing vineyards. The dreaded root louse had virtually wiped out the vineyards of France in the mid–nineteenth century, when California viticulture could barely even be called fledgling. Phylloxera-resistant rootstock from the New World had then been used to replant the French vineyards.

"Yeah, phylloxera is back again with a vengeance because of a throwback rootstock, AxR1. It's ironic, because that rootstock was originally planted to help increase production. You could get up to a ton of grapes more per acre on it. But it turned out that half its parentage was nonresistant to phylloxera, after all. They've been losing vines all over the state."

"Not a pretty picture," Lynne agreed. "But you said there's something *worse* than phylloxera?"

"I heard a rumor not too long ago—and mind you, it's *just* a rumor—that they found glassy-winged sharpshooters at Villa Belladuce. And you know what *that* could mean."

"Bad news. Very bad news." Lynne appreciated the horror of this possibility both as a gardener and occasional connoisseur of fine wine. The glassy-winged sharpshooter wasn't a tipsy refugee from a frontier bar in a Wild West town. Instead, it was a hardy flying insect that carried Pierce's disease, an incurable bacterial affliction that attacked and killed wine grapes by shutting down their ability to conduct water from their root systems. Pierce's disease had already destroyed significant acreage in the Temecula vineyards just north of San Diego, and the sharpshooter's northern migration was being tracked with the diligence once reserved for monitoring Soviet missile systems. The sharpshooter was a restless traveler, often hitchhiking on innocuous nursery stock. Controversy raged in Sonoma County over state intentions to spray pesticides in the event of serious infestation, plans that infuriated the county's organic farmers.

"But enough already," Wendy said. "Listen, you can take

the newspapers with you and read all about it, though there isn't much of anything there that you don't already seem to know. Why don't you come back in now and cook a little?" She grinned. "I'll let you whip the cream for the cream puffs."

Wendy had discovered, on an earlier visit, that Lynne's favorite sinful cooking ingredient was heavy cream, which Rosemary & Thyme stocked by the gallon.

"You're on," Lynne told her, following the young woman back into a kitchen now filled with enticing aromas and the carefree chatter of her Sonoma Sojourners.

**ELEANOR** Whitson had listened carefully as the young chef outlined steps in the preparation of the phyllo chevre packets her group was assigned to make for lunch. The goat cheese was acrid and unappealing to work with, though she didn't complain. Nor had she made any fuss when asked to slice a plate of incredibly ugly mushrooms. Her son, Jimmy, had been fond of exotic mushrooms and had sometimes gone to gather them in the wild, but he'd warned her repeatedly about eating strange mushrooms. If you didn't know what you were doing, he'd say, you could end up eating something that would land you in line for a liver transplant, if it didn't kill you outright. There was no reason to think these mushrooms were unsafe, but Eleanor had no intention whatsoever of tasting the bisque they'd be part of.

Alice Harper was mincing herbs and chatting with Pat Martell on the other side of the workstation.

"I can't remember," Pat said to Eleanor now, "if you told us where your kids live."

The two women had been prying all morning, though they probably thought they were just being friendly. "Seattle. And yours?"

"Omaha, Miami, and Anchorage, Alaska," Pat replied with the ease of long practice. "We've got just about every climate and time zone covered. Alice is the lucky one, though. Her kids and grandkids are all in the San Diego area, so she can see them anytime she wants."

"Which isn't always the same times that *they* want," Alice admitted. "I was never very good with little babies, and neither is my daughter. I keep telling her that she grew up, and so will her little ones. I prefer them when they can communicate with you. I'm the only person I know who actually liked her children better when they were teenagers."

"The little Rutledge baby is sweet," Eleanor said. Maybe she could deflect this entire conversation somehow. "And she really does look just like her mother."

"She's a beauty, all right. But any resemblance is just coincidental. Lynne told me the baby's adopted." Pat nibbled on a grape. "Mmmm."

Eleanor stiffened involuntarily. "Sorry. I didn't know."

"No reason why you would," Pat said easily. "My kids were adopted, too, so I'm particularly attuned to it, that's all."

"I didn't mean to offend," Eleanor answered, wanting the floor to open and swallow her. She continued to carefully brush melted butter on the paper-thin sheets of phyllo, to trim them meticulously, to line them up with geometric precision. "Is that filling ready?"

Alice folded the herbs into the cheese mixture. "Yes, ma'am."

And as they all wrapped globs of cheese into neat phyllo packets, Eleanor once again withdrew, allowing the two old friends to chatter as she quietly completed her culinary chores.

The big, bright kitchen was filled with laughter and conversation, with aromas she might once have found appealing and people she might once have enjoyed knowing. Certainly Pat and Alice were nice enough, and both seemed wonderfully content. Same thing with the kids stuffing bay shrimp into tomato shells and constructing cream puffs over at the next workstation. They all seemed to be having a grand time, the Atherton boy unselfconscious as the girls giggled and chattered. They were a cheerful and wholesome lot, those kids, and their laughter twisted knives in Eleanor's heart.

It was almost too much to bear, having the courting rituals so close at hand, watching the young man grin at his female companions, a chef's hat perched jauntily on his head, a smear of chocolate on one of his cheeks. The girls beamed back, lighthearted and flirtatious, spreading chocolate frosting on the cream puffs, all of them deliciously carefree.

Eleanor knew now that this entire trip had been a colossal mistake, misbegotten and destined to create more problems than it could ever solve. She couldn't imagine now what she had thought she might accomplish, could scarcely believe the lengths she had gone to to be in this place she now desperately wanted to flee. But now that everything had gone so terribly and unbelievably wrong, all she could do was sit tight and wait, pretending to be something she wasn't, hoping and praying that nobody would make the connections that now terrified her.

It had been one thing to plan this all, sitting in the big, empty house in Pasadena, a house filled with bitter memories and restless ghosts. It was something else altogether to be here, in the midst of this nightmare, waiting.

What Eleanor wanted to do more than anything in the world was go home, to lock herself in her house and not come out for a month, or maybe forever. Yesterday at one of the wineries they visited, she'd seen a whimsical freestanding door and frame, just sitting beside the roadway, labeled Door to Nowhere.

If only, she thought now, there were some way to walk through that door and never come back.

*Chapter 8*

"**MRS**. Rutledge, why was Lance Belladuce on your property the other night?"

Angela looked at Detective Lauren Shaw wearily, wishing she'd gone with the Sonoma Sojourners to that cooking class, wishing she'd told the policewoman that she was indisposed, wishing that she'd never heard of Villa Belladuce. There was no point in hoping that Stephanie would rescue her, either. The baby had just gone down for her nap and was good for at least two hours. And Jeff had gone storming off to InRut in Sunnyvale, to deal with some alleged problem.

"I already told you," she answered. "I don't have any idea. He just showed up out of the blue."

"And when was the last time you saw Lance Belladuce before the other night?"

Angela thought for a moment. "It was probably about three weeks ago. We were bottling Chardonnay, and I went over to the winery to watch."

Funny how exciting it had seemed at the time, the notion of her own wine going into her own bottles in her own winery.

Jeff hadn't been interested, but that was nothing new. He was immersed in some technical problem, working round the clock, forgetting to eat, going down to InRut for days on end. When he got engrossed that way, he became essentially oblivious to the world, and Angela had learned over the years that it was easier just to wait him out. Once he'd solved whatever it was he was working on, he'd be ebullient in ways that reminded her of their courting days at Berkeley.

"I thought you told me that Lance wasn't supposed to be involved with the winery operation." The detective sounded puzzled.

Angela looked around, hoping for a distraction, depressingly certain there wouldn't be one. She and the detective sat in rich brocade wing chairs flanking the stone fireplace in the living room of the main house, a room Angela had furnished with carefully selected heavy traditional pieces, things that had an antique look without actually being old. A Revolutionary War musket, one of Jeff's oldest and most valuable pieces, hung over the fireplace.

The ability to buy everything new was one of the things she liked best about being rich, and since Jeff didn't really care so long as there was one comfortable chair in every room, she'd had free rein decorating this house, which was very different indeed from the Craftsman furnishings she'd emphasized in Palo Alto. The best of those things remained here, in the media room.

"We hired his uncle to run the winery," Angela explained. Vincent Belladuce ran a first-class operation. A wizard at using native yeasts for fermentation, he was opposed in principle to fining or filtering his wines. He'd actually seemed pleased when the Rutledges sold off the low-end operations to concentrate on quality rather than quantity. "Vincent always handled operations when the Belladuces owned the place, and he's a master vintner. Vincent had a couple of men there working with him that day, but I didn't realize that Lance was going to be there until he walked through the door."

*Swagger* was actually a better description, but there was no need to share that observation with Detective Shaw. Lance had a presence that filled any space he inhabited. Angela hadn't even needed to turn around to realize that he'd come through the open winery door.

"You were surprised to see him?"

"I suppose. But it didn't matter."

"Why not?"

Angela shrugged. "Vincent had everything under control. He certainly didn't need any help, and he seemed kind of surprised when Lance showed up."

"He wasn't expecting him?"

"Nobody ever *expected* Lance. He'd just sometimes be there and sometimes not."

"Did you talk to him that day?" Detective Shaw asked.

"Well, sure. I mean, I don't remember any specific conversation or anything, but we said hello, and he hung around for a while, and then he split."

"How did his uncle react when he showed up?"

Angela laughed. "Vincent said something like, 'Look what the wind blew in,' and kept on working. Lance poured himself some of the Chardonnay we were bottling and said he thought it was even better than the last two years they'd bottled, and those had been outstanding."

"Was it better?"

"It was excellent," Angela told her. "Villa Belladuce wines are always good, and our Chardonnays are some of the finest in the county." She'd seen mixed cases of estate-bottled Villa Belladuce Chardonnay going for thousands on Internet auction sites.

"Wasn't it Chardonnays that Lance relabeled for export?"

Angela sighed. "I don't know. That was all years ago, and my only interest was in whether anything had actually been shipped under the winery label that might come back to hurt us after we bought the place. There didn't seem to be a problem like that. Whatever might have happened, it was never made public, and the wines were recalled."

"How did you hear about it?"

"The realtor mentioned it." Angela sighed again. "But she

really downplayed it. And at the time, it seemed much less significant than the possible phylloxera problems."

"Which turned out to be more than just possible. You wound up replanting, I understand, and you're in litigation with both the realtor and the Belladuces about it."

It made Angela uncomfortable to realize how much this woman knew about Villa Belladuce's business problems. Sonoma wine making was so gossipy, a true grapevine, so to speak. When somebody sneezed pruning zinfandel vines in Healdsburg, a chorus of "Gesundheits" echoed from the four corners of the county.

"Sometimes it's necessary to take out unproductive vines," Angela said. "If you live here, you must realize that."

Detective Shaw nodded sympathetically. "Sure. I've lived in Sonoma County all my life, and I have friends in the business. I know how difficult it can be. Those AxR1 vines caught all kinds of people off guard. The folks out at Davis really screwed up on that one."

"That's for sure," Angela agreed. By law, any stock used to grow California wine or table grapes had to first be tested and approved at the University of California's Davis campus out in the agricultural San Joaquin Valley. Enforcement was problematic, however, and some growers actually smuggled in budwood from France.

"When you bought this place, were you aware of Villa Belladuce's problems with the IRS?"

Angela nodded. "Who wasn't? The reason they had to sell was because they'd been playing fast and loose with the tax man. But we made certain that any encumbrances were taken care of before we assumed ownership."

"Some folks in the area were surprised that you kept the B and B operation open."

"We're just honoring a reservation for this one group."

However, Angela wasn't sure what she and Jeff would do with half a dozen empty guest cottages, after they closed down the B and B. Jeff had talked about doing high-level computer workshops, using the cottages for housing. An educational program for prodigies, kids born with the same kind of freakish intelligence he himself possessed. But at this point, he was probably more inclined to raze the lot of them.

"Do you know of any other business problems that Lance or the winery had?" the detective asked, interrupting Angela's thoughts. "Things you might have found out while you were negotiating to buy this place?"

Angela offered a winsome smile. "A couple things. Generally, that he had terrible business judgment, and he didn't pay his bills. Have you looked into his restaurants? I understand he opened several using other people's money and his family's wines, but they kept going bust." She stood up. "Do you mind if we walk over to the winery while we talk? When the group gets back here, they're supposed to have a little tour and a tasting. Now that you folks are finished there, I need to set things up."

Detective Shaw rose with surprising grace. She was one of those tall, physically fit women who most likely lived at the gym. "Sure. Your housekeeper will take care of the baby?"

Angela nodded as she led the detective out the front door and around to the path that led through the grove to the winery. It was another beautiful day, fluffy clouds floating aimlessly around a clear blue sky. The climbing roses on the fences along the driveway were in full bloom now, exuding spicy fragrances. She wished she had the heart to enjoy them.

As they passed through the woods, Detective Shaw spoke. "Actually, I should warn you that you may find the place a bit . . . disordered. We try not to make too big a mess, but our crime scene people checked the building interior pretty thoroughly, since Mr. Belladuce had an unauthorized key for the winery."

"I wish I knew how he got that key," Angela said, almost to herself.

"Apparently his Uncle Vincent gave it to him. In any event, you may want to get somebody in to clean up a bit before you bring your bed-and-breakfast guests over."

"No problem," Angela assured her as they rounded the corner of the winery building. She forced herself not to think about yesterday morning, about Lance's body lying over there in the gravel. She wondered fleetingly what they'd done with his car. It was a nice little car. One of his ex-wives would surely want it.

But wait. What was that smell? She stopped abruptly and sniffed, frowning.

A strong, acrid odor, the scent of wine.

She quickened her pace and moved rapidly toward the door, Detective Shaw hurrying along with her. Now Angela could see that the concrete pad outside the door was stained red, and the dusty ground at its edges was darker than the rest of the lot.

Muddy, Angela realized, as she rushed toward the building.

She had her key out to open the door, but it wasn't necessary. The door swung open on its own, letting out an overpowering smell of wine.

Angela let out an involuntary shriek of horror. "Oh my God!"

The floor was inches deep in dark red liquid.

"Step back," Detective Shaw ordered, and Angela was vaguely aware that the woman had a gun out, had pushed her aside, and was now stepping cautiously into the building. "Where's the light switch?"

Angela reached around the side of the doorframe.

"No, don't touch it. Get back outside. *Now*."

As Angela reluctantly backed away, the detective used the back of a fingernail to flick the lights on. Artificial light filled the cavernous winery, and the extent of the devastation was immediately apparent.

Somebody had systematically trashed the entire place, using brute force and blunt instruments. Several somebodies, probably, judging from the extent of the destruction.

They hadn't been in a hurry, either. The more closely Angela looked, the better she could see that what had happened here seemed almost systematic.

The ends of barrels on the racks had been hacked and smashed open, sending rivers of wine to the floor. Barrels on the ends of rows had been rotated and the bungs removed, a slower but also effective way of draining their contents. Bottles from the cases packed for shipping had been removed and broken, in some cases by hurling them against the barrels. The bottling equipment was battered and smashed, and something was wrong with the floor drains, which should have sucked away all this excess liquid.

Angela watched in a state of shock and fascination as the detective sloshed cautiously up and down the aisles of barrels, holding her gun in front of her just like in a movie. She even kicked open the door to the office and found it empty. After a few moments, she returned to the doorway.

"There's nobody here now. When was the last time you were here?"

Angela's mind was blank, frozen.

"Mrs. Rutledge? Are you all right?" Detective Shaw had lowered her gun but still held it firmly. Angela was surprised to find that vaguely reassuring.

The caves! What if those had been vandalized, too? It wasn't merely affectation or historical sentiment that led Villa Belladuce to age and store many of its finest wines in those caves. They were a perfect, naturally cool location, sixty degrees year round.

"We have to check the caves," Angela told her urgently. "The best wines are out there."

"As soon as I get some backup here," Detective Shaw promised.

Angela nodded numbly as she slowly turned to look around the room. The winery was awash in wine. Fine wine, expensive wine, Villa Belladuce varietal wine.

Ruined wine.

"Who would do something like this? Why?" Detective Shaw asked.

"I can't imagine." But even as she spoke, she knew the answer, could see it staring down at her from the large framed photos of generations of Belladuces that hung on the winery walls.

*Chapter 9*

**PAT** Martell and Alice Harper waited contentedly for Lynne in the circular rose garden near the old City Hall in the large, heavily shaded central plaza of the town of Sonoma. As veteran chaperons of far too many fourth-grade California history field trips, they'd decided to forgo the Mission tour and other historic buildings, at least for today. The plaza had a timeless feel and was packed with historic significance—the official California state flag had been born here, during the Bear Flag Rebellion, just for starters—but the horticulture was right up to the minute. A flourishing Betty Boop floribunda rose bloomed just behind the bench where Alice sat.

"I love waving the guys off in the morning, knowing they won't be back till dinnertime," Alice said. Bodega Harbor, where Don and Mark were golfing today, was clear across the county on the Pacific Ocean. "It reminds me of the good old days, when Don went to work in the morning, and all I had to do was run the house and chauffeur the kids and lead the Scouts and do fund-raisers for the PTA."

Pat laughed. "Ah, yes. Return with us now to those thrilling days of yesteryear. Four hundred thousand rolls of gift wrap in the gym and three hours to get it all to the right kids in the right classrooms. On your marks, get set, *go!*"

"Piece of cake compared to keeping Don from reorganizing the kitchen one more time. Not that I'm complaining," Alice added hurriedly. "I mean, I look at Lynne, and I think how easily it could have been any of us."

At moments like this, even though she hadn't attended church regularly since her kids left home, Pat always involuntarily crossed herself. Alice was right, of course. Whatever problems either of them had—and husbands in their sixties at home full-time was no stroll in the park—at least their guys were healthy and alive. Pat knew that only full-blown Alzheimer's would ever erase her memory of Lynne's hysterical call the morning that Monty died.

"Next time, let's have her find someplace where we can send the guys to go golf on their own for a few days, and then the three of us can go somewhere else," Alice said. "Lynne needs a vacation of her own, when she doesn't have to ride herd on a bunch of people."

"Seattle?" Pat suggested.

"Actually, I was thinking Paris," Alice admitted. "But Don would have a cow if I told him we were going to Europe by ourselves. Not that he'd want to come himself, of course." Don preferred his vacations in English-speaking locales that offered McDonald's, where the native cuisine featured no suspicious vegetables or mysterious sauces.

"Hey, guys!" Lynne came around the corner, beaming and cheerful, with Eleanor Whitson in tow.

Eleanor looked wan, dressed in beige slacks and an olive-green fleece jacket with a dispirited beige stripe. Pat and Alice had found it so difficult to maintain a conversation with the woman during the morning's cooking class that eventually they stopped even trying. Eleanor had labored like an automaton, folding the cheese-and-herb stuffing into phyllo packets as snug and tidy as the hospital corners Pat's mother had taught her to make in the olden days, before fitted sheets.

"Been shopping?" Pat asked Eleanor, who was carrying a small paper bag.

"I looked around a bit," Eleanor said. Her voice, like her hair, was wispy and colorless. Pat wondered if she'd have the hair done tomorrow afternoon when they went to the spa. Nobody would deliberately be so drab. "I didn't really see much. Just got a scarf for my neighbor, who's watching the house." Though Eleanor probably wasn't more than a few years older than the three Floritas friends, she had the demeanor and mannerisms of someone in her nineties.

Lynne plopped down beside Pat on the bench and inhaled the rich perfume. "I sure do love rose gardens. But I kind of miss the chickens here."

"Chickens?" Eleanor asked, frowning. It seemed to be her default expression.

"There used to be chickens running free here in the plaza," Lynne explained. "But parents complained that the roosters were chasing their kids, so they finally just got rid of them."

"Coq au vin?" Pat wondered.

"Quite possibly, though those roosters would have been pretty tough old birds."

"Just like us," Alice said. "You're right about this rose garden, Lynne. I really like it. And I also like the way so many of the vineyards incorporate roses. Is that really supposed to be functional?"

Lynne nodded. "Used to be, anyway. Roses are susceptible to a lot of the same diseases and pests as grapes, only the roses are afflicted first. They'd plant them by the vines as a kind of early warning system. When the roses got sick, it was time to pay more attention to the grapes."

"Like coal mine canaries," Pat said.

"Exactly. But nowadays, viticulture has become such a science that the roses are mostly kept around for good luck, and 'cause they look pretty."

"Also like us," Alice said with a grin. She turned to Eleanor, who had perched tentatively on one of the benches. "Do you go to the rose garden at the Huntington very often,

Eleanor? I'd want to be there all the time if I lived where you do."

Eleanor Whitson shook her head slightly. "I don't go much anymore. Where are we going for dinner tonight, Lynne?"

Pat watched Lynne subtly change gears at the graceless change of subject. Lynne was really good at making folks feel comfortable, at anticipating needs and interests. This was part of what made her such a bona fide, late-blooming business success story in their circle of empty-nesters. Of course, her nest was emptier than most, since Monty's death, but Lynne had already been working for Maggie Chambers at Booked for Travel when Monty died. Pat would always wonder if Maggie—who was seventy-eight but a really *young* seventy-eight at the time—had actually been ready to retire or if she had offered to sell out to Lynne because she knew the young widow needed a passion on which to reanchor her life. But it wasn't the kind of question you'd ask Maggie, one of the original Crusty Old Broads.

"Hunter's Hideaway," Lynne told Eleanor now, as warmly as if the woman had been her dear friend for decades. That kind of graciousness was a gift, one that Pat had not been given and wasn't sure she envied. It took so much energy to be nice all the time. "It's over in Glen Ellen, near where we went to the Benziger Winery for the tram tour. We passed it on the way in, as a matter of fact, and we'll be going through there again when we tour Jack London's ranch Friday morning."

"Don is really looking forward to that," Alice put in. "He's been reading Jack London for weeks now." She chuckled. "And feeling very virile, I might add. But being a lady, I won't elaborate."

"A pity," Lynne told her wryly. "I was hoping for details."

"What kind of restaurant is it?" Eleanor asked, rising above the veiled ribaldry, as befit a Pasadena matron.

"I guess you'd have to call it California cuisine," Lynne said. "Everything is nice and fresh, and your vegetable and protein and starch will be separated on the plate. Though there's a fifty-fifty chance they'll come with some pretty sauce artfully drizzled over everything."

Alice laughed. "Drizzle away, just so long as there's enough of it. This isn't going to be one of those meals where two perfectly arranged green beans constitute the vegetable course, is it?"

Lynne shook her head. "No way. I think that whole age of culinary minimalism is over, anyhow. At least I hope it is."

"What I want to see over is haystack cuisine, this business of piling everything on top of everything else," Pat said. "All the different parts of the meal layered in a tower in the center of your plate with different sauces on different levels and one perfect mushroom cap on top. It all looks really nice until the first time you take a knife or a fork to it, and then it collapses into an ugly little mess. When Ricky was a kid, he'd pile his food all up that way, and I punished him for it. How was I supposed to know he was simply ahead of his time?"

Eleanor Whitson shifted her weight in ladylike irritation, then glanced at her watch. "When are we going back, Lynne?"

Lynne was instantly alert. "We're informally scheduled to go back in about forty-five minutes, Eleanor, with a stop on the way at the Ravenswood tasting room. But Villa Belladuce's just up the road. I could run you back right now if you'd like."

"I wouldn't want to impose." Her tone was just whiny enough to suggest that she didn't give a hoot if she imposed or not.

"No imposition at all," Lynne assured her, wearing her most congenial tour guide smile. "Sit tight for a minute, and I'll get the van."

❦

**RYAN** Atherton quietly closed the connecting door behind him. Gran had fallen asleep in the reclining chair, and he'd debated rousing her to suggest she get into bed, but that sounded too much like the old jokes about nurses waking patients to give them sleeping pills. He turned on the TV in his own room and idly channel-surfed, stopping briefly at a soap opera with some glossy-looking women arguing about a cad named Chad. He settled on a CNN financial report, feeling vaguely virtuous.

The chirp of the cell phone startled him. Lynne had given each of them one when they arrived, to facilitate communication when they went off on different activities. But this was the first time that his had actually rung.

"Hey, Bro." Kelly sounded perky, not necessarily a good sign. He was worried about his sister, who remained tightly wound even now, on vacation, when there was minimal stress and no particular cause for alarm. "Gran okay?"

"She's fine. Taking a nap right now. Whatcha doing?"

Kelly had brought Ryan back after lunch, then returned to Sonoma to meet Jessica and Sara. The three of them had decided to go shopping, an activity Ryan ranked right up there with scrubbing toilets. "Watching CNN."

"For this you came to California?" Even though it hadn't been her idea, Kelly had embraced the trip with a ferocious enthusiasm. Her rationale had been simple: They could each have the semblance of a vacation while indulging Gran's desire to visit California for what all of them knew would be the last time.

"You called to criticize my viewing habits?" he countered.

"Actually, I called for two reasons. First to tell you we found a place in town that sells cheese curds, and we bought a bag."

"Trying to turn this into a busman's holiday for me, are you? I hope the second reason's better."

"For those of us who can't wander into the production area and pick up a bag of cheese curds it *is* a big deal. Your girlfriends are both fascinated. But listen, the main reason I called was to see if you wanted to go with us to Ravenswood in about an hour. I can pick you up, if you think Gran wouldn't mind."

"Of course she wouldn't. She was kind of annoyed that I came back this afternoon."

Without formally planning it, the twins had managed to tag-team staying with Gran, whose strength was almost nonexistent. Neither had said so out loud, but Ryan knew that he and Kelly each feared their grandmother would die alone while they were off having fun.

"Ravenswood has some really nice wines," Kelly went on, as if she thought Ryan could tell the difference between a Chardonnay and a chateaubriand. He was a Wisconsin native, a beer-and-brats boy. "Jessica and Sara are kind of hoping you'll come back."

Hmm. He'd let the remark about "your girlfriends" go, but Kelly seemed determined to make an issue out of this. "Is that your guess?"

"Not at all, Romeo. They both asked, separately. You aren't going to have those poor girls fighting a duel at sunrise, are you?"

Ryan laughed. "Sorry there aren't any guys our age here, Kel. I wasn't exactly expecting this, you know." Ryan had a girlfriend back in Wisconsin, a pleasant young brunette in the accounting department. In rare moments of objectivity he could admit—though only to himself—that the relationship was going nowhere at a very leisurely pace.

"So is that a yes? C'mon, I sneaked off to make this call. They're going to miss me."

"Okay, okay. Come pick me up whenever. I'll be here."

Kelly had always been more hyper and intense than Ryan, a difference accentuated when the two entered the labor force after graduating from the University of Wisconsin. Kelly went from Madison to Chicago, where she carved herself a profitable niche as a headhunter in the tech fields. She was young enough to understand electronic technology as it existed right now and sharp enough to realize that it changed so quickly that conventional businesses couldn't possibly understand or keep up with the evolution. Kelly's talent was determining a company's current needs and translating those into techie employees who'd be appropriate for both now and a year from now, and maybe even five years from now.

His own talent, however, was a good deal more down to earth: marketing cheese. Muenster for the masses, via mail order and the Internet. Not exactly what he'd had in mind, but he hadn't really had anything in mind, so this was okay.

Ryan thought he heard a distant car door slam and went to the door of the cottage, wondering for just a moment if Kelly had tricked him by calling from just down the road. To his relief, he saw Eleanor Whitson coming onto the patio from the parking area. She trotted down the path toward her own cottage, and he went back to CNN.

About five minutes later, he heard a knock on his door. Was this Kelly? He was going to be really annoyed if she started playing matchmaker games on him.

But it wasn't Kelly at all. Lynne Montgomery stood outside with the woman cop he'd talked to yesterday morning when they found the dead guy over at the winery. Neither one of them looked happy.

The detective nodded a greeting. "Good afternoon, Mr. Atherton. I'm glad I caught you. Do you suppose I could talk to your grandmother for a minute?"

Ryan frowned. "She just fell asleep. Can't it wait?"

Detective Shaw smiled and waved a hand. "Of course. But while I'm here, could I come in for a minute?"

Ryan shrugged and opened the door wider.

Lynne turned to the detective. "I'm going back down into town, all right?"

"Sure. I'll talk to you later." The detective came in and sat in the chair by the window.

Ryan flicked off the TV and sat on the edge of his bed. "What can I do for you?"

"I was wondering if you'd had any more thoughts about what time you heard the cat on the night before last."

Ryan shook his head. "I woke up really thirsty, and I was getting a drink of water when I heard it. But I didn't look at the clock, or if I did, I don't remember it." His head had been throbbing, and he'd popped three ibuprofen with the water. "Does it matter?"

"Actually, it does. We found cat hairs on the body, and the cat didn't go out again till after the body was discovered in the morning. If we can determine when the cat was let in, we'll know for certain that he was killed before that time."

"I don't suppose you could ask the cat?" Ryan wondered. He put a hand up. "Sorry, that was in really poor taste. But wouldn't whoever let the cat in be able to tell you when it was?"

"The housekeeper let him in, but she didn't notice the time. When were you last over at the winery?"

Ryan blinked at the rapid change of subject. "Never, actually. We were supposed to have a tour yesterday morning, but that got canceled because you folks were here. We're going over there later this afternoon, before dinner. Why?"

"I'm afraid you won't be going today, either. There's been some vandalism at the winery. Do you know if anybody from your group has been over there?"

"What happened?"

"Do you know if anybody from your group has been over there?" she repeated.

"No idea whatsoever," he said. "Are you going to tell me what happened?"

She smiled thinly. "Somebody wrecked the equipment and poured out a lot of the wine that was barreled in the main winery building. We're not sure exactly when, but we know it was all right late yesterday afternoon when our crime scene technicians finished down there."

*Oh, man. That truck last night.* Ryan took a deep breath. "I may actually be able to help you. I was out walking last night after dinner." He felt a strange hesitation at bringing Jessica into this. After all, they hadn't really *seen* anything. But there'd been an odd feel to that truck roaring down the highway with its lights out, odd enough that he had instinctively moved to protect her.

He told the detective everything he could remember, leaving out only the part where he kissed Jessica good night by the roses in the moonlight.

*Chapter 10*

**AS** Mark Martell climbed contentedly back into the rented golf cart, he looked out over the Pacific shoreline and decided that his was an exceptionally fine life. He didn't even mind so much anymore that he was retired. Mark would have preferred to keep working until he dropped at his desk one day in his eighties, but that wasn't how the work world operated these days, and the choice had been taken out of his hands.

He'd been sixty-two when the ax fell, senior accountant at Bio Beginnings, a biotech firm in La Jolla, when the company restructured. Don had been working with him there, running the labs, with responsibility for overseeing technical operations, ordering equipment, hiring junior staff, and keeping the egomaniacal senior researchers contented. The lab had made some significant breakthroughs, though nothing on the scale they'd hoped for, and for a while it looked as if the entire place was doomed. That happened a lot in biotech: ambitions loftier than achievements, dead ends on roads that once appeared promising, tents silently folded in the night. Just when it was starting to look as if Bio Beginnings was at the tent-folding stage, a long-shot process turned out to work beautifully. The firm was bought out by a major player in the field, and old-timers like Mark and Don were strapped into golden parachutes. Both had been accumulating stock options through the lean years, and Mark figured out the best timetable for them to redeem those. They'd cleaned up financially.

He missed going to work, however. He did a spot of consulting here and there and even got a little wistful when all the storefront tax places opened in the first quarter of the year. But he was too old to get a job working for anybody else now, and he'd learned how to create his own structure for his days.

And there was something to be said for being able to golf 365 days of the year if you felt like it.

◦═══◦

**GUIDO** Ambrosino could tell that Maria wasn't really enjoying herself. She hadn't said anything, of course, and it wasn't in her nature to complain. In fact, he suspected that she'd probably deny it if he'd asked her directly, but you didn't spend half a century with somebody without knowing when she was uncomfortable.

Yesterday had been a different matter, with the entire group out on the tour together, and Lynne Montgomery along. That had been fun, an adventure, a new experience. Of course there'd been undercurrents from the strange and terrible death of that young man. But in an odd and spooky way, that had only made the day more exciting.

Today, in this smaller group, the differences were more pronounced. The Texans, Guido knew, would have preferred to be alone. They paid almost no attention to the Ambrosinos and were only slightly more civil to Ginger Conner, that nice young woman from San Diego. She seemed to drink far more than was respectable for a lady, but she was polite to everyone and respectful to Maria, which was all that really concerned Guido.

Before reaching the large and imposing Chateau Souverain, where they had now settled in for a late lunch, the group had visited two wineries on the Alexander Valley appellation tour. The Chalk Hill Winery, technically in the separate Chalk Hill appellation, was interesting in the way that all of these places were interesting: small, determined operations dedicating themselves to the production of fine wine.

The Field Stone Winery, however, had stolen Guido's heart, and he suspected that no vineyard or winery that followed would affect him the same way. The physical plant was odd—dug into the ground, more or less—but it wasn't the subterranean architecture at Field Stone that had so captured him, or the efficient way the operation was designed. No, it was something altogether unexpected that set this winery apart from others that were all beginning to blur in his mind.

At Field Stone they were bottling wine made from sangiovese grapes, the same red grapes used in Chianti production in Tuscany.

Guido and Maria had seen sangiovese grapes growing in central Italy five years ago on their forty-fifth anniversary trip, had sat on stone terraces under ancient olive trees overlooking those vineyards. They'd sipped Chianti and eaten exquisitely prepared local specialties. It all had been rather magical, and it was their enthusiasm for that trip, he suspected, that had led the kids to set up this one.

For the first time on the trip, Guido found a wine he wanted to take home, and he'd bought four bottles.

There was something else going on today, however, something that he found confusing and a bit unsettling. Hake Sandstrom kept asking their guide and limo driver to make special detours so he could look at wineries that weren't on the day's schedule, and he seemed a lot more interested in those other places than the wineries that they were actually visiting. The guy was up to something, no question about it, and Guido wouldn't have cared, if it weren't for the fellow's attitude that whatever he wanted was so obviously more important than anything the others might have in mind.

So he had surprised everybody, including himself, by insisting that he and Maria have their own table for lunch at Chateau Souverain. Hake and Heidi Sandstrom sat at the next table over with Ginger Conner, and their guide was having a sandwich out in the limo. As Guido listened to the next table's spirited consideration of which wines they wanted with lunch, he knew that sitting apart had been a smart move. The others couldn't decide whether they wanted a flight or a vertical tasting, and Guido wasn't about to admit that he had no idea what either one was. Nor did he care.

The Ambrosinos stuck with iced tea and ordered Caesar salads that came with roasted chicken, more food than either of them could possibly consume in the middle of the day. They could have split one order, truth be told, and he wished they'd done that. Guido had worked too hard for too many years to ever be comfortable with waste, but Maria just whispered to him to eat what he wanted and leave the rest.

At the next table now, the others were trying another wine. Hake Sandstrom's annoying twang carried a little too well. "This has no nose at all," he pronounced disdainfully.

Guido winked at Maria, and she smiled back at him, the corners of her dark eyes crinkling.

"Would you mind too much," she asked softly, "if tomorrow I stayed behind?"

He frowned at her. "What do you mean?"

She gave a little shrug. "At Villa Belladuce. This"—she waved a hand briefly around the café, and he understood immediately that she meant the traveling around and not the winery here or any other specific location—"is just the same thing over and over. I'd like to rest, to spend some time with the baby."

"They may not want you spending time with the baby," he told her gently. "They have a lady who takes care of the baby."

"So you think they wouldn't want me?" She sounded hurt.

He reached a hand across the table and covered her own hand, trembling now as she clenched her napkin. "Maria, Maria, you know that's not what I mean. But this is your vacation, your holiday."

She leveled a steely gaze at him, and he realized that he had no say in the matter whatsoever.

"I could stay with you," he offered.

She shook her head. "Tomorrow is the garden tour. I know you want to see that."

And indeed he was intrigued by the idea of the Luther Burbank Gardens, though nowhere near as enthusiastic as some of the others. Guido had spent much of his life trying to grow the perfect tomato, first in pots on a fire escape and then later in the small patch behind the house where he and Maria had raised five children.

"You're right," he admitted. "But after that, I will stay with you. Surely we have the right to not do something as much as to do it, no?"

She squeezed his hand. "We'll tell the children we visited a thousand vineyards."

He laughed. "We'll tell the children we did exactly what we wanted to do."

**SARA** Conner was finally feeling human again.

She wasn't sure exactly what she'd been thinking of, or if she'd been thinking at all, that first night when she got so appallingly drunk. Thirty-six hours of near abstinence, however, had cleansed her system. Now she cautiously sipped one of the magnificent zinfandels that Ravenswood specialized in and realized that it was indeed a remarkable wine.

It didn't appear that she was going to meet Prince Charming on this trip, but getting out of Atlanta had been an excellent idea. Though she hated to admit that Ginger was ever right about anything, her sister had been square on the money about that.

As she watched Ryan and Jessica now, it occurred to her that Jessica seemed seriously smitten and that Ryan appeared to be reciprocating. Well, wouldn't you just know it? She'd all but forced Jessica to come along on this trip. First, she'd argued that they ought to move, run away, start over somewhere else, like California. When that didn't work, she backpedaled to a suggestion that a simple vacation couldn't hurt anybody.

Now here was Jessica, slipping right into the role Sara had

envisioned for herself, and where was it all going to leave Sara? By her stony lonesome in Atlanta, slaving away in the litigation department by day and arguing about custody arrangements with her ex-husband by night. With somebody who didn't even want custody, but desired it only to inconvenience Sara.

Men could be such slugs.

Jessica remained firmly focused on California. "It really creeps me out, thinking how close we came to surprising those vandals who busted up the winery," Jessica said with a shiver. They'd been delayed nearly half an hour when they went to pick up Ryan, waiting for Jessica to give the police her version of what she'd seen—or, apparently, what she *hadn't* seen—last night. "They might have killed us."

A trifle melodramatic, Sara thought, but what she said was, "I thought you weren't anywhere near the winery."

"But we might have been."

*You might have been in Bangladesh, too, but you weren't,* Sara thought bitterly. *Enough already.*

Ryan looked like he wanted to sweep Jessica into a reassuring embrace, and Sara had sudden visions of being asked to move into Ginger's room in the Umbria cottage so that the lovebirds could have a little privacy. She dismissed the thought. Ryan didn't seem like the kind of guy who'd behave that way a hundred yards away from Saint Granny.

Kelly leaned back against the polished blond bar and cocked her head. "I think the only person in real danger is already dead," she announced. Kelly had a way of cutting through the bull that Sara found very appealing.

"I'm sure he didn't think anyone was going to kill him," Jessica answered in a tiny, little voice.

Ryan draped a reassuring arm around Jessica's shoulders, and Sara saw an expression she couldn't quite read pass across Kelly's face.

Kelly looked around the tasting room, which they had pretty much to themselves. "I like this place," she announced. "I like the No Wimpy Wines slogan and the whole attitude. I think I may need to buy me some souvenirs here."

They'd spent some time when they first arrived, looking at the corner of the room that featured pictures of celebrities wearing or drinking Ravenswood products, and of regular folks clad in No Wimpy Wines shirts in places like Fiji, Tangiers, Galapagos, and China.

"Then if I ever take a trip someplace exotic," Kelly continued, "I can send them a picture of me in a No Wimpy Wines T-shirt, and they can put up in the photo gallery. I've also decided"—Kelly held her nose to her wineglass and gave it a little swirl—"that my favorite red wine is zinfandel."

"This may be a really dumb question," Ryan said, "but why do they call it white zinfandel when it's pink?"

"There are no dumb questions," Kelly pronounced with mock seriousness. Then she grinned. "Just dumb questioners."

Ryan shrugged. "Guilty as charged. I was just wondering."

"It all has to do with how the grapes are handled when they're crushed," Sara explained. "But you need to know that blush wines are really looked down on by serious wine drinkers. Mr. Sandstrom would probably snort you into the next county if you even suggested drinking white zinfandel."

Kelly laughed. "The next county is Napa, so that would be okay by me. Ryan, white zin is like those rosé wines that Gran used to drink. Mateus and Lancer's, remember? And she'd save the bottles?"

He nodded. "Oh, yeah. I guess the part I don't understand is—" He looked befuddled and then a bit sheepish. "Actually, I don't think I was paying attention at all when they told us how wine was made. If they even did."

"Me, neither," Jessica admitted. *Now there was a shocker.*

Sara smiled. "Do you want to know?"

"Sure," Ryan said, just as Jessica shrugged her shoulders and answered, "Not really."

"He spoke up first, Jessica. Sorry. This is something I actually know, so brace yourself. Wine making 101, the CliffsNotes version. You grow some grapes. Then you harvest the grapes, ideally in cool weather and sometimes at night if it's a particularly warm region. You crush them. Up till this point, it's the same for red or white wines. For white wine, you remove all the skins and seeds and stems right after the grapes are crushed, so that only the juice is left to ferment. You add yeast and put it all into some kind of container to ferment for a while. It's called *must* at this stage.

"Anyway, the fermentation releases a lot of carbon dioxide and turns the sugar in the grapes into our old buddy, alcohol. When the grape juice finishes fermenting and the sugar's gone, it's technically wine. But then, unless it's real rotgut, you put it into another container to age for a while. Later on, you filter and bottle it."

"And red is done differently?" Ryan asked.

Sara couldn't tell if he was just being polite, and she didn't really care. This beat hearing Jessica tell them one more time how scary it had been to see that stupid truck. "Red wines are fermented with the skin and seeds still mixed in. That's how it becomes—duh!—red. From the skins. When it's the color and tannin level you want, it goes through a press to remove the skins and stuff. Then it goes into aging containers and eventually it's filtered and bottled. Red wines are usually aged longer than whites to mellow out the tannin."

"Tanning?" Ryan sounded confused.

Sara shook her head and spoke with a deeper-than-usual drawl. "Cultural communications breakdown here. I'm not dropping the *g* cause there isn't one. It's tannin." She spelled it. "Which is a natural acid from the skins. It's part of what gives red wine its flavor, and it mellows as the wine ages."

"So the longer it ages, the mellower it gets?"

"To a point. Eventually, I think it all turns into vinegar. You know, you hear every now and then that somebody's going to open a bottle of hundred-year-old wine, but I don't think it's any good when they do."

Ryan shrugged. He seemed to have absorbed all that he was going to. "So, does that mean the white zinfandel is, what, half and half?"

"Ryan, please! Mr. Sandstrom would have you shot for asking that." She flushed. "Oops. Guess that's a bad way to put it, under the circumstances. But no, it's not a mixture. It's made from regular zinfandel grapes, but the skins are removed pretty quickly, so it stays pink instead of becoming this beautiful, rich red." Sara held her glass up to the light to admire the deep ruby liquid.

"And that's all there is to it?" Jessica asked. "The wineries always make it sound so complicated."

"Oh, there are plenty of differences and variables, starting with all those different varieties of grapes. How it's aged, what it's aged in, the kind of yeast, how long it's aged, whether it's filtered and with what. But that's the crash course, all you really need to know."

Ryan shook his head. "All I really need to know is when's dinner. I'm starving."

**ELEANOR** Whitson was packing when she heard the knock on her cottage door.

She looked around in a panic. Her suitcase lay open on the bed, her clothes jumbled haphazardly into it, looking as if they belonged to somebody else altogether. She'd unpacked and put everything neatly away when she arrived on Sunday, arranging her dresses and blouses in the closet on hangers, folding slacks and sweaters tidily into drawers the way she always did when she traveled. She'd been mildly panicky at the time, wondering why she was here, realizing how different things appeared when you were actually on the scene.

Sunday felt like a hundred years ago, Sunday's anxiety a tiny breeze compared to the force-ten gale of her current emotions.

The knock came again, sharper and more insistent.

"Mrs. Whitson?"

She stood paralyzed as she recognized the lady detective's voice. Shank, Sherwood, what was her name? Shaw, that was it.

"Mrs. Whitson, open up, please." The detective's tone was sharper and more insistent the second time.

Eleanor smashed everything into the suitcase, tried unsuccessfully to zip it closed, then cast her eyes about frantically. The suitcase was huge, and there was nowhere she could hope to hide it. She tried to lift it off the bed, but it was too heavy and bulky, and it slipped through her hands, banging noisily onto the floor. Desperate now, she pushed it into the corner with her foot.

"Mrs. Whitson, this is Detective Shaw. Please open up now." Impatience and a bit of irritation sounded now in the detective's voice. How did she know Eleanor was in here? The others were gone, after all. She was alone except for Ruth Atherton, who seemed too sick and tired to notice anyone else's comings and goings.

She had to get out of here somehow. She looked around and realized the hopelessness of it all. There was no escape. She knew the connecting door was locked because she'd checked it just before she started to pack, fearful that Lynne might open it unexpectedly and discover her preparing for flight. Not that Lynne was even here. Now she realized that even if she could leave via Lynne's room, she'd have to exit the cottage through the front door, which sat right beside her own front door, where Detective Shaw was waiting right now, none too patiently.

She was trapped.

The detective banged a third time, a heavy thudding that sounded to Eleanor like the advance of absolute and total doom.

Slowly, as if in a trance, she moved toward the door. She twisted the deadbolt open and turned the knob deliberately, then pulled the door open a crack, yearning for the false protection of a chain lock.

"Mrs. Whitson?" Detective Shaw stood a full head taller than Eleanor and looked past her into the room. Could she see the suitcase?

"I'm busy," Eleanor said, holding onto the door. She didn't have to let her in, did she? A person had rights in her own home. Though of course this wasn't Eleanor's home, wasn't anybody's home, really, except maybe the Rutledges'.

But there wasn't time to really think about that or about anything else. The detective pushed the door open and stepped inside, her eyes scanning the room quickly and taking in the overflowing suitcase on the floor, the empty hangers scattered on the bed. She stuck her head into the bathroom long enough to observe Eleanor's vanity case open on the counter, fully packed and ready to be closed.

"Were you going somewhere?" the detective asked. It was hard to read her tone. What did she know? What did she suspect?

"No, no," Eleanor protested weakly. Her eyes strayed to the Yellow Pages open on the dresser, and the detective followed her gaze.

"Airport shuttles?" Detective Shaw closed the outside door firmly and took her time looking around the room. "Why are you leaving, Mrs. Whitson? Your tour doesn't end until Saturday."

Eleanor felt all her strength melting away. Tears formed in her eyes and ran silently down her cheeks. "I couldn't stay here. I shouldn't have come. I didn't mean—" She stopped abruptly, and her own silence seemed to grow in her ears like some creature that puffs itself up in the face of attack by a predator.

"You didn't mean what?" Detective Shaw's voice was mild, conversational. "Why don't you have a seat, Mrs. Whitson?"

Eleanor moved blindly to a chair and sat down. Detective Shaw sat in the companion chair, a little too close.

"When I asked you the other morning if you knew Lance Belladuce," the detective went on, her voice gentler now, "you told me you didn't. You didn't mention your son, James, or the Belladuce restaurant down in Monterey."

Tears were sliding down Eleanor's cheeks now. She wasn't sure when they'd started. Sometimes it felt as if she'd been crying for years. "I forgot," she offered feebly.

Detective Shaw cocked her head, moved a little closer, and frowned. "You forgot? Mrs. Whitson, I have a son myself. And if he'd lost two hundred thousand dollars in a restaurant and then killed himself, I know I'd never be able to forget it."

Eleanor felt words pouring out of her, words she couldn't control and knew she would regret. "Of course I didn't forget it. But I didn't kill Lance Belladuce. I just thought if I could . . . I don't know . . . I thought if I could see this place, maybe see *him,* then I could finally put it all behind me. I had my reservations before the Rutledges bought this place. But it was all different than I thought it would be. He didn't even recognize me. . . ." Her voice trailed away, and she raised desperate eyes to meet the detective's cool, impassive stare.

"But I didn't kill him. Really, I didn't. I just *wanted* him dead."

"Mrs. Whitson," Detective Shaw said in a firm tone that was somehow also gentle and kind.

Eleanor thought she might faint, and she swayed momentarily.

The detective caught her arm, and Eleanor felt the woman's strong fingers close just above her elbow. "Mrs. Whitson, I think you'd better come with me."

*Chapter 11*

A cool mist had drifted into the Valley of the Moon, and the early evening air hung chilly on the Villa Belladuce patio as the Sonoma Sojourners gathered for a bit of wine and cheese before dinner. Lynne shivered, momentarily regretting that tonight she was driving the van to dinner. A warming nip of wine would be welcome right now. A cup of coffee would be even better.

The tour of the Villa Belladuce caves had been postponed again, following some unspecified vandalism over at the winery. Angela had left a vague note of apology on Lynne's door.

Lynne was more than a little curious about what had happened at the winery, but unfortunately, Angela hadn't put in an appearance since Lynne returned with Alice and Pat after meeting up with the kids at Ravenswood. Lynne had walked over to the windowless winery building to check out what was going on, but the place was buttoned up tight. Only a muddy patch by the doorway that smelled of wine suggested the havoc within.

"Are you sure it's August?" Sara Conner drawled, tightening a pale green shawl around her tiny shoulders. The shawl was a loose weave shot through with a thread of copper, and it seemed designed more for appearance than warmth. "I mean, I know that Ginger said it would be cool here, but this is ridiculous! I've been freezing ever since I got off the plane."

Lynne regarded the girl thoughtfully. She had no meat on her bones to speak of, so it wasn't much of a surprise that she chilled easily. And her wardrobe was definitely oriented toward summer patio parties in Atlanta, all skimpy little dresses and short shorts.

"Northern California's a fairly mild climate year round," Lynne told her, "but the problem is that there aren't any extremes on either end. It doesn't get too terribly hot in the summer or too terribly cold in the winter."

"What was it Mark Twain said about San Francisco?" Alice asked. "I can never remember that line when I want it."

"That he spent the coldest winter of his life there one summer," Don answered. He was a fount of arcane literary information, which no longer surprised Lynne. Don read more than any adult male she knew, and when he became engrossed in a subject, he'd research it to death.

A chirping from her purse startled Lynne. The cell phone. But who'd be calling her now? The Sonoma Sojourners were all either on the patio or in their cottages getting ready for dinner. Could it be her son David again, following another query from Detective Shaw? More likely it was a wrong number, somebody trying to reach a pizza parlor or soccer coach in Floritas. The phones were all programmed with the Floritas area code.

"Lynne Montgomery," she answered offhandedly.

"Lynne?" The voice was soft and tremulous, and she didn't recognize it immediately. "It's Eleanor. Eleanor Whitson."

Lynne looked across the patio toward Campania, the cottage she and Eleanor shared. She'd assumed Eleanor was taking a nap and would be out shortly. Perhaps she'd overslept and was afraid they'd leave without her.

"Oh, hi, Eleanor. Are you about ready for dinner?"

Eleanor gave a strangled sob. "Lynne, I'm not going to dinner. I'm not going anywhere. They arrested me."

"What?" Lynne wouldn't have pegged Eleanor for a practical joker, but surely she wasn't serious. "Who arrested you? Where are you?"

"I don't know. I mean, I'm at the police station." She was definitely crying, and her words came out in strangled little clumps. "They told me I could make a phone call, and I didn't know who else I could call or what I should do."

"I don't understand." Lynne stood up and moved away from the others. This seemed to call for at least a modicum of privacy. "Why would anybody arrest you?"

"For killing Lance Belladuce."

*Oh, my goodness.*

"But I *didn't,*" Eleanor went on. "I swear it. Only I didn't tell them I'd met Lance before, or about my son."

This was crazy. Eleanor had known *Lance*?

"There must be some kind of mistake," Lynne told her, trying to sound calm and reassuring. "We'll get it all straightened out; don't worry. What can I do?" This was uncharted territory. Lynne had taken a client to the emergency room on more than one occasion while on tour, but she'd never had to get anybody out of jail before. And if Eleanor actually was in jail, and for murder at that, what on earth could she do about it, anyway?

"I don't know," Eleanor wailed. "Will you . . . will you call my daughter? She'll know what to do. I guess I need a lawyer, too. This is just so horrible, I don't know what to do."

Lynne thought fast as she dug in her purse for a pencil and paper. "Give me your daughter's number," she said, "and I'll call her right away. Do you have a lawyer you want me to call?"

"Just my lawyer at home, but he only does wills and things. I don't know what to do."

Neither did Lynne, but she'd watched plenty of TV cop shows. "I'm sure this is all some kind of silly mistake, Eleanor, so let's see if we can't get it straightened out right away. You don't have to say anything to the police without a lawyer. You know that, don't you?"

"They told me that. But the more I explain, the meaner they get. And now they took my fingerprints, and they won't let me leave, and I don't know what I'm going to do."

As Lynne began wondering how on earth one went about finding a criminal attorney in a strange town, she turned and caught a glimpse of Hake Sandstrom's rented Jaguar out in the parking lot. *Hmm.* "Eleanor, for heaven's sake stop talking to the police until you have a lawyer with you. Was it Detective Shaw who arrested you?"

"Yes. I was going to go home because I just had to get away from here, and she came in and saw me with my suitcase all packed and brought me down here. They keep asking me all these questions, and I don't know what to tell them."

"Don't tell them anything, Eleanor. I'll find you a lawyer somehow. I'm sure this is all some terrible misunderstanding, but you need a lawyer to straighten it out."

By the time Lynne hung up, everyone on the patio was watching her, mesmerized. "That was Eleanor Whitson," she told them, as if they might not have figured it out on their own. "I don't understand exactly what's happened, but she seems to be in jail."

Then she marched down the path to Abruzzi.

**HAKE** Sandstrom listened to Lynne Montgomery's report with astonishment.

"Still waters run deep," he said, shaking his head. Of all the people in this sorry little group, Eleanor Whitson would have been his last choice as a likely murderer.

"I can't believe she's guilty," Lynne told him, frowning. "I don't think we should assume the worst until we know exactly what's going on."

"Well, if these local rubes arrested her, they must have pretty solid evidence." Hake knew that even if the woman had been arrested in error, it could be mighty difficult to shake her loose now. He'd never done criminal work himself, but he knew enough about it to realize that once the cops had some-body in custody, they tended to focus all their attention on making their case and spent almost no time looking into other possibilities.

"Does she have money?" he asked Lynne.

Lynne narrowed her eyes slightly. "I don't think she'll re-quire a public defender, if that's what you mean. I assume she can afford to pay a good attorney."

Hake shook his head and offered a hint of a smile. "A good attorney can cost a bundle. But I do know a fellow down in San Francisco, Len Morelli. If he's available, he'd be just the ticket."

Hake rather liked Leonard Morelli, a high-profile criminal attorney who'd won acquittals for any number of wealthy clients who were guilty as hell. He'd met him two years ago when Morelli defended a Fort Worth restaurant owner ac-cused of commissioning the murder of an ex-wife and her boyfriend. The restaurateur was a high-rolling corporate client of Hake's firm, which farmed out the case because Tam-merville, Carr and Barnes handled only civil litigation and didn't soil its hands with criminal matters.

The restaurateur—whom Hake had assumed fell into the guilty-as-hell category—was convicted of malicious mischief because there was no way to get around the fact that he'd posted naked pictures of the ex-wife on half a dozen Internet sites. But Morelli walked him on the murder solicitation charges. The restaurateur had since opened two more estab-lishments, in San Antonio and Houston, and all three places were doing a booming business.

Hake picked up his little electronic datebook, pushed some buttons, and peered at the tiny screen. "Keep your fingers crossed," he told Lynne as he dialed the cell phone. It was nearly six o'clock, but a secretary picked right up. Hake gave her his name, and after a moment, he heard Morelli's smooth voice on the line.

"Hakester!" Morelli exclaimed. "How's it going? Don't tell me you've got another one of your wacky Texans in a jam?"

Hake had been drinking an estate-bottled Merlina Merlot—

which sounded to him more like a hot starlet than the surprisingly acceptable wine that it had turned out to be—when Lynne knocked on the cottage door. He topped off his glass now. Heidi still hadn't emerged from the bathroom, where she'd been primping for almost an hour. He'd never figured out what took her so long, though he was willing to concede that the results were usually worth the wait.

"Not a Texan this time, Len. I'm up here in Sonoma on vacation, and there's a lady from Pasadena got herself arrested for murder. Any chance you could come on up here and lend the lady a hand?"

"Murder in Sonoma? You wouldn't be talking about Lance Belladuce, would you?"

Hake raised an eyebrow. He'd been so concerned about maintaining his own low profile here that he hadn't really stopped to think this was a major regional news story. For all he knew, it could be a major *national* news story. This was not good.

"Got it in one," he answered. "Heidi and I are staying at Villa Belladuce, and the lady they've arrested is one of the other guests here. Gestapo took her away this afternoon, I guess, and she just now got her phone call."

"Did you tell her to keep her mouth shut?" Morelli asked.

"I didn't talk to her." Now that he thought about it, Hake realized that he'd never spoken to Eleanor Whitson. He'd barely been aware of her. The lady was like wallpaper. "She called and talked to the tour guide."

"Tour guide? This gets more and more interesting, Hakester. Let me see here. I had dinner plans, but nothing that can't be rain-checked for a good cause. Give me her name, and I'll make a couple calls, find out where she is, and get on up in the next couple of hours. Traffic crossing the Golden Gate is still all jammed up. I can see it from my window here. But you can tell that little lady that the cavalry is on the way."

⚜

**BEFORE** they left for dinner at Hunter's Hideaway in Glen Ellen, Lynne did go bang on the back door of the mansion. As she waited for a response, she admired the window full of African violets in full bloom. Somebody in this house paid attention to them. Lynne no longer bothered with house plants of any sort, and she'd never had much luck with African violets, which she considered unreasonably fussy.

The maid, Rosalita, opened the door cautiously, and Lynne could smell garlic and olive oil simmering inside the kitchen. Rosalita was very short and very plump and had a pretty smile with gleaming white teeth. She looked about twenty-three, and Lynne wondered fleetingly what she was doing here, why she wasn't off enjoying her own life somewhere instead of living in with a couple of Silicon Valley refugees. When she spoke, her English was excellent and unaccented.

Lynne explained that it was important that she talk to Angela, and Rosalita left her standing outside the screen door. While she waited, Lynne took in as much of the interior of the kitchen as she could and gave herself a good sniff of whatever the garlic thing was. She was starting to get hungry.

Lynne had never been inside the mansion, and it looked like she wasn't going to get in now. Tradespeople to the rear, please. Too bad, too, because it looked like a classy and comfortable place.

Angela hurried around a corner into the kitchen, a long white terry-cloth bathrobe tightly belted at her waist, turned-up Ugg boots on her feet, her hair hanging in damp tendrils around her face. Without makeup, she looked weary and wan.

"What is it?" Angela asked, anxiety hovering at the edges of her voice.

"I just wanted to let you know that one of the people with my tour, Eleanor Whitson, was arrested this afternoon. She's charged with killing Lance."

Angela's eyes widened. "Come in, come in," she said, as she turned and sat down at a burnished cherry table in a corner of the large, airy kitchen.

Once inside, Lynne was pleased to see that the room lived up to her first impression of it. Angela (or her decorator) had excellent taste, or anyway taste similar to Lynne's own. She lingered for a moment admiring the African violets, which were even more impressive up close. This was a room she could live with quite easily. "Your violets are beautiful."

Angela barely seemed to hear her. "Tell me what happened."

"I don't know too much. I brought Eleanor back here from town early this afternoon at her request, and Detective Shaw was already here. But you know that, of course. I assume she was here because of whatever it was that happened down at the winery." Lynne paused a moment, but Angela didn't seem inclined to jump in with details. "Apparently, Detective Shaw took her in for questioning and then arrested her."

Angela was frowning. "Which one is she? This is all kind of confusing. What'd you say her name is? Ellen?"

*How to put this?* "Her name is Eleanor. Eleanor Whitson. She's the rather quiet little lady who's here by herself. She's been staying in the other room of my cottage, Campania."

Angela shook her head. "I still can't picture who you mean. Are you talking about the kind of heavyset woman with the dark hair?"

"No, that's Alice Harper. Eleanor is little and trim, and her hair is a sort of platinum beige. She doesn't say much, so you might not have really noticed her."

"Why did she kill Lance?"

"I have no idea, and anyway, she says that she didn't. I have trouble picturing it, myself, but I guess you never know. Anyway, I'm about to go call her daughter and give her the bad news, which I don't mind telling you I dread. Her daughter lives in Seattle, and I assume she'll want to come down here. If she does, would you have any objection to her staying in her mother's room?"

Angela seemed to think about this for a moment, then shook her head. "Of course not. Though she'd have to leave on Sunday when the rest of you go."

"Oh, sure. Things should be resolved somehow by then."

"Well, keep me informed," Angela said, just as a speaker on the wall beside the stove emitted a plaintive wail. "Gosh, that's Stephanie already."

Lynne knew an exit line when she heard one. She thanked

her hostess and let herself out as Angela hurried off to fetch her baby.

⎯⎯✦⎯⎯

**LYNNE** retired to the privacy of her own room to make the call to Eleanor's daughter. Dr. Rebecca Whitson's service first tried to tell her that it wouldn't be possible to reach the doctor until morning. Informed this was an emergency, in Lynne's most authoritarian playground-monitor tones, the service then left Lynne on hold with soft-music radio for three minutes.

"This is Dr. Whitson," a clear, slightly nasal voice announced suddenly.

Lynne took a deep breath, introduced herself, and then cut to the chase. "I'm afraid I have some difficult news for you, about your mother."

"What? Is Mother sick? Was there an accident? What? What's happened?" Doctor or no, a panicky tone laced Rebecca Whitson's voice. Well, she'd been a daughter before she was a doctor.

"No, no, there's nothing wrong with her health. But I'm afraid . . . well, I'm afraid she's been arrested."

"Arrested? *Mother?* What on earth for?"

Lynne took another deep breath. "She's accused of killing a man here at the place where we're staying in Sonoma."

"Sonoma?" Then Rebecca Whitson gasped. "Sonoma! Oh my God, did she kill Lance Belladuce?"

Goodness gracious. How did it happen that a Seattle opthalmologist knew the name of a rural California murder victim? And why did Eleanor's daughter phrase her question in a way that made it sound like she believed this was possible? "She says she didn't do it, that it's all a mistake. Do you . . . uh . . . know Lance?"

"I only met him once," Rebecca Whitson said. "So did my mother. Meet him once, that is. He's really dead?"

"Yes, I'm afraid he's really dead. But how did you know him?"

"Through my brother, Jimmy. He had a restaurant with

Lance Belladuce in Monterey. It failed. Jimmy'd always suffered from depression, and after the restaurant closed, his depression got worse. We didn't know he was in such bad shape, of course, until it was too late."

Lynne didn't like the sound of this, and she had a terrible feeling that she knew where it was going. "What happened?" she asked softly.

Rebecca Whitson's voice was barely a whisper. "Suicide."

*Chapter 12*

**LONG** ago, Lynne had taken a journalism course and learned the five Ws: who, what, when, where, and why. Of these, her favorite had always been *why,* because it seemed that when you knew the reason behind something, everything else tended to fall right into place.

Learning that Eleanor Whitson actually had a motive for killing Lance Belladuce—and a humdinger at that—answered a great many other questions, some of which Lynne hadn't even realized she was asking herself.

It explained why Eleanor had come on this tour in the first place. Lynne remembered now that Eleanor's travel agent had asked very specifically about the accommodations when she made the arrangements, had emphasized that Eleanor was only interested in coming if they were assured of staying at Villa Belladuce.

It explained why Eleanor had seemed so uncomfortable once she arrived, as well. Why she'd been so stunned the morning that Lance's body was discovered when she came out to breakfast and found the police on the patio.

Her discomfort made absolute sense, of course, if Eleanor had actually killed him. Still, Lynne simply couldn't make the mental leap that would have this timid woman confronting and slaying anybody.

Just before Lynne was about to gather everyone together so that they could leave for dinner, Detective Shaw arrived with two other detectives and a search warrant for Eleanor's room. She was efficient and methodical and noncommunicative. No, she couldn't say anything about the investigation. No, it wouldn't be possible for Lynne to see Eleanor, though Rebecca Whitson probably could when and if she arrived. No, Leonard Morelli hadn't yet arrived to see his newest client. There was something in the clipped way she made that statement that suggested she knew exactly who he was and was less than thrilled to have him involved in the case.

Which was, Lynne decided as she joined the others and revved up the engine of the van, probably the best news possible for Eleanor.

**DINNER** at Hunter's Hideaway in nearby Glen Ellen was initially rather somber. Everybody spoke quietly among themselves at first, conducting hushed discussions of menu choices and wine selections and the particulars of their individual day's activities. Their experiences were universally good, it seemed. Lynne was interested to notice that Jessica and Ryan now seemed to be a couple, sitting together in the van and the restaurant, giving each other long, soulful glances when they thought nobody else was looking. When she and Pat and Alice had arrived at Ravenswood in late afternoon and found the kids there, Lynne had gotten the distinct impression that Kelly and Sara were both relieved to have somebody else to talk to.

Mark and Don had loved golfing overlooking the Pacific, the gang on the Alexander Valley appellation tour seemed pleased with their experiences, and everybody who'd fixed lunch at Rosemary & Thyme raved about Wendy Carr. Except for Eleanor—a major exception, to be sure—the Sonoma Sojourners seemed to be having a grand time.

"Is there any reason we shouldn't go ahead with the party for the Ambrosinos?" Pat asked Lynne quietly at dinner.

The fiftieth anniversary celebration was scheduled for the following day, Wednesday, on the Villa Belladuce patio in late afternoon. That way, everybody could participate in the day's planned activities—hot-air balloon rides, the Luther Burbank Gardens, and golf at the Sonoma Mission Inn in the morning, followed by miscellaneous spa indulgences in the afternoon—and still have sufficient time for the previously scheduled dinner afterward. Alice and Pat had hired Wendy Carr to provide Italian-themed hors d'oeuvres for the event, and up until the moment they learned of Eleanor's arrest, had been immersed in all manner of cheerful party plans.

"None at all," Lynne told her. "I think it's probably just what we all need. And who knows? If this really is all a mistake, Eleanor might even be back with us by then."

But she knew the statement sounded hollow, and Pat cocked her head skeptically.

"Oh right," Pat said. "They're going to let her out of jail, and she's going to come back and stay at Villa Belladuce? I wouldn't imagine she'd be too terribly welcome."

Alice shook her head. "It's all a shame, of course, but could we not talk about it anymore now? This is really selfish of me, and I'm terribly sorry about what poor Eleanor must be going through now, whether she did it or not, but this *is* supposed to be our vacation."

"You're absolutely right," Lynne told her, fully aware that she herself wouldn't be able to stop thinking about any of it for more than a minute or two at a time until she was safely back in Floritas and the others had returned to their various homes.

She lifted her glass of tea and offered it to her friends, grateful once again to have them with her in this odd and difficult time. "To vacations."

❦

**JESSICA** Kincaid was starting to realize that on her journey of life, this trip was just about the only time she had taken a hand in plotting the itinerary. As the middle child of a suburban Atlanta cardiologist and a former Junior League president, she had followed a brother who was an overachieving athlete and preceded a sister who was breathtakingly beautiful. When she thought about herself, she always used terms like *average* and *ordinary* and *unremarkable.*

Least resistance was an easy enough path to take, all things considered. She was an adequate student, a passable tennis player, a presentable debutante. She never quite managed to live up to her mother's expectations, and her failed marriage had only served to cement the notion that she wasn't *quite* good enough. Other girls, her mother reminded her repeatedly, worked at their marriages.

Well, Jessica had worked at hers, all right, but it had proven to be menial and unrewarding labor. Ken was considered a catch, her mother claimed, but after Jessica caught him and endured a wedding that consumed the better part of a year, she found herself looking down a road she no longer cared to travel. Ken was handsome but vapid, wealthy but irresponsible, charming but cruel-hearted. All of this she might have learned to tolerate if he hadn't also proven utterly incapable of fidelity.

Only with her divorce had Jessica moved into territory that was exclusively her own. As the first divorcée on either side of her family, she might have enjoyed the illusion that she was a Bad Girl, if it hadn't been for the irrefutable fact that Ken was the only one having any fun. Daddy had seen to it that she had the finest divorce attorney in Atlanta, and nobody had been more surprised than Daddy when Jessica decided she was no longer interested in teaching kindergarten and had enrolled in paralegal school.

Now here she was: thirty years old, damaged goods, self-supporting only because of her alimony, and closer to independence than she'd ever been in her life. As she walked down into the moonlit vineyard holding Ryan Atherton's hand, she felt wonderfully free.

*Chapter 13*

"YOU told her *what*?" Jeff asked, staring at Angela in astonishment. Had his wife taken total and absolute leave of her senses?

"I told her that woman's daughter could stay here in her mother's room if she comes down here. The daughter lives up north somewhere. Portland or Seattle, something like that. I can't remember."

"Angie, why? That's ridiculous! What were you thinking? This isn't a hotel, and it isn't going to be a bed-and-breakfast anymore, either, not once this week is over. You want to run a hotel, buy one somewhere else, and go to work in the morning like most people do. Our home is our home, and that's that."

Jeff saw no inconsistency in the fact that he himself had never gone to work like most people do. Indeed, his home was also his workplace and had been for years. Nonetheless, he held rigid and admittedly retro opinions about other people's employment. Maybe that was what Angie really needed, anyway: a job. She had too much time on her hands here, even with the baby. It made her moody and unpredictable. Back when she'd been working at Chem-o-lex, there'd been a certain rhythm to their life together. Of course, there was no financial need for her to work now or ever, but maybe she ought to be thinking about it anyway. Rosalita could watch the baby. That's what they paid her for, after all.

He looked at Angela, curled up at the opposite end of the sumptuous tan leather sectional in the media room. They were watching a video on the huge screen that dominated the opposite wall, a recent sci-fi release with a lot of awesome computer-generated special effects, the kind of movie that both of them usually loved. A lithe brunette actress was gliding through a stainless steel wall without mussing a single hair on her head. Jeff realized he'd lost track of where she was coming from or what she intended to do.

"She caught me off guard, I guess," Angela said apologetically. "I suppose if I'd thought about it, I might have said no, but so what? Does it matter?"

"Does it matter? This whole thing is a nightmare, Angie, like quicksand. We're caught up in this huge mess, and it keeps getting worse. There's a dead man on our property and a gang of strangers overrunning the place. There's nighttime prowlers destroying the winery, which was the reason you wanted to move here in the first place, and when it looks like maybe one small part of that is finally resolved, you tell the killer's daughter to come stay here for a while?"

Angela turned to look at him with curiosity. "Honey, I didn't realize you'd feel so strongly about it."

Strongly didn't begin to describe Jeff's feelings. "I hate this, Ange. I hate it all. I hate having all those people running around here and having Lance Belladuce show up strutting his sorry ass around our property."

"He won't be doing it again," Angela answered mildly.

"But he's still making trouble for us, even dead. You said yourself that the Belladuces were responsible for what happened to the winery. Though I don't understand why you say that."

Angela picked up the remote and paused the movie, stopping two androgynous men wearing black bodysuits from dealing with a pulsating chartreuse blob that had just appeared outside their window. She turned, tucked her legs underneath her, and faced Jeff.

"Not everything was damaged or destroyed, Jeff. The equipment was all banged and smashed up, but that can be replaced. What can't be replaced is the wine. Most of the barrels were hacked open on their ends, probably with axes. However—and it's a big however—some of the barrels in the barrel room and all of the ones in the caves were left untouched. The ones the vandals left alone in the winery are the really special ones—the ones the Belladuce family wouldn't be able to bear destroying. The ones that arrogant ethnic familial pride would dictate they leave alone."

"Did you tell the police that?"

"Well, of course I told the police that. Not that I think they really listened. And now that they've arrested that Whitson woman, I don't think they're going to pay much attention to what happened in the winery. Detective Shaw asked very pointedly about insurance."

Jeff snorted. "So, if we're adequately insured, that's a substitute for competent police work?"

"Honey, I don't know. I'll talk to her about it tomorrow, all right? And I'll tell Lynne that the daughter can't stay here. Will that satisfy you?"

He shook his head. "No, but it's a start. While you're at it, why don't you tell them all to leave?"

"I can't do that now."

"Why not?"

"Because. It would just make it more complicated."

He regarded her with disbelief. "I'd say it would make everything a whole lot simpler. And then we put this wretched albatross on the market and get the hell out of Sonoma County. You want wine, we'll buy wine. We'll buy warehouses full of the stuff, and it can be estate-bottled and limited pressings and any other kind of special you want. You can bathe in it if you feel like it. But this is no good, Angie. You know it just as well as I do."

She started to cry now, and he felt helpless, the way he always felt helpless when she cried. Jeff was all too aware that Angela had overcome horrors he couldn't even imagine. The scars on her body, even after all the restorative surgeries, spoke of unspeakable agony. All he'd ever wanted to do was make her happy, erase the memories of the hideous hospitalizations and keep her smiling and looking toward the future. Toward their future. Angela's smile touched a part of his soul that he hadn't even realized was there before he met her. He adored this woman.

"C'mon, honey," he told her, sliding down on the couch and gathering her in his arms. She was sobbing now, heaving huge, wrenching sobs that shook her body and tore his heart. "We have everything that matters right here. You and me against the world. And we've got Stephanie, and we can get more babies if you want." He listened to himself with incredulity. The last thing he wanted was a wing full of squalling babies and smelly diapers and two A.M. feedings. But he'd do it to make Angie happy. He'd do anything to make Angie happy.

"We may not even be able to keep Stephanie," she wailed. "What if they take her away from us?"

He smoothed her hair and spoke soothingly. "Nobody's going to take her away. It's just harassment, those E-mails." Vile harassment, though. He'd concede that readily. The last one had been an unequivocal threat: "STEALING INNOCENT INFANTS IS EVIL AND THE LORD WILL PUNISH THE EVIL, WILL SMITE THEM FROM THE FACE OF THE EARTH." All in caps, the Internet equivalent of rude shouting.

"I talked to Sean O'Brian again this morning," Angela said through her sobs, speaking into his shoulder.

"That's good," he told her, wondering if it was.

Sean O'Brian was the family law attorney in Los Angeles who had arranged Stephanie's adoption. He'd come highly recommended and, until the threatening E-mails began, Jeff would have called him a miracle worker. Within three weeks of their first meeting, O'Brian had found them a UCLA coed about to deliver a married physics professor's child, a girl who didn't believe in abortion and was willing to relinquish all rights to her baby.

That had been part of what Angela wanted, what she had insisted upon. No shared custody, no open adoption, nobody showing up on the doorstep in two years, or ten years, or twenty to claim parental privilege and rip apart their family. A clean and irreversible adoption at any price. And the price had been substantial.

At the time, Jeff had wondered a bit. The business about the coed and the professor seemed a bit too perfect, a trifle too trite, exactly the kind of information any adoptive parent would want to hear. He'd half expected O'Brian to add that the mother was also a National Merit Scholar in line for a spot in the next Olympics, that the father had just accepted a Nobel Prize.

Still, the baby tested healthy and she was beautiful and O'Brian maintained the paperwork was in perfect order. Jeff didn't believe you could trust lawyers, but the problem was that there was nobody to ride herd on them but other lawyers. Somewhere you had to stop checking and second-guessing and make a leap of faith. He'd stopped and made that leap after he consulted three other attorneys who vetted the paperwork and pronounced it acceptable.

But Angela was shaking her head. "He said there's nothing he can do to stop the E-mails, that you should trace them and bring suit or get a restraining order."

"I already tried to trace them," he reminded her. "They come from free accounts that change each time. I can't get info on them without a court order, and vague threats aren't enough reason to get a court order."

She pulled back and stared him right in the eye, her face blotchy and tear-streaked. "Do you mean to tell me you can't hack into a simple E-mail database and find out who's sending those?"

A part of him wanted to tell her the truth, to acknowledge that of course he could. That he'd already taken care of it and discovered who was behind the threats. Jeff knew people who could find out just about anything, no questions asked. But it would only complicate matters to tell her now. "Honey, that's not the kind of thing I *do*. I'd probably get caught, and then we'd look like paranoid idiots."

"So hire somebody."

"Who?"

"I don't know. I don't care. But I do know that I can't stand much more of this. Every time I get one of those messages, I have this image of a gray Ford pulling up the driveway and some horrible social worker coming in here and snatching Stephanie out of my arms. Taking her away to a birth mother who's a crack addict living in a dive with her out-of-work boyfriend." Angela had never bought the coed-seduced-by-professor story, either. "We can't let that happen. It would kill me."

"It's not going to happen, honey. I promise. And I bet there won't be anymore threatening E-mails, either." His voice rang with certainty.

She looked at him first with curiosity and then with confidence. "Thanks, honey. I love you." She burrowed into his arms, and for a long time they held each other in silence.

**IN** the morning, Angela came out to the breakfast room, carrying baby Stephanie. Maria Ambrosino, who'd finished eating and was sitting quietly with Guido at a table for two, stood up and went to greet the baby. Angela handed her over without hesitation, then crossed to where Lynne was sitting with the Harpers and the Martells.

"Could I speak you for a moment?" Angela asked.

"Sure." Lynne left her coffee and croissant and stepped out onto the patio with their hostess. "What's up?"

Angela gazed off across the vineyards, still shrouded in morning mist. "I talked to my husband last night," she began, looking mildly uncomfortable, "and he doesn't think it's a good idea for that woman's daughter to be staying here."

Lynne had seen this one coming from the moment Angela

walked through the door, but she decided to push a little, anyway. "Why not?"

"He doesn't want to create bad feelings with the Belladuce family, since they're still so involved in winery operations."

Fear of bad feelings with the Belladuces didn't seem to have entered into the scene on the patio Sunday night, but Lynne merely nodded. "I can understand that."

"I'm really sorry," Angela went on. "Have you heard anything more about what's happened with her?"

"Not a peep, though there really isn't any reason why the police would be sharing any details with me. One of our guests arranged for a lawyer to come up and represent her, at least temporarily. If I hear any more, I'll let you know."

"Thanks," Angela said, "and I'll reciprocate, of course."

⌒═╳═⌒

**A** good night's sleep seemed to have convinced the Sonoma Sojourners that it was in everyone's best interests to move forward with enthusiasm and vigor. After breakfast, folks set out on their various adventures in what could almost have been called a festive mood. The Conner sisters, the Atherton twins, and Jessica Kincaid headed north in Kelly's rented Buick for their hot-air balloon ride. Once they'd departed, with Don Harper, Mark Martell, and the Sandstroms following shortly thereafter to keep their golf date, the garden tour group seemed to heave a collective sigh of relief.

Maria Ambrosino, who was staying behind for the day, waved them off, little Stephanie in her arms. Guido blew his wife a farewell kiss. Life could only get simpler, Lynne thought.

She hoped so, anyway.

⌒═╳═⌒

**SUNLIGHT** hadn't yet cracked through the clouds when they arrived at the Luther Burbank Home and Gardens just after the ten o'clock opening. The site sat smack in the middle of downtown Santa Rosa, within spitting distance of the municipal buildings. Once Lynne brought the Sonoma Sojourners through the brick entry walls past a gently bubbling fountain, however, urban life simply disappeared.

They waited a few minutes beside a rose garden bursting with fragrant blooms, until their guide joined them. The plump, sixtyish woman introduced herself as Marian.

"We take a lot of things for granted when we garden and eat today," Marian explained as they stood outside the carriage house, now converted into a gift shop. Behind her, another worker arranged plants for sale on a rack of outside shelving. "A remarkable number of those things are directly traceable to Luther Burbank, and some of them aren't even associated with his name. The russet potato, for instance, paid his way from Massachusetts to California in 1875 when he sold the rights for one hundred fifty dollars. This was a *huge* innovation, because Burbank had grown the original from a rare potato seed pod, in a period after the Irish potato famine. You might say he's the father of the modern french fry. He was also responsible for developing or introducing over two hundred different varieties of fruits and nuts, including one hundred thirteen different varieties of plum. He crossed apricots and plums to develop the plumcot, and he developed some really wonderful freestone peaches."

"What do you mean, he 'introduced' these things?" Pat Martell asked.

"Well, at that time, many of the plums came from Japan, including such famous varieties as satsuma, my personal favorite," the guide said. "He was always trying to find newer or better versions of familiar plants. He did a lot of grafting, to grow varieties he liked on sturdier, disease-resistant rootstock. One of his most amazing feats was filling an order for twenty thousand plum trees. He sprouted twenty thousand almonds, got the baby almond trees established, and then grafted plum budwood onto the almond rootstock. It was quite an accomplishment at the time."

It seemed to Lynne that growing twenty thousand of anything would be a major accomplishment any time. Just planting the sprouted almonds would take forever. But then she had never been a very patient gardener.

Marian pointed to a fruit tree over near an enormous stand of spineless cactus. "We keep this cherry tree to demonstrate one of his most favored techniques. Several different types of cherry are grafted onto the same tree. Very space efficient for determining what will or won't produce well."

They passed the paradox walnut tree, named because it was unusual for a hardwood to grow so quickly, and went by raised beds where volunteer gardeners cheerfully weeded and deadheaded and did the kind of picky detail work that Lynne never quite got ahead of in her own garden back home in Floritas. Maybe it was easier when you worked in a legendary garden, she thought.

Or maybe she just wasn't meant to have perfect-looking flower beds.

⌐══✦══⌐

**MARIA** Ambrosino was enjoying the peace and quiet at Villa Belladuce. Baby Stephanie had gone down for her morning nap in a magical bedroom filled with stuffed animals and lacy pillows and a lot of bold black-and-white designs. Angela said the black-and-white designs were supposed to somehow make her smarter. That notion seemed a bit far-fetched to Maria, but there was no doubt in her mind that Angela adored this baby girl, and rightly so. She was a treasure.

Now Maria sat in the chair outside her little cottage, looking out over the vineyard. She was pleased that Guido had so enjoyed the place yesterday that had Chianti, even though it was called something else. Everything here seemed to be called something else, actually, not that it really mattered.

She shifted her weight and felt the cell phone in her pocket, then pulled it out and looked at it thoughtfully. The phones seemed rather silly, since Lynne did such a good job of organizing everything all the time, but she and Guido were carrying them, nonetheless, as they'd been told to. What would Guido say if she called him up now, like a teenager?

She concentrated a moment to remember the combination of numbers to reach him directly. The phones were set up to communicate with each other through short codes that Lynne had called speed dial. She pushed the Power button to turn on the phone and impulsively dialed Guido's number.

The phone rang twice and then was answered.

"Lynne Montgomery." The guide's voice came clearly in her ear, and Maria was embarrassed by her mistake.

"I'm sorry," she said. "This is Maria. I didn't mean to bother you."

"No bother at all," Lynne assured her. "Is there a problem? Can I help you with something?"

Maria laughed self-consciously. "I was trying to call Guido, just to say hello. I must have the numbers wrong."

"An easy mistake to make," Lynne said. "His code is thirty-four, and mine is thirty-three. Would you like me to get him for you? He's just up ahead with the others. Or would you rather call him directly?"

"I'll call him," Maria said. "But don't tell him it's me. I'd like to surprise him."

A few moments later, after she tried again, she heard her husband's anxious voice. "Hello? Hello? Who's there?"

Maria told him. Then, feeling wickedly playful, she whispered endearments that she imagined would have him blushing in front of the other ladies.

**JEFF** was checking his E-mail when he heard a soft knock on the workshop door.

"Yes?" he called.

The door opened slowly, and Rosalita entered, stopping just inside the door. She was not allowed to clean in here and was under instructions not to enter the room under any circumstances. "Mr. Jeff, the policewoman is here to see you."

He leapt up. "Did you let her in?"

Rosalita hurriedly shook her head. "No, no. She's waiting outside."

Jeff turned back to the computer, exited his E-mail program, and hurried to the door. "Thanks. Where's Angela?"

"She said she was going to lie down while the baby took her nap."

He nodded. "Good. Don't bother her."

He ushered Rosalita out and locked the door behind them.

Detective Shaw was sitting on the patio. She rose as he strode out to join her.

"You wanted to see me? You've arrested somebody for destroying our winery?"

She shook her head regretfully. "Not yet, but we will. Could we go inside?"

"What for?"

"To talk a bit. Something's come up that seems rather curious."

He considered his options. To refuse to speak to her altogether was stupid and pointless; it would only make her more determined. And while he didn't particularly want to bring her into the house, that seemed a good way to give at least the appearance of cooperation.

"Sure," he said. "Come on into the kitchen."

Once seated at the kitchen table, she declined his offer of a beverage, then got right to the point. It was worse than he'd feared.

"Something curious turned up when we examined Lance Belladuce's computer," she began.

"Oh?" He wasn't going to help her here. Better to find out just what she knew.

"We went through his 'Sent E-mail' messages from three different accounts and found a number addressed to you and your wife."

He pasted on a frown, looking concerned. "E-mail to us from Lance Belladuce? I guess that would be from when we were negotiating to buy the place."

She shook her head and looked steadily at him. "No, this is much more recent, and it seems to have been sent anonymously. The messages were rather unpleasant, actually. Threatening, you might say."

Okay. At this point she'd be more suspicious if he didn't admit he knew what was going on. In some fashion. He opened his eyes wide. "Are you telling me that Lance Belladuce was the one sending those hateful messages about our baby?"

"That surprises you?"

He gave it a moment. "Maybe not. It's the kind of sneaky, underhanded thing he might have done." He didn't have to work at having righteous indignation in his tone.

"Not 'might have,' Mr. Rutledge. He *did* do it, and you got the messages. Didn't you?"

"They were meaningless," he told her. "Somebody in my position hears from crackpots all the time. I just hit Delete and forget about it."

"But these weren't all addressed to you. In fact, most of them seem to have been addressed to your wife."

"And I told *her* to just hit Delete and forget about it." He decided it was time to take control of the conversation. "My wife is a very gentle, kind woman. The messages upset her terribly. They were always full of harsh Biblical illusions, but I guess you know all that, if you've read them."

"Most unpleasant," Detective Shaw agreed. "Any parent would find them upsetting."

"There haven't been any new ones since last week," he said slowly.

"And it would seem unlikely that there'll be any more in the future. How long have you known Lance Belladuce was sending you those messages?"

He looked pointedly at his watch. "About two minutes."

"Oh, come on. You expect me to believe that you wouldn't track down the origin of something as malicious as that? It's right up your alley."

"What's up my alley? Slander? Libel?" The statement itself was libelous, or would have been if it didn't happen to be true.

"Computers."

Jeff leaned back and looked at Detective Shaw. "It's illegal to access somebody else's personal E-mail. I would never do that."

"Oh come on," she said again with a mild tone of exasperation. "I'm not here to bust you for hacking. I don't care how you got the information. But I know you had it. And I want to know how long you've known."

"I could only answer that question hypothetically," he said after a moment. "If it were possible for me to obtain that sort of illegal information, I'd probably have been inclined to seek it out after the first two or three communications. Hypothetically."

"Hypothetically." She pulled out a sheet of paper and looked at it thoughtfully. "The first E-mail was sent on May thirtieth."

He shrugged. "If you say so."

"I say so. The second was June thirteenth, and the third was June twenty-fifth. That was the one that mentioned fire and brimstone, if it will refresh your memory."

Jeff Rutledge's memory was a superlative machine, but now was not the time to show off. "I remember. It would have been after that one, hypothetically. Up until then, it seemed like random hate mail. Some sick kind of spam." Angela was not rational on the subject of fire, which was hardly surprising. She had gotten fairly hysterical.

"And how long would it have taken you to find out where it was coming from?"

He smiled at her. "About half an hour, once I got in touch with the right person."

"So you've known for six weeks that Lance was responsible for this, and you didn't do anything about it?"

He swallowed. "I did do something. I called him. I told him I knew what he was doing, and he should stop it, or I'd report him to the authorities. He laughed and hung up."

"And changed to a different anonymous free E-mail account."

He nodded. "And changed to a different anonymous free E-mail account."

"But you didn't tell your wife?"

"I didn't want to disturb her any further. I was assuming that once he'd been unmasked, he'd stop." He shrugged. "And he did, for a while."

Detective Shaw glanced at the paper in her hand. "Until

July eleventh." When he gave no response, she continued. "Followed by July nineteenth, July twenty-fourth, and July thirty-first. Not only did he not stop, he stepped up the pace."

"It didn't matter. I just deleted them."

Jeff was starting to feel a little antsy. This woman was calm and matter-of-fact, actually rather pleasant. She might have been explaining an insurance policy to him or outlining a marketing plan. Except that in this encounter, she had all the power, and they both knew it.

"I'd really rather you not bother my wife about this," he said. "It's been very stressful for her."

"You did tell your wife when you found out, didn't you?"

He said nothing.

She seemed prepared to wait him out. After a while, she leaned back and smiled. "I don't have any choice about talking to her. But I'm a little confused here. You say this has been so stressful, but you could have alleviated that stress. You knew six weeks ago who was responsible."

"I thought it would be better this way. That he'd stop."

"Well, he did, didn't he?" After a moment, she offered a wide smile. "I've heard that you have a Singer 1911 forty-five."

He started. "What does that have to do with anything?"

"Nothing whatsoever," she told him with a grin. "It's just that if you did, I'd love to see it sometime."

"Why?"

" 'Cause it's got an incredible rep. Only five hundred made, and it's worth twenty grand if you can find somebody willing to part with one."

"You know guns?" He shouldn't have been surprised. She was a cop, after all. And Angela had told him how Detective Shaw had stalked into the vandalized winery with her weapon drawn.

The grin widened. "I know guns. Do you keep your collection here?"

Pride battled wariness for a moment, and pride won. "I do. It's all locked up, of course." Angela insisted, somewhat irrationally, that to protect Stephanie, they had to have everything under double and triple lock. Stephanie was six months old. She couldn't even walk. "But I'm afraid I don't have time right now."

❦

**RUTH** Atherton had pushed herself as far as she could. The problem was that at any given moment, she had a finite amount of energy and no way of knowing how much of it remained. It was as if the energy were gently pouring out of an opaque bottle until suddenly, with no warning whatsoever, the bottle was empty.

"I think I'll sit for a while," she told Lynne, moving slowly toward a bench and seating herself carefully, propping the cane beside her. The docent was leading the rest of their group off to look at drought-tolerant beds in the back of the garden, and Ruth didn't care about that, anyway.

"By all means," Lynne said immediately. "I'll wait with you."

Ruth shook her head, but Lynne was already sitting down. "I don't want to be a burden. Please. Go on so you won't miss the tour."

"Don't be silly."

There was something about Lynne Montgomery that reminded Ruth of the twins' mother, Barbie, who'd died with her husband twenty years ago. She liked to think that Barbie would have grown into a cheerful, competent, middle-aged woman like Lynne. She'd barely gotten to know her daughter-in-law at all, since the young couple had lived in Indianapolis through most of their marriage.

"I've been here lots of times," Lynne went on. "Would you like me to go get the wheelchair so you can join the others? This place seems pretty accessible."

Ruth hated the wheelchair, currently folded up in the back of the van, just in case. They had brought it with them from Wisconsin, using it in the airports and the long corridors of Kelly's high-rise apartment building overlooking Lake Michigan. It was a simple manual model, nothing fancy, no motors or anything, but it symbolized a loss of independence that

Ruth simply couldn't reconcile herself to. She knew that it would be essential tomorrow for the visit to the redwood grove in the western part of the county.

"No, really. I can see plenty from right here. It's like that plaque: 'One's nearer to God in a garden than anywhere else on earth.'" Ruth looked up at the sky, which was starting to clear, then waved a hand at a bed of blindingly white Shasta daisies. Their guide had told them this Burbank innovation was the first man-made species of flower, a concept that brought to her mind a workshop filled with Santa's elves, painstakingly gluing petals onto stems. "It's always puzzled me that flowers seem more vivid when the sun isn't shining."

"I'm sure there's some technical scientific reason, something about refraction or diffusion or something," Lynne answered easily. "But I figure it's just that the flowers have to try a little harder to get your attention then. What do you grow in Wisconsin, anyway? I've been meaning to ask."

Unmasked. Ruth had been waiting for this ever since she heard some of the others discussing obscure varieties of split-corolla narcissus imported from the Netherlands.

"Not much," she admitted. "I never was much of a gardener, and the last few years I haven't even put petunias in my planters. Actually, my favorite plant at home is entirely impractical. It's a great big flowering crab apple outside my dining room window." She thought about the crab apple in full bloom and of all the springs that it had heralded for her, then turned to more practical matters. She had Lynne to herself just now, an opportunity that might not come again. "What do you know about the Kincaid girl, Lynne?"

Lynne turned to look her right in the eye, smiling mischievously. "You mean other than that she seems extremely attracted to your grandson?"

Ruth laughed. "Oh, girls have always been attracted to Ryan. That's nothing special. It was tough on Kelly for a while in high school, when Ryan always seemed to have a girlfriend, and Kelly almost never had a beau. But with Jessica, he seems to be attracted back, so I can't help but wonder."

"I really don't know much," Lynne admitted. "She and Sara Conner work together for some big law firm in Atlanta, and they're both divorced. Sara has a little boy, but Jessica doesn't have any kids that I know of."

Ruth Atherton furrowed her brow. "There was a time when divorce would have bothered me more than it does now, I think. Although I'm old-fashioned enough that it always disturbs me that divorce seems so easy for these young people."

"I'm not sure divorce is ever easy for anyone, Ruth. Don't you think maybe it's that young people are more willing to admit they've made a mistake?"

Lynne's childhood had been filled with friends of her parents who didn't seem to get along at all. Or who got along only because the man was overseas alone for years on end. A lot of these couples, she knew now, had remained together only because divorce was generally a bad career move in the military, signaling instability and a lack of control over subordinates.

"Maybe. And yet . . . I used to worry that the kids would marry too young. Ryan had a serious girlfriend his senior year of high school, and I lay awake nights wondering what I'd do if he ran off and married her. Or if she got pregnant and he *had* to marry her. And now, here I am, with my days literally numbered, and I'm just afraid that neither one of them will ever find the right person." She shook her head. "Listen to me, the melancholy old lady, trying to manage people's lives on her deathbed. I always thought that kind of pressure from the dying was a cheap exercise in power. Extortion." She shrugged. "Oh, well. So, do you like Jessica, Lynne?"

Lynne considered. This was a serious question, grandma to grandma. "Yes. I do. She has a down-to-earth quality that I find very refreshing. Her friend doesn't have it. If it were Sara that Ryan had his eye on, I'd be more inclined to worry, I think. Not that anything will necessarily come of any of this, of course."

"Stranger things have happened."

Ruth's pocketbook jingled on the bench beside her, and she involuntarily jumped. Lynne watched her face mirror her fears, the eternal, maternal worry that something awful had happened to the kids. Ruth had lived that nightmare, had lost a child twenty years ago. She understood the terror of an unexpected phone call. She reached toward the pocketbook, then pulled her hand back.

Lynne regarded her quizzically as the phone continued to ring. "Would you like me to answer that?" Not that her luck was much better on this score. Maria's misdirected call to Guido hadn't begun to obliterate the dreadful call she'd taken from Eleanor in jail.

"I don't think I remember how," Ruth admitted as she grabbed her purse and dug out the phone, handing the still ringing device over to Lynne. "It's so tiny, I don't see how it can work. A deck of cards is bigger." She watched anxiously as Lynne pressed buttons.

"Lynne Montgomery," she announced briskly. She listened for a moment. "No, she's fine. She's right here. What's that?"

She listened a few moments longer as Ruth watched anxiously. Then she extended the phone.

"If you're taking calls," she said, "I think this is one you'll like. It's Kelly and Ryan, floating across Sonoma County."

**JESSICA** clutched the woven wicker railing of the gondola that hung from the enormous rainbow-colored hot-air balloon, watching workers in the vineyards below doing something to grapevines, seeing cars meander down a backcountry road. She reminded herself one more time that there was no reason to expect the balloon to plummet from the sky, that travel by hot-air balloon was actually extremely safe. She turned to watch Ryan talking into the cell phone. He shared a section of the partitioned gondola with Jessica, and for a while had stood behind her, his hands on the railing on either side of her. Last night after dinner, they'd taken another walk, out into the vineyard itself. When he kissed her then, he hadn't wasted any time on her forehead.

"It's pretty amazing, Gran," he was saying. Simple words from a fundamentally decent guy. A guy she had yet to see say or do anything that seemed even remotely duplicitous or insincere.

A guy with a cheese watch, for crying out loud, who knew less than she did (though not by much) about wine and wasn't the least bit concerned about his ignorance. A guy who wasn't embarrassed to take a vacation with his grandmother, who considered Jessica's accent fantastically exotic, and who had offered her cheese curds with a straight face as one of his favorite foods in the world.

A guy about six inches taller than she was, with a funny little scar over his right eyebrow and thick bushy hair the color of buckwheat honey, with soft brown eyes that reminded her of velvet.

This was ridiculous. She was falling in love.

*Chapter 14*

**THE** Sonoma Sojourners had just wrapped up their guided tour and were milling around the gift shop at the Luther Burbank Gardens when Lynne's phone rang again. As she stepped outside to answer it, she passed the counter where Alice and Pat were swapping volunteer stories with the Burbank docents. Alice and Pat worked together in the Friends Bookstore at the Floritas Library, and on a normal Wednesday morning, they'd be moving into the home stretch of their weekly three-hour shift right about now.

For her part, Lynne was starting to yearn for the olden days when you went out somewhere and you couldn't be reached by phone until you got back. Being accessible twenty-four hours a day was the pits.

She wasn't surprised to find Rebecca Whitson on the line, sounding fairly despondent. "I don't know why I called you, actually," Rebecca apologized. "But I have to talk to somebody about this and . . . oh, I don't know."

"I'm sure this is all just awful," Lynne told her, moving out of earshot of the others. Not that it mattered with her people, but there were some other visitors to the gardens who didn't need to know the sorry particulars of the Sonoma Sojourn. "Is your mother still in custody?"

"Oh yeah. She's not going anywhere. She was arraigned this morning, and bail was denied because she's considered a flight risk. That horrible detective said she was preparing to flee when she was arrested yesterday."

"That horrible detective" had to be Lauren Shaw. It was difficult for Lynne to think of her as malevolent, though the woman was undeniably tough. Lynne had gotten along just fine with Detective Shaw and so, now that she thought about it, had all the others in the group. "Did you meet with her attorney? Leonard Morelli? Was he at the arraignment?"

"Yeah. He's a real piece of work, too."

Lynne wasn't surprised to hear a friend of Hake Sandstrom's thus described. "What did he tell you?"

"That he'd try to get the judge to reconsider the bail issue, but that even if he did, Mother would probably have to stay here in Sonoma County. Which she can't bear the thought of."

Staying in Sonoma County was probably more pleasurable than staying in the Sonoma County Jail, but Lynne kept her mouth shut. "What can I do to help?" Other than offer a place for Rebecca to stay, of course. She crossed her fingers that request wouldn't come up first.

"Is there any way you could meet with me and the lawyer? He's going back to San Francisco this afternoon, but he suggested that you might be able to provide some information that would help him. And he wants to see where everything happened."

"That might be a little tricky," Lynne said, "and I have some responsibilities with my tour group that I have to take care of first." Like getting the hot-air balloon and Burbank Gardens contingents connected for lunch, feeding everybody, and then delivering them to the spa in Sonoma for miscellaneous indulgences.

"We could meet you somewhere. I'm at a hotel here in Santa Rosa. Mother said I should go use her room since it's

already paid for, but I can't bear the thought of being anywhere that Lance Belladuce ever was. Dead or alive."

Not surprising, since it was Rebecca's brother who'd committed suicide. And also convenient, saving Lynne the awk-
wardness of passing along the Rutledge edict. She thought
fast. "Tell you what. If you can give me half an hour or forty-
five minutes, enough time to get everybody settled in for
lunch, I can meet you then."

**IT** actually took closer to an hour, because the hot-air balloon
contingent was delayed. Lynne packed Ruth's wheelchair into
Kelly's trunk, and the two of them drove directly back to Villa
Belladuce, skipping lunch. Then Lynne deposited the others at
Chevy's in downtown Santa Rosa, promised to be back as
soon as possible, and headed for Rebecca Whitson's hotel.

She found Rebecca in the hotel dining room with Leonard
Morelli. They were easy to spot: She was a younger, slightly
more vivacious version of her mother, and he was a handsome, black-haired, black-eyed Italian with a diamond earring, wearing a three-thousand-dollar suit. If he was a piece of
work, it was a slick and finely crafted one. She took a moment
to admire him as he stood and extended a well-manicured
hand in greeting.

"Mrs. Montgomery, I'm Len Morelli," the attorney told her
in a tone that was just a little too unctuous. She told herself
not to dislike him because he was successful, or because he
represented criminals, or because he was too aware of his own
good looks. She had a feeling she'd find sufficient reason to
dislike him on his own merits soon enough. Smarmy always
irritated her.

"Call me Lynne." She shook his hand and turned to Rebecca, who remained seated. "And you must be Dr. Whitson,"
she said, extending her hand.

"Rebecca," the young woman said. Her handshake was
cool but firm, though overall, she looked a little limp. Having
your mother arrested for the murder of the guy you blamed for

your brother's suicide could do that, Lynne supposed. What a sorry can of worms this was.

Once they'd ordered, Len Morelli wasted no time. "Based on the evidence presented this morning, the state has a fairly strong case, Lynne, and we're hoping that you'll be able to provide information to help refute that evidence. Unfortunately, Mrs. Whitson didn't exercise her right to remain silent nearly soon enough, and she made some extremely damaging statements to the arresting officers concerning motive."

"She should never have come here," Rebecca said softly. "If she'd told me what she was planning, I would have told her not to do it."

"Why do you think she came?" Lynne asked.

"I don't really know. I'm sure she didn't come to kill Lance Belladuce, if that's what you mean. Maybe she thought if she could just see him, that would give her some kind of closure. You see, my parents never were able to accept that my brother's depression wasn't just a lack of what my father always called 'get-up-and-go.' I've had a lot of time to think about this, and even in childhood, Jimmy suffered from depression. Moodiness, lethargy, sleeping for days on end. Once he got to be a teenager, I think he tried to self-medicate with recreational drugs, and that just made matters worse. He ended up in rehab when he was nineteen, and he was suicidal then, too."

Lynne could see that Len Morelli was listening intently, and she hoped he'd know to keep his mouth shut for a while. Rebecca Whitson needed to unload, and she'd tell him anything he needed to know if he just gave her enough time.

"Was he ever treated for the depression?" she asked.

Rebecca shook her head. "Not until he was in his late twenties, and by then he'd gone through a bunch of self-help and rehab programs. He tried antidepressants for a while, but he didn't like the side effects, so he'd always go off them. It was a vicious cycle. When he stayed on long enough for the meds to have any impact on the depression, he'd decide that he really wasn't depressed after all, and he'd go off the meds. And he had a terrible time holding a job while this was going on."

"What did he do?"

The question seemed to catch Rebecca off guard, and it was obvious that there was no simple answer like *He was a plumber* or *He networked computers.*

"He was a very gifted amateur chef," she said after a moment. "He had a degree in business, but it took him about seven years, and at the end, he just finished it up to shut up my father. My father had a very strong work ethic, and it drove him nuts that Jimmy didn't have the same kind of ambition."

Lynne would also have bet that Rebecca Whitson's father had issued frequent public comparisons of his good child, the doctor, and her brother, the mentally ill screwup. And that the comparisons rankled with the luckless Jimmy.

She'd seen the scenario many times growing up, the difference being that officers with sons like Jimmy tended to dump them into military school at the first real sign of trouble, to shape them up. That the shaping-up process didn't usually work was a dirty little secret of military family life. Everybody moved all the time, and that fluidity destroyed continuity of personal relationships. You might not run into a family again for years, if ever, would only hear second- or third-hand what happened to these kids. A lot of them wound up enlisting, but not many became officers themselves.

"Did Jimmy get involved with the restaurant with Lance Belladuce as a chef?" Lynne asked.

Rebecca smiled, as if glad that Lynne had taken note of Jimmy's awkward talent. "Partly. The place was down in Monterey, and he'd been living there for a while when all of this came together. He had money from our grandparents, both of us did, and so he made a substantial investment in the place. But what he was really excited about was that he could plan and control the menus. The place was called Belladuce, and its theme was Italian seafood. Jimmy didn't want to be the primary chef, because that was way too much work, and he always was a bit on the lazy side, even when he wasn't depressed, but he had . . . well, I guess it's not too corny to say that Jimmy had a culinary vision for the place. He really seemed alive when he was talking about it, during the planning stages."

"You said you and your mother only met Lance once. Was that at the restaurant?"

Rebecca nodded. Their entrées arrived, and she took a cursory look at her chef's salad, speared and ate a single piece of hard-boiled egg white, then pushed her plate away.

"We went to the grand opening, all of us. Daddy was still alive, and he and Mother flew up from Pasadena. I was finishing my residency in Seattle, and I flew down. It was a big hoopla, and Jimmy was really excited about what was happening. I hadn't seen him that enthusiastic in years. It seemed like a wonderful opportunity, and at that point, we didn't realize that most of the money in the place was his."

"And you met Lance there?"

"Yeah. He was just as warm and effusive as can be. He was serving fancy wines from his family's winery, and the food was fabulous. Lance had a couple of Italian starlets up from Hollywood, girls who supposedly were actresses but who looked more like hookers."

Rebecca shifted her shoulders slightly in embarrassment. "I guess I'm pretty provincial. Jimmy always thought so, anyway. But I hadn't heard of these supposed actresses by name, and the girls looked cheap. I remember Lance started talking about some movie he was producing and saying that Jimmy might associate produce it with him, and my father was very upset about it. He didn't say anything right away, but later that night, he made a point of telling Jimmy he'd be a damned fool to invest in any movie, ever. And I could see it just raised Jimmy's hackles. In all the years they fought with each other, my father never once realized that Jimmy would be bound and determined to do the exact opposite of anything he told him. Their entire relationship was reactive."

"What was your impression of Lance Belladuce, Rebecca?" Len Morelli's question was soft and slid neatly into the conversation. Lynne upgraded her opinion of him a couple of notches. So far, he'd been quiet and gracious and had paid close attention to everything Rebecca had to say. A man who was a good listener could name his own price.

"That he was really full of himself," Rebecca answered immediately. "Oh, and that he was handsome and charming enough. He thought it was really interesting that I was a doctor, and he kept asking why I'd want to be an opthalmologist."

*Not an unreasonable question,* Lynne thought, since she'd never understood how doctors picked their specialties, apart from such obvious pairings as good-natured folks with cheerful dispositions gravitating toward pediatrics. What made one person go into urology and another choose internal medicine? One become a neonatologist and another an oncologist?

"Did you see him any other time while you were in Monterey?" Morelli asked.

She shook her head. "I had to be back at work, so I left first thing in the morning. Mother and Daddy did stay over a couple more days to see the aquarium. The butterflies were there, too, and Daddy was always fascinated by them."

The Monterey peninsula served as a wintering and breeding ground for monarch butterflies, a phenomenon Lynne had seen a couple of times when she was in college at UC Santa Cruz. When the monarchs were in town, trees and shrubs dripped with black-and-orange-striped bodies, like a spread in *National Geographic*, except that it was right there in front of you, alive and undulating.

"Did they see your brother and Lance again while they were in town?"

"You'd have to ask Mother. I have no idea. Although my guess would be yes, because this was kind of a milestone for Jimmy. Making good of something and all. They'd want to bask in that, I imagine, but I've never discussed it with Mother."

Rebecca offered an apologetic half smile, a sad intelligence reflected in her hazel eyes. "Communication was never a strong point for the Whitson family."

"So they probably did go back to the restaurant and eat there again," Morelli said. "Do you know of any other trips they made to visit before the place closed? How long was it before the restaurant went out of business?" Morelli had taken over the questioning unobtrusively and effectively. Lynne was starting to feel pretty good about Eleanor Whitson being in his hands.

"A bit less than a year," Rebecca said. "I never did understand exactly what the problem was. The location was a little out of the way for tourists, and I think that hurt them. We found out about all this after the fact, though. We didn't even know that the place had gone bust. Jimmy didn't tell us. From what I was able to piece together, after it closed, he just shut himself up in his apartment in Monterey and stopped taking his meds and slipped into a funk he never came out of."

"Was he still in Monterey when he killed himself?" Len Morelli asked.

Rebecca nodded. Her mouth was quivery, and it looked to Lynne as if she was about to lose control. "In his apartment. They didn't find him for a few days afterward." Now she did start to cry. "He didn't even have any friends to check up on him."

Len Morelli pulled a neatly pressed white cotton handkerchief out of an inside pocket and handed it to Rebecca. Did he carry those routinely? Lynne wondered. For clients and relatives of clients who dissolved into sloppy tears? It was a nice touch.

Rebecca Whitson took the handkerchief gratefully, buried her face in it for a moment and then looked up, composed once again. "I'm sorry," she said. "This is very hard. I feel so utterly helpless."

"We'll do everything we possibly can to get your mother released on bail quickly," Morelli promised. "Unfortunately, everything you've just told me contributes to a pretty strong motive for her. But," he said, turning his attention to Lynne, "tell me what happened Sunday night."

Lynne gave them the unabridged version of the scene on the patio. "You know," she finished, "I bet it was Eleanor who broke the wineglass. Because she was so startled at seeing him. I should have realized that before."

Morelli smiled. "You had no reason to think it. And I don't think it matters, anyway. But she could have gone out on her own to meet him later, and nobody would have known she was gone."

Lynne nodded. "That's true of just about anybody in the group, though. The cottages are set up for privacy. There's no more than two people in any room. So if the other one's asleep . . ."

"The biggest thing we have going for us right now," the lawyer said, "is that they haven't found the murder weapon. Did your mother have a gun, Rebecca?"

The young woman looked horrified. "Heavens, no! Mother's always hated guns. Jimmy liked them, and that scared her. I think she always knew having a gun around wasn't good for somebody with a dark side like his. And he did end up shooting himself."

"Did your brother keep guns at your mother's house?"

"She wouldn't permit it." Rebecca thought for a moment. "Though he might have. But if he did have any guns there, he'd have hidden them pretty carefully so she wouldn't find out about it."

"But it's possible that he did that? Hide weapons at her home?"

Rebecca nodded. "I might not have said that yesterday. But today I'm starting to think that even the most ridiculous things are possible. I mean, my mother—*my mother!*—has been arrested for murder. She's a very gentle soul, you know. She uses those little Havahart mousetraps because she can't bear to kill anything."

"And we're operating under the assumption that she's innocent," Len Morelli pointed out. "That means that somebody else killed Lance Belladuce, and that's where I'd like to concentrate my efforts right now. Lynne, can I come out and visit you at Villa Belladuce this afternoon?"

Lynne shook her head. "Sorry. First of all, I'm not going to be there this afternoon. I'm going to be in the town of Sonoma with some of my clients. But even if the afternoon were open, I have a feeling that Jeff and Angela Rutledge would be very angry if I brought you there without their permission. You'll need to talk to them first."

He frowned. "I just want to get the lay of the land, to see where everything is."

"I could draw you a little map," Lynne suggested. "I'd even be willing to take some pictures for you. But I can't bring you onto their property without permission. My whole group is in danger of being tossed out already. I think the Rutledges would love to have an excuse to make us leave, and I can't afford to eat that expense and provide alternate accommodations for everybody for the rest of the week. It's only Wednesday, and we're scheduled to be there for four more nights."

"I understand," he said, though his disappointment was obvious. "Do you have a camera?"

"In my cottage," Lynne said. "I brought it along to shoot souvenir pictures for everybody, but I don't normally take shots of group activities." Or of accommodations, though the Rutledges wouldn't know that.

"Is it digital?"

She shook her head. "Nope. Thirty-five millimeter. Color me old-fashioned."

"Hey, that's fine," he said. "You're probably pretty good with a camera, doing what you do."

"I'm adequate," she told him, starting to get annoyed.

"Much more than adequate, I'm sure. And I'll be happy with anything and everything you can shoot for me. The winery, the patio, the grounds, whatever. Anything you can get me will be a big help. Shoot a ton of film, and I'll reimburse you, of course."

*Actually,* Lynne thought, *Rebecca Whitson and her mother would.*

"Once you people leave Villa Belladuce," Morelli went on, "I'm willing to bet they turn that place into a fortress, and I'll have to get a court order to get in."

Rebecca hadn't eaten any more of her salad after that first speck of egg white, but Lynne was nearly to the bottom of her own salad bowl. And somehow or another, without appearing to ingest anything, Morelli had disposed of an enormous club sandwich. Lynne sneaked a peek at her watch. Time to get back to the gang at Chevy's and move them down the travel pipeline to Sonoma. Mud baths all around.

"What I really need right now," the lawyer said, "is a record of exactly what the entire place looks like at this point in time. Before anything can be changed or destroyed." His tone suggested that the Rutledges might well vacate the premises and then call in an air strike, destroying any evidence that could save Eleanor Whitson's skin.

"I'll do what I can," Lynne told him, looking at her watch quite pointedly this time. "I can't stay any longer. I'm sorry. Call me if you need more information. Rebecca, how long are you going to be in town?"

"I don't know. I've got patients scheduled all week, and my partner said he'd try to cover for me, but I need to get back, unless there's something I can actually accomplish here. I told Mother I'd stay through tomorrow, but after that, I need to leave. Do you know where her things are?"

"No, but I'll find out," Lynne promised, as she started to stand. "Nice to meet you, Len. Rebecca, I'm so sorry about all of this, but I'm sure it's all a huge misunderstanding. Len seems like just the fellow to get everything straightened out."

Len Morelli was on his feet first, pulling back Lynne's chair, a paragon of perfect manners.

"With the aid of your pictures, Lynne," he reminded her. "And do give my regards to Hake Sandstrom. He here in town with you today?"

"Nope, he's golfing down at the Sonoma Mission Inn. I'll tell him you said hello."

"Time permitting, I'll stop by there on my way back to the city and say hello in person. Haven't seen him in a while. And I'd never have expected to find him here in Sonoma, either. I saw his wine cellar when I was trying a case in Dallas a couple of years ago. Very impressive, but not much California representation. The Hakester was strictly a Francophile where the fruit of the vine was concerned. Wonder what changed his attitude?"

*An interesting question,* Lynne thought as she hurried out to the van and raced to pick up her charges.

*Why* was *the Hakester here, anyway?*

*Chapter 15*

"**YOU** know, I always wanted to do this," Ginger Conner announced from the vat where she lay immersed in goopy black mud. "It's so incredibly contradictory. You want to be more beautiful, so you coat your entire body with filth."

"Warm filth," Lynne murmured from the tub beside Ginger's. "Warm, aromatic, revitalizing filth." Aromatic was stretching matters it a bit. It actually just stank. And there was something a little too symbolic about going directly from a meeting with a criminal attorney to a warm cauldron of vile, primordial goo.

"But I know what you mean," Lynne said. "When my boys were little and it rained, they'd go out and roll in the mud sometimes, and I could never bring myself to get too mad. I always wished I dared do the same thing." And now, for a fantastic fee, she could. Life was grand.

Lynne was actually multitasking here and felt particularly pleased that she'd been able to combine this self-indulgence with her tour guide chores. Ginger Conner was the Booked for Travel client she had most neglected so far on this trip, and the one whose good graces she most needed to maintain for business reasons. Most of the folks on this tour would never use Lynne's professional services again. The Sandstroms and Ambrosinos and Athertons were all one-shot clients, the girls from Atlanta wouldn't need her again, and Eleanor Whitson wasn't likely to be a repeat customer, even if the police released her right this minute. Lynne had the Harper and Martell accounts no matter what, by virtue of long friendship.

Only Ginger Conner was a repeat business customer, a corporate account for a company whose executives and sales force all did a lot of traveling. The account was steady and reliable and had generated additional business from others in the shiny new industrial complex where Ginger's firm was located.

In a way, of course, it was Ginger's own fault that Lynne hadn't paid more attention to her. She was too competent, too self-sufficient, a take-charge woman with none of her sister's vulnerability. Ginger was one of the new breed of career women, girls who had always known they would work, who majored in business as a matter of course, who segued effortlessly from college into middle management. Girls like Dr. Rebecca Whitson and Lynne's own daughter, Jenny, who had taken it as a given that they would be able to do whatever they wanted.

Whereas Lynne, now in her midfifties, had spent much of her life trying to adapt to continual changes in the ground rules. Part of the first wave of the postwar baby boom, she'd been born too late to be entirely comfortable in the happily harnessed housewifery of the fifties, too soon to fit neatly into the anything-goes anarchy of the sixties. That she grew up a military brat only compounded the identity crisis. She'd attended eleven different schools by the time she finished high school, had stood up in classrooms on several continents introducing herself to boys and girls she knew would be part of her history before the semester ended. Her family had lived in Norfolk and San Diego and Oslo and Guam and Italy, had once moved from Florida to Washington, D.C., and back again in the space of a single year.

And then, after years of being rootless, she had planted herself in Monty's native Floritas. The world continued to change more quickly than she could ever keep up with, but it no longer mattered so much, and she could pretty much pick her own pace for playing catch-up with general societal changes.

"Is the heat bothering your sunburn?" she asked now. Ginger had returned from her hot-air balloon ride with patches of pinkened skin on her cheeks and forearms. The young woman was fair-skinned and probably never ventured outdoors in San Diego without a meticulously applied protective coating of industrial-strength sunblock. At a guess, even her lipstick would contain sunscreen. All the better cosmetics did in melanoma-plagued Southern California.

"I can't really tell. But it was pretty stupid of me to get burned like that. It never occurred to me how exposed we'd be up there. I mean, *duh*. You're closer to the sun. You're actually *above* the clouds part of the time. I'm lucky I didn't come out of this looking like a boiled king crab leg." But Ginger didn't sound too terribly concerned, and though her face was flushed from the heat of the mud bath, the sunburn looked quite manageable.

"It looks like it'll fade out in a day or two," Lynne said. "I kind of miss getting suntanned, to tell the truth. I used to flat out love it. I'd get really dark and wear little white dresses and my hair would bleach out really light. I'd take the kids to the beach for the day and none of us would even use sunscreen. Dark tanning oil, if anything. I'd never dare say this to my dermatologist, but I think just about everybody looks better with a tan."

"I wouldn't know. I always burned."

"Did you grow up in Southern California?" Lynne was starting to realize that despite numerous conversations with Ginger at Floritas Chamber of Commerce Sundowners, she really knew very little about her. Cocktail chatter often worked that way.

Ginger shook her head. "Uh-uh. Pittsburgh. But once I got out here and spent my first winter, I knew I couldn't go back.

I came west, and Sara went south, and neither of us ever gave a backward glance. We come from one of those Irish families that put the *fun* in *dysfunctional.*"

At a minimum, Lynne thought, that meant alcoholism. And at worst, she simply didn't want to know. It was time to change the subject. "So what was your favorite part of the hot-air balloon ride?"

"You mean other than lunch?" Ginger asked. "I must say, getting some good Mexican food up here was a real surprise. I love Chevy's at home. I go to the one in Del Mar all the time."

"Me, too. I was sorry I couldn't join you." Lynne immediately regretted the statement, fearful that Ginger would now want to know all about Eleanor Whitson.

But Ginger, bless her heart, was still focused on the balloon ride. She was quiet for a moment, then spoke very deliberately. "I think what I most liked about riding in the balloon was the sense of possibility. I mean, on the one hand, everything was very controlled, at least at the beginning of the flight. How fast we went up and how high and all of that. But once we were up, everything was also subject to the forces of nature. We came down in an entirely different area than I thought we were going to, and I'd checked out all kinds of maps before we ever left."

"I know what you mean," Lynne told her. "I've only done it once, and I don't think I'd ever do it again, but it was so . . . so *free.* I remember thinking there should be some kind of sense of movement, but there really wasn't one."

"Did you do it in Del Mar? I can see the balloons from my office window sometimes." Ginger worked just off I-5 on the southern edge of Floritas.

"Yeah. It was a surprise from my husband on our twenty-fifth anniversary." Lynne knew she could close her eyes right now and put herself back there if she wanted, dangling beneath a swirl of crimson and orange and vibrant yellow, sunset colors on an enormous balloon. Warmth on their heads from the flames roaring in the burner above them, the Pacific shoreline sculpted off to the west. Tiny horses galloping around the Del Mar racetrack far below and Monty's golden face reflected in the warm August sunlight. Monty in particular was someone who looked great with a tan. They'd gone from there to a seafood dinner and then walked the beach hand in hand in the moonlight, giddy from champagne and love, watching the surf break while they talked in non sequiturs about a future filled with more beaches and more seafood and each other.

Best to close the door on that particular set of memories right now.

"Is your sister enjoying herself, do you think?" Lynne asked. Sara and Kelly and Jessica were off in another part of the spa having aromatherapy body treatments and facials, while the Sandstroms, after a morning of golf, had opted for his-and-hers two-hour full-body massages.

"Not as much as I'd hoped," Ginger said, "but the change has been good for her. Any change would be. I'd like to see her get the hell out of Atlanta and away from that controlling son of a bitch ex-husband, but it ain't gonna happen. And it's not like I'm in a position to be giving matrimonial advice. Sara might be divorced, but at least she *had* a husband. A loser to be sure, but a rich loser."

She laughed. "Listen to me. I'm lying here buried in mud saying it was a good thing that my baby sister married a moron."

⊂━━━▶━━━○

**ANGELA** stood in the middle of the ruined winery and willed herself not to cry.

It was just about twenty-four hours since she and Detective Shaw had discovered the devastation here, and this was the first opportunity she'd had to get in and start cleaning up. The cops had sealed everything up yesterday afternoon, and the crime scene technicians had finished shortly before noon today, leaving a swath of nasty black fingerprint powder that drifted down into the remaining puddles of wine and turned them murky. The room looked as if a hurricane or a flood had swept through and then receded, one of those terrible Eastern cataclysms that show up on the nightly news as evidence of the ultimate force of nature.

Except that this flood had been wine, and the smell of it was still so strong it made her dizzy.

Maybe she would have been dizzy anyway.

She knew that the police had spoken with Vincent Belladuce and the other employees who had access to the building, and that all of them had denied any knowledge of the vandalism. Well, what did the cops expect them to say? *Sure, I came in with a couple of friends and a couple of axes and hacked out the ends of dozens of wine barrels. Poured out about sixty thousand bottles worth of wine, and now I'm going to Disneyland.*

Angela had not yet talked to Vincent, nor did she intend to until she was certain she could remain in icy control throughout the entire conversation. He was an imperious old man under the best of circumstances, the kind of old-country sexist with little use for women in any role but subordinate. This attitude was made tolerable by an innate charm, the same charm that had made Lance so maddeningly irresistible.

Though charm hadn't, she reflected, proven an asset for Lance in the long run.

According to Detective Shaw, the police hadn't found any useful fingerprints here. This was the second time in as many days that they'd been through here, and all they'd determined was that various employees—including numerous Belladuce cousins and a couple of guys who'd married into the clan—had indeed handled equipment in and around the building. Whoever had vandalized the place had apparently worn gloves.

When the Rutledges bought Villa Belladuce, Angela had immediately upgraded the mediocre stereo system in this building. She never stinted on sound systems. Now she had a bootleg CD of a Springsteen concert playing, pounding loud to help keep her moving and to fill her brain so she didn't have to think about what she was doing and what had happened here.

Can't start a fire without a spark.

Thunderous, driving, pulsating music reverberated through the building. Sheer oblivion music, like she'd used to sustain herself in the first months after the accident, blasting through earphones in her hospital bed. "You'll damage your eardrums," the older nurses had chided, but she wouldn't let them turn it down, and the younger ones seemed to instinctively understand. Damage her eardrums, indeed. And what if she did? Most of her young body was already in hideous suppurating ruin. Why spare her ears?

She'd used the music to carry her through that suspended time, the endless minutes that melted into endless hours that ever so slowly evolved into endless days. She'd played a lot of Janis Joplin then, a singer she'd just discovered before the accident, a woman dead before Angela was even born. When they warned her of potential hearing loss, she countered that Joplin had refused to compromise when doomsayers warned she'd destroy her vocal chords. That they'd told her to protect her voice for later in life, for a time that turned out never to come at all.

The music sustained Angela through the worst of that dreadful period as she alternated the blessed fog of painkillers with the searing pain of debridement and the phantom agonies of the amputated foot. She'd been terrified of the pain but even more frightened of addiction, which a year later would kill her brother, who overdosed in a one-room apartment in the Hollywood Hills at twenty-three.

But even the music failed her now, as it moved into the dreary sadness of "My Hometown."

Two of Rosalita's friends, Mexican men with little English, had come in to help clean up and were now busily engaged in sweeping up the broken glass and splintered barrel staves, in hauling loads of soggy corrugated cardboard out to the dumpster. Raul and Manuel had replaced some of the toppled barrels on their racks and very slowly, the winery was regaining a grudging sense of order. There were times when it was useful to be fluent in Spanish, which she'd sometimes spoken with Latina girlfriends at Venice High School a lifetime ago. The words were a little rusty, particularly since she insisted that Rosalita use only English with the baby, but she could find enough of them when she needed to.

She stared for a while at the smashed bottling equipment, where apparently they'd used sledgehammers. The damage was extensive and didn't look fixable. Most likely they'd have to replace it completely, and God knows if their insurance company would give them trouble.

She caught herself. There were times, like right now, when it was useful to remind herself that it didn't matter what *anything* cost. Because she could afford it.

The concrete floor was stained, and dark splotches discolored the unfinished wooden paneling on the walls by the door, as if someone had splashed through in rain boots. Now she slogged furiously across to the corner where a dozen barrels remained in their racks, bungs intact, ends untouched by the wildly swinging ax marauders. The wine continued quietly aging inside fine French oak. Here was the proof. As far as Angela was concerned, those untouched barrels were stronger evidence of the identity of the vandals than a videotape of the actual rampage in the winery.

The vandalism had been entirely systematic.

To prevent the wine from running off too quickly, someone had created a little lake by blocking the heavy drains in the concrete winery floor with towels jammed into the openings after the metal grates were unscrewed and removed. The cops had removed those blockages, and most of the wine on the floor had drained away, hundreds of thousands of dollars worth of runoff. In the ultimate irony, it would seep into the earth and water the vines outside from which some of the wine had originally come. The circle of life, with a criminal assist.

"Mother of God!"

Angela turned to see Vincent Belladuce in the doorway, staring into the winery with a look of consummate horror on his face. He walked in slowly, moving his eyes up and down, back and forth, pacing mechanically. He looked truly stunned.

"I suppose you're going to say this surprises you?" Angela didn't bother keeping the anger from her voice.

He ignored her, crossing to inspect the smashed and battered bottling assembly. He shook his head darkly and turned to examine some destroyed barrels that Raul and Manuel had rolled over to the wall by the doorway and then turned to stand on end. Other barrels had been pushed off the racks after their contents drained and then hacked at a bit more. Those were beyond repair, not even suitable to slice in half and use as patio planters.

Vincent ran his fingers lightly across some of the broken and splintered edges, then reached down and picked up the neck of a smashed Chardonnay bottle from a glittering pile of debris that Manuel was sweeping into an enormous dustpan.

Vincent Belladuce was a strong-featured and robust man with thick, silver hair, a bushy moustache, and dark eyes that glittered with wisdom and experience and often, as they did now, with more than a touch of danger. His navy-and-green plaid shirt was tucked into belted dark cotton work pants, which were, in turn, tucked into heavy rubber boots, the kind of boots they wore to walk the vineyards during the rainy season. Someone had told him very specifically what had happened here, she realized, or he wouldn't be wearing the boots. Would the police have passed on that information? Or had it come from the vandals themselves, second cousins thrice removed or whatever. All the regulars who worked in the winery were related one way or another, whether by blood or by marriage or by simple cussedness.

Vincent turned the broken bottle neck over in his hand, then carefully deposited it in one of the trash barrels positioned at random intervals across the floor for the cleanup.

Angela realized that suddenly he looked old.

"It more than surprises me," he said slowly, turning to look at her with raw pain in his eyes. "It sickens me as well. It twists knives in my heart. This winery has been my life. These wines are like my children, and to see this happen . . ." His voice trailed away as he slowly looked around again. His eyes, Angela noticed, lingered on the racks of barrels behind her, the barrels undamaged in the otherwise wholesale destruction. But he didn't mention them.

"The caves?" he asked.

She shook her head, feeling an entirely unexpected wave of pity for him. This place *had* been his life. Vincent Belladuce had been making wine in this room for over fifty years. "Untouched. I don't know why. Maybe they ran out of energy, or maybe they didn't know how to get in, but somehow I think that whoever did this knows just about everything there is to know about the wine making operation at Villa Belladuce." She could feel the acid rising again in her voice, and she didn't bother to try to stop it.

He went over to a barrel still lying on its side on the floor, its bung removed and its end hacked open with sufficient vigor to leave fist-sized holes. The barrel had contained a year-old cabernet. He leaned down and rubbed his hand absently along the staves, then looked up at her. His eyes were deep and empty.

"You are angry," he said, "and upset. But so am I. I've lost a nephew who was like a son to me, my dead brother's oldest boy. Lance was maybe too careless with the ladies, maybe more willing to chase a wild idea than to follow a simple path. He was a foolish boy sometimes, but I loved him. I know that your husband didn't like him and that there was bad blood between them, but tomorrow we bury him, and out of respect for his memory, I'm going to let all that go."

But he didn't seem to be letting anything go, actually. He seemed to be getting angrier and angrier. Now he gave the empty barrel a furious shove, and it rolled crookedly toward the doorway.

He watched it roll away, and suddenly his eyes widened. He strode toward the barrel in a few short steps, and Angela found herself holding her breath. Something about the way he moved and the glint in his eye paralyzed her. A song was just ending on the Springsteen CD, and the room fell into a sudden hush.

Vincent Belladuce squatted beside the end of the barrel and looked through the splintered holes into the empty interior. Shaking his head, he rolled up his right sleeve and thrust his arm inside the hacked-open end.

The music crashed into the opening chords of "Born in the USA," but Raul and Manuel—who almost certainly had not been, who probably didn't even have green cards—ignored the music and moved slowly toward Vincent and the barrel.

Angela listened to Bruce Springsteen growl as Vincent Belladuce slowly withdrew his arm from the end of the broken, emptied barrel.

In his hand was a gun.

*Chapter 16*

**KELLY** Atherton was beginning to despair of ever actually meeting Jeff Rutledge.

She didn't have to, of course. It didn't have anything to do with why they were here, other than pure serendipity, but serendipity had to count for something. And it had seemed so easy before she actually arrived: a secluded Sonoma winery, host welcomes guest, mission accomplished. In more advanced versions of the fantasy scenario, she and Jeff Rutledge had hit it off immediately, discovering shared interests and ideas, brainstorming ways she might put her talents to use working for him.

Well, scratch *that* notion. At this rate, she'd never even get to shake the guy's hand.

Still, here she was, positioned to have a full view of the patio and the mansion and the wing of the mansion where she'd determined Jeff Rutledge kept his workshop, so who knows? Maybe she'd get lucky. It didn't need to be a lasting encounter, after all. She'd been able to tell from the ugly scene on the patio that this was an archetypical geek sadly deficient in social skills. But she found him fascinating, nonetheless, and someone working in the field of corporate technical employment could only benefit from being able to say, "When I met Jeff Rutledge . . ."

Of course, that wasn't absolutely essential. Having actually been here—and at an exceptionally verifiable point in history—she could probably claim any kind of interaction she wanted, and nobody'd ever be the wiser. Jeff Rutledge wouldn't surface to counter the assertion of a Chicago headhunter. He hadn't even surfaced to greet guests staying at his own vineyard, the rude creep.

Still, lack of manners notwithstanding, Kelly Atherton was willing to cut Jeff Rutledge a lot of slack. Long before she ever heard of Villa Belladuce or Booked for Travel, Kelly had been familiar with his story. It was a fairly remarkable saga, actually, a modern technological legend.

Kelly'd read up on him before the trip, this man whose name brought up some 438,000 hits on Google.com, her preferred search engine. The only child of a Kansas grocer and an obstetrical nurse, Jeffrey Alan Rutledge possessed an IQ of 173 or 164 or 181, depending on your source, or perhaps only on which time he'd been tested. Mighty darn high, no matter how you counted it, however, up there in the mega-genius range. He'd joined Mensa at the age of six and was an electronic tinkerer from his earliest days, the kind of kid who would have built ham radios a generation earlier. Coming of age in the final decades of the twentieth century, he worked instead with microchips and motherboards and then began compulsively developing software.

He had a sense of the missing link, Jeff Rutledge did. A way of looking at a problem and finding a way to bridge the gap, to move beyond the familiar into the unknown, and to find things in the unknown that nobody had believed possible. An idea man in the purest sense. He'd once told *Fortune*: "My most important innovations come to me in a kind of gestalt, and I'd love to take the credit, but I don't know where the information comes from. It's as if I were channeling."

*Channeling.*

Kelly chuckled now at *Fortune*'s reaction to that answer.

California goofball, they'd implied. Lucky flake. Never mind that he was a Kansan whose brand of flaky luck had brought him three separate fortunes, each resulting from a process so valuable he could name his own price with full confidence that no matter how outrageous, that price would be met.

Twice Bill Gates had paid his price, and there'd been a picture of the two men together in the *Fortune* article. Rutledge was taller, his features more angular, his glasses more trendy. But they were cut from the same geek cloth.

It was the third fortune that most interested Kelly, the company and processes he had thus far declined to sell. InRut, a double entendre that also screamed nerd, geek, dork. InRut was working in the realm of true artificial intelligence, both here and at the company compound down in Sunnyvale. No more operating systems for Jeff Rutledge. No more intuitive leaps to make life easier for the guy at home putting his checkbook into Quicken, the secretary importing Excel tables into Word, the teenagers in chat rooms at three A.M.

Jeff Rutledge had moved squarely into the future.

Not that any of this was going to do Kelly much good. She was starting to realize that if Lance Belladuce hadn't crashed their opening night party, she might never have seen Jeff Rutledge at all. It was possible he'd put in an appearance at the Ambrosinos' anniversary party, scheduled for the patio before dinner tonight, but a meteorite smashing into the patio was also possible and perhaps more likely.

Still, she'd been happy to come back early from the spa this afternoon. Mostly to be with Gran, of course, but this way she was also available, just in case. Gran had worn herself out this morning and was sound asleep, so Kelly had carried one of the patio chairs down to the little paved area outside their cottage and had just started the third Harry Potter book. She couldn't believe that she hadn't read these years ago, actually, but somehow she'd thought she was too mature until Ryan brought her a complete set when he drove down with Gran. Now she was grateful to be a very slow reader, and wasn't sure what she'd do when she finished.

Too bad she couldn't send Jeff Rutledge an owl.

**UNAWARE** that he was being ever-so-politely stalked by one of the tourists he despised, Jeff Rutledge wandered down to the kitchen from his workshop and put a package of popcorn into the microwave. He liked this kitchen, which retained a certain old-world sensibility, despite the presence of a Sub-Zero refrigerator and a six-burner restaurant stove. Beautifully burnished copper pans and kettles and bowls hung over a blue marble center island. Extensive glass shelving in a bank of southwestern windows held the African violets Angela loved.

When the popcorn was ready, he poured it into a copper bowl and started upstairs, by way of the grand staircase just inside the large double front doors. He nodded to Rosalita, who was lovingly rubbing some kind of lemon-scented oil into the ebony baby grand piano in the music room, which sat behind the staircase. Neither Jeff nor Angela played the piano—or any musical instrument other than the stereo—but the Belladuces had designed this as a music room, and Angela had decided it would remain one, with a piano ready and waiting when Stephanie was old enough to take lessons.

The mansion had originally featured three master bedroom suites, two on the second floor and one downstairs that they'd converted into a media room. They'd kept one of the upstairs ones as their own bedroom and torn out a few walls to combine the other with two smaller bedrooms into a large space for Jeff's workshop. As he started down the hall now to the workshop, he was startled to hear someone singing softly in Stephanie's room. He stiffened and felt the hair stand up on his neck. Rosalita was downstairs, and Angela had gone over to the winery to clean up the latest mess the Belladuces had visited on them.

Who was with his daughter?

He reached Stephanie's door in four long strides, flung it wide, and was rewarded for his vigilance by a piercing wail from his daughter. The baby sat propped on one end of a white wicker love seat, and a strange old lady that he'd never seen before sat beside her. The old lady picked the howling baby up and rocked her in a soothing kind of bounce while Jeff stood in the doorway feeling like a perfect idiot.

Except, what was this stranger doing in this house, holding his child?

"Who the devil are you?" he asked, a little louder than he'd intended. The baby started crying louder, and the old lady glared daggers at him.

"Oh, there, there, there," she told the baby, putting her face close to Stephanie's. The crying slowed a bit, then diminished to a whimper as Stephanie grabbed a set of plastic keys that the old lady dangled in front of her.

Then, and only then, the old lady looked up at him. "I am Maria Ambrosino, a guest with the Sonoma Sojourn group," she told him in a thick Eastern accent. New York, Boston, one of those extraordinarily ethnic accents he could never differentiate, other than to know they weren't British. Jeff had a bit of a tin ear, actually. "Your wife said I could stay with Stephanie for a while today. I didn't want to go out with the others."

This was absurd. Angela was out of her mind. She'd refused to hire a nanny, stating that she was the mother here, and she didn't need or want to share Stephanie with anyone but him. She'd agreed to having a live-in housekeeper, however, precisely so there'd always be somebody here to watch the baby. There was certainly no need to bring in the damned tourists to baby-sit.

The old lady stood up, holding a now-contented Stephanie and looking a little frightened. She offered the baby to him. "Here, please take her, I don't mean to intrude."

Jeff realized he was backing away and hated himself for it. This baby business scared the bloody blue hell out of him. He had never held an infant in his arms until the day that Stephanie arrived and had not once felt comfortable holding her. She seemed so impossibly fragile. He was always certain that he'd do something horrible, drop her on her head or break one of her delicate little bones with his innate clumsiness.

He forced himself to smile, to reassure the woman who

now looked genuinely terrified and who, truth be told, also looked absolutely at home holding his baby. "No, no, you're fine," he said. "I just didn't realize you were here. You surprised me."

He retreated from the baby's room and hurried down the hall to the sanctuary of his workshop. Angela wouldn't have left the baby with someone she didn't trust absolutely, he realized now, so there was no reason for his apprehension, though she certainly should have mentioned it to him.

He bolted the door behind him with an absurd sense of relief. Whose house was this, anyway? Who was he hiding from? His own six-month-old baby? A plump, white-haired lady who looked like she'd been sent from central casting for the role of the grandma in the flour-smudged apron?

Or was he hiding from all of his own long-buried fears and demons, clawing their way to the surface of his mind through the wreckage of the last few days?

c⟩━━⟨ɔ

**MOMENTS** later, the phone began to ring, the number that only Angela knew, the one that played "Zippity Doo Dah." All their phones were programmed with different musical rings so that they could differentiate incoming calls. This was the one Angela called "the direct spousal link."

"You'd better get over here," Angela told him now, without preamble. She sounded frantic, edgy. "The cops are on their way. Again. Vincent Belladuce came to the winery, and he found a gun in one of the emptied barrels."

"Found?" Jeff asked scornfully. "A gun in a wine barrel? What kind of nonsense is that?"

"I don't know exactly," his wife said briskly, "but Vincent is really furious, and he's waving the gun around, and I never thought I'd say this, but I wish the cops would hurry up and get here."

c⟩━━⟨ɔ

**KELLY** was engrossed in Quidditch practice when a door slammed on the far side of the mansion. She looked up and saw Jeff Rutledge running down the outside staircase leading from his workshop.

Now. The perfect opening. She closed the book and started walking swiftly toward the patio, mentally rehearsing a statement of surprise at encountering him there. But before she could even reach the patio, he'd sprinted past the breakfast room and across the parking area.

She followed him far enough to watch him lope down the path that led through the wooded area to the winery. When she couldn't see him anymore, she walked slowly back to the Tuscany cottage, poked her head in long enough to see that Gran was still sleeping, and picked up Harry Potter again.

Five minutes later, she heard a siren growing louder and caught a glimpse of flashing lights whizzing past the mansion. This time, she crossed the property and went through the woods herself, going far enough around the front of the winery to see the sheriff's car sitting out front and to hear Bruce Springsteen echoing from inside the building.

*Chapter 17*

**ANGELA** couldn't take her eyes off the gun.

It was a tiny thing, dripping red wine, looking more like a toy than a lethal weapon. A lady's purse gun, maybe, something cute to tuck into a garter or a brassiere.

And yet it was frightening to watch Vincent Belladuce brandish the tiny pistol, swinging it wildly around the room as he ranted. At first it sent a shower of wine drops into the air. Angela was afraid to move, uncertain what Vincent might say or do.

Raul and Manuel had wisely retreated outdoors and maybe even had fled the premises, a departure she could hardly fault them for. She didn't want to be here herself, after all, and she particularly didn't want to be here while Vincent Belladuce, who had served time in prison for manslaughter, was waving around a firearm.

"I'm calling nine-one-one," she told him in a low, level voice as she moved cautiously toward the phone. He nodded, made no objection, and lowered his hand and the gun to point at the floor. He wasn't relinquishing it, but once Angela had the 911 operator, she didn't care. Then she pressed her luck by dialing Jeff's number in the workshop at the house.

But now that she'd finished these notifications, she was stuck here with a greatly agitated, armed man in a room filled with wreckage and broken sharp objects. She moved slowly to the controls to turn down the music, though she couldn't bear to turn it off altogether. At the moment, the music was the only thing that made any sense, and Vincent didn't seem to be aware of it at all.

"What in the hell is going on here?" Jeff stood outlined in the doorway, and relief washed over Angela at the sound of his voice. She couldn't remember any time she'd been happier to see him, and this was a man whose mere existence brightened her every day.

Vincent turned toward Jeff's voice, swinging the gun. Jeff put both his hands in the air, like an old-style Western movie, and halted abruptly. "Vincent, what are you doing? Put that thing down."

Vincent looked at the gun in his hand as if noticing it for the first time. He lowered the gun once again so that it pointed at the ground and walked slowly across to the table where Angela stood beside the phone.

"Move away," Vincent told her, and she scurried backward, heading toward the door where Jeff still stood. Jeff slowly lowered his hands, eyeing Vincent cautiously, then walked quietly and deliberately toward Angela. They met halfway, and she collapsed into his arms, trembling.

Vincent laid the gun on the table and looked slowly around the wreckage in the winery. "My whole life I put into this place, and for what?"

Angela didn't think he expected an answer, and she didn't have one, anyway.

She hoped the 911 operator had taken her seriously, had understood the urgency in her tone. She could call again, she supposed. Maybe she should call again. Vincent might not be holding the gun now, but he remained irascible and volatile. Lance had been volatile, too. Maybe the Belladuces were all that way, unpredictable powder kegs of raw emotion and hot-blooded passion.

In the distance she could hear the whine of a siren, and she exhaled in relief, stealing a glance at Vincent, who had moved away from the gun on the table and was now walking up and down the rows of ruined barrels as if in a trance.

The Boss moved into "Hungry Heart" just as the cops arrived.

⚬━◆━⚬

**ALICE** Harper had quickly realized that it wasn't going to be easy to squeeze a fiftieth anniversary party for Guido and Maria Ambrosino into the Sonoma Sojourn schedule, and that was even before anybody was murdered or arrested.

Significant obstacles were built into the schedule itself. Every single night was spoken for already, with long-standing reservations at carefully selected restaurants. Lynne went to a lot of trouble to offer a choice of interesting daytime activities on her tours, and while the schedule was elastic, it was never really empty.

So she and Pat had huddled, devised a plan, and issued written invitations to every member of the group. Early Wednesday evening, they'd have a gathering on the patio. Add some elegant hors d'oeuvres to the regularly scheduled wine hour, attach a bouquet of helium balloons to the antique wine press, present the couple with a few token gifts. Alice was pleased that everybody had gotten into the gift idea, though she was not really surprised. There was something so fundamentally appealing about the Ambrosinos that even that annoying Hake Sandstrom seemed mildly respectful. Heidi'd been carrying a huge, elegantly wrapped gift when she returned from the spa.

Now Alice and Pat assembled their party materials on the patio and set to work. It was about four P.M. and still warm and sunny, the perfect day for a celebration.

Pat had finished dozens of volleyball-sized white tulle bows by now, fluffy and airy and as ethereal as the clouds drifting overhead. Alice was attaching them by their pipe cleaner feet to chairs and bushes and planters around the patio.

"What do you suppose the cops are doing down at the winery?" Alice asked. There'd been three patrol cars there when she and Pat returned from Santa Rosa.

"I can't imagine," Pat said. "Lynne told us somebody had trashed it, but I thought that was all taken care of yesterday morning, while we were still at the cooking class. This has got to be something new, but what?"

The sound of approaching footsteps across the gravel parking area caught their attention, and they stopped in midmotion and watched as Jeff and Angela Rutledge came up past the breakfast area and marched into the kitchen door of the mansion without speaking to each other or acknowledging the presence of Alice and Pat. Jeff looked pretty much as he had the only other time Alice had seen him, that first night, also on the patio. But Angela had a dirty, depressed, and defeated look to her. Her hair was dull and lifeless, her face was drawn and smudged, her jeans were splotched and stained.

When they'd disappeared into the kitchen, Alice let her breath out and turned to Pat. "So," she said brightly, "do you think our host and hostess will be joining us tonight?"

Pat opened a flat tissue paper bell and clipped its edges together to create a three-dimensional wedding bell. "I hope not," she said, looking at the back door. "I don't think I can take much more of Mr. Rutledge's charm. I don't care how rich he is or how smart. He looked just now like he'd eat you for breakfast. I don't want anything or anybody spoiling this party."

"Well, at least we can be sure that the guy who disrupted the party the other night won't be here," Alice noted. "On account of he's dead."

Pat lowered her voice. "The guy who really disrupted things the other night is the guy who just stalked past us like he owned the universe and was thinking of ejecting lower life forms like us. And *he's* still very much alive."

Pat carefully moved the floral centerpiece back a few

inches on the table they'd set up for it. "Does this look all right?"

Alice stopped, looked, and nodded. "Of course. Has Lynne ever made a bad floral arrangement?"

Lynne had a feel for flowers and an amazing knack for creating incredible bouquets and centerpieces. Her particular gift was the ability to wander around your yard—a yard that you'd swear didn't have anything remotely attractive in it, that couldn't provide enough raw materials to fill so much as a bud vase—and pull together an arrangement that would cost you fifty bucks at the florist. The floral arrangements she created out of her own wonderfully abundant yard were awesome, in demand year round.

"Good point," Pat said. "I do love to watch her do it, too."

They'd picked up several prefab bouquets at a grocery store in town, and Lynne had deftly turned them into a single grand arrangement, discarding the brighter, gaudier blooms so that the final result was comprised exclusively of airy pastels. Alice had watched the process with awe. She would never have the nerve to throw away part of a bouquet. She was even uneasy about removing flowers that were unquestionably dead after a few days in an arrangement and usually just pitched the entire thing when any part of it started looking tired. Whereas she'd seen Lynne whittle a huge bouquet down systematically over nearly a month until it consisted of a single perfect bloom. Every rearrangement was significantly different from the others, and they all looked swell.

What Lynne had created for this party also coordinated perfectly with the plantings in the various containers on the patio. The simplicity of the pastel snapdragons and dwarf cosmos and sweet William made just the right counterpoint. A dozen silver-and-white helium balloons floated in the patio center above the antique wine press.

Pat stepped back, put her hands on her hips, and looked around the patio. "You know, we ought to think about doing this more often."

Alice chose to be obtuse. "More often than what? We just met these people."

"You know what I mean. We could put on parties for other people, back home."

They'd talked about this before, very casually. "Pat, I don't want a job. I have a job. He retired last year."

Pat laughed. "But don't you see, Alice? That's the beauty of it. We'd only have to do the things we wanted, when we wanted. It'd give us a sense of purpose."

"I have a sense of purpose. I've always had one." Alice laughed. "And if I forget what it is sometimes, I figure that's just part of the aging process."

**SARA** had been observing Jessica in action all day.

Jessica had devoted extra time to her hair and makeup this morning and was visibly disappointed to learn that the Athertons were breakfasting in their cottage. She'd also seemed less than thrilled, had almost gotten pouty, when Ryan jumped into the front seat beside his sister for the ride north to the hot-air balloon launch site.

Things had warmed up considerably once the balloon was in the air, however, and Sara had seen enough guys in action to realize that Jessica's interest in Ryan was being reciprocated big time. She'd been annoyed yesterday at Ravenswood, but that irritation had passed, and now she was willing to concede that maybe this was The Real Thing.

Or A Real Thing, anyway, which would almost be good enough. Jessica definitely needed something good to happen to her. She was due.

This afternoon, they'd been pampered and massaged, aromatherapied and pedicured, treated like absolute royalty by all sorts of deferential spa employees. When they got back to Villa Belladuce, where there was nothing to do for over an hour till the Ambrosinos' anniversary party, Jessica plopped down on her bed and closed her eyes.

An hour later, there she remained.

Sara finished dressing for the evening and looked at Jessica thoughtfully. She was breathing evenly, but Jessica usually emitted a wheezy little snore when she was really asleep. "You awake?" she asked softly.

"Sort of," Jessica mumbled.

"I was just wondering—" Suddenly her curiosity felt like prying, her interest seemed intrusive, almost prurient. "Never mind."

"What?" Jessica's eyes remained closed, but her voice was clearer. She was definitely awake now and probably had been all along.

"—if this thing with you and Ryan is going somewhere." There, she'd said it.

Jessica's eyes opened slowly, and her lips spread in a small, thin smile, reminiscent of the Mona Lisa. "Lordie, I sure hope so."

Sara laughed despite herself. "Me, too. He's a real sweetie, Jess, and he sure seems interested in you. Though I don't know what you guys can do about the geography thing. He doesn't seem like he's in any hurry to leave Wisconsin, and your mother will have a hissy fit if you try to move away from Atlanta."

"My mama's been having hissies about one thing or another my entire life," Jessica drawled, "and you know what? This time, I don't think I care." She began softly singing the University of Wisconsin fight song. "On, Wisconsin, on Wisconsin, dum da dum dum dum."

"Please! Spare me! I'll be out on the patio when you come to your senses," laughed Sara as she turned away from the bed and gave herself a last-minute inspection in the full-length freestanding mirror. She wore a bitsy little white eyelet mini-dress with apricot ribbon woven through the bodice and spaghetti straps of embroidered rosebuds. Her hair floated in a smoky cloud, and her lipstick was the precise apricot of the ribbons and rosebuds. She looked great, even if there wasn't anybody to notice.

It was like a tree falling in the woods when nobody was around to hear it, she decided after a moment. The tree definitely made a noise, and she definitely looked terrific.

She headed for the door.

**OUT** on the patio, Sara discovered that Pat Martell and Alice Harper had worked magic. The patio had taken on a fairyland quality, all white and silver and delicate. What's more, it didn't look like they were nearly finished yet. There were piles of decorating materials on two of the tables, spilling out of large white plastic bags.

"You two are really incredible," Sara told the older women. "What can I do to help?"

Pat stepped back and smiled at her. It was a rather maternal smile, but Sara didn't mind maternal smiles unless they actually came from her own mother. "Why don't you help me bring out one of the tables from the breakfast room to put the gifts on while Alice finishes with the paper bell doohickeys?"

"That's me," Alice acknowledged cheerfully. "The doohickey queen. I keep thinking I'm going to get to do a wedding for my younger daughter, but she's not holding up her end of the bargain. I'm starting to get a complex. I'm always a friend of the family, never the mother of the bride."

Sara cringed. "Let her take her time," she said after a moment. "You don't want her messing up like I did. Trust me, it's worth waiting."

By the time Pat and Sara had set the table up and moved the gifts onto it, Alice had spread paper wedding tablecloths on all the tables and strewn them with little silver stars. Then Wendy Carr from the Rosemary & Thyme Cooking School arrived with a trunk full of hors d'oeuvres. When Sara'd been playing with cream puff filling yesterday, it seemed, these ladies had been planning an event and ordering party food. Amazing.

They hauled various trays and coolers and containers into the breakfast room, where Wendy unveiled a beautiful red-white-and-green Italian torte made of blended cream cheeses and pesto and sun-dried tomatoes. Its top was decorated with more pesto and tomatoes to emulate the Italian flag.

"Gorgeous!" Pat told her. It was kind of cute how excited she was.

"I tried to keep it simple and Italian," Wendy explained. "Of course, the problem with doing ethnic food for ethnic people is that they usually have very specific ideas about what things are supposed to taste like."

"That looks like it's going to taste like heaven," Sara said.

"Here, try a taste. I kept out a sample for quality control." Wendy opened a little Tupperware container holding a miniature, slightly messy version of the torte, then produced crackers and a little serving knife with a lug of grapes on its handle. Everybody tasted and admired.

Meanwhile, Wendy unpacked a platter of mixed olives and a tray of assorted hors d'oeuvres. "I dropped the cake off at the Sonoma Bistro on my way over here. They'll have it ready when you all finish your dinner tonight."

"You are awesome," Sara told her with absolute sincerity. "This makes me almost wish I'd had a real wedding myself, instead of running off to Vegas like we did." Then she shrugged and offered a rueful little smile. "But maybe that was best, after all. A disposable start for a disposable marriage."

"You can give yourself a big wedding next time," Alice suggested. "Give Pat and me a call, and we'll come do your decorating. Lynne can come along to do the flowers."

Wendy leaned in and spread a bit of torte on a cracker. "Where is Lynne, anyway? I was hoping she'd know what's going on down at the winery."

"I'm right here," Lynne said from the doorway, "and I know less than nothing, and it's driving me crazy."

*Chapter 18*

**MARIA** Ambrosino looked around at all these people she barely knew, people who had thrown a party for her and Guido, even though they were strangers who would most likely never meet again. Who would have thought that something like this could happen? And to think she'd been nervous about going to California.

On the table in front of her were the gifts she'd just finished opening: a pair of crystal champagne flutes and a bottle of champagne, a beautiful coffee table book about the wine country, a CD called *Songs for Young Lovers,* a royal blue velvet wine bottle carrier, a funny-looking gizmo for opening wine bottles, a small framed print of a vineyard scene, and a pair of hunter green sweatshirts embroidered with "Sonoma" in creamy script. Lynne had been taking pictures that she promised to get developed tomorrow.

The young man who'd been bartender the first night was back again, and Maria noticed that everybody had now settled into different wine preferences. She herself was drinking a cabernet, which went nicely with that scrumptious pesto, cheese, and dried-tomato torte. When Pat told her the torte had been made by the woman who gave the cooking lessons the other day, Maria was almost sorry she'd missed the class. But only almost. She'd done a lot of cooking in her day, more than enough for several lifetimes. Maria was quite content to cut back rather than learn new recipes. She'd feel obligated to try to make them again, and then Guido probably wouldn't like them anyway.

"Happy Anniversary!" Angela's voice trilled behind them, and Maria twisted in her seat, surprised and delighted. Mr. Rutledge hadn't been particularly cordial this afternoon when he came upon her in the baby's room, and she thought he might not want Angela to attend. But here was Angela, beautiful and smiling. "Stephanie insisted that we had to come out and congratulate you."

Angela wore a long, black, peasant dress with full sleeves and scarlet smocking on the yoke, and she had the baby on one arm and a bottle of Dom Perignon in her other hand. Maria reached instinctively for the baby, and Angela handed her over without a murmur, the folds of her dress draping gracefully as she bent down to transfer the precious cargo. She was still as striking as she'd been the first night they were here, but now the young woman had dark smudges under her eyes and an anxious air that hadn't been present Sunday night when they all first met on this patio.

"You can save this for later, if you'd like," Angela told Guido as she handed him the chilled champagne bottle. "And don't tell the chamber of commerce, but it isn't from Sonoma."

Guido beamed as he took the bottle. Maria thought he looked fantastically handsome in his navy suit, with a crisp white shirt and a burgundy and navy and gold striped tie. He'd insisted that they wear their fanciest clothes once he realized what was happening, that these ladies actually intended to put on a party in their honor. Maria was glad he had.

"This should be shared with all of you," he announced. "You have touched my heart tonight."

The bartender took the bottle, opened it with a flourish,

then poured the first glasses for the anniversary couple. Most of the others declined, sticking with their various preferred vintages, but a few moments later, everyone but baby Stephanie was holding a glass. Maria noticed that Angela herself had opted for the champagne, which pleased her. The girl needed to relax.

Guido stood and raised his glass. "A toast to my bride," he said, looking down at Maria with such love and intensity that she felt her eyes fill with tears. "For fifty years she has been the light of my life and the center of my world." He clinked his glass to hers, then leaned down and kissed her. When he stood up, he smiled and looked around at all of them. "And all these years, anyplace we've ever been, if there's a baby, that's where you'll find my Maria."

Everyone laughed, including Angela, and after a certain amount of glass clinking all around, people drank.

"Where were you married?" Alice Harper asked.

"Our parish church," Maria said, "in Boston. I had the most beautiful dress that my aunt made, with satin and lace and a thousand tiny seed pearls on the bodice. Aunt Luisa was such a wonderful seamstress. All my daughters wore that same dress. And all of them were married in that same church."

"What nice roots you've put down," Angela told her.

"It's just our life," Maria answered with a shrug. "All of you, any one of you would have a story just as interesting."

"I don't think so," Pat Martell said. "We got married at Travis Air Force Base right before Mark shipped out. I wore a simple little beige suit and a Jackie Kennedy pillbox hat. Mark was in uniform, and none of our family was there. The entire service took seven minutes."

"I was in a wedding one time when the groom passed out right in the middle of the ceremony," Heidi Sandstrom said in a pronounced Texas twang. Everybody looked at her in mild surprise. This was the first public statement she'd made since arriving. "There we were in this stinking-hot little chapel in the middle of the summer in San Antonio, and all of a sudden, the groom starts swaying. The best man grabs one of his arms, and the bride gets the other, but he's fading really fast. Next thing you know, they've dropped to their knees and the minister's racing through the service so fast you can hardly even tell he's talking English. And then, just as he says, 'I now pronounce you man and wife,' the groom passes out completely. Flat out, facedown, out cold on the ground."

"Did the marriage last?" Lynne asked, sounding truly fascinated.

"Nope. Though I don't really believe it had all that much to do with the wedding itself. Sometimes a relationship is just doomed from the get-go, you know?"

"Do I ever," Sara Conner drawled, and everybody laughed.

**JEFF** Rutledge looked down at the crowd of strangers assembled on his patio and watched Angela laughing and talking with these people, giving every indication that she enjoyed their company. The old lady from back East was holding his baby again, while Angela sipped from a champagne flute.

If anyone had tried to tell him twenty years ago that he'd be a billionaire vineyard owner with a beautiful and accomplished wife, he'd have thought them daft. Back in his childhood, he hadn't believed he'd ever be anything but miserable and a misfit.

It wasn't easy being smart in the suburban neighborhood where he grew up in Kansas City. Nor was it easy being too tall and too skinny and too nearsighted to read the blackboard even in first grade, when the letters were six inches tall.

Not that he needed to read those letters. Jeff had been reading since he was two, had worked his way from Aachen to Zygote in the *World Book Encyclopedia* his parents had purchased on the occasion of his birth. He loved science fiction, and when the cranky librarian at their neighborhood library tried to force him to check out picture books, his mother raised a bit of polite hell and obtained special dispensation for him to access the adult collection. He needed a stool to reach the top shelves.

Some of his earliest and fondest memories were of taking things apart. Household appliances, radios, blenders, electric shavers, the stereo. A picture in the upstairs hall of his parents' house showed seven-year-old Jeff in the basement, surrounded by hundreds of parts that had once comprised a broken television set. Jeff wore scruffy chinos and a striped T-shirt, flashing a big grin and missing four front teeth. Beside it hung a picture taken the next day, when he'd reassembled the old Motorola, and it worked for the first time in years. Jeff wore the same clothes, and the TV showed the opening credits for *Charlie's Angels*.

He tired of being the neighborhood fix-it kid by the time he was ten. His teachers urged his parents to have him skip a grade, or maybe two, perhaps even to home-school him. He was bored in class, years ahead of his classmates in every subject but PE, forever buried in one fat sci-fi paperback or another. His parents did permit him to take one course each semester at the junior college, but they insisted he remain with his grade level in regular public school, their argument for keeping him there well-intentioned though ultimately misguided. "He needs the socialization," they'd tell his teachers, "to have interaction with other children." They couldn't, or wouldn't, understand that this interaction mostly consisted of being taunted and bullied and teased, of being beaten up regularly by miniature psychotics who later went on to careers in factory assembly and truck loading.

Liberation had come for Jeff Rutledge in the form of a personal computer, a primitive model that he put together from a mail-order kit. At the time, of course, he had no idea that this would be his ticket out of Kansas City, a key that would open worlds that hadn't yet been invented. That he himself would invent some of those worlds.

Every now and then, however, he wished he were back in the safety of his misfit childhood, working on Mrs. Blake's broken blender.

⚬━✕━⚬

**ANGELA** sipped her champagne and watched Maria holding Stephanie. With all the fuss about Vincent finding that gun, and the cops coming yet again, and the implications of finding a firearm that the police seemed to think might be the murder weapon—well, with all that, she'd been totally caught off guard when they got back to the house and found Jeff upset. And why? Because he'd found Maria in the baby's bedroom this afternoon.

Angela really didn't care what he said about it, though, and she'd soothed him into a semblance of civility before she came out here. There was something so wonderfully calming about Maria's presence that Angela had decided to take full advantage of her interest in the baby. Too bad there wasn't some way to pick a baby's grandparents, rather than just take the ones that were issued. Angela would have chosen Maria in a heartbeat.

Jeff's parents hadn't even seen Stephanie yet, not that it would mean anything to his dad, whose Alzheimer's was progressing so rapidly he could no longer travel. Jeff's mom, a nice enough woman, declined any offers of help, declared that she'd never put her husband in an institution, and refused to leave Kansas City while he was sick. Stalemate. Angela's mom, divorced for the third time, had come to visit two weeks after Stephanie arrived, stayed four interminable days, and worked her way through enough wine to float the houseboat she was living on with her current boyfriend down at Lake Havasu.

Maria and these other folks would all be gone in a few more days, anyway, and Angela didn't mind taking full advantage of her presence right now. While everything was so stressful and chaotic, it was a relief to have one less thing to worry about. Rosalita was perfectly adequate, of course—Angela had interviewed dozens of potential housekeeper/nannies before selecting her—but she didn't seem to have the psychic bond with Stephanie that Maria did.

Lynne Montgomery was wandering over now, looking just a little too casual for Angela's liking. "I hear there was some more excitement over at the winery today," Lynne said nonchalantly.

Angela nodded, reluctant to volunteer anything. She suddenly realized that she'd left the promised tour of the wine caves hanging. She polished off her glass of champagne and wished she'd brought out two bottles. The first one was already empty.

Lynne continued to stand there expectantly, taking an occasional sip from her own wineglass, smiling at her. Angela realized she had two possible courses of action: Tell her something to make her go away, or grab the baby and run. The second option was far more appealing, but the first was probably easier in both the short and long runs.

"Vincent Belladuce came by while we were cleaning up the mess in the winery, and he found a gun," she told Lynne, realizing that in ten minutes every one of these people would probably hear the story. She was half tempted to clap her hands and make a general announcement, but she didn't want to spoil Maria's party.

Lynne raised her eyebrows. "A gun that the police missed when they searched there the other day? I thought you said they searched really thoroughly, practically tore the place apart."

"The reason they didn't find it was they weren't looking in wine barrels," Angela explained tersely, and then she recounted the discovery as briefly as she was able. "For all I know, Vincent planted the gun when he pretended to find it. It was a tiny little thing, small enough so he could easily have palmed it."

"You think he planted the gun?" This raised a lot of interesting possibilities.

"Oh, I don't know. But I do know the police think it's probably the gun that killed Lance."

"They don't know for sure?"

Angela looked at her watch. "They probably do by now, but they don't seem in any hurry to share much information with me. It's some kind of rare, special little gun that only one company makes. A mini-twenty-two revolver. They were going to take it off and do ballistics tests or something to it."

"What about fingerprints on the gun?"

"They didn't seem too hopeful about that. Wine's extremely acidic, so anything metal that's immersed in it might not retain fingerprints. If it was immersed, that is, not just dunked when Vincent pretended to find it. I really don't know. But regardless, Vincent had his paws all over it, so they'd probably only find his prints on it, anyway." She frowned, then muttered, "Which maybe was his idea."

"Are you saying you think he killed his nephew?" Lynne asked.

"Stranger things have happened. That family's all a bunch of hotheads. If Vincent got mad at Lance, I could see him doing that in a fit of passion and then trying to get rid of the evidence. It wouldn't be the first time he killed somebody, you know."

"I only found out about his previous conviction yesterday," Lynne said. "I must say I was rather surprised."

"Nothing about that family would surprise me anymore. And Vincent lives just down in the town of Sonoma, so he can get here easily anytime."

"Why would somebody hide a gun in a wine barrel?" Lynne wondered. She looked genuinely baffled.

"Beats me. If it were my gun, I'd be more inclined to just toss it in a ditch."

Lynne still looked puzzled. "Does this mean Lance was in the winery? I thought you said he didn't have access anymore."

"That's what I thought, too. He wasn't supposed to," Angela answered, scowling. "But they found a master key on his key ring, and Vincent admitted that after we changed the locks and security codes, he gave a key and the new code to Lance."

"What for?"

Angela threw up her hands. "Why do the Belladuces do anything? Don't ask me to come up with rational answers for the stuff that family does. They're all crazy." Time to change the subject. "So, where are you folks going for dinner tonight?"

"Sonoma Bistro," Lynne answered. "You know, I never did get entirely straight what happened in the winery. Obviously, I haven't been over there this year, but I remember the place having dozens of barrels on racks. Was all of that wine poured out?"

Angela shook her head. "Nope. You couldn't really pour it

out, because the only opening on most of the barrels is the bung-hole on top. Even turning it sideways it would take a long time to drain. We pump it out to bottle it. No, the bungs were removed from the barrels, and then they took an ax to the ends of the ones that were opened. That's how it all poured out. Of course, there were about two dozen barrels of really special vintages that weren't emptied, weren't bothered at all. Which suggests to me that this wasn't exactly a random act of vandalism. That whoever did it knew which were the best wines and left them strictly alone." Would Lynne pick up the implications of this? Or would she be as dense as that Detective Shaw?

Apparently, she'd be dense. "Well, isn't that good news?" she asked with a puzzled expression. "That those barrels were spared?"

"It just makes me figure that it was an inside job. I don't think the police really understand that those barrels were very deliberately left undamaged. And that putting the gun into the particular barrel where Vincent found it made it unlikely that anybody would find it for a long time. That barrel was full of last year's cabernet, which wouldn't have been decanted and bottled for at least another year and probably even longer than that."

Lynne made a dismayed face. "Yuck! Wouldn't it ruin the wine to have a gun in it?"

Angela nodded. "Of course. But even then, we wouldn't necessarily realize what had happened, at least not till we drained the barrel. Now and then, a barrel just goes bad. Vincent uses wild yeasts for fermentation, and sometimes those just turn weird on their own. The wild yeasts make a finer wine when they work, but there's some risk involved. You have more control with a commercial strain of yeast."

"Will they be able to tell whose gun it is?" Lynne asked

"You'd have to ask Detective Shaw about that, but don't expect her to actually tell you anything significant. I find out more about what the police are doing from watching the nightly news than from anything they tell me." She looked pointedly at her watch. "You folks had probably better get going, and I need to give Stephanie her bath. But listen, I promised to show you all the caves, and I haven't forgotten. What's your schedule tomorrow?"

"There's an all-day Russian River appellation tour that some of the folks are going on. I'm taking a small group in the morning to see the redwoods at Armstrong Redwoods State Reserve, and we'll all have lunch together at Korbel's."

"You'll enjoy that," Angela said. "It's really pretty there, over by the Russian River."

"I know. It's one of my personal faves. Anyway, after that, I'll bring Ruth Atherton back here for the afternoon and probably connect with the others somewhere on their afternoon travels." She smiled. "Or maybe I'll play hooky and take a nap. Think I can get away with it?"

"Probably," Angela agreed. "You want to try to go see the caves when everybody gets back? Or would it be better to do that in the morning before everybody leaves?"

Lynne cocked her head. "It's tough enough getting everybody going in the morning as it is. Why don't we do it late afternoon, if that'll work for you? It looks like we'll have leftover hors d'oeuvres from tonight, so we can just schlep those over and open a bottle of wine and call it happy hour."

"Sounds good to me," Angela told her, hoping she sounded more sincere than she felt. "And now I really do need to feed Stephanie and give her her bath."

As she turned to get the baby, she glanced up at Jeff's workshop and saw a man-sized shadow behind the partly open miniblinds. The shadow abruptly disappeared.

A few minutes later, she heard the rumble of the garage door opening on the other side of the house, followed by a muffled roar as Jeff's Porsche sprang to life. She fought the impulse to run after him, to ask where he was going and why he was abandoning her yet again. Buy why bother? He'd tell her he was going down to Sunnyvale, to deal with problems at InRut. Maybe he was, and maybe he wasn't. She wouldn't give in to her paranoia by calling down there to check on him, and if he was leaving at this hour, he probably wouldn't be back before morning.

She felt terribly, totally alone.

*Chapter 19*

HEIDI Sandstrom was bored silly.

Sometimes Hake just didn't realize how ridiculous his scheming and plotting could be, how much easier things could be if he'd just come out and say what he wanted. He made everything so much more complicated than it needed to be. All this skulking around looking at vineyards while pretending to be interested in the tour was utterly pointless, as far as Heidi could tell. They were all pretty much alike, the places in Hake's price range, and none of them were too terribly appealing when you got right down to it.

This was pretty country, though, she had to admit that. Green and rolling, with grapevines everywhere you turned. Couldn't exactly imagine herself living here, though it would be all right to visit now and then, she supposed. Hake had already commissioned a dozen designs for the labels on his private reserve wines, wines that at this point existed only in his mind. He had also cleared a section of the locked, climate-controlled wine cellar in the basement of their Highland Park home, preparing to fill it with his private stock.

That was really Hake's goal, of course. Possession. To have his own wines in the wine cellar, not to be here watching the stupid grapes grow. Once Hake bought one of these vineyards, Heidi was fairly certain he'd lose interest in the place itself. He didn't even really like California wine, but once he realized he couldn't ship it to his home, that was that. Nobody told Hake Sandstrom he couldn't do something. He'd been determined to find a way to get his wine, and owning a stupid vineyard was his solution.

He certainly didn't want to move here. Hake was a fourth-generation Texan, with ancestors who'd fought at the Alamo and a longhorn tattoo on his butt. His heart was in Texas, and his work was in Dallas, putting in long hours at the office and even longer hours on the golf course with clients and potential clients.

Heidi wouldn't be expected to relocate, thank goodness. The level of slovenliness in this area was decidedly unappealing. Women didn't wear makeup, and men didn't hold doors, and everybody wore jeans all the time. Old jeans, at that. It was very tiresome.

There'd hardly been any drinking today, since they'd golfed in the morning and spent most of the afternoon being pampered at the spa. But it hadn't taken long to get buzzed once they returned to Villa Belladuce. Hake had a couple of half-empty wine bottles in the room—all the oxygen meticulously removed, of course—and they'd finished off most of them before coming out to that silly anniversary party.

Not that Heidi objected to the party, which was sweet in its own little way, but she was growing very tired of this bunch of people, and the end of the week couldn't come soon enough to suit her. She was going to have to start paying more attention to how much she drank, too, since wine calories were calories nonetheless, and she didn't look forward to dieting on her return home to work off a trip she hadn't even enjoyed.

Hake's capacity for alcohol had increased dramatically in the three years that they'd been married, although Heidi secretly believed that *she* was the one with true reason to drink:

Hake's wretched children from his marriage to that pudgy hag Susan. The kids were Heidi's contemporaries, in fact, which had created some awkward moments. Hake Jr. was two years older than she was, and Lizbet a year younger. Age was not a subject they discussed, however, not since that difficult conversation when both realized that Lizbet's sorority house at UT had been only one door down from her own, and that they'd both been in residence at the same time.

A bigger problem than age was that Hake's kids had hated Heidi from day one, as if it were her fault that Hake had tired of their frumpy mother. Her husband was determined that everyone would get along, and he pretty much ignored the undercurrents of antagonism. Hake chose to believe that all was merry and bright whenever his happy family was assembled, and Heidi did her part by bombarding her stepchildren with exaggerated affection. Their discomfort made it all worthwhile.

"Let's go by Merlina," Hake suggested as they left the Sonoma Bistro when dinner finally ended. He'd been pleased to find baby lamb chops on the menu, had wolfed down both of his and one of Heidi's, and seemed exceptionally chipper.

"I'm tired," Heidi said. "It's been a long day, sugarplum."

Actually, it had seemed considerably shorter, since they weren't cooped up in a limo, racing from one winery to another, but had been calmly rooted in one general location for the duration.

The high level of social energy required here was starting to really get to her. Ginger Conner had attached herself like a barnacle to the Sandstroms at dinner, polishing off close to two bottles all by herself. Ginger was, she had to admit, a good enough drinking companion. She knew a million jokes and at least half of them were funny. Even so, Ginger had a coarse mouth and thick thighs and talked far too much about her dreary job. She was not someone Heidi would voluntarily choose to party with or even to know.

"It'll only take half an hour," Hake promised, revving the engine.

But naturally it took longer. Everything always did. Hake

was really flying in the Jaguar, so they got to the Merlina vineyard and winery fast enough. But once he'd cut his lights and slipped down the roadway into the deserted grounds, he seemed to think they had all the time in the world. They got out and walked around, circling the winery building and the unimaginative little house behind it.

The outside lights were on sensors that lit the grounds up as they walked around. They'd already looked at this place once in daylight, and Heidi wasn't sure what Hake thought he'd accomplish by seeing it at night. She could have told him it would feel spooky and saved them both a trip. She also suspected she was ruining a brand-new pair of silver sandals.

"I'll wait in the car," Heidi told him. "I'm freezing." Which was true enough.

"Just a few more minutes," he promised. When Hake said "a few more minutes," Heidi had learned to translate that into half an hour, minimum. So she got back into the Jag, took off the sandals, and closed her eyes for a moment's rest.

She was half asleep in the front seat when Hake got back in and roared out to the highway. But they hadn't gone half a mile when a wailing siren pierced the night, and a wild display of flashing lights exploded behind them.

Some days it just didn't pay to get up.

**LYNNE** had decided not to wait up for the Sandstroms when everyone returned to Villa Belladuce from dinner. What she really needed and wanted was a good night's sleep, with no cats yowling or bodies being left at the winery or clients being arrested for murder. As she drifted off, she thought about the high school student who had come to Booked for Travel on Career Shadow Day, a sweet, vivacious girl who had been convinced that Lynne's job was the most glamorous in the world. The illusions of youth, she decided, were truly precious.

When the cell phone rang some time later, interrupting a perfectly lovely dream about visiting the redwoods with

Monty, she awoke confused and disoriented. Hearing Heidi Sandstrom's twang brought her instantly awake.

"Something awful has happened," Heidi announced. "Hake's been arrested."

Lynne shook her head like a dog coming out of the lake, hoping to get her brain engaged more quickly. "What are you talking about? What happened?"

"We went for a drive," Heidi said, "and I guess Hake was maybe speeding a little, and he got pulled over. They busted him for driving under the influence."

Lynne made a mental note to send a check to MADD. There was a sweet kind of justice to this, after all of Hake's arrogant statements about not requiring a driver, thank you very much. She was fleetingly grateful that her clients for this trip all signed waivers stating that any time they didn't use Booked for Travel transportation, the agency had no liability.

"Do you want me to call your lawyer? Mr. Morelli?"

"Well, of course," Heidi answered irritably. "Why do you think I called? And as soon as you do that, come pick me up."

**FINDING** Mr. Morelli turned out to be surprisingly easy. When she told his service it was an emergency concerning Hake Sandstrom, she was patched through in less than two minutes.

Len Morelli didn't even sound sleepy. "I'll come on up and bail him out," he promised. "I live in Marin, so it won't take me that long to get up there. By the time I get there, he should be sobered up enough that they'll let him go. Where's Heidi?"

"Tapping her little toe at the jail, waiting for me to pick her up."

Morelli laughed. "I won't keep you then. Did they wreck the car or anything?"

"Not that she mentioned."

"Then tell Heidi I'll take care of getting the car back, too. You get me any pictures yet?"

"I shot some at the anniversary party for the Ambrosinos,

yeah. But I couldn't go down to the winery, because the cops were there again this afternoon."

"Really?" He sounded genuinely interested. "Why?"

"Ask them," she told him. "I've got to go pick up Princess Heidi."

⚬══╪══⚬

**IN** the morning, Lynne might have thought it was all a bad dream except that the clothes she'd stripped off to get back in bed were lying on the floor, and a dispirited paper coffee cup from a twenty-four-hour convenience store sat on her dresser.

She found the Sandstroms' Jaguar back in the Villa Bella-duce parking lot when she left for her morning walk and decided she'd let the happy couple sleep as late as they wanted. The Texans weren't much on breakfast, even on good days.

Lynne sat at breakfast with the Harpers and Martells and quietly filled them in on her nocturnal adventure, concluding with the news that Heidi had told her last night that the Sandstroms would not be on today's Russian River appellation tour.

"Hallelujah," Pat said, shaking her hands in the air as if attending a revival. "I must say I wasn't looking forward to spending the day with them." The Harpers and Martells were taking the appellation tour today as couples.

"Oh, I had it set up so you four would have your own limo," Lynne told her, "but now that it's just six of you, I called and changed it to a single stretch limo."

"I wish I could have seen Heidi in jail," Alice said wistfully. "Trophy wives don't generally construe 'for better or worse' to include spending the night in the pokey."

"She wasn't really in jail," Lynne clarified, "and she wasn't arrested. They just brought her along because she wasn't sober enough to drive the car after they arrested Hake."

"Did she prattle all the way back?" Alice asked.

"Actually, I think she passed out for a while. Though she called it 'dozing off.'" Lynne smiled wickedly. "You want more details, maybe you could take her a breakfast tray."

"That's okay," Alice said quickly. "But I must say, Lynne,

if I'd known your tours were this exciting, I'd have started taking them ages ago."

"If this one gets much more exciting," Lynne told her, "I'll consider looking for another line of work."

"Maybe the problem is that you billed this as a full-service tour," Pat suggested.

"You may be right," Lynne said. "I definitely need more fine print."

⟨━━━✦━━━⟩

**DETECTIVE** Lauren Shaw arrived at Villa Belladuce shortly before they were scheduled to leave for the redwoods. The Russian River appellation tour had just departed in a long, white limo carrying the Harpers, Martells, and Conner sisters. After the morning visit to the redwoods, everybody would meet up for lunch at Korbel's.

"I'm glad I caught you," Detective Shaw said. "I see Mr. Sandstrom's car in the lot. Is he here?"

Lynne nodded. "As far as I know, though I haven't seen him this morning. Did you know he got popped for drunk driving last night?"

"That's part of the reason I'm here," Detective Shaw said. "Before I go talk to him, do you have a minute?"

"We were about to leave, but nobody'll mind if we're delayed a few minutes. You want some coffee? I think there's still some breakfast stuff out, too."

"Only if you'll join me."

"I already ate," Lynne told her, "and I try to be careful not to eat more than three meals a day on this trip, or I'd come home twenty pounds heavier."

She led Detective Shaw into the breakfast room, where Farrah was breaking down the buffet. The detective selected a gooey pecan roll, poured herself some coffee, and followed Lynne onto the patio. "Now," she said, "about Counselor Sandstrom. I understand you picked his wife up at MADF last night." The Main Adult Detention Facility, beside the Santa Rosa Courthouse, was a big, grim place.

"Quite true," Lynne told her. "You know, I've never had a

client arrested on a tour. And now I've got two of them. This is not going to be good for business." She realized suddenly that she was babbling, and babbling to a cop, at that. The Sandstroms had really gotten to her.

Detective Shaw laughed. "Extenuating circumstances, at the very least. What I need to know now is why Hake Sandstrom is on your tour."

"I have no idea," Lynne admitted, "and I've given it a lot of thought. There are certain types of people who enjoy taking organized tours, and the Sandstroms don't fit any of the usual categories."

The category they fit best, actually, was Obnoxious Rich Jerks.

"We have information that he was planning to buy a vineyard," Detective Shaw said. "Were you aware of that?"

Lynne shook her head slowly. "No, I sure wasn't." Random bits of information suddenly dropped neatly into place. "But I don't have any trouble believing it, now that you bring it up. This morning, the Ambrosinos told me that he detoured to look at some places when they were out with the Alexander Valley tour. Maybe those were places he was interested in. He and Heidi kept going off on mysterious drives, too. His secretary made their reservations for this tour, and she called back about four times to reconfirm that we'd be staying at Villa Belladuce, but I didn't have any contact with either of them until they arrived. However, his being here makes a lot more sense if he had a hidden agenda."

"Did he ever mention anything about a syndicate that he was part of that made an offer for Villa Belladuce?"

"You mean before the Rutledges bought it? Or now?"

"Before." Detective Shaw considered for a moment. "I wonder if he's expecting it to go back on the market. I'll let you go now, Mrs. Montgomery, but until I get some clearer answers on what they're doing here, I'm going to tell the Sandstroms not to leave the county without permission. Can you give me a hand with that?"

Lynne snorted. "How do you think I could force them to stay? I'm a tour guide, not a nanny, and they're adults. They wouldn't even need to make airline reservations. They flew up in their own plane. I can't very well fling myself onto the tarmac."

The detective smiled. "Of course not. But you could give me a call if you think they intend to leave."

"Sure. Will you stop them?"

The detective shrugged. "Maybe."

"Maybe's good enough for me," Lynne said. "But I probably won't see them till we get back here tonight. And I'm glad you came by, because everybody has been really curious about that gun that turned up down at the winery yesterday afternoon." Somebody had, in fact, brought up Jeff Rutledge's fabled gun collection.

Detective Shaw didn't say anything for a moment.

"If you can't tell me, I understand." Lynne held her breath. On the one hand, she was frantically curious. On the other, ignorance was bliss.

The detective looked at her thoughtfully, then seemed to make a decision. "Have you ever met Vincent Belladuce?"

Ah, yes. Vincent Belladuce, that charming vintner who'd done hard time for manslaughter. "Yeah, I've met Vincent. He was usually around when we used to come for tastings, back before the bed-and-breakfast. I believe he's the one who actually makes the wine. Why?"

"He's the one who found the gun in one of the damaged wine barrels."

Lynne frowned at her. "*In* the wine barrel?"

Detective Shaw nodded. "So he says. It's a twenty-two-caliber Magnum minirevolver that he claims must have been slipped into the barrel through the bunghole."

"You mean through that sort of cork thingy on the top of the barrels? Those things are awfully small, I thought."

"Yeah, they are. The standard wine barrel bunghole is two inches in diameter, and these were standard barrels. Like I said, it was a very small gun."

"I don't really know anything about guns, other than that my son always says I should learn how to shoot just in case, and I keep telling him I don't want to. How small is small?"

The detective used her hands to illustrate. "A bit over five inches long and a little less than three inches tall. But the way the handle's curved, it would slip right in."

It sounded like the kind of goofy novelty a gun collector might own.

"Is it the gun that killed Lance Belladuce?"

"It looks that way, though I won't have the ballistics results till later this morning. He was killed with a twenty-two, we do know that."

"Can you trace the gun?"

The detective nodded again. "We already have. It was reported stolen from a residence in Los Angeles eighteen years ago."

"You can tell for sure it's the same gun?"

The detective nodded. "We can. And I'm keeping you from whatever you're supposed to be doing right now, aren't I? Where are you folks going today?"

Lynne smiled contentedly. "Well, you probably know more than I do about where the Sandstroms are going. Some of my people have already left to tour some Russian River wineries, and they'll meet up with my other group at Korbel's for lunch. Today should be a lot of fun, I think. We're going out to Armstrong Redwoods State Reserve. Then later this afternoon, Angela told me that she'll be ready to give us a little tour of the wine caves here. I'm not counting on that happening, though."

"No reason to think it won't," Detective Shaw said. "There wasn't any damage down in the caves." She stood and gathered her dishes. "Thanks for the breakfast. And enjoy the redwoods. I wouldn't mind coming along myself, except I think that I'd probably put a bit of a damper on things for you folks."

Lynne stood, too. "Not if you let people think that you were the one responsible for arresting Counselor Sandstrom. That might earn you a medal."

## Chapter 20

**HAKE** Sandstrom was already awake when Detective Lauren
Shaw knocked on the door of Abruzzi on Thursday morning.
He'd been yearning for the kind of hotel with a coffeemaker
in his room and a room-service waiter a phone call away. He
desperately wanted coffee, but he didn't want to run into any
of the Sonoma Sojourn yahoos this morning. Normally, he'd
send Heidi, but Heidi was still sleeping, and he wanted to
keep her that way for now. She'd been plenty unhappy when
he got back last night.

Hake opened the door just a crack. "Yes?"

"Mr. Sandstrom, I need to speak to you for a moment," Detective Shaw told him. She seemed awfully alert and determined.

"My wife's asleep. Come back later."

"I'm afraid I need to talk to you now, sir. Why don't you
come out and join me on the patio?"

Hake considered his options, hated them all, and said, "I'll
be right out."

He dressed hurriedly, careful not to disturb Heidi. By the

time he got out to the patio, all the Sonoma Sojourners seemed to be gone, and Detective Shaw was sitting at a table looking out over the vineyard.

"What can I do for you?" he asked, pulling out a chair and sitting down.

When she told him, it was even worse than he'd feared.

⚬━━✦━━⚬

**THE** last time Ruth Atherton had visited the redwoods, she was nineteen and in love.

She hadn't told the twins that, hadn't really shared any of the details of her earlier trip, other than that she'd come to California by bus with her friend Doris and that she'd been captivated by the majesty of these enormous and extraordinary trees. That had been enough to satisfy Ryan, at least, and while she suspected that Kelly wondered what she'd left out, her granddaughter had never asked directly. Ruth had chosen not to volunteer the information.

Now, as she sat beside Kelly and Ryan in the center row of Lynne's van, passing through endless acres of grapevines, she wondered why she hadn't. There was nothing shameful or improper about any of it, other than that Ed Masters, the object of her young love, was not the man she eventually married. But it had always seemed somehow disloyal to her husband, and then to her husband's memory, to discuss this other man, whom she had loved with all of her young heart and soul.

And so she hadn't.

Impulsively, she decided to rectify that omission now. She knew she could speak comfortably in this small group. Jessica Kincaid, seated up in the front passenger seat, might be slightly embarrassed, but it would be interesting to see her reaction. And the Ambrosinos, in the far backseat where Ruth could only feel their presence, without actually seeing them, would surely appreciate the story. They were far and away the most romantic couple on the tour.

"I don't think I ever told you," Ruth began tentatively, "just how it happened that I came out here all those years ago."

Kelly turned to look directly at her. "I thought it was some kind of high school graduation present from your parents."

Ruth smiled. "In a way. But I'd already finished a year of college at Lawrence by then, and my friend Doris, the girl I traveled with, was even older. No, I think that my parents were hoping that I'd stop moping about a beau who'd gone off to war." There, she'd said it. For clarification, she added, "Not your grandfather. I hadn't met him yet. This was another young man altogether."

"Really?" Kelly's gray eyes widened in shock, and for some reason, that pleased Ruth enormously. It was nice to know that she could still surprise the kids after all these years. Ryan, seated directly behind Jessica, didn't react. His eyes were aimed forward, watching his new girlfriend as he listened. For her part, Jessica kept her eyes on the road, straightened her back just a little, and politely stayed out of the conversation.

"Really. His name was Ed, and he'd gone up to Canada to enlist in the Royal Army to fight Hitler. The United States wasn't in World War Two yet, but quite a few of the boys from northern Wisconsin went to Canada to join up. It all seemed like a grand adventure at first." She sighed, remembering how Ed Masters's blue eyes had blazed with fervor for the cause. She had never tried to dissuade him from going, even though her heart was breaking at the thought of his departure. "Anyway, after a while, I slipped into a bit of a funk, and so my parents got together with Doris's. She also had a beau who'd gone up to Canada to enlist, and she was even droopier than I was. Her dad found a nice chaperoned tour for us to take, to see the western United States.

"I didn't think Ed would approve, but he wrote and told me he thought it was a wonderful idea, and that I should find a place where we could honeymoon when he came home. None of us had any idea how long that war would go on, of course. And so, off Doris and I went, in a big blue bus, and we saw all kinds of wonderful things. Geysers that shot up toward the stars in Yellowstone National Park and the Columbia River gorge, and Crater Lake, which was so impossibly blue it didn't look real. And then we got to the redwoods."

She shook her head as the memory washed over her. "It was so extraordinary, I don't think I can even find words to describe it. There was a tree that was big enough to drive a Chevrolet right through the middle of. I wrote and told Ed that I'd found our honeymoon spot, and he wrote back and said we'd get engaged when he came home on leave." She fell silent then, realizing she'd led herself and the twins down a path that none of them might be ready to travel.

After a while, Kelly spoke softly. "What happened, Gran?"

Ruth closed her eyes. "Ed was killed in a Luftwaffe raid on an English airfield a few months later. He never did come home." She could feel tears seeping through her closed lids, as Kelly's strong arm crept around her shoulders. When she opened her eyes a moment later, Jessica was wiping away tears in the front seat, and Kelly was also crying.

Ruth opened her pocketbook, found a pack of tissues, and passed them around. "I'm sorry. I didn't mean to put a damper on the day. I just felt I was being somehow dishonest about why I wanted to come here."

"Not at all, Gran," Kelly told her, toughened up again. "Thanks for telling us."

⚬━✦━⚬

**"WE'RE** almost here, folks," Lynne told her passengers ten minutes later as the van headed up a winding road toward the Armstrong Redwoods State Reserve, not far from Guerneville in the northwestern part of Sonoma County. Other, more spectacular stands of redwoods grew up north—a few hours up Highway 101, for instance, stood the stunning Avenue of the Giants, featuring that drive-through tree Ruth had mentioned—but this old-growth redwood forest was hard to beat for convenience.

They stopped briefly at the tiny visitor's center, gathered maps and brochures, then climbed back into the van and entered the park itself. A State of California pickup truck passed them, dragging its tailgate and spewing fumes. It felt like sacrilege.

"These are the tallest trees in the world," Lynne told her passengers. "There's one up north that's taller than the Statue of Liberty. These coastal redwoods can't take freezing weather, and they require a lot of water, so they only grow within about thirty-five miles of the ocean."

She suggested opening all the windows to enhance their appreciation, then drove slowly through the woods to give her passengers a sense of the majesty of the park.

"They're so straight!" Jessica marveled, craning her neck out the window. "And so incredibly tall. I can't even see the tops of them. There aren't any branches anywhere near the ground. This is amazing."

"Are these the oldest trees in the world?" Ryan asked.

"The oldest of these coastal redwoods are maybe two thousand years old," Lynne said, "but most of these trees are considerably younger than that. The giant sequoias that you find farther inland on the western slope of the Sierra Nevada are older and larger in diameter, but not quite as tall. The biggest one of those is the General Sherman. It's a hundred feet in circumference at the base and around thirty-five hundred years old. These redwoods are youngsters in comparison, and mostly only ten or fifteen feet in diameter."

"Only," Ruth murmured. "Only."

"I'm going to turn around at the picnic area up here and then come back to the Discovery Trail. That's set up so that we can take the wheelchair along it and get a sense of what this forest is really like."

"Awesome," Kelly proclaimed. "That's what it's like."

**WHAT** Hake Sandstrom wanted right now was a Jacuzzi and a pitcher of Bloody Marys. What he was getting was a lecture over greasy eggs at a hotel coffee shop. Heidi sat silently in dark glasses and had barely acknowledged the presence of Len Morelli.

"I can't represent you on this," Morelli told him.

"What the—of course you can. It's just a simple DUI."

"Not all that simple, Hake. Your blood alcohol was almost three times the legal limit."

"But I wasn't drunk. I felt just fine."

"Look, being functional at point two three isn't a very compelling defense, but that's neither here nor there. You need to talk to your new attorney about that."

Hake could feel the walls closing in on him. After he'd gotten rid of that bitch detective this morning, he'd called Morelli in a panic. But before he could get anywhere, Morelli cut him off, gave him some BS about conflict of interest, and suggested he call another lawyer.

This late breakfast was a compromise, but Hake noticed that Morelli had only ordered coffee. Not a good sign.

"Any plan I might have to buy property here is purely coincidental," Hake began. "It's just a misunderstanding, that's all."

"Hakester, there are prisons from coast to coast crammed with the misunderstood." Morelli held up a hand to forestall any reply. "I already have a client, and it's a conflict of interest for me to represent you. You should have told me from the beginning that you were interested in buying a vineyard."

Hake glowered. This was no fun at all. Heidi removed her glasses and stared down at a plate of fresh fruit. It wasn't going to be easy to wipe this experience out of her memory banks. At the very least, it would be expensive, though he was used to that. Heidi was a very expensive woman. "It didn't seem relevant."

"My client told me yesterday afternoon that Lance Belladuce recognized you and said hello that first night you all got here. Then he winked at Heidi."

Heidi tensed beside him, and Hake filed that away for future reference. "So?"

"So I'm looking for ways to get her off on a murder charge, and that means looking for alternate suspects. And like it or not, Hakester, that includes everybody else who was there when Belladuce got killed. Particularly if any of them knew the victim before they arrived."

"I barely met him—" Hake began. This was unbelievable.
He tried to do a favor for that mealymouthed little lady, and
now all of a sudden Len Morelli was fitting *him* for a lethal
injection?

Morelli shook his head and held up both hands this time to
stop him. "Don't want to hear it, Hake. Can't listen. I called
Jim Lassiter, and he said he'd be willing to take on your case.
If you want him, of course. Jim's an excellent attorney, and
he's local, which will help if you're dealing with local law enforcement."

Hake knew when he was beaten, though he generally didn't
like to admit it. He knew he'd be catching hell from Heidi
about this for months to come, maybe even years. But he felt
an overwhelming need to explain.

"I never met him alone," he began, speaking hurriedly before Morelli could shut him up again, or stick his fingers in his
ears or whatever. "I was in a syndicate that tried to buy Villa
Belladuce, and for a while we had the inside track." He didn't
like to think of the earnest money Lance Belladuce had pock-
eted just before he made the Rutledge deal. Sub rosa earnest
money, alas, that the young slimeball refused to return or even
to acknowledge. It had been a bite, and an exasperating one at
that. Hake didn't mind losing nearly as much as he minded
being snookered.

Hake spread his hands, palms up, and offered a disarming
smile. "Then the Rutledges swept in with their damned Internet fortune. And that was all she wrote."

Morelli shook his head. "I wish you hadn't told me that. I
wish you'd learn to keep your mouth shut. So I'm going to
leave you two in a moment. But before I go, you get Legal
Lecture Number Forty-seven, free of charge."

Hake sighed. Heidi looked up for a moment, seemed about
to say something, then turned her gaze back to her melon
balls. A wink? He wished he'd been smart enough never to let
Heidi within a thousand miles of Lance Belladuce.

"Your new attorney could tell you all this, too, and maybe
he will. But the rules are different in criminal law. In civil law,
you want to inconvenience the other party as much as you

possibly can. In criminal law, the other party is the state, and the State of California has more resources than you can begin to imagine. So if you want all this to go away like you say you do, you make nice to Detective Shaw or anybody else who wants to talk to you. In the presence of your lawyer, of course."

"Stupid bitch," Hake muttered. He looked at Morelli in his exquisitely tailored pinstriped suit, supple Italian loafers, and diamond ear stud. He'd made his chops at twenty-nine by springing a convicted murderer from death row on the basis of newly available DNA evidence, and he had never looked back.

"That's not relevant," Morelli went on mildly. "But here's what you need to remember. Lawyers make terrible clients, because we all think we know more than we do, and some of us just can't resist the tendency to get too cute. However, you're way past that point here. You're at the point where it needs to be 'Yes, ma'am' and 'No, sir' and at least the illusion of cooperation. Ask Jim. He'll tell you the same thing. The time to volunteer that you'd previously met the decedent was Monday morning, when they found his body. All you can do at this point is damage control."

He stood up. "Here's Jim Lassiter's number. Call him, and listen to him, and do what he says. And when this is all over, we'll tie one on and laugh about it. You can bring the wine. Heidi, I'm looking forward to spending time with you under more pleasurable circumstances. You take care of this rascal, all right?"

Heidi looked up at Len Morelli. "Don't you worry about that," she assured him in a voice dripping acid. "I *will* take care of him."

As Morelli left the coffee shop, she turned to Hake, and her eyes were like stilettos. Hake added another zero to the figure he'd projected it would take to buy his way back into her good graces.

"Come to Sonoma County," she told him, in what he recognized as a parody of his own original suggestion. "We'll have us a grand old time and buy us a vineyard. You know, if

I didn't think it would make us have to stay here even longer, I'd be tempted to kill you myself. Hakester."

◦━╼╾━◦

**JESSICA** had noticed that in California, places seemed to go out of their way to be accessible to the handicapped, above and beyond the grudging compliance with the Americans with Disabilities Act she'd seen in Atlanta. The Discovery Trail here was a classic example, expressly designed for the handicapped and featuring signs in both standard English print and brass-plate Braille. A rope was strung along the side of the trail to serve as a guide and handrail. They'd encountered other people in the parking area, but here, the Sonoma Sojourn group had the trail pretty much to themselves.

"Hey, this mulch looks like string cheese!" Ryan exclaimed. The mulch on the ten-foot-wide trail was long, flaked, and . . . well, stringy. "I can't get away from work even in the untouched wilderness."

Everyone laughed as they began wandering around, then started down the trail. A split-rail fence on either side of the ten-foot-wide nature trail was only partly finished, with supports bolted into Xs at intervals between long rails lying on the ground, awaiting assembly. Giant clover, in keeping with the scale of everything else, sported individual leaves two inches across.

Signs at regular intervals warned: Fragile Area—Stay on Trail. Strange to think that something could be this strong and regal and imposing and yet be genuinely fragile at the same time. It felt like a metaphor, Jessica realized suddenly, one she didn't want to think about just now.

She stayed back and out of the way as Kelly swung Ruth Atherton's wheelchair out of the rear of the van and opened it with a single expert sweep of her wrist. There was no doubt about one thing: Kelly was incredibly competent.

Jessica wasn't sure how she felt about Kelly right this moment, having changed her mind about Ryan's sister several times in the few short days they'd been at Villa Belladuce. Her first impression had been of Kelly as a wonderful, doting granddaughter, and Jessica had liked that a lot. Doting had quickly escalated into officiousness, however, with Kelly hauling her grandmother back and forth across the county, synchronizing watches, eternally edgy, refusing to leave the poor old woman alone. That Kelly was considerably less appealing.

Things had really changed, however, when it became apparent that—however briefly—Jessica and Ryan had some kind of minor-league romance in play. Kelly had immediately withdrawn as if scalded, becoming distant and cautious and ever so polite. Which might, Jessica supposed, simply be her customary initial reaction to Ryan's girlfriends. He said he didn't have anybody special in his life right now, but Jessica was willing to bet that Ryan had always had a girlfriend when he wanted one. He had such a charming, puppy-dog quality to him. Kelly, on the other hand, reminded her of a jungle cat.

Of course, it was entirely possible that nothing more would come of this, that Jessica and Ryan would kiss each other good-bye, head for Atlanta and Wisconsin respectively on Sunday, and never cross paths again. Falling in love on vacation might make a nice movie plot, but in the real world, it seemed fraught with complications. Starting with going home to different cities. Not to mention being associated in Ryan's mind with his grandmother's last days. He might prefer simply to put all of this California trip behind him, Jessica included, not so far down the line.

Jessica ordered herself to stop making future projections and predictions and think about something nicer. The story Ruth had told in the van on the way over here, for instance. The simple recitation of facts had moved Jessica to the core, had given her a sense that love was too precious a commodity to squander.

Kelly was back to being officious today, as she pushed her grandmother's wheelchair along determinedly, all upbeat and peppy. This was why they'd come, and by golly, she was going to make sure they all had a real peak experience. Ryan walked with Kelly and Ruth as they approached the Colonel Armstrong tree, proudly identified as being 308 feet tall, 14.6

feet in diameter, and 1,400 years old. Everywhere she went on this trip, people were spewing statistics.

"How can they know how old the trees are without cutting them down? I thought you had to count the rings to know for sure," Ryan said. He wasn't exactly ignoring Jessica, but he certainly wasn't paying her much attention.

"They guesstimate," Lynne told him. "Enough of them fall down or have been logged. Those they can count. Based on that, they have a pretty good sense of what size translates into in years."

"So many," murmured Maria Ambrosino. She and Guido walked slowly at the rear of the motley, wheelchair-led procession. "I'm glad we came to see this." She twisted her head and squinted up toward the faraway patches of sky.

Jessica looked up, too, through the thick canopy to streaks of sunlight breaking through branches hundreds of feet above the earth. "It doesn't seem real. And it's all so incredibly quiet."

"Very few animals live in these groves," Lynne explained. "There's so little light that there's not much for them to eat."

When Kelly pushed the wheelchair up a ramp so that her grandmother could see and feel the bark of a redwood tree, Jessica held back. She wasn't sure how she fit into this group or if she did at all. Ryan had invited her last night. He claimed that his grandmother had suggested she come along, and while that was enormously flattering, it also raised more questions than it answered.

She decided now to concentrate on the nature hike elements of the excursion and tentatively touched the thick red bark of a tree that grew directly on the side of the trail. "It feels like cork," she noted with surprise.

"Redwood bark is actually rather spongy, as much as anything from a tree can be. And the bark can be as thick as a foot," Lynne said. "Redwood itself is very disease-resistant and these trees are tough. The last major fire through here was in 1926, and you can see some of the trees that burned out at the center near their bases but still survived."

She pointed at a tree just off the trail that was almost completely hollowed out, like the places where Piglet and Pooh lived in the Hundred-Acre Woods. Jessica looked skyward. Sure enough, a hundred feet or so above the earth, branches grew out of the trunk, offering vivid green vegetation to the sun.

Ryan's grandmother was right about at least one thing: This would be an incredible place for a honeymoon.

———

**AT** a souvenir shop just outside the park, a crowd of French tourists swarmed about, examining redwood burl clocks and boxes and bowls and odd jewelry. The red and white vans in which the French group had arrived sat out front, labeled Van Rouge and Van Blanc, respectively. Everyone was jabbering away in French, consulting conversion tables for francs and dollars, purchasing expensive items that more often than not were remarkably tacky.

Kelly wandered among them, oblivious to the noise and the crowd. She was looking for exactly the right souvenir, something she could keep forever to remember this day. She settled finally on an exquisitely patterned little redwood burl bowl and didn't even turn it over to look at the price. When the harried man behind the counter rang her up, she was surprised at the cost. But she knew it didn't matter, that she would have paid ten times as much without blinking.

There was no price anyone could put on today. Like her grandmother over half a century ago, she was building a memory.

## Chapter 21

**ELEANOR** Whitson had lost track of what day it was, and she was having trouble telling the time of day because they never turned her lights out, and all she wanted to do was sleep. Sleep wasn't an answer, of course. Her dreams were filled with people who were gone—her husband, her son, her parents—and were sometimes worse than the reality of being awake. Still, sleep passed the time.

Her attorney, Mr. Morelli, was very nice. That much had registered, and she was grateful for his efforts on her behalf, even though she had no real sense of what those efforts were. Rebecca seemed to think that he was the right person to be helping her, and Rebecca's judgment was generally sound.

This business with the photo line-up that Mr. Morelli had set up now made her very nervous, however.

On Monday night, after dinner, Eleanor had decided to go back down to the winery and look around again, to see the place where Lance Belladuce's body had lain that morning, to try to wrest some sense from the long and baffling day.

Eleanor had hated Lance Belladuce for so long that when she first learned he was dead, for a strange and horrifying moment she thought she had willed it to happen.

It was a simple enough matter to slip out of her cottage and move through the shadows to the pathway that led through the woods to the winery. She was too strung out to sleep, even after drinking quite a bit of wine throughout the day and at dinner.

But when she got there, she found a pickup truck outside the closed winery door and heard the sound of indiscriminate banging and crashing coming from inside the building. Whatever was happening, she knew, was something she wanted no part of. And yet she couldn't make herself leave. So she stood paralyzed in the shadows, she had no idea how long, and waited while the noises went on and on. For a while there was also a lot of crashing that sounded like breaking glass.

She was so mesmerized that she almost didn't notice when the noises stopped.

When the winery door opened and three men came out into the night, she shrank back behind the shrubbery in terror. Whatever they were doing, it was obvious they weren't supposed to be there any more than she was. The men carried large tools—axes, sledgehammers, mauls, she wasn't sure what—which they tossed into the back of the truck with a cacophony of clanging that brought a series of vulgar epithets from the man who got into the driver's seat. The other men climbed into the pickup, and they drove off, creeping down the drive with no headlights.

When they had finally gone, she found herself so weak and frightened that she could barely muster the strength to go back to her cottage. And then, to top it all off, she practically stumbled over the Atherton boy and one of the girls, necking behind the cottages.

Eleanor had told the police about seeing the men early on, shortly after they first took her away for questioning. They hadn't seemed very interested. Mr. Morelli, however, believed that what she'd seen was extremely important. Now he'd arranged with the police for her to look at photographs and see if she could identify the men. He was a comforting presence beside her in the little room, across the table from Detective Shaw and another officer whose name she couldn't remember.

She had sent Rebecca back to her hotel because it was too painful to see her, had urged her to go home to Seattle. If there was anything good about this wretched situation, it was, ironically, that Eleanor was far from home. She might not know anybody here, but nobody here knew her, either.

"Mrs. Whitson," Detective Shaw began, "I'm going to show you some sets of pictures, and I'd like you to tell me if you recognize anyone in them from Monday night at the winery."

"It was dark," Eleanor said. Her voice sounded faint and feeble.

Mr. Morelli placed a hand on Eleanor's forearm. "But there were lights outside the building, and those lights were on, weren't they?"

She nodded.

"Then just do the best you can." He'd told her earlier that this was important. Anything she could do to help resolve questions about what else had been happening at Villa Belladuce might also help redirect police attention toward finding out who actually had killed Lance Belladuce. Since Eleanor knew that she hadn't—no matter what the police or anybody else might believe—this seemed an excellent idea, and one of the few things she was currently able to focus on.

Detective Shaw placed a set of six pictures in a little holder in front of her. "Do you recognize any of these people?"

Eleanor peered at the photographs. She'd been so sure before, and now they all looked so much alike. Dark-haired men, head shots, some that seemed to be police photographs and others that might be simple snapshots.

"I'm not sure," she said, "but I think this one might have been one of them." She pointed at a picture of an angry-looking fellow with a shock of black hair falling onto his forehead. It was one of the snapshots.

"Okay," Detective Shaw told her, giving no indication

whether she'd identified a legitimate suspect or an Italian movie extra. "Now look at these."

The second set of pictures had nobody who looked familiar. She gasped in dismay when the third set was put out.

"That's Lance Belladuce," she said in a tiny voice, pointing at a picture.

Detective Shaw nodded. "Do you recognize anyone else?"

There was another man in that set who might have been at the winery that night, and the fourth set held a photograph of the large, ferocious man who had been the driver. The fifth set had nobody familiar.

"Is there anybody else in any of these photographs that you recognize, or who looks familiar?" Maybe it was her imagination, but Eleanor thought that Detective Shaw sounded much friendlier now.

Eleanor pointed hesitantly at one picture. "This man looks like somebody I saw on a television program, but I guess that's not what you mean. No, just those three. And Lance, of course."

"Do you think you might be able to pick these men out of a lineup if we showed them to you with a group of others?" Not just friendly. Actually encouraging.

What did she have to lose? "I can certainly try," Eleanor promised.

⊙━✦━⊙

**LYNNE** had always been charmed by the Korbel Champagne Cellars. The collection of lushly landscaped, nineteenth-century buildings was far off the beaten path, nestled in a grove of redwoods on the north shore of the Russian River up near Guerneville. Joyous blossoms flowed out of beds and spilled down hillsides: airy cleome and graceful cosmos, lemony marigolds and short yellow sunflowers, pink nasturtiums and drooping purplish amaranth, scarlet zinnias and pink bedding begonias. Such a floral jumble ought to have appeared too busy, but it didn't. The place had a peaceful feel to it, a sense that whatever went on here had nature's blessing.

Plus, of course, this winery produced only sparkling wines,

the ones the ever-persnickety French didn't want anybody else calling champagne. Lynne had associated these since childhood with happy times and celebrations. Any time her father brought home a bottle of champagne, there'd been good news tied to it, and if that good news usually meant that the family was moving, at least it meant they'd be going because her father was moving up, or out, or somewhere that he wanted to be going. She learned quickly enough not to associate the champagne with the unhappy aspects of these moves, things like leaving everyone behind one more time, since most likely they'd have been moving anyway, happy news or no.

She and Monty had continued the tradition, even in the early days when all they could afford was cold duck. The two of them had even come to Korbel once before they had kids, on their way up the coast to camp in the redwoods. It had been a fairly soggy experience overall, but she still fondly remembered drinking champagne by their campfire and then zipping the sleeping bags together.

Now she sat with Ruth Atherton in a sunny spot outside the deli, where they'd be meeting up within the hour with the other Sonoma Sojourners, fresh from various Russian River wineries. The Ambrosinos sat at a nearby table, endearingly engrossed in each other. The kids were off taking the tour of the winery, one of the best anywhere.

"So, was your visit to the redwoods what you'd hoped for?" Lynne asked Ruth, who seemed less worn out than she had after previous excursions. Who seemed, actually, rather invigorated.

Ruth nodded slowly. "I think so. I tried not to have expectations, because I had so much emotional baggage going into this, and for some reason, I was terrified that the kids would disapprove if they found out I had a boyfriend before their grandfather. I know it sounds ridiculous when I say it like that, but there you are. An irrational fear is a fear nonetheless. Once I decided to just tell them, it all seemed much easier."

"For whatever it's worth, I think everyone was charmed. I know we were blubbering up there in the front seat. I come from a military family, so I can appreciate that your young man ran off to enlist in Canada. And I also know how difficult it must have been for you to have him go."

Which wasn't entirely true. Lynne's memories of her father's tours overseas and his other extended absences were actually rather tranquil. There'd been less excitement with him gone, but also less anger and formality. While he was gone, her mother always managed to negotiate the knife edge between relaxation and lack of discipline, an ability she'd passed along to her children. When Daddy came home again, however, everybody shaped up in a big fat hurry.

Ruth Atherton shrugged. "It was a long, long time ago, and it really doesn't matter much now. I'm actually far more upset about that poor Whitson woman. If she didn't kill that fellow, which I have great difficulty imagining, then it's absolutely dreadful to think of her locked up with a bunch of drug addicts and . . . well, you know. Criminals. And even if she did kill him, it's still hard to think of her under those conditions. She struck me as a rather mousy little thing, but she had her dignity."

*Dignity.* It wasn't a word Lynne would have attached to Eleanor Whitson, but it fit better than *murderer,* the other current choice. Lynne wondered fleetingly how the Sandstroms were doing, if Len Morelli had sprung them and if they'd hopped onto their private plane and gone back home. Detective Shaw would be mad if they split, but that was just too bad. If she wanted them to stay, she could keep them here herself.

"Well, there really isn't anything we can do for her, I'm afraid," Lynne said. "She's got a lot of money and a really good lawyer. If you have to be in trouble with the law, those are both good things to have."

Kelly and Ryan and Jessica rounded the corner to join them, full of sparkling wine and good cheer.

"You wouldn't believe what they're selling in the gift shop," Kelly announced. "Champagne shampoo, wine body lotion, and wine/glycerine soap."

"For the girl who thinks it's attractive to smell like a rescue mission," Jessica added. As everyone laughed, Lynne noted that the two young women seemed to have achieved a new level of comfort with each other. Though perhaps it was just tasting half a dozen varieties of bubbly, which would comfort almost anyone.

"There's a microbrewery here," Ryan announced. "Finally an alcoholic beverage that I understand."

"You seemed to be understanding that champagne pretty well," Kelly told him easily. Whether it was having success-fully visited the redwoods, or simply the champagne, Lynne noticed that the young woman was significantly mellower than she'd been all week.

"Before they grew wine grapes here, this was a major hops-producing area," Ryan went on. "The beer came first."

"Actually," Lynne said, "I think the grapes were here ear-lier, unless the hops grew wild. The Franciscans planted mis-sion grapes all up and down the King's Highway, El Camino Real, when they were building the California missions. But those weren't the high-quality wine grapes grown today, of course."

Ryan shrugged. "Whatever. They've got four different kinds of Russian River Ale here, and I plan to sponsor a little tasting of my own tonight. For whoever wants to join me."

"We're going to see the caves," Kelly reminded him.

"So? We can't carry bottles of beer into a cave?" Ryan asked.

"Maybe we can stop in Sonoma," Jessica suggested, "and pick up some more of those cheese curds."

Lynne watched as Kelly and her grandmother met each other's glance and grinned. It was a pretty good day all around, she decided. Old love exposed and approved, new love blossoming with familial blessing. Not half bad.

⊶⊰✦⊱⊷

**THE** Jaguar was in the parking lot when they returned to Villa Belladuce after lunch. The group Lynne had taken in the van immediately broke into smaller clusters, the kids talking about going back to Ravenswood or maybe down to Carneros, an area they had yet to explore. Ruth assured the twins that she would be sleeping soundly all afternoon and all but ordered them to leave.

Lynne braced herself and went to knock at Abruzzi, the Sandstroms' cottage. She had no interest whatsoever in seeing either of the Sandstroms, but she needed to know whether they intended to participate in any further activities. She wouldn't refund any of their fees, no matter what their plans. The contract all guests signed covered that issue pretty specifically, though an attorney might challenge it reflexively. Mostly, she was going because it was politic to make nice.

Hake grudgingly admitted her, wearing navy slacks and a white cardigan with an ostentatious gold monogram. Heidi, the mistress of pretension, probably had his initials sewn on his boxers as well.

Counselor Sandstrom, now thoroughly cleansed of whatever jail cooties he might have picked up last night, held a glass of red wine and did not seem happy to see her. Nothing in his demeanor approximated remorse for anything. Water ran behind the bathroom door.

"Yes?" Hake said irritably. "Did I forget to get my activities card punched?"

*Oooh. Things weren't going well. How nice.* "I just wanted to see how you and Heidi were doing, and if there was anything I could help you with."

His imperious glare was clearly intended to reduce her to a quaking little glob of jelly, but having grown up around Navy officers, she found it merely amusing.

"Was Mr. Morelli able to resolve your problems?" she asked delicately.

"I fired him. I have different counsel now."

Lynne thought about that for a moment. Len Morelli had been actively strategizing at lunch yesterday. Had this somehow backfired on Hake? Was Morelli trying to pin Lance's murder on either or both of the Sandstroms? It was an intriguing notion, if a rather implausible one.

"I see," Lynne answered, though of course she didn't.

Heidi emerged from the bathroom, clad in an expensive

little casual-wear outfit fashioned from cream and fuchsia silk with shiny gold buttons, fresh makeup troweled into place. It wouldn't be long before she started taking the occasional nip and tuck on her facial features and any other body part that displeased her. In a few more years, Heidi'd have her plastic surgeon on speed dial.

Right now, she looked even less happy than her husband.

"I was wondering if you planned to join us for dinner tonight," Lynne told them both, the essence of cordiality. "We're going to Marino's again." Marino's, the restaurant just down the road where they'd eaten the first night, was one of Lynne's favorites in the region. She liked to schedule Sonoma Sojourns for dinner there twice, since there was always more than one entrée she really wanted to try. Tonight she planned to have the portabello mushroom ravioli in basil cream.

The couple exchanged a glance.

"We'd be delighted," Hake told her expansively. "That was one of the best meals of the trip, wasn't it, sugarplum?"

Heidi offered a smile so radiant it had to be artificial. "I do believe you're right. It's bound to be a yummy meal."

A yummy meal? This was moving into *Twilight Zone* territory.

"That's good news," Lynne told them, matching Heidi's phony smile. She could play this game easily. "I know the others will be as happy as I am to have you joining us again." A neatly ambiguous statement.

Heidi crossed to the dresser where several half-empty recorked bottles of wine stood beside a clean glass, picked up the open bottle without even looking at it, and poured herself a hearty slug. Then she gave Lynne another dazzling smile. It was downright creepy.

"I've just learned of a crisis at my firm in Dallas," Hake announced smoothly. "I'm doing everything I can, however, to avoid having to go back and put out some fires."

*Yeah, right.* "We'd certainly hate to have you leave before the tour ends."

"That would be a pity," Heidi purred.

"We're finally going to have the tour of the Villa Belladuce wine caves," Lynne went on, "before we go to dinner tonight. And then there's a nice appellation tour scheduled for tomorrow up in the Dry Creek region, unless you'd rather come along on the Jack London tour."

"Who's Jack London? Does he have a winery?" Heidi asked.

"At one time he owned some vineyards," Lynne answered with a smile, "but he's been dead since 1916. Jack London was a famous writer."

Heidi's features contorted in a pretty little frown. "Books by dead people are so boring."

*Chapter 22*

MARIA could tell that Guido was tired, worn out from trying to keep up with all of these youngsters for the past five days. He was so young at heart that it always surprised and disappointed him when his body refused to cooperate.

When the Ambrosinos got back to Villa Belladuce early Thursday afternoon after lunch, he told her rather sheepishly that he thought he might like to lie down for a while.

"That's a good idea," she agreed immediately, turning down the bed and fluffing up his pillow. "You go right ahead. I think the young people have gone off somewhere again, so it should be nice and quiet." Ruth Atherton had gone directly to her cottage on returning, and even Lynne had announced her intention of taking a nap. "I may just rest a little bit myself."

Once Guido was settled, Maria closed the curtains, turned out the light, and lay on top of the covers. After a few minutes, Guido began to softly snore. Maria, however, found herself increasingly more awake. Finally accepting that she wasn't going to be able to sleep, she got up, put her shoes back on, and quietly went outside.

There was nobody on the patio, though a few tulle bows remained attached to chairs and shrubbery. She smiled as she remembered the party last night, the generosity and good wishes of all these dear people.

Now she stood outside her cottage, wondering if she had sufficient nerve to go knock on the Rutledges' back door, realizing there was no excuse whatsoever she could make for dropping by. And then, wonder of wonders, the back door opened. Angela came out, pushing one of those elaborate navy blue strollers that the young mothers all had these days, so different from the big, black baby buggy Maria had filled with her own children. Angela parked the stroller on the patio and went back inside.

By the time she emerged a few moments later, pulling an empty red wagon, Maria was leaning over the stroller. Stephanie beamed up at her, gurgling in delight.

◦━━✦━━◦

**ANGELA'S** first reaction on seeing Maria was annoyance. Enough was enough.

But then Maria looked up at her with frightened dark eyes, and Angela felt like an insufferable bully. It was ironic that in this crowd of people that was making her life so miserable, there was also someone who was so good with Stephanie, who made the baby's care seem so effortless. Because while she wouldn't admit it to anyone in the world, Angela was really quite insecure about her ability to care for this child. She'd always believed that motherhood was something that every female was hardwired to do, the proof being that the physical equipment was issued so indiscriminately. Not that Angela had the equipment herself anymore, of course. Which probably could be classified as irony, too, though not as readily.

She offered Maria a tentative smile. "I was just going down to the caves to set things up for your tour and tasting later. Would you like to join us?"

Maria's entire face lit up. "If I can be of any help."

"Well, of course you can." Angela gestured toward the

stroller. "I need to pick up some things in the breakfast room here, and then we can head on down. Could you push Stephanie's stroller?"

A few minutes later, as she rummaged around in the big Sub-Zero refrigerator selecting hors d'oeuvres to pack into a cooler, Angela thought about irony, a subject she understood all too well.

Given a choice, she'd have preferred to know nothing about the subject. This was knowledge she had gained at a terrible, incalculable price. She'd had plenty of time to ponder the implications of it all, however, when she lay in the hospital in excruciating pain after the accident. And then, much later, she had taken an entire course in the subject at Berkeley.

Because being at Berkeley at all was part of the irony. A big part. She certainly hadn't been headed in that direction as a teenager in Venice, California. She hadn't been heading in any direction at all, really, had been simply pointed forward in a vague way along with most of her friends and classmates at Venice High. She was a pretty good student, better than most, and she liked her math and science courses, though it wasn't cool to admit that in her circle. Occasionally she got genuinely enthusiastic about an academic project, but mostly she just skated.

Even as she seemed to be doing now. She'd always been good at it.

She finished packing the cooler and a case of wineglasses into the little red wagon and rejoined Maria and the baby outside. They started across the parking area toward the path through the trees, Angela in the lead. Then it happened.

"Are you limping?" Maria asked. "Did you hurt yourself?"

Oh, God. Had she hurt herself? *Just a bit, Maria. Just enough to change everything in the world.* Normally, Angela would brush off anyone rude enough to ask such a question, but she couldn't bring herself to be unkind to Maria. It seemed easier to just tell her the truth.

"I have an artificial foot," she explained, looking back over her shoulder, suddenly aware of the scars that ran in ribbons of shiny, welted flesh across her body, feeling them as if she were naked and they were outlined in hot, phosphorescent paint. "I was in a really bad automobile accident, and I lost my right foot."

*Lost* made it sound like something she'd misplaced, but she was accustomed to the euphemism after all these years, though nobody ever asked anymore, now that she and Jeff were so insulated from the world.

Maria gasped in dismay. "How terrible! You poor thing! What on earth happened?"

Her distress was so genuine, her interest so sincere, that Angela found herself telling the story she almost never told anyone.

"I was just a teenager," she said slowly, "not really a bad kid, but maybe a little wild." Though *maybe* was a gross understatement. Angela Lester had been right on the borderline between precocious and incorrigible, sliding toward real trouble.

She and her mother lived in a too-small Venice bungalow, in a schizoid neighborhood plagued by drive-by gang shootings, even as yuppie gentrification projects piled grotesque second stories onto decrepit 900-square-foot cottages. Police helicopters constantly thup-thup-thupped through the night air, beaming powerful searchlights on the yards and alleys below. Angela was fascinated by the choppers and often went outside to see where they were searching, to imagine who they were trying to catch. Sometimes, she knew, they were after her friends, kids who had cast their lot with adventure rather than conformity. That awareness was part of the thrill as well.

Her father was long gone, and most of the time, her mother had a boyfriend living in, guys who alternated between ignoring her altogether or paying creepy, revolting attention. Her mother waitressed nights, which left Angela at home with the boyfriends, an entirely unsatisfactory arrangement. The boyfriend who was living with them at the time of the accident worked at a sleazy auto shop on Lincoln Boulevard, turning back odometers and falsifying smog certificates. Ray watched a lot of sports on TV and drank cheap beer by the case.

When Ray started making passes at Angela, she deflected them at first by making smartass remarks and then by keeping her bedroom door locked and once, just before the accident, by having a couple of her male friends waylay and beat the crap out of him as he drove into the garage from the alley. When Ray staggered into the house, bloody and furious, Angela had expressed dismay as she sprang to dial 911, careful to keep the triumphant lilt out of her voice as she reported the assault.

"We were going up to Hollywood," she went on, editing frantically so as not to unduly shock Maria. "My friend Penny and me. It was a couple of weeks before Thanksgiving, Friday night, and my mom was working late. I was sleeping over at Penny's, and we were kind of bored, so we decided to go see my brother." To score some weed, actually. Bobby always had dope, and he always was generous. He had a little apartment in the Hollywood flatlands, running with a rough but exciting crowd, setting himself up for what Angela could see with the horrible clarity of hindsight was inevitable disaster.

"It had just started to rain, kind of a drizzle, the first rain at the tail end of a long, dry summer. That always makes the roads really slick, though I don't think either one of us realized it. We were just cruising along in the fast lane on the Santa Monica Freeway when it happened." The radio was blasting, and they were going eighty, buzzed on a couple cans of Bud they'd filched from the fridge, laughing at what a crummy job the windshield wipers were doing.

"You don't need to tell me," Maria said quietly. "It's all right."

But suddenly Angela felt an enormous urge to explain, to tell the story, to prove to Maria that she wasn't just another careless teenager. Though that was, of course, precisely what she and Penny had both been. Cocky teenagers with a deadly sense of immortality.

"I think I want to tell you," Angela said. "But what I know about the accident itself is only what I was able to reconstruct much later. It was all kind of fragmented and disjointed. I remember the car spinning out and Jenny screaming and a horn blaring, and a huge grinding crash, and heat and flames. The last thing I remember hearing was a man's voice, all panicky, saying, 'Forget about her, the car's gonna blow.' And after that, I don't remember anything for a solid week."

"Did the car explode?" Maria asked. They were almost at the caves now, coming along the back side of the winery.

"No. There was a fire, but I don't think the car actually blew up. You see, the gas tank in those old VW beetles is just in front of the seats, practically in your lap. And when we started getting smashed up, that tank cracked. Penny's cigarette started a fire. The only reason I survived at all was that there was a trucker a couple cars back who was stuck in traffic and had a fire extinguisher in his cab. He moonlighted as a welder, and he wasn't afraid of fire. He emptied that fire extinguisher into the car and saved my life. Fortunately, the gas tank wasn't very full. Penny was always running on empty."

"What happened to Penny?" Maria asked.

"She was killed instantly." Cold, hard words that, even after all this time, hadn't lost their horror.

"Oh my dear, I'm so sorry."

Angela tried to smile. "In the long run, it probably saved me. And if it hadn't happened, I don't know what I'd be doing right now, but I probably wouldn't have ended up here." She looked around. "Not that being here seems like such a great thing just now."

They'd reached the caves. As Angela stopped to find the correct key on her key ring, Maria leaned close to the window on the large, oaken door and peered into the dark interior. It was a double-wide door, large enough to bring a forklift in to haul the wine barrels around, but crafted to have an old-world look and feel, with wrought-iron hinges and heavy, distressed wood on the exterior.

Angela opened the door, stepped inside to disarm the alarm system, then pulled the red wagon inside. "C'mon in," she told Maria, "and I'll give you a sneak preview of what the others have to wait till tonight to see."

She showed Maria the layout of the place. Then, while Maria wheeled Stephanie down the various tunnels, speaking to her in Italian, Angela set up the tasting room. She devoutly hoped this would be the last Sonoma Sojourn group activity requiring her involvement.

And she thought about the road that had led from an inferno on the Santa Monica Freeway to a winery in Sonoma County, how unlikely it all seemed in retrospect and how totally her life had changed in the moment Penny's Volkswagen began its final, fearful skid.

During her long and difficult recovery, once she got past the first waves of bitterness and anger and despair, she had realized that whatever she might have intended to do with her life—and the plans had been fairly vague, centering on parties and hanging at the beach and maybe taking a course or two at Santa Monica Community College—things were very different now. She would never again be the carefree girl who had climbed into the little blue bug that November night.

It was September before she returned to Venice High on crutches, painfully adjusting to the first prosthetic foot and acutely aware that people whispered and stared and speculated about the horrific damage beneath her loose jeans and long-sleeved shirts. She didn't talk about the accident, and after a while, people stopped asking. She had finished her junior year's coursework with private tutors in her mother's newer, larger house in Mar Vista, purchased with part of the insurance settlement. Ray, the live-in boyfriend, was no longer interested in her.

She nailed the SAT, wrote an application essay about the accident that reduced her guidance counselor to tears, was accepted at seven colleges, and enrolled at UC Berkeley the following September. Three weeks into her second semester, she was hurrying down the steps of a classroom building when the wretched prosthetic foot detached and sent her sprawling into Jeffrey Alan Rutledge.

The first thing he said, after she assured him that she was all right, was, "How interesting." He was looking at the inadequate fake foot that had fallen off and rolled away when she fell. He helped Angela up and settled her on the steps, then re-trieved the wayward prosthesis, examining it as an exercise in physics, not as a handicap. He was very polite and sweet, and he was totally unlike the guys she had always run with.

He didn't know how to talk to girls, and couldn't make small talk, and disappeared for days on end when he was working on one of his computer projects. He wasn't even a student, officially, just a hanger-on who audited courses that appealed to him, and he had no interest in a college degree.

Nobody was more surprised than Angela when they fell in love. Each had been wounded by the world and each found comfort in the other's understanding. They learned ways to protect each other, and after living together three years, they went to City Hall on an April morning and got married. An-gela expected a quiet life in Silicon Valley, working at a biochem lab while Jeff developed operating systems, maybe adopting a child one day, since the accident had ended her childbearing prospects.

What neither had anticipated was that Jeff Rutledge's vi-sion was just quirky enough to be unique, and that a decade later, they would be absurdly wealthy.

*Chapter 23*

**BEFORE** Lynne left her cottage to resume her guide duties on Thursday afternoon—before she got out of bed after her nap, actually—she called attorney Len Morelli to find out what, if anything, she could do for Eleanor Whitson. Obviously, her official responsibilities had ended once the woman was carted off to jail, but Eleanor had paid a lot of money for this trip, and Lynne felt obligated to at least try to help. Besides, she felt sorry for Eleanor and didn't believe for a second that she'd ever killed a higher life form than a mosquito.

But Len Morelli wasn't in.

One down.

Next, Lynne called Detective Shaw. "You wanted to know if I thought the Sandstroms were getting ready to leave California," she told her. "Well, they say they're planning to stay, and they're all gushy and excited about participating in group activities. Which tells me that they're up to something. Oh, and Hake made a point of mentioning a crisis in his office, so he's definitely laying the groundwork to split, I'd say."

"Thanks for the heads-up," Lauren Shaw said. "And while

I'm talking to you, I might as well let you know what I just told Angela Rutledge. We've arrested two of Lance Belladuce's cousins for the vandalism in the winery. There's a warrant out on another man, who seems to have left town rather suddenly."

"Cousins. Would those be Vincent's sons?"

Lynne had never paid much attention to the Belladuce family tree prior to this visit, other than to know it extended back into nineteenth-century California, a relative rarity in the Golden State. Even with the help of contemporary newspaper accounts, she had trouble keeping them all straight. It would have been useful to consult the wall of family photos in the winery, but that didn't seem to be a likely option this year. And future visits weren't too terribly likely, either, unless the place changed ownership again.

Though, come to think of it, that wouldn't surprise her. Owning a winery didn't seem to be working out too well for Jeff and Angela Rutledge.

"No. These guys are second cousins on Lance's mother's side of the family."

"Have they admitted doing it?"

Detective Shaw laughed. "Not hardly. But they were identified by an eyewitness."

"Who?"

"I can't say right now, Mrs. Montgomery."

"Well, what about that gun?"

"What about it?"

"Did you get your ballistics tests back, or whatever? Is it the gun that killed Lance?"

A moment's hesitation. "I can't talk about that, either, I'm afraid. It's all part of an ongoing investigation."

Which sounded like a *yes* to Lynne.

Two down.

⚬━┼━⚬

**REBECCA** Whitson didn't answer her cell phone, but she called back half an hour later, as Lynne was dressing to meet the Sonoma Sojourners for the much-delayed Villa Belladuce wine caves tour.

"I'm going back to Seattle tonight," Rebecca said. "I don't know what else I can do here, and Len Morelli says there's likely to be a long wait before anything else happens. Mother keeps telling me to leave, and she won't talk to me when I go see her. If all I can do is feel helpless, I might as well do that at home." She sounded exhausted.

"I'm so sorry about all of this," Lynne told her. "Is she allowed visitors? Would you like me to go see her? I'll be in town through Sunday." The last thing Lynne wanted to do was visit Eleanor Whitson—or anybody else, for that matter—in jail. But she knew she had to offer.

"That's very kind of you, but she doesn't even want to see me. You don't have any of her things there, do you?"

"As far as I can tell, the police took all her personal effects. You should check with Len Morelli about getting them back. He'd know what to do. What's supposed to happen next? With your mom's legal situation?"

"He's going to try again to get bail. I have a feeling that's hopeless right now, because they keep arguing that she's a flight risk because she was packing to leave when she was arrested. I'm probably going to have to go down to L.A. and get a power of attorney or something to take care of her affairs there. In the midst of all the rest of this, I'd sure hate to find out that her phone or water were cut off because the bills didn't get paid."

**THE** way everyone had been carrying on all week about the caves tour, Heidi had expected something a bit grander. Maybe not as spectacular as Carlsbad Caverns, which she had visited with her North Dallas Girl Scout troop in fourth grade. Carlsbad Caverns was amazing, with dripping water and enormous underground rooms and huge, otherworldly displays of stalactites and stalagmites. Whichever was which, she could never remember. Either it was that stalactites held on "tite" so they wouldn't fall down, or that stalagmites "mite" fall down. Not that it mattered, and now that she thought about it, Carlsbad Caverns also had bats, which was a distinct negative.

No, it didn't have to be Carlsbad Caverns, but she had hoped for something a bit more interesting than this boring, phony-baloney cellar. In any cause, she suffered from mild claustrophobia and would never have considered coming if Hake hadn't insisted. It was part of their lawyer's join-in-and-have-a-swell-time instruction, which sucked big time.

It was downright chilly in here, and she was grateful the new pants outfit had such a clever little jacket, though she already regretted wearing the delicate bone sandals that went so nicely with it. This ground was dirty and dusty, and she could practically feel the fabric of her sandals inhaling the filth. Sonoma County was turning out to be very hard on her shoes. She'd be barefoot by the time she got home at this rate.

Lynne yammered on about different configurations used in wine cave operations, some of them apparently quite complex, and it amused Heidi to watch Hake nodding thoughtfully as if the information were new and exciting. The Villa Belladuce caves were a simple series of tunnels, shaped rather like a hand and lined with wine barrels stacked three high, marked on their ends with cryptic information about the contents.

It was, she supposed, atmospheric. At least if you liked dingy places that were likely to harbor spiders. The path sloped downward at a gentle angle, with low-wattage electric lights glowing softly on the walls. About twenty feet inside the cave, the ground leveled and opened into a large room, the palm of this underground hand.

"What do you use these giant barrels for?" Heidi asked Angela Rutledge, who was showing them around in her most annoying lady-of-the-manor way.

The room was filled with enormous ancient redwood wine barrels. They'd seen similar ones at some of the wineries, though she couldn't remember which. They'd even told a story at one of those places about pouring the wine out of one of them to put out a fire, sometime long ago.

"We don't use them for anything right now," Angela told her, rather dismissively. She was awfully snotty for somebody married to such a dweeb. And never mind how much money he had, either. Heidi had realized early on that it was just as easy to find a rich man with savoir faire and charm as one without. Though maybe that hadn't been an option for Miss High and Mighty who, according to Hake's research, had some really horrible scars.

"Off this central room," Angela went on, "half a dozen branches fan out down into the hillside."

And so the caves tour went, with Hake working overtime to charm Angela Rutledge, and Heidi counting the seconds till Sunday. Sunday, their bossy new lawyer had told them, was the absolute earliest they could leave Sonoma if they didn't want to complicate matters even more. Hake had resisted the advice at first and had privately told Heidi they could get to the airport and into the air in less than an hour if need be. It was nice to have options.

But meanwhile, they had been instructed—no, ordered—to stay with the tour group and go on all the stupid little excursions and act as if they couldn't be having a nicer time. This daunting and infuriating challenge would be easier, Heidi hoped, if she just kept a bit of a buzz on.

Accordingly, she began imbibing generously when the group returned from various solo excursions down the tunnels and gathered in a small tasting room located just off the central room. Everyone was here except the old lady with cancer and, of course, that mousy little lady who was in jail. She was so bland that Heidi couldn't even remember what she looked like.

They spread out around two simple oak tables. Angela brought out leftover hors d'oeuvres from last night, which Heidi avoided pointedly. She didn't do leftovers, not even doggy bags of shrimp. Meanwhile, Angela removed glassfuls of wine from three barrels on the wall of the tasting room, using a device called a wine thief. It looked something like a turkey baster.

That cute little Ryan seemed to be conducting some kind of

simultaneous beer tasting. He'd brought along chilled bottles of various beers that he proudly proclaimed had come from the Korbel microbrewery, though why you'd want to get beer made at a winery Heidi couldn't imagine.

He'd also dumped a bag of something called cheese curds rather inelegantly onto a plate. They looked disgusting, resembling big yellow toothpaste nerdles. Mindful of her instructions from their new lawyer, however, Heidi was the model of politeness as she declined to try them. Miss Noblesse Oblige herself.

"These are so fresh they squeak," Jessica Kincaid announced as she moved closer to Ryan on the bench and nibbled the cheese curds. Apparently, she was the winner in the Date Ryan Atherton Derby, though Heidi would have thought he'd go for the tiny brunette.

"You can warm them just a little in the microwave, and they'll squeak even more," Ryan told her.

Now Heidi simply couldn't contain herself, and she knew Hake wouldn't dare try to shut her up. "Why on earth would you want your food to squeak?"

Jessica gave a rather embarrassed little laugh. "Just because, I guess. I never even heard of cheese curds before this week."

"The name doesn't sound very appealing," Heidi said, pushing her empty glass toward Angela and pointing at the barrel of cabernet she wanted her next glass to come from. Angela looked annoyed, but she filled the glass.

"It's just a stage in the cheese-making process," Ryan explained. "These are the curds that separate from the whey. Then they're pressed together in wheels or molds to form cheese. That's all."

Heidi frowned. "Curds and whey. You mean like Little Miss Muffet?"

Ryan looked right at her and grinned. He *was* awfully cute. "Exactly."

His sister spoke up now. "You know, I thought these caves would be . . . well, more dank. Really cold and clammy." She swirled a glass of a four-year-old Villa Belladuce zinfandel, took a deep whiff, then drank.

"Well, it is kind of chilly," Sara pointed out, pulling a white cashmere cardigan more tightly closed across her chest. "But I think that's the point, isn't it?"

Angela Rutledge nodded. At least for once she didn't have that stupid baby with her. Heidi had briefly considered having a child, but Hake didn't seem very interested, and she'd decided not to push it. She wasn't that excited about the idea herself. Children seemed to be a great deal of work. Babies smelled nasty and kept you up all night, and it went downhill from there.

"Absolutely," Angela said. "The first caves were dug in an era before the invention of air-conditioning, when you had to either find a way to keep wines cool naturally or risk having them suffer from the summer heat here. Which hasn't been too bad during your visit, but this area can get pretty warm. This particular cave system varies from fifty-seven to sixty-one degrees, but it never gets out of that four-degree range, whether it's the middle of summer or the middle of winter."

"Were these caves dug by the Chinese?" the fat lady from Southern California asked.

"The original section was," Angela answered. "The Chinese laborers earned about eight dollars a month and were responsible for most of the early cave systems. Nowadays, there's been a revival in cave-digging hereabouts, so when the Belladuce family expanded this cave fifteen years ago, they hired a contractor who actually specializes in digging wine caves."

Angela leaned back and tapped lightly on the wall. "This is supposed to look like the natural limestone, but it's actually a concrete mixture that gets sprayed on the walls after they're dug. It's called shotcrete."

"What if there's an earthquake when we're down here?" Kelly Atherton asked.

Heidi shuddered. *Thanks so very much for bringing that up.*

"We'd wait it out," Angela told her, "but there isn't likely to be real danger down here. Sections of this cave predate the

San Francisco earthquake of 1906, and there've been all kinds of other quakes in this area since then. It's a pretty stable system, and they added some steel reinforcement at strategic points when they expanded down here."

Heidi, feeling a resurgence of claustrophobia, swiftly calculated the distance to the exit and how quickly she could reach it. Then she consulted her watch and did some math in her head to figure out how many hours were left before the tour would end.

Sixty-five. Surely she could manage for sixty-five hours, at least part of which she'd be asleep.

Assuming, of course, that she wasn't buried alive in an earthquake in the next hour. The fun just never stopped here in wine country.

*Chapter 24*

JACK London's Beauty Ranch reflected a time when writers could live large.

The magnificent spread ranged over the hills above Glen Ellen, with spectacular vistas all around and no sign of civilization—not even vineyards—in any direction. The portion of London's original property now maintained as a California state park retained the isolated charm and splendor that must have first appealed to the writer when he bought the initial 130 acres in 1905.

Lynne was pleased to have so many folks along for today's tour of London's ranch. Some years, nobody on the Sonoma Sojourn was interested in this particular side trip at all, and she had to skip it or go on her own after the tour ended. She felt doubly rewarded today because she was so utterly comfortable with the folks in this group: Pat and Mark Martell, Alice and Don Harper, and Kelly Atherton.

One of the treats of the visit to London's ranch for Lynne was seeing Don Harper spring to life. He seemed more genuinely excited about today's excursion than anything else since his arrival. He'd even dressed for the occasion, in the kind of hiking ensemble that looks nice in an ad in the *New Yorker* but a bit silly if you're actually hiking.

Don often became obsessive about an interest, reading and researching it exhaustively, till he had wrung every scrap of interesting information from his subject. Jack London was his most recent mania.

Kelly was the only real surprise in today's group. Lynne suspected that she was along less out of interest in hard-living writers of Very Masculine Fiction than because it was much closer to Villa Belladuce than San Francisco, where the rest of the young people had gone on a spur-of-the-moment trip. Kelly had driven her own car today, in case her grandmother called from Villa Belladuce, where she was taking the day off and resting.

Maria and Guido, claiming the privilege of age, had also remained at Villa Belladuce. "We will walk the vineyards," Guido had told Lynne shyly last night after dinner, "and sit outside our little hillside cottage and enjoy God's beautiful country." He smiled then. "And of course Maria will be with the baby."

The Sandstroms, it turned out, were the only ones intending to take the Dry Creek appellation tour, for which a limo and driver were reserved. Hake had gone public at breakfast that morning with his hope and dream of buying a Sonoma vineyard. He was outing himself, Lynne suspected, as a form of damage control, since he'd been so secretive up till the very moment he got busted. He remained jovial and effusive until Detective Lauren Shaw arrived, wearing her grimmest expression yet.

⚬━✦━⚬

**FOR** once, Hake was smart enough to keep his mouth shut.

The minute Detective Shaw asked him to tell her again what he'd done after dinner on Sunday night, he knew something was going south in a hurry.

He forced himself to be casual. "We returned from dinner, said good night to Lynne Montgomery—she was out on the patio—and went to bed. I made love to my wife, and then we fell asleep."

"Did you leave your cottage at any time between your return from Marino's and when you came to breakfast on Monday morning?"

He shook his head. This was not good. "Slept like a baby."

"Did you have occasion to go down to the winery at any time between your arrival at Villa Belladuce on Sunday and breakfast on Monday?"

Even worse. He shook his head again. Would it be overdoing things to offer a big smile? He didn't think so. He beamed at her. "Nope."

"Then how does it happen, Mr. Sandstrom, that your fingerprints were on Lance Belladuce's Miata when we found it parked beside his dead body?"

That was when he told her he wanted to see his attorney. Her lips turned upward in a tiny, little smirk as she offered him her cell phone. He wanted to smack her, but that didn't seem prudent.

⊙━━━◦

**ANGELA** was reading through the vicious E-mail messages once again.

Jeff had made a big show of deleting them, of course, but he didn't seem to realize that she wasn't a total dunce where the computer was concerned and that she'd already saved them in a file labeled "Phylloxera Symptoms" on her computer. She hadn't looked at them for a couple of days now, though she continued to check her E-mail several times a day. There hadn't been a new message since this last one, on July 31. Eight days now, and before that, they'd been coming more and more frequently.

She read the message displayed on her monitor through tears that blurred its hateful letters:

NO AMOUNT OF MONEY CAN PROTECT GUILTY SINNERS FROM JUSTICE. THEFT OF A CHILD IS PUNISHABLE BY DEATH. GOD ALLOWS NO MAN TO HIDE BEHIND FILTHY LUCRE.

She had no idea how long she'd been sitting there, sobbing, before Jeff came into the room. When had he gotten home? His side of the bed was still empty when she got up this morning.

"What is it?" he asked, though surely he knew. She pointed at the screen. "I thought I got rid of that."

"You can't just make it disappear, Jeff, pretend it isn't there by pushing a button." She tried to stop crying. He hated it when she cried.

"It's nothing, Angie. It's some lowlife trying to make trouble, but you can't let it bother you. And you know what? There haven't been any new E-mails since Lance Belladuce died. It wouldn't surprise me to find out that he was behind this all along."

She used a couple of keystrokes to bring up her current screen saver, a slide show of nature scenes that she normally found extremely soothing. Today, she knew, nothing would soothe her. "Why?"

"Does it matter? It's stopped now."

"You think it's stopped. It could start again anytime."

"It won't." Jeff crossed to the window that looked out on the front yard and drive. Gazing through the glass, he spoke flatly. "We're getting rid of this place. I've had it."

She didn't know what to say. She stared at the computer screen as a photograph of a tropical island dissolved into one of an Arctic glacier. The screen was huge, though not as large as the hatred that fueled the E-mail messages hidden behind these serene images

"We'll get rid of these people," he went on, "and the minute they leave, we're out of here. We can stay in the condo down in Palo Alto until you find another house."

"We can't just walk away from this," she protested feebly. She didn't think she had the strength for this argument anymore.

"Of course we can. It's too far from my work, anyway. It takes hours to get down there, and going through San Francisco takes forever."

This was a new argument, one that had only recently come

into play, and she wasn't sure how to counter it. Villa Belladuce was indeed several hours away from Sunnyvale, which
to her mind was a virtue. Jeff hadn't minded the distance at
first, and he loved to drive the Porsche, anyway. It always
seemed to please him to have an excuse to roar off. Sometimes he'd even drive all the way around the East Bay, taking
I-680 through the countryside so he could really crank up the
speed.

But it did take hours, even on the fastest, most direct route
in the dead of night. Jeff was gone more frequently now than
ever before. Last night he'd gone off again, in the middle of
the night, not even leaving a note on her bathroom mirror.

And now he was back, without a word of explanation.

**WHEN** Don Harper walked through the door of the Jack London Bookstore in Glen Ellen, he felt as if he'd come home.

The bookshop also served as headquarters for the Jack London Research Center Foundation. Don chatted up the propri-
etor, the widow of an Oakland ad exec who'd been hired to do
some work for the Jack London Association and had wound
up as the nerve center of an entire industry of Londonalia.

Then he took his time perusing the current wares, which included first editions under glass and endless shelves of more
plebian hardcovers and paperbacks. The place stocked picture
books and photo essays, short story collections and transla-
tions into an amazing range of foreign tongues, including
Russian and Japanese.

Eventually, Don became aware that the others were growing politely restless. He bought a leather-bound short story
collection, a limited edition of *Valley of the Moon,* and an appealing brown card that copied a sign on London's office
door:

PLEASE DO NOT ENTER WITHOUT KNOCKING.

PLEASE DO NOT KNOCK.

Once they were out of the van, Lynne let Don lead the tour. At the farm buildings, he lingered over the Pig Palace, with a central feed house and seventeen surrounding piggie apartments, each designed to house a separate hog family.

"Unfortunately," Don told the group, "we can't get into the cottage, where he wrote so many of his later stories and novels. It's closed weekdays, though I may just have to come back tomorrow."

"You know, I don't believe I've ever read anything he wrote," Pat Martell admitted. "But the kids all read *Call of the Wild* in junior high. Their English teacher would lower the classroom air-conditioning as far as it would go to get them into the mood of the frozen north." She grimaced. "Of course, that was back when energy was cheap."

Kelly Atherton laughed. "All we had to do in Wisconsin was open a window. I read *Call of the Wild* and *White Fang* when I was a kid. Our next-door neighbors had malamutes, and I'd go over and act out the books with them in the winter. I liked to play the part of Buck, and the dogs always let me have my way. And that's the full extent of my knowledge." She pulled out a photographic postcard she'd bought at the Jack London Bookstore, looked at it, and smiled. "Oh, and that he was a major-league hunk."

Don glanced at the card she was holding and also smiled. "Read the quote on that picture, Kelly."

She looked down and read. " 'The proper function of man is to live, not to exist. I shall not waste my days in trying to prolong them.' "

"Which turned out to be pretty prophetic," Lynne noted as they turned back toward the museum. "He barely made it to forty."

"Really?" Pat sounded startled. "I had no idea he was so young when he died."

"Kidney failure," Don explained, "though over the years there've been those who claimed he committed suicide."

"Why'd they say that?" Kelly asked, frowning.

"He was found in a coma." Don felt surprisingly defensive. The Jack London he'd grown to appreciate in recent months was a fighter, not a quitter. And surely suicide was the ultimate form of quitting. "He'd been suffering from serious kidney problems for years, and his health was going downhill. He'd been taking morphine for the pain, but there was no reason to think he overdosed either deliberately or by accident. If it happened today, there'd be an autopsy and an investigation, and they'd smear the medical details all over the Internet. But back then, it was just a discussion among a couple of local doctors. It's a damned shame that his reputation was dirtied this way, that's all I have to say about it."

He actually had quite a bit more to say about it, but he realized he was starting to sound a little hysterical. Also, he wanted to pace himself physically, and there was no good to come of getting riled up. He concentrated on walking till they reached the museum.

"This may just be my own prejudice," Lynne told them as they entered, "but I can't help but wonder what Jack London would have to say about all the scholarly attention folks pay him. College courses, books of literary criticism, English dissertations, a Jack London Society whose directors are all university professors. All this for a guy with almost no formal education himself."

"He was extraordinarily prolific," Pat Martell noted. "It says here he published fifty books. How could he possibly do all that writing along with everything else?"

"Some men," Don told her, puffing his chest up a bit, "are simply larger than life."

**THE** remains of Wolf House stood half a mile away, swallowed by the woods.

As they moved eagerly down the trail through stands of oak, madrones, redwood, and Douglas fir, Don imagined Jack and Charmian riding horseback on this trail on a crisp autumn morning, heading down to monitor the progress in the construction of their dream house. The place had been destroyed by fire just before the Londons were scheduled to move in.

"It was all constructed from native materials," Lynne told

them as they hiked, "most of them from right here on the ranch grounds. Huge rocks, redwood trees with the bark still on them for the exterior walls, lots of stone."

They rounded a curve then, and Wolf House rose suddenly in front of them. Don was stunned. He'd read extensively about this place, had pored over photographs and blueprints. None of it prepared him for the breathtaking magnitude. Towering chimneys with stone fireplaces that opened into thin air jutted above the treetops. Even in ruin, it was enormous.

The extravagance of the place was oddly troubling, and Don could barely imagine what it must have seemed like nearly a century earlier. What had he been thinking, this hardy adventurer, this chronicler of wild and fantastic experiences, as he planned and built such a colossus?

As he wondered what it must have felt like to stand by and watch it burn and burn and burn, taking days to fully consume itself, he heard one of the cell phones ring.

And then Lynne was standing beside him, looking worried, holding her phone. "I think something's wrong," she said. "We need to go back right away."

*Chapter 25*

**MARIA** was just as glad they'd decided to stay at Villa Belladuce today, because Guido was up much of the night with an
upset stomach from something he ate at dinner. He normally
didn't suffer these problems; indeed, he prided himself on
being able to eat anything from calamari to freshly dug clams
to their nephew's heavily peppered sausages. Maria, always
suspicious of fungi, faulted the mushrooms in the ravioli,
though Lynne and a couple of the others had eaten the same
thing and seemed unaffected.

Maria suspected, actually, that Guido was less bothered by
indigestion than by simple exhaustion. Yesterday afternoon's
nap had been good for him, and she realized now that she
should have insisted all along that he rest regularly during the
daytime hours. There was no way either of them could keep
up with Lynne and her sprightly friends from Southern California, much less with the children who were always racing
off on some breathless errand or another. Though they always
looked out first for Ruth Atherton, she amended hastily, lest
she be judged for unfairness.

Angela had even offered her lunch, which was sweet of her, since they had no car and no way of going out for any kind of midday meal. Angela had left the kitchen door to the mansion unlocked and instructed the young Mexican girl to let Maria have whatever she wanted. It had seemed an imposition when Angela first suggested it, but now that Maria's stomach was growling, she was glad she hadn't argued. Guido had merely groaned when she asked if he wanted any lunch, so she headed on up to the mansion by herself.

She rapped lightly on the kitchen door. When nobody answered, she rapped again, a little louder. Still no answer. The Mexican girl must be off cleaning somewhere or—Maria was surprised to feel a pang of jealousy—she might be tending to baby Stephanie.

Maria gingerly turned the knob and walked inside slowly, calling a soft, "Hello?"

No answer, and no sign of anybody. She waited for a few moments, then shrugged and went to the big stainless steel refrigerator that Angela had shown her earlier. She opened it with a sense of wonder. It held a lot more food than Maria would have imagined, since Angela had said more than once that she didn't like to cook.

One shelf was given over exclusively to baby food, with several bottles of formula there as well. There was also quite a lot of carefully labeled homemade baby food, which Angela had told Maria proudly she pureed herself, from organic produce only. Pureed carrots, applesauce, pears—all in little jars, some of them fuzzed by frost.

Maria sneaked a peek into the freezer and found dozens more, lined up like soldiers. It both fascinated and confused Maria that a young woman with so much money would go to this kind of trouble. She herself had fed her babies and her babies' babies Gerber and Beech-Nut without reservation, and there'd been no more doting mother in all of Massachusetts than Maria Ambrosino.

She fixed herself a sandwich with ham and some of that jack cheese that looked like mozzarella but was softer, selected a pear from a copper bowl of fruit on the counter and, after a moment's hesitation, helped herself to a bottle of peach-flavored Snapple. There were glasses in the cottage, and she'd stop by the ice machine in the breakfast room on her way back.

She was about to leave when she heard a door slam upstairs and the angry voice of Jeff Rutledge yelling, "Wait!"

Maria froze.

Now came Angela's voice, also loud and furious. "Just give it a rest, will you? It doesn't matter, and I might ask you exactly the same question."

"I don't care if they think I did it. They'll never prove anything." A moment's silence followed.

Maria, both horrified and fascinated, strained to hear. She knew she had no business listening to this private disagreement, but she found herself unable to ignore it and definitely unable to leave. Without thinking about what she was doing, she stepped out into the hall so she could hear more clearly.

Jeff's voice now was softer, less angry. "I just need you to tell me where you were, Angie. Why I couldn't find you."

Angela's voice remained harsh. "I don't see how you can be so authoritative about my whereabouts, since you're gone half the time yourself."

"I wasn't gone then. I was right here. And you weren't," he shot back.

"If you don't trust me after all this time, there's not much I can do—"

The piercing wail of a baby interrupted Angela.

"Oh great," Angela shouted. "Now look what you've done. Thanks a whole hell of a lot."

"I haven't done anything," Jeff answered, sounding almost whiny.

"Just forget about it," Angela snapped. Then her voice changed, became lower and more soothing, even as the baby's cries grew louder. She must have opened the door to Stephanie's bedroom. "Hey, baby darling, you're awake! Hush, sweetie pie, hush, hush, hush. C'mon, let's go get you a bottle."

The baby continued to howl, and the crying grew louder.

Maria retreated hastily to the kitchen, realizing that Angela would bring Stephanie down that big stairway in the front hall any minute now. What should she do?

She was perfectly justified in being here, of course. She'd been invited. But there was nothing to be gained from intruding on a personal argument, and she didn't want to embarrass the Rutledges. She started to gather her sandwich and Snapple, then realized she couldn't possibly get out before Angela reached the kitchen.

She stood there, frozen, as Angela stalked into the kitchen, carrying the squalling Stephanie.

"Rosalita? Warm a bottle." Angela's voice was hard and authoritative. She stopped abruptly at the sight of Maria. "Oh! I didn't realize you were here."

Well, obviously not. Maria lowered her head apologetically. "I just came in to make a sandwich. I'm sorry. I'll go now."

Stephanie kept wailing as Angela bounced her irritably in her arms.

"No, don't go. Could you just grab a bottle out of the fridge?"

Maria set down her own food, then turned to the refrigerator and removed one of the bottles. "Shall I warm it?"

"Please. Thirty seconds." Angela pointed to a huge microwave built into the wall. She continued to jiggle Stephanie, who continued to screech.

Maria put the bottle in the microwave, thinking that she'd never heard the baby cry this long before. "Maybe she's wet?" She gestured to the changing table in a back corner of the kitchen set up as a baby service area. That monstrous stroller sat beside it, awaiting the next journey. "I could change her."

"No, I'll do it. You just get that bottle."

Angela laid Stephanie on the changing table, ripped open the snaps on the bottom of her little pink-and-white-striped sleeper, and stripped off the wet diaper, expertly resealing it into a tight white package. As she stepped on the foot pedal to open the trash can beside the changing table, Maria found herself wondering which foot she was using, the real one or the fake, and she realized that Angela had never said which was which. Maria caught herself in shame. What possible difference did it make, and how could it be any of her business?

None of this was her business. She needed to get out of here, to go back to the cottage. Guido might be awake, might need her.

Angela didn't bother with powder, just taped the baby into a new diaper as Maria hesitantly approached with the warmed bottle. Angela snatched it from her hand and all but shoved it into the baby's mouth. Stephanie began to suck greedily, clasping her tiny hands to the bottle.

The sudden silence was shocking.

For the first time, Maria looked at Angela. Her hair was mussed, and she wasn't wearing any makeup. She wore white jeans and a long-sleeved lavender turtleneck with white tennis shoes. Her breathing was fast and shallow. Maria wondered if she should apologize for eavesdropping but thought that mentioning what she'd overheard might only make matters worse.

"I should go," she said softly, looking around to find where she'd set down the sandwich and drink.

"No, don't leave." It was an unmistakable order. Angela picked up Stephanie, cradling her in her arms, making sure the bottle was plugged securely into the baby's greedy mouth. Then she looked around the kitchen, as if she were seeing it for the first time. Finally, she turned her gaze to Maria. "I left some things down in the caves last night," she said. "Would you mind coming along while I pick them up? I was going to run down before Stephanie woke up, but I guess she wasn't very tired."

"Of course," Maria said. "Would you like me to—" She gestured toward the stroller. At Angela's nod, she released the brake and brought the stroller over to mother and daughter. Angela settled Stephanie, grabbed a large key ring from a hook beside the back door, and started to open the door. Then she closed it again.

"Oh, wait," Angela said. "Your lunch! Or is that for your husband?"

Maria shook her head. "No, Guido isn't eating anything. His stomach is still bothering him. He's probably still sleeping."

Angela opened a cabinet, revealing the largest collection of Tupperware that Maria had ever seen. She pulled out a round container, the size of a single layer cake, and thrust it toward her. "Put your plate in this and bring it along. You can have a little picnic."

❦

**HAKE'S** new lawyer, Jim Lassiter, wasn't very prepossessing, didn't have the natty sophistication of Len Morelli, and looked, in fact, like somebody you'd hire to fix your parking tickets in Cleveland. But he seemed to know everybody at the police station, and they all greeted him jovially. Even Detective Shaw was cordial to him. Which was fine right now, Hake decided, when there was still a chance of getting out of this on charm and evasion. If matters escalated any further, however, he'd need far bigger guns than this little cap pistol.

They sat in Lassiter's office now, in some anonymous building in downtown Santa Rosa. It was a small partnership, just two criminal lawyers and a girl with an overbite and orange lipstick, chewing gum at the front desk.

"The problem," Lassiter said, "is that your story doesn't leave any wiggle room. And being alibied by your wife doesn't do you much good, since there are a lot of people who saw her get pretty loaded on Sunday night. Meanwhile, there's no way to explain what your fingerprints are doing on that car. You're lucky, you know. If they'd been a little quicker when you were booked the other night, checked your prints then against unknowns from the crime scene, you might be talking to me through glass right now. It'll be harder to put you back in custody now that you're out, but don't think it can't be done."

"They've already charged somebody with that murder."

"True, but I think they may realize the case against Eleanor Whitson is a little bit flimsy. If you weren't a lawyer, you'd probably already be in custody." He offered a thin little smile.

"They like to make sure their ducks are all lined up before they arrest attorneys. Now, I know they've still got several people digging into Lance Belladuce's business dealings, which is how your name came up in the first place. That syndicate thing."

Hake had given his options considerable thought and hated them all. But anything he told this guy was protected under attorney-client privilege. "What if I told you that he was already dead when I got there?"

Jim Lassiter looked at him shrewdly. "I'd ask you when you were there, and why."

Hake decided to go for broke. "Okay, here's what happened. There were nine of us in this syndicate that was trying to buy Villa Belladuce, 'cause the place was so big and expensive. I met with Lance a couple of times, and the last meeting we had, I gave him quite a lot of cash as . . . well, as an incentive, I guess you could say. It was earnest money, though we didn't exactly call it that."

They hadn't exactly called it anything. Lance had told him he wanted fifty large in small bills. And Hake had delivered. Three weeks later, Lance called to say that Villa Belladuce was being bought by a computer geek with more money than God. And that the earnest money was nonrefundable.

"I wanted to look at some other vineyards in this area anyway, smaller ones that I could afford on my own, so when I found out about this tour, we signed on. But mostly I wanted that fifty thousand back, and Lance was being evasive. I figured my chances of getting it back could only improve if I was staying at his family's old stomping ground."

Lassiter was listening attentively. "Did you tell him you were coming?"

Hake shook his head. "Nope. I was planning to call him once I was here, but then he simplified things by showing up Sunday night."

"Did you talk to him on the patio?"

"No. But I called him from the men's room at the restaurant at dinner that night and told him I wanted the money back. He suggested that I meet him down by the winery later, and we set a time." Hake kept his eyes steadily on the lawyer. This was where he had to really sell the guy. "But when I got there, he was already dead. I actually stumbled over his legs, and that's when I lost my balance and must have touched the car."

"How do you know he was dead?"

"I had a little flashlight. I shone it on him and looked for a pulse, and when I didn't find one, I hauled ass back to my cottage and stayed there till breakfast the next morning."

Jim Lassiter winced. "It didn't occur to you to call the police?"

Hake offered a sheepish little grin. "I guess that wasn't very smart of me, not raising the alarm." No need to mention that he'd patted down the body, looking for a fifty thousand dollar bulge that wasn't there. "But they can't arrest you for stupidity, can they?"

Now Lassiter chuckled. "On the contrary, that's why most people get arrested. Whose idea was it to meet at the winery?"

"His."

"Who set the time?"

"He did."

"Were you on time?"

"I was actually a little late. I had to wait till Heidi fell asleep before I could leave."

"Did he give any reason for wanting to meet under those circumstances?"

Hake started to shake his head, then stopped. "No, wait. He did say something about planning to be in the neighborhood anyway."

"When you called him, was he at home?"

"I assume he was. That was the only number I had." He went back to the sheepish expression. "Got myself in a mell of a hess here, don't I?"

Jim Lassiter nodded somberly. "You do indeed."

☞━✦━☜

**AS** they retraced yesterday's path down to the wine caves in silence, Maria remembered how touched she'd been to have the girl share the terrible details of her accident. It had been as if some kind of hard shell had peeled back for just a little while, revealing the young woman's vulnerable side.

Today there was nothing vulnerable about Angela, and Maria felt saddened at the difference. Now there was only the cloud of the overheard argument and Angela's obvious foul mood. Stephanie, bless her, remained oblivious to it all. She'd polished off her bottle and was playing with a ring of brightly colored keys as Maria pushed the stroller. Youth and innocence could be such a blessing.

When they reached the caves, Angela unlocked the door and stepped inside to fix the alarm system, as she had yesterday. The afternoon was cool, and the contrast in temperature wasn't as obvious as it had been before. Maria pushed the stroller inside and followed Angela to the tasting room.

Angela had closed up the barrels of wine they'd been tasting before leaving last night and had removed the perishable hors d'oeuvres. Ryan Atherton had taken away his unopened beer bottles, but the empties remained, along with dirtied wineglasses and a sack full of used paper plates and plastic cutlery. As Angela bustled around the room, repacking the glasses, bagging the rest of the trash, she looked desperately unhappy.

Maria decided to try to make amends.

"I wasn't trying to listen," she began carefully. "I was just making myself a little lunch, like you told me to."

Angela stiffened. "What are you talking about?"

"Just now, up at the house. When you and the mister—" She wasn't sure where to take it from here and stopped.

"You were *eavesdropping*?"

"Not on purpose," Maria whispered, suddenly frightened. There was a look in Angela's eyes that suggested a cornered animal. Maria was aware of Stephanie gurgling happily in her stroller in the corner, of the cool, dry air in the cave, of the absolute silence surrounding them. She could hear Angela's breathing, hard and fast.

"Why would you—" Angela began.

*Deetaleet-deetaleet.*

The chirpy ring of a cell phone startled both of them.

Maria's hadn't rung before, but she watched enough TV to know what they were supposed to sound like. As she moved her hand cautiously to the pocket where she was carrying hers, she saw Angela whip a royal blue phone out of her own pocket and flip it open.

"Yes? Yes, dear. I'll be back in a minute. Just tidying up from last night." Angela's voice was bright and cheerful, utterly different from its tone moments earlier. The sudden change frightened Maria even more. "No, honey, I'm fine. Love you." She pushed a button and tucked the phone away again.

Maria began moving cautiously toward the doorway. "I should go back, see how Guido is doing."

Angela stepped between Maria and the exit. "Not yet. I want to know why you were listening."

As Maria started to explain once again that it had been an accident, that she hadn't meant to intrude, she suddenly understood the implications of Jeff Rutledge demanding to know why he hadn't been able to find his wife. She realized when he must have been looking for her, and why it mattered so much.

"It was you!" Maria blurted. "You killed that man!"

Angela's face shut down totally. It was absolute confirmation. When she spoke, her tone was flat and tinged with sorrow. "I wish you hadn't listened," she said. "I wish you could have minded your own business."

"But why? You already have this place, when it used to be his." In the brief time Maria had seen him, Lance Belladuce had been young and handsome and utterly without cares. Suddenly, Maria understood, and it broke her heart. "You were in love with him."

Angela shook her head. "No."

"You poor thing," Maria soothed. She was terribly frightened, but she also felt enormously saddened for this girl, this young woman who had endured so much, had conquered pain and disfigurement and disability. She had the money and the house and the vineyard and the husband and then, finally, the baby. But there was nothing in what Maria had seen of Jeff

Rutledge that could ever match the sensuality and passion of Lance Belladuce. "He shouldn't have mistreated you."

"It was all just a game for him," Angela suddenly spat out. "A stupid game he played while we were trying to buy the place. Jeff wouldn't have anything to do with it, didn't want to come here at all. He barely looked at the place before we signed the papers to buy it. It was all me doing everything, and Lance negotiating for the Belladuces. But I didn't . . . I never . . ."

She stopped abruptly, and Maria suddenly realized she was saying that she'd never been physically unfaithful to her husband.

"Handsome men don't always understand their power," Maria said slowly, "or sometimes they understand it too well."

Angela cocked her head as she considered this. "I suppose you may be right. And I'm sorry about this, really. But I can't let you go tell people what you heard, and now that you've figured it out . . ."

Maria felt tears slipping from her eyes as she realized the danger she was in. Guido, her children, the grandbabies—all would be lost, and she would never be able to tell them how much she loved them. "I won't say anything. Please don't shoot me."

Angela's laugh echoed in the room, harsh and not quite sane. "Don't be silly. I *can't* shoot you. I made Jeff lock all his guns up so tight *I* can't even get at them. I only had the one gun, a silly little thing that I had for a million years, and the police have it now."

Maria shook her head in confusion. "It was your gun all along? Not your husband's? And you put it into that wine barrel?"

"Well, of course I put it into the wine barrel. I had to do *something* with it, just in case they could trace it, which it turned out they could. Not that they could trace it to me, I don't think, but I wasn't sure. My brother gave it to me when we were teenagers, before the accident. I didn't always feel safe in our neighborhood. I never knew where he got it, but he called it Angie's Little Equalizer, and he showed me how to use it."

As Maria listened, her heart sank. She knew Angela couldn't tell her these things and then let her go. There was no way to overpower the girl, who was less than half her age, strong and healthy. She couldn't stop the tears now, didn't bother to try.

"I never told anybody I had it," Angela went on, "not even my best friends, and when my brother died, nobody knew about it at all. Jeff's guns have all been fancy one way or another. Investments, he says, and I guess that's true, 'cause he almost never shoots any of them. So I just held on to this all these years and what do you know? It turned out to be absolutely perfect for . . . for what I used it for. As if I'd had it all along just for this."

Angela's features hardened into the ugliness of hatred. "It took care of that laughing, lying Lance Belladuce, and it was small enough to hide where nobody would ever find it. I made sure the winery was locked up tight before I left that night. It should have worked. It would have worked, if those damned Belladuces hadn't busted up the winery the next night and hacked open all those barrels."

The movement was so sudden that Maria almost didn't notice it. The mallet that Angela had used to hammer the bungs back into the barrels last night was lying atop the barrel closest to the door. She swept it up and brought it around behind Maria, smacking her on the back of the head.

Maria felt only a moment of surprise before she crumpled to the ground.

*Chapter 26*

**MARIA** awoke in total darkness.

She was cold, and her head hurt, and she knew instinctively that she was in great danger. Though she seemed to be in an upright position, she was slumped over, with something biting cruelly into her waist. She tried to straighten herself, and as she did so, the pressure around her stomach eased. She realized now that she was sitting on the ground, with her feet out in front of her, and that her hands were both free.

Not that that did her any good. She felt cautiously around herself, trying to figure out where she was and what had happened. The blackness surrounding her was absolute. She explored the constriction around her waist and found a thick chain that she traced behind her to a padlock.

The caves.

She was in the caves, and Angela was gone. The baby was gone, too, thank the good Lord, off with her mother. Her mother, who had killed a man.

Maria knew now where she was and what had happened,

and her tears began again. Angela had rushed off hurriedly, but she would be back. And when she returned . . .

Maria decided not to let herself think about that. She twisted and pulled the chain around her waist until the padlock was in front of her, but then there was nothing more she could do. She felt the lock and determined that it wasn't the kind that you twirl to certain numbers but rather a large, solid device opened only by a key.

A key she didn't have.

She was stuck here, and surely Angela would return any minute. There was no telling how long she'd been gone. She'd answered a phone call, Maria remembered, and gone off to assuage her suspicious husband.

The phone call! Maria's hand went to her pocket and found her own cell phone. She carefully worked it out of the pocket, clutching it tightly, fearful to drop and lose it. It could be her lifeline, if she could only figure out how to use it in the dark. She had to remember how the face part was set up, so she could call for help.

She carefully brought it to rest in her lap and gingerly opened its cover. There was a power switch here somewhere on the bottom, and she probed the face with her fingers until she found what she thought was the right button.

She pushed it and nothing happened.

She pushed another button, and a third. Just as she was about to howl in despair, she pushed one more button, and the face lit up as the phone gave a cheery little *deetaleet*.

The light on the phone felt like a gift from God, a sign that the Almighty meant for Maria to escape this horrible cave. She pressed thirty-four, the speed-dial code for Guido, and held her breath. There was only part of a ring, and then a tinny voice—not Guido's—saying she should leave a message. She realized that he probably hadn't touched the phone for days, that most likely it was in his pants pocket and turned off.

Now she tried thirty-three, for Lynne. It rang twice, and then she heard a voice.

"Lynne Montgomery."

Maria began to weep for joy. "Lynne, Lynne! It's Maria, you've got to help."

"Hello? Hello?"

The light on the face of the phone dimmed suddenly, and she read "Call dropped." What did that mean? She pushed the power switch again and tried the thirty-three code. She got a busy signal this time, and wept again.

◦══✦══◦

**AS** Lynne sped back to Villa Belladuce from Beauty Ranch, she listened again and again in her mind to the faint sound of Maria Ambrosino's voice as she'd heard it in the woods by Wolf House. Reception had cut in and out, so she could only hear snatches: "Lynne . . . Maria . . . got to . . ."

Then her voice was gone, along with the call.

Lynne hadn't worried at first. "That's odd," she told Pat and Alice. "That was Maria, but I lost the call before I could ask her what she wanted."

"Maybe she misdialed again," Pat suggested. "Remember how she called you at the Burbank Gardens when she was trying to reach Guido?"

"Easy enough to make a mistake," Mark Martell agreed.

Lynne had then dialed the code for Maria's phone and gotten no answer, just the irritating voice mail that signaled the phone was busy, or out of range, or turned off. Guido's phone gave the same response, as did Ruth Atherton's. Nobody answered the Rutledge line at the mansion. Something felt very wrong about this.

"She wouldn't need to call Guido," she told them, thinking out loud. "They're both at the same place. And she sounded upset. C'mon, let's get Don and go back."

The ride to Villa Belladuce seemed to take forever, but it was less than half an hour before Lynne raced up the drive to the parking area. By now, she was frantically worried. She jumped out and dashed across the patio to Veneto, the honeymoon cottage where the Ambrosinos were staying.

She banged at the door. "Maria? Guido?" Her shouts and knocks went unanswered for a moment, and then Guido slowly opened the door. He wore pajamas and the vague, dis-oriented expression of one just awakened.

"Guido, is Maria here?"

He shook his head, puzzled. "No. She must be with the baby."

"You're sure she isn't in the bathroom or something?" Lynne craned her neck to look past him.

He stepped back and raised both hands in groggy bewil-derment. Lynne crossed the room in two strides and opened the bathroom door. Empty.

"You think she's over in the mansion? With the baby?"

"I guess." He was awake enough now to realize that some-thing was amiss. "What is it? Is something wrong?"

"She called me," Lynne told him hurriedly, "and the call was cut off. I tried to call her back, but there was no answer. But it sounded as if she needed help."

His eyes opened wide in alarm, and Lynne caught him as he swayed. "I'm sure she's fine," Lynne reassured him automat-ically. She stuck her head out the door and spied Alice Harper coming across the patio toward her own cottage. "Alice! Can you help me here? Hurry!"

Alice was a large woman, but Lynne knew her friend could really move when she wanted to. She was there in seconds, surveyed the scene with a swift glance, and then took Guido's other arm. "Let's sit down, shall we?" she told him, and he let her lead him to a chair.

"I'm going to look for her," Lynne said hurriedly. "You stay with him, and call nine-one-one if he looks the least bit shaky."

Next, Lynne ran to the back door of the mansion and banged there. After a moment, Jeff Rutledge opened the door, looking perturbed.

"Yes?" His tone was even more brusque than usual.

"Is Maria here?" At his vague expression, she said, "Maria Ambrosino, the woman from my tour who's been helping with your daughter?"

He frowned. "I haven't seen her all day."

"Could you ask your wife?"

He rolled his eyes and stepped back inside. Lynne hadn't been told to stay outside, so she followed him into the kitchen and heard him calling somewhere past the door that seemed to lead to the rest of the house.

"Angie? Have you seen that Maria woman?"

Angela's voice was faint but clear. "Not since early this morning, honey. Why?"

"The tour lady's looking for her."

"Sorry, I don't know where she is."

As Lynne looked around the kitchen, she saw Stephanie's stroller sitting just inside the back door. A box of wineglasses and some empty beer bottles from the Korbel microbrewery rested on the otherwise immaculate granite island. The last time Lynne had seen those beer bottles was the night before, down in the caves, when Angela told them not to worry about cleaning up, that she'd take care of it all later.

Jeff Rutledge returned to the kitchen. "Angela hasn't seen your lady," he said firmly. He opened the door and held it pointedly for Lynne. "She's probably gone for a walk in the vineyard or something."

Outside after this bum's rush, Lynne stopped for a moment and ran her eyes up and down the rows of grapevines. There was nothing and nobody out there. She thought again of the beer bottles and wineglasses on the island. If Angela had brought them back last night, surely they wouldn't still be sitting out, not in a tidy household with live-in help. And she didn't remember the stroller being out in the middle of the room the last time she'd been in that kitchen.

The caves!

She turned and ran across the patio and parking lot, down the path through the woods to the winery. She kept to the back side of the winery, the shortest route to the caves, realizing dimly that she was reversing the run she'd made Monday morning after finding Lance Belladuce's body.

As then, she was winded when she reached her destination. The heavy wooden door to the caves was locked. She banged on the door and yelled, then looked around, trying to decide what to do next. A bright flash of color in the ground cover caught her eye, and she bent to investigate.

Colored plastic keys. A baby toy, one she'd seen clutched in Stephanie's tiny fingers on more than one occasion. Including this morning.

So Angela and the baby had been here today.

Then, from behind the door, Lynne thought she heard a faint crash. She hesitated a moment, wondering if her imagination was working overtime. When she heard a second crash, she no longer hesitated. She picked up a rock and smashed the glass window at the top of the heavy double door.

"Maria?" she called.

"I'm here!" came the faint answer, and Lynne felt relief wash over her.

"Are you all right?" She knocked the glass out of the opening and reached in carefully, trying to open the lock from inside. It didn't seem to be that kind of lock. There was no knob, no deadbolt, no latch, only an interior hole for a key that matched the exterior location.

"I think so." Maria's voice sounded very far away.

"I'm trying to get in, but the door is locked. What happened?"

"Angela—"

But just as Maria started to say whatever she was going to say, the alarm went off. *Eet-a eet-a eet-a* reverberated inside the cave. It couldn't, Lynne realized almost immediately, do more than frighten off someone breaking into this cave. Nobody could hear it who wasn't already on the property, though presumably it was wired in to some security company.

"I'm getting help," she yelled in to Maria, as she pulled out her own cell phone and dialed 911.

⌁

**FIFTEEN** minutes later, Villa Belladuce was once again overrun by police.

It all happened quickly once it began, and later, Lynne remembered what had happened only as flashes of activity, a montage of brief clips.

Maria Ambrosino, being wheeled out of the caves on a gurney by burly young paramedics, while she protested that she was fine, really she was.

Guido, his pajama top tucked hastily into slacks, walking alongside the gurney, holding Maria's hand and leaning down to whisper into his beloved's ear.

Detective Lauren Shaw arguing with Jeff Rutledge at the kitchen door, then telling him he was under arrest if he didn't let her into the house that very minute.

Jeff Rutledge had, in fact, stepped aside as Detective Shaw and two other officers entered the kitchen, weapons drawn, and headed into the house. He trailed the police officers, looking dazed and terrified. Lynne was waiting on the patio when all this started, and she took advantage of the confusion to slip inside herself.

By the time she got indoors, the cops and Jeff Rutledge were all upstairs. She stopped at the base of the stairway, remembering too late that this household had an arsenal in it somewhere, Jeff Rutledge's fabled gun collection.

Then she heard Detective Shaw's clear voice announce, "Angela Rutledge, you're under arrest. You have the right to remain silent . . ."

As the Miranda warning continued, Angela Rutledge gave up her right to remain silent in a piercing wail that Lynne knew she would hear in her nightmares for years to come.

Lynne backed slowly against the wall opposite the staircase, then, and stood aside as the officers brought Angela down. The young woman shuffled along in a daze, looking drained and defeated, her hands cuffed behind her, eyes blank and empty.

Following the motley entourage, looking every bit as lost and frightened as his wife, came Jeff Rutledge. He walked carefully, carrying his daughter, speaking soft words of reassurance into her tiny ear.

*Epilogue*

**LYNNE** slammed the side door of the van and went back for one last check of the cottages. Villa Belladuce's deserted and abandoned atmosphere seemed unrelated to the departure of the Sonoma Sojourners. The vines still hung heavy with ripening fruit, the patio furniture sat in its casual groupings, the mansion loomed strong and tall and proud.

But that mansion sat empty now. Jeff Rutledge had taken his baby and his nanny and had gone to stay in his Silicon Valley condo. It was difficult to imagine him ever returning, not even to fetch whatever equipment he kept in that workshop upstairs. The Jeff Rutledges of the world hired minions to pack and transport their possessions, and the only possession that really seemed to matter to him was beyond his reach, awaiting a bail hearing on Monday morning in Santa Rosa.

Lynne had collected everyone's keys as they left, her final task for the tour. The Harpers and Martells had taken off at their customary oh-dark-thirty departure time this morning, and were probably halfway to Floritas by now. The shuttle had arrived at eight for the Ambrosinos, and Lynne smiled as she pictured them holding hands on the plane, looking out the window at the Rocky Mountains. Maria had survived her ordeal more easily than Guido, all things considered, and the dear old man had refused to let his wife out of his sight for a moment since he'd climbed into the back of her ambulance for what turned out to be a totally unnecessary trip to the hospital.

Hake and Heidi Sandstrom had simply left, slipping away the moment it became clear that Hake was—while far from innocent—at least not guilty of anything beyond drunk driving and poor judgment. In the confusion after the police and paramedics arrived at Villa Belladuce, only Lynne had seemed to notice that Hake was making repeated trips to the rented Jaguar with luggage. She considered pointing this out to some of the cops who remained after Detective Shaw left with her prisoner, then decided it was no longer her business. She had, indeed, taken great pleasure at watching the taillights of the Jaguar heading away from both the vineyard and herself. It was anyone's guess if Hake possessed sufficient chutzpah to try once again to acquire Villa Belladuce in the fire sale that would surely follow this week's events.

In any event, somebody new would be buying the place, and the possibility of Lynne returning with a new group of Sonoma Sojourners in another year seemed far likelier than it had a week before.

Purely by chance, Lynne had witnessed Jessica and Ryan's tearful farewell. The Athertons were leaving for San Francisco International in Kelly's rental car at almost exactly the same time that Jessica, Sara, and Ginger were taking their rental car back to the airport in Oakland. While Kelly and Ginger packed their respective trunks, Ryan and Jessica had slipped behind the Sandstroms' emptied cottage. When Lynne happened upon them, they were clinched in a good-bye embrace that suggested somebody would soon be accumulating a whole lot of frequent flyer miles.

Now Lynne went from cottage to cottage, making sure nobody had left behind anything obvious, marveling at all her group had experienced and endured in the space of a week.

She gathered two partially consumed wine bottles from the dresser in the Sandstroms' cottage and found a sweater on the floor of Ginger's closet.

She deliberately chose to end her rounds at Veneto, the honeymoon cottage occupied by the Ambrosinos. While most of the other cottages had the feel of hastily departed motel rooms, here the bed was neatly made, the towels hung evenly in the bath, the water glasses washed and drying by the bathroom sink.

The room had the feel of love and care and commitment. Lynne shed a few tears of her own before she walked out, climbed into the van, and headed for home.

> And now
> an exclusive preview of
>
> # Savage Run
>
> the new Joe Pickett Novel
> by acclaimed mystery writer
> C. J. Box

*Chapter 1*

**Targhee National Forest, Idaho**
**June 10**

**ON** the third day of their honeymoon, infamous environmental activist Stewie Woods and his new bride, Annabel Bellotti, were spiking trees in the Bighorn National Forest when a cow exploded and blew them up. Until then, their marriage had been happy.

They met by chance. Stewie Woods had been busy pouring bag after bag of sugar and sand into the gasoline tanks of a fleet of pickups that belonged to a natural gas exploration crew in a newly graded parking lot. The crew had left for the afternoon for the bars and hotel rooms of nearby Henry's Fork. One of the crew had returned unexpectedly and caught Stewie as Stewie was ripping off the top of a bag of sugar with his teeth. The crewmember pulled a nine-millimeter semiautomatic from beneath the dashboard and fired several wild pistol shots in Stewie's direction. Stewie had dropped the bag and run away, crashing through the timber like a bull elk.

Stewie had outrun and out-juked the man with the pistol, and he met Annabel when he literally tripped over her as she sunbathed nude in the grass in an orange pool of late-afternoon sun, unaware of his approach because she was listening to Melissa Etheridge on her Walkman's headphones. She looked good, he thought, strawberry blond hair with a two-day Rocky Mountain fire-engine tan (two hours in the sun at 8,000 feet created a sunburn like a whole day at the beach), small, ripe breasts, and a trimmed vector of pubic hair.

He had gathered her up and pulled her along through the timber, where they hid together in a dry spring wash until the man with the pistol gave up and went home. She had giggled while he held her—*this was real adventure,* she'd said—and he had used the opportunity to run his hands tentatively over her naked shoulders and hips and had found out, happily, that she did not object. They made their way back to where she had been sunbathing and while she dressed, they introduced themselves.

She told him she liked the idea of meeting a famous environmental outlaw in the woods while she was naked, and he appreciated that. She said she had seen his picture before—maybe in *Outside Magazine?*—and admired his looks: tall and raw-boned, with round, rimless glasses, a short-cropped full beard, and his famous red bandana on his head.

Her story was that she had been camping alone in a dome tent, taking a few days off from her freewheeling cross-continent trip that had begun with her divorce from an anal retentive investment banker named Nathan in her hometown of Pawtucket, Rhode Island. She was bound, eventually, for Seattle.

"I'm falling in love with your mind," he lied.

"Already?" she asked.

He encouraged her to travel with him, and they took her vehicle since the lone crewmember had disabled Stewie's Subaru with three bullets into the engine block. Stewie was astonished by his good fortune. Every time he looked over at her and she smiled back, he was pole-axed with exuberance.

Keeping to dirt roads, they crossed into Montana. The next

afternoon, in the backseat of her SUV during a thunderstorm that rocked the car and blew shroud-like sheets of rain through the mountain passes, he asked her to marry him. Given the circumstances and the supercharged atmosphere, she accepted. When the rain stopped, they drove to Ennis, Montana, and asked around about who could marry them, fast. Stewie did not want to take the chance of letting her get away. She kept saying she couldn't believe she was doing this. He couldn't believe she was doing this either, and he loved her even more for it.

At the Sportsman Inn in Ennis, Montana, which was bustling with fly fishermen bound for the trout-rich water of the Madison River, the desk clerk gave them a name and they lookd up Judge Ace Cooper (Ret.) in the telephone book.

**JUDGE** Cooper was a tired and rotund man who wore a stained white cowboy shirt and an elk horn bolo tie with his shirt collar open. He performed the ceremony in a room adjacent to his living room that was bare except for a single filing cabinet, a desk and three chairs, and two framed photographs—one of the judge and former president George H. W. Bush, who had once been up there fishing, and the other of the judge on a horse before the Cooper family lost their ranch in the 1980s.

The wedding ceremony had taken eleven minutes, which was just about average for Judge Cooper, although he had once performed it in eight minutes for two Indians.

"Do you, Allan Stewart Woods, take thee, Annabeth, to be your lawful wedded wife?" Judge Cooper had asked, reading from the marriage application form.

"Anna*bel,*" Annabel had corrected in her biting Rhode Island accent.

"I do," Stewie had said. He was beside himself with pure joy.

Stewie twisted the ring off his finger and placed it on hers. It was unique; handmade gold mounted with sterling silver monkey wrenches. It was also three sizes too large. The judge studied the ring.

"Monkey wrenches?" the judge had asked.

"It's symbolic," Stewie had said.

"I'm aware of the symbolism," the judge said darkly, before finishing the passage.

Annabel and Stewie had beamed at each other. Annabel said that this was, like, the *wildest* vacation ever. They were Mr. and Mrs. Outlaw Couple. He was now *her* famous outlaw, although as yet untamed. She said her father would be scandalized, and her mother would have to wear dark glasses at Newport. Only her Aunt Tildie, the one with the wild streak who had corresponded with, but never met, a Texas serial killer until he died of lethal injection, would understand.

Stewie had to borrow a hundred dollars from her to pay the judge, and she signed over a traveler's check.

After the couple had left in the SUV with Rhode Island plates, Judge Ace Cooper had gone to his lone filing cabinet and found the file. He pulled a single piece of paper out and read it as he dialed the telephone. While he waited for the right man to come to the telephone, he stared at the framed photo on the wall of himself on the horse at his former ranch. The ranch, north of Yellowstone Park, had been subdivided by a Bozeman real estate company into over thirty fifty-acre "ranchettes." Famous Hollywood celebrities, including the one who's early-career photos he had recently seen in *Penthouse,* now lived there. Movies had been filmed there. There was even a crack house, but it was rumored that the owner wintered in L.A. The only cattle that existed were purely for visual effect, like landscaping that moved and crapped and looked good when the sun threatened to drop below the mountains.

The man he was waiting for came to the telephone.

"It was Stewie Woods, all right," he said. "The man himself. I recognized him right off, and his ID proved it." There was a pause as the man on the other end of the telephone asked Cooper something. "Yeah, I heard him say that to her just before they left. They're headed for the Bighorns in Wyoming. Somewhere near Saddlestring."

⚬══✦══⚬

**ANNABEL** told Stewie that their honeymoon was quite unlike what she had ever imagined a honeymoon to be, and she contrasted it with her first one with Nathan. Nathan was about sailing boats, champagne, and Barbados. Stewie was about spiking trees in stifling heat in a national forest in Wyoming. He had even asked her to carry his pack.

Neither of them had noticed the late-model black Ford pickup that had trailed them up the mountain road and continued on when Stewie pulled over to park.

Deep into the forest, Stewie now removed his shirt and tied the sleeves around his waist. A heavy bag of nails hung from his belt and tinkled while he strode through the undergrowth. There was a sheen of sweat on his bare chest as he straddled a three-foot-thick Douglas fir and drove in spikes. He was obviously well practiced, and he got into a rhythm where he could bury the six-inch spikes into the soft wood with three heavy blows from his sledgehammer; one tap to set the spike and two blows to bury it beyond the nail head in the bark.

He moved from tree to tree, but didn't spike all of them. He attacked each tree in the same method. The first of the spikes went in at eye level. A quarter-turn around the trunk, he pounded in another a foot lower than the first. He continued pounding in spikes until he had placed them in a spiral on the trunk nearly to the grass.

"Won't it hurt the trees?" Annabel asked as she unloaded his pack and leaned it against a tree.

"Of course not," he said, moving across the pine needle floor to another target. "I wouldn't be doing this if it hurt the trees. You've got a lot to learn about me, Annabel."

"Why do you put so many in?" she asked.

"Good question," he said, burying a spike in three blows. "It used to be we could put in four right at knee level, at the compass points, where the trees are usually cut. But the lumber companies got wise to that and told their loggers to go higher or lower. So now we fill up a four-foot radius."

"And what will happen if they try to cut it down?"

Stewie smiled, resting for a moment. "When a chainsaw blade hits a steel spike, the blade can snap and whip back. Busts the saw teeth. That can take an eye or a nose right off."

"That's horrible," she said, wincing, wondering what she was getting into.

"I've never been responsible for any injuries," Stewie said quickly, looking hard at her. "The purpose isn't to hurt anyone. The purpose is to save trees. After we're done here, I'll call the local ranger station and tell them what we've done. I won't say exactly where we spiked the trees or how many trees we spiked. It should be enough to keep them out of here for decades, and that's the point."

"Have you ever been caught?" she asked.

"Once," Stewie said, and his face clouded. "A forest ranger caught me by Jackson Hole. He marched me into downtown Jackson on foot during tourist season at gunpoint. Half of the tourists in town cheered and the other half started chanting, 'Hang him high! Hang him high!' I was sent to the Wyoming State Penitentiary in Rawlins for seven months."

"Now that you mention it, I think I read about that," she mused.

"You probably did. The wire services picked it up. I was interviewed on *Nightline* and *60 Minutes*. *Outside Magazine* put me on the cover. My boyhood friend Hayden Powell wrote the cover story for them, and he coined the word 'eco-terrorist'." This memory made him feel bold. "There were reporters from all over the country at that trial." Stewie said. "Even the *New York Times*. It was the first time most people had ever heard of One Globe, or knew I was the founder of it. Memberships started pouring in from all over the world."

*One Globe.* The ecological action group that used the logo of crossed monkey wrenches, in deference to late author Edward Abbey's *The Monkey Wrench Gang*. One Globe had once dropped a shroud over Mt. Rushmore for the president's speech, she recalled. It had been on the nightly news.

"Stewie," she said happily, "You are the real thing." He could feel her eyes on him as he drove in the spiral of spikes and moved to the next tree.

"When you are done with that tree I want you," she said, her voice husky. "Right here and right now, my sweet, sweaty . . . *husband.*"

He turned and smiled. His face glistened and his muscles were swelled from swinging the sledgehammer. She slid her T-shirt over her head and stood waiting for him, her lips parted and her legs tense.

⊙━◆━⊙

**STEWIE** slung his own pack now and, for the time being, had stopped spiking trees. Fat, black thunderheads, pregnant with rain, nosed across the late-afternoon sky. They were hiking at a fast pace toward the peak, holding hands, with the hope of getting there and pitching camp before the rain started. Stewie said they would hike out of the forest tomorrow and he would call the ranger station. Then they would get in the SUV and head southeast, toward the Bridger-Teton Forest.

When they walked into the herd of cattle, Stewie felt a dark cloud of anger envelop him.

"Range maggots!" Stewie said, spitting. "If they're not letting the logging companies in to cut all the trees at taxpayer's expense, they're letting the local ranchers run their cows in here so they can eat all the grass and shit in all the streams."

"Can't we just go around them?" Annabel asked.

"It's not that, Annabel," he said patiently. "Of course we can go around them. It's just the principal of the thing. We have cattle fouling what is left of the natural ecosystem. Cows don't belong in the trees in the Bighorn Mountains. You have so much to learn, darling."

"I know," she said, determined.

"These ranchers out here run their cows on public land— our land—at the expense of not only us but the wildlife. They pay something like four dollars an acre when they should be paying ten times that, even though it would be best if they were completely gone."

"But we need meat, don't we?" she asked. "You're not a vegetarian, are you?"

"Did you forget that cheeseburger I had for lunch in Cameron?" he said. "No, I'm not a vegetarian, although sometimes I wish I had the will to be one."

"I tried it once and it made me lethargic," Annabel confessed.

"All these western cows produce about five percent of the beef we eat in this whole country," Stewie said. "All the rest comes from down South, in Texas, Florida, and Louisiana, where there's plenty of grass and plenty of private land to graze them on."

Stewie picked up a pinecone, threw it accurately through the trees, and struck a black baldy heifer on the snout. The cow bolted, turned, and lumbered away. The rest of the herd, about a dozen, followed it. The small herd moved loudly, clumsily cracking branches and throwing up fist-sized pieces of black earth from their hooves.

"I wish I could chase them right back to the ranch they belong on," Stewie said, watching. "Right up the ass of the rancher who has lease rights for this part of the Bighorns."

One cow had not moved. It stood broadside and looked at them.

"What's wrong with that cow?" Stewie asked.

"Shoo!" Annabel shouted. "Shoo!"

Stewie stifled a smile at his new wife's shooing and slid out of his pack. The temperature had dropped twenty degrees in the last ten minutes and rain was inevitable. The sky had darkened and black coils of clouds enveloped the peak. The sudden low pressure had made the forest quieter, the sounds muffled and the smell of cows stronger.

Stewie Woods walked straight toward the heifer, with Annabel several steps behind.

"Something's wrong with that cow," Stewie said, trying to figure out what about it seemed out of place.

When Stewie was close enough he saw everything at once: the cow trying to run with the others but straining at the end of a tight nylon line; the heifer's wild white eyes; the misshapen profile of something strapped on its back that was large and square and didn't belong; the thin reed of antenna that quivered from the package on the heifer's back.

"Annabel!" Stewie yelled, turning to reach out to her—but she had walked around him and was now squarely between him and the cow.

She absorbed the full, frontal blast when the heifer detonated, the explosion shattering the mountain stillness with the subtlety of a sledgehammer bludgeoning bone.

**FOUR** miles away, a fire lookout heard the guttural boom and ran to the railing with binoculars. Over a red-rimmed plume of smoke and dirt, he could see a Douglas fir launch like a rocket into the air, where it turned, hung suspended for a moment, then crashed into the forest below.

Shaking, he reached for his radio.

*Chapter 2*

**EIGHT** miles out of Saddlestring, Wyoming, Game Warden Joe Pickett was watching his wife, Marybeth, work their new Tobiano paint horse, Toby, in the round pen when the call came from the Twelve Sleep County Sheriff's office.

It was early evening, the time of night when the setting sun ballooned and softened and defined the deep velvet folds and piercing tree greens of Wolf Mountain. The normally dull pastel colors of the weathered barn and the red rock canyon behind the house suddenly looked as if they had been repainted in acrylics. Toby, a big, dark bay gelding swirled with brilliant white that ran up over his haunches like thick spilled paint upside down, shone deep red in the evening light and looked especially striking. So did Marybeth, in Joe's opinion, in her worn Wranglers, sleeveless cotton shirt, and her blond hair in a ponytail. There was no wind, and the only sound was the rhythmic thumping of Toby's hooves in the round pen as Marybeth waved the whip and encouraged the gelding to shift from a trot into a slow lope.

The Saddlestring District was considered a "two-horse dis-

trict" by the Game and Fish Department, meaning that the department would provide feed and tack for two mounts to be
used for patrolling. Toby was their second horse.

Joe stood with his boot on the bottom rail and his arms
folded over the top, his chin nestled between his forearms. He
was still wearing his red cotton Game and Fish uniform shirt
with the pronghorn antelope patch on the sleeve and his
sweat-stained gray Stetson. He could feel the pounding of the
earth as Toby passed in front of him in a circle. He watched
Marybeth stay in position in the center of the pen, shuffling
her feet so she stayed on Toby's back flank. She talked to her
horse in a soothing voice, urging him to gallop—something
he clearly didn't want to do.

Persistent, Marybeth stepped closer to Toby and com-
manded him to run. Marybeth still had a slight limp from
when she had been shot nearly two years before, but she was
nimble and quick. Toby pinned his ears back and twitched his
tail but finally broke into a full-fledged gallop, raising the dust
in the pen, his mane and tail snapping behind him like a flag
in a stiff wind. After several rotations, Marybeth called,
"Whoa!" and Toby hit the brakes, skidding to a quick stop
where he stood breathing hard, his muscles swelled, his back
shiny with sweat, smacking and licking his lips as if he was
eating peanut butter. Marybeth approached him and patted
him down, telling him what a good boy he was, and blowing
gently into his nostrils to soothe him.

"He's a stubborn guy—and lazy," she told Joe. "He did *not*
want to lope fast. Did you notice how he pinned his ears back
and threw his head around?"

Joe said *yup.*

"That's how he was telling me he was mad about it. When
he's doing that he's either going to break out of the circle and
do whatever he wants to, or stop, or do what I'm asking him
to do. In this case he did what I asked and went into the fast
lope. He's finally learning that things will go a lot easier on
him when he does what I ask him."

"I know it works for me," Joe said and smiled.

Marybeth crinkled her nose at Joe, then turned back to

Toby. "See how he licks his lips? That's a sign of obedience. He's conceding that I am the boss. That's a good sign."

Joe fought the urge to theatrically lick his lips when she looked over at him.

"Why did you blow in his nose like that?"

"Horses in the herd do that to each other to show affection. It's another way they bond with each other." Marybeth paused. "I know it sounds hokey, but blowing in his nose is kind of like giving him a hug. A horse hug."

"You seem to know what you're doing."

Joe had been around horses most of his life. He had now taken his buckskin mare, Lizzie, over most of the mountains in the Twelve Sleep Range of the Bighorns in his district. But what Marybeth was doing with her new horse, Toby, what she was getting out of him, was a different kind of thing. Joe was duly impressed.

A shout behind him shook Joe from his thoughts. He turned toward the sound, and saw ten-year-old Sheridan, five-year-old Lucy, and their eight-year-old foster daughter April stream through the backyard gate and across the field. Sheridan held the cordless phone out in front of her like an Olympic torch, and the other two girls followed.

"Dad, it's for you," Sheridan called. "A man says it's very important."

Joe and Marybeth exchanged looks and Joe took the telephone. It was County Sheriff O. R. "Bud" Barnum.

There had been a big explosion in the Bighorn National Forest, Barnum told Joe. A fire lookout had called it in, and had reported that through his binoculars he could see fat dark forms littered throughout the trees. It looked like a "shitload" of animals were dead, which is why he was calling Joe. Dead game animals were Joe's concern. They assumed at this point that they were game animals, Barnum said, but they might be cows. A couple of local ranchers had grazing leases up there. Barnum asked if Joe could meet him at the Winchester exit off of the interstate in twenty minutes. That way, they could get to the scene before it was completely dark.

Joe handed the telephone back to Sheridan and looked over his shoulder at Marybeth.

"When will you be back?" she asked.

"Late," Joe told her. "There was an explosion in the mountains."

"You mean like a plane crash?"

"He didn't say that. The explosion was a few miles off of the Hazelton Road in the mountains, in elk country. Barnum thinks there may be some game animals down."

She looked at Joe for further explanation. He shrugged to indicate that was all he knew.

"I'll save you some dinner."

**JOE** met the Sheriff and Deputy McLanahan at the exit to Winchester and followed them through the small town. The three-vehicle fleet—two County GMC Blazers and Joe's dark green Game and Fish pickup—entered and exited the tiny town within minutes. Even though it was an hour and a half away from darkness, the only establishments open were the two bars with identical red neon Coors signs in their windows and a convenience store. Winchester's lone public artwork, located on the front lawn of the branch bank, was an outsized and gruesome metal sculpture of a wounded grizzly bear straining at the end of a thick chain, its metal leg encased in a massive saw-toothed bear trap. Joe did not find the sculpture lovely but it captured the mood, style, and inbred frontier culture of the area as well as anything else could have.

**DEPUTY** McLanahan led the way through the timber in the direction where the explosion had been reported, and Joe walked behind him alongside Sheriff Barnum. Joe and McLanahan had acknowledged each other with curt nods and said nothing. Their relationship had been rocky ever since McLanahan had sprayed the outfitter's camp with shotgun blasts two years before and Joe had received a wayward pellet under his eye. He still had a scar to show for it.

Barnum's hangdog face grimaced as he limped aside Joe through the underbrush. He complained about his hip. He complained about the distance from the road to the crime scene. He complained about McLanahan, and said to Joe sotto voce that he should have fired the deputy years before and would have if he weren't his nephew. Joe suspected, however, that Barnum also kept McLanahan around because McLanahan's quick-draw reputation had added—however untrue and unlikely—an air of toughness to the Sheriff's Department that didn't hurt at election time.

The sun had dropped below the top of the mountains and instantly turned them into craggy black silhouettes. The light dimmed in the forest, fusing the treetops and branches that were discernable just a moment before into a shadowy muddle. Joe reached back on his belt to make sure he had his flashlight. He let his arm brush his .357 Smith & Wesson revolver to confirm it was there. He didn't want Barnum to notice the movement since Barnum still chided him about the time he lost his gun to a poacher Joe was arresting.

There was an unnatural silence in the woods, with the exception of Barnum's grumbling. The absence of normal sounds—the chattering of squirrels sending a warning up the line, the panicked scrambling of deer, the airy winged drumbeat of flushed spruce grouse—confirmed that something big had happened here. Something so big it had either cleared the wildlife out of the area or frightened them mute. Joe could feel that they were getting closer before he could see anything to confirm it. Whatever it was, it was just ahead.

McLanahan quickly stopped and there was a sharp intake of breath.

"Holy shit," McLanahan whispered in awe. *"Holy shit."*

The still-smoking crater was fifteen yards across. It was three feet deep at its center. A half dozen trees had been blown out of the ground and their shallow rootpans were exposed like black outstretched hands. Eight or nine black baldy cattle were dead and still, strewn among the trunks of trees. The earth below the thick turf rim of the crater was dark and wet. Several large white roots, the size of leg bones, were pulled up from the ground by the explosion and now pointed at the sky. Cordite from the explosives, pine from broken branches, and upturned mulch had combined in the air to produce a sickeningly sweet and heavy smell.

Darkness enveloped them as they slowly circled the crater. Pools of light from their flashlights lit up twisted roots and lacy, pale yellow undergrowth.

Joe checked the cattle, moving among them away from the crater. Most had visible injuries as a result of fist-sized rocks being blown into them from the explosion. One heifer was impaled on the fallen tip of a dead pine tree. The rest of the herd, apparently unhurt, stood as silent shadows just beyond his flashlight. He could see dark, heavy shapes and hear the sound of chewing, and a pair of eyes reflected back blue as a cow raised its head to look at him. They all had the same brand—a V on top and a U on the bottom divided by a single line. Joe recognized it as the Vee Bar U Ranch. These were Ed Finolla's cows.

McLanahan suddenly grunted in alarm and Joe raised his flashlight to see the deputy in a wild, self-slapping panic, dancing away from the rim of the crater and ripping his jacket off of himself as quickly as he could. He threw it violently to the ground in a heap and stood staring at it.

"What in the hell is wrong with you?" Barnum asked, annoyed.

"Something landed on my shoulder. Something heavy and wet," McLanahan said, his face contorted. "I thought it was somebody's hand grabbing me. It scared me half to death."

McLanahan had dropped his flashlight, so from across the crater Joe lowered his light onto the jacket and focused his Mag Light into a tight beam. McLanahan bent down into the light and gingerly unfolded the jacket; poised to jump back if whatever had fallen on him was still in his clothing. He threw back a fold and cursed. Joe couldn't see for sure what McLanahan was looking at other than that the object was dark and moist.

"What is it?" Barnum demanded.

"It looks like . . . well . . . it looks like a piece of *meat*." McLanahan looked up at Joe vacantly.

Slowly, Joe raised the beam of his flashlight, sweeping upward over McLanahan and following it up the trunk of a lodgepole pine and into the branches. What Joe saw, he would never forget. . . .